DANCING BENEATH YOU

ROSANNE BITTNER

DANCING BENEATH YOU
By Rosanne Bittner

This book is a work of fiction. All characters and their names, and all incidents, are a product of the author's imagination. Any resemblance to real persons or real incidents is coincidental. Contains violence, sex, and other adult content.

Cover design by The Write Designer and Mandy Koehler Designs.

diting by CEOEditor, Inc.

For my devoted beta readers, Patti Matthys and Tonya Lucas, who put up with my constant changes and editing and patiently waited for each "next" chapter as I wrote it. No story is set in stone until it shows up as a published novel. It is always a good feeling when you reach THE END, and your readers beg for more, especially your beta readers. Thank you, Patti and Tonya for helping me with my very first contemporary story.

CHAPTER ONE

Rhythmic drumming greeted Carmen and her friend Val as they entered the Spirit of Fire Theatre at Indian Trails Casino/Resort. Soft flute music, the distant cry of an eagle, and the occasional howl of wolves added to the mystical atmosphere inside, promising an exciting show unlike anything Carmen had seen before. Spectators who'd lined up earlier inside the theater lobby visiting and laughing, were now quiet and whispering, as though they had entered a church.

The aura of another world and another time inside the theater posed a stark contrast to the modern world of traffic, computers, crime, cell phones, hip-hop, rap music, and political chaos just outside the doors. For Carmen, the worst chaos had been her own life the last four years ... a living hell no twenty-eight-year-old should have already suffered.

She pulled a light sweater around her shoulders against the chill of the air-conditioned room as she and Val searched for the seat numbers shown on their tickets. "I'm already lost in this show, and it hasn't even started," she told Val.

"I'm just glad that I finally got you out into the world of the living again," Val answered. "It's time for you to start enjoying life." She found their seats, only eight rows back from the stage and right beside center aisle, and moved in to sit down. "This show is supposed to be entirely Native American," she told Carmen. "I'm not really sure what to expect, but it looked interesting."

Carmen tucked her small handbag between her thighs. "It does feel good to get out," she admitted, "but I still can't get over the feeling that Jerry is watching me from some secret place. Maybe he is even here in the theater. He continues to find ways to threaten me."

Val scowled. "And ways to keep you from enjoying that beautiful home on Reed's Lake that you won in the divorce. You shouldn't let that sonofabitch keep you from enjoying life, Carmen. You are divorced, and if Jerry hurts you or even comes near you, he will go straight to jail. Remember that."

"And it would be *after* he beats the hell out of me again. I'm afraid to take that chance, which is why I can't enjoy the lake house anymore. I'm safer living with my dad, and besides, he needs help with Grandma and Grandpa, especially since Mother died. He's trying to stay away from putting his parents in a home, but Grandma's Alzheimer's is getting so bad, I don't think it's long before he will have no choice."

"That's too bad." Val set her handbag on the floor between her feet. "Try not to think about those things for tonight, Carmen. Relax and enjoy the show."

"Thanks for inviting me." Best friends since grade school, Carmen and Val grew up together, but during Carmen's volatile marriage, they hardly saw each other.

Jerry forbade Carmen to go anywhere without him or to hang out with old friends.

"We are going to eat at the Three Feathers Restaurant afterward," Val told Carmen as she watched the stage. "You will *love* their food. Maybe we will even have time to play the slot machines for an hour or so after we eat."

"You always have everything planned, don't you?" Carmen teased.

Val shrugged. "Sid and I already had the tickets and the Three Feathers reservation. He was disappointed that he was called to the emergency room at Spectrum, but that's life for a doctor on call. I'm glad you and I can do more together again. Seems like it's always when we have something great planned that Sid gets called to the hospital."

"You're the one who fell in love with a neurosurgeon and married him," Carmen reminded her. "Meantime, it's only late June. We have the whole summer to catch up on all the things we used to do together. But give me some time to adjust to having my life back." The realization of how alcohol and drugs had changed the man she once loved into a brutal stranger still tore at her emotions. Being raised in a quiet, Christian home hadn't prepared her for the violent turmoil her marriage became. She believed marriage was forever, but when things reached the point where her very life was at stake, Jerry hadn't left her much choice but to divorce him. She shivered at the ugly memories.

"That music and drumming is eerie, isn't it?" Val commented. "That eagle's cry sounded real."

"I suspect it *was* real," Carmen answered. Time to stop dwelling on things better forgotten.

Val nodded toward the stage. "Look at those drummers. They look mostly young, but you can tell every one of those guys sitting around that big drum is Native American." She looked at Carmen with teasing fear in her brown eyes. "*Warriors!*" She exaggerated the word as though they were in danger.

"This is the twenty-first century, and you are a nut case!" Carmen joked, waving her off. "I don't know how we became such good friends. We are as different as night and day."

"That's why we do get along," Val answered. "You need me to bring out your wild side."

"I don't *have* a wild side."

"And there is my point, you poor thing. So beautiful but so shy and introverted."

Others settled into their seats and stopped talking as the lights dimmed. Carmen felt lost in a time forgotten, a world of dreams and visions made more real by the howl of wolves —somewhere. Was that real, too, or just a recording? Then came the piercing cry of what sounded like a *real* warrior, so startling that she turned to look toward the back of the theater, but it was too dark to see anything.

"Did you look at the picture in the brochure of the man responsible for these shows?" Val whispered close to her ear.

"No. I haven't even opened the program."

"His name is Ben Colter, and he's *gorgeous!* He's a Harvard graduate, summa cum laude, no less. He's an attorney and an AIM activist who spends a lot of time in Washington, DC. And besides these shows of Native dancing, he and the same group of young people perform regular concerts that are a combination of Native songs mixed with modern music. I'd kind of like to see that. The man went to Julliard. When it comes to the arts, you don't get much more prestigious than that. This guy must be both brilliant *and* talented."

"When on earth did you get a chance to read all that?"

"When we were standing in line. Some promoter handed me a program in advance. You were busy blabbing with the lady ahead of us."

Carmen shook her head as the drumming and flute music combined with soft singing continued. Everything went dark, and suddenly a fake campfire lit up center stage. The Native drummers, some in full Native American dress, others wearing just jeans and T-shirts, began drumming harder. The flute music and singing stopped, and the drummers softened their rhythmic beat again as the announcer's voice came over the loudspeakers.

"Ladies and gentlemen, welcome to Indian Trails Casino-Resort, Michigan's newest casino, owned by the northern Potawatomi. Most of the proceeds from tonight's show, *Dancing Beneath You,* will go toward programs for Native American youth, as well as to the new Sunrise Reservation in South Dakota, which exists solely due to the hard work of the man who sponsors these young people and this program here tonight: Attorney Benjamin Red Wolf Colter, a Lakota man who has dedicated his life to Native American causes. Sunrise was established strictly for teaching the arts, the ancient culture, songs, dances, and languages of the Lakota. Mr. Colter's youth program is called YESS, which stands for Youth, Education, Self-confidence, Success."

The audience applauded Colter's efforts.

"Be sure to check your brochures for information about how you can donate to Mr. Colter's programs. For now, because real wolves and an eagle are used in some segments of this performance, we ask you to refrain from taking pictures that produce a flash when animals are present, as that could startle them. Pictures from this show can be purchased in the lobby, so turn off your phones, sit back, and be prepared to be transported into another world ... another time ... another culture."

Anticipation filled the theater and its two tiers of spectators as the Native American drumming and music grew louder again. A platform from beneath the stage slowly rose, and on it stood a gloriously painted warrior, his powerful arms outstretched. He looked upward, head tilted back, eyes closed, his long, black hair hanging to his hips. The platform began turning, and Carmen's eyes widened with a mixture of admiration for the man's physique and feelings of guilt that she shouldn't be looking at all. The white buckskin leggings he wore covered only the front and back of his legs. The sides were open, exposing bare but powerful thighs and hips. Carmen could hear women whispering their admiration.

"*Damn!*" Val said under her breath.

Carmen nudged her arm. "I think it's a good thing Sid *isn't* here," she joked.

"That must be Ben Colter. It's hard to tell with all that paint on his face, but the brochure says he's the lead dancer."

A large screen to the right gave the audience a close-up picture as the platform continued to turn. Other than beaded moccasins and the open-sided leggings, the warrior wore a white, fringed vest embellished with Native symbols. His hair was decorated with feathers and beads, and he wore several silver and feathered earrings, silver rings, and a choker necklace that looked like it was made of wood and turquoise.

As the platform turned the man full front again, a Skycam that freely panned the stage focused on the warrior's face. Carmen studied his incredibly handsome features, full lips, square jaw, high cheekbones—the classic looks of a Native American man. She couldn't help noticing very distinct abs where his vest fell open. Silver cuffs around his upper arms accented his powerful biceps. White stripes with a red stripe between them were painted across his cheeks, and studded leather bracelets decorated his powerful wrists. He wore a wide, thick leather cuff that covered his left forearm. "That cuff on his arm looks like it's for a large bird," Carmen commented.

"I don't care what it's for. I think I'm in love," Val muttered.

Carmen snickered, trying to avoid her own base attraction to the man. After what she'd been through with Jerry, being sexually attracted to any man was the last thing on her mind when she agreed to come to this show.

The platform stopped turning, but the drumming and singing continued in the background. Colter stood still for a moment longer, eyes still closed, while a now-silent audience waited for his next move. Everyone gasped and *oohed* and *aahed* and looked up when an eagle flew overhead then, giving out the beautiful and lonely cry that could not be mistaken for any other type of bird. It put out its feet, spread its wings, and landed on Colter's left forearm. The whole room seemed momentarily bathed in spirituality and an aura of commanding power.

Colter flashed open his eyes then, so suddenly that a few people gasped. On the big screen he was looking directly into the Skycam. His dark eyes glittered with spirituality, as though, deep inside, he carried the knowledge of an ancient past, the spirits of warriors from two hundred years ago. He was a young man with old eyes—eyes that could see right through a person and into their mind. The strangest part was that Carmen truly felt as though he *was* looking straight at her ... *only* her.

"Remember this," Colter spoke, his voice rich and deep. "Everywhere in this land you say is yours, beneath the earth, the bodies of the true People are buried—Lakota, Santee, Apache, Comanche, Ute, Crow, Potawatomi, Blackfoot, Nez-Perce, Cherokee, Iroquois, Choctaw, Huron, Seminole, Mohawk—and too many more to name. They are there, dancing beneath you, celebrating the fact that one day ... maybe a day not so far off ... this land will again belong to them. A day of reckoning is coming, and only the true Human Beings will survive to dance again." A teasing grin passed over his lips, and his dark eyes sparkled with what seemed a mixture of humor and prophecy. "Perhaps one day *they* will dance on *your* graves. *Hetchetu welo!* May it be so!" On those words he jerked his arm upward, and the eagle flew to the back of the theater.

Gasps, laughter, whistles, and applause moved through the audience as the singing, drumming and flute music grew very loud. The stage lit up, and a troupe of beautifully dressed dancers whirled and gyrated and danced to a rhythmic beat in feathered, beaded regalia so colorful it was difficult not to stare in awe. Through it all, an older Native American man carried a long pipe to Colter and helped him light it, after which Colter walked from center stage and down a runway that brought him farther into the audience and only two rows away from Carmen. He raised the pipe and offered it to the four directions, blowing smoke in each direction before handing the pipe back to the older man.

"Good God, he's even more magnificent up close," Val said excitedly. "I need a cold shower."

Carmen nudged her to keep quiet, although the drumming and music was loud enough that Ben Colter likely did not hear her. Within minutes, every person in the audience was captivated by the rhythmic drumbeats that seemed to match their pounding hearts. Secretly, Carmen thought maybe her own heart was pounding hardest of all.

Colter rejoined the dancing. At one point, he looked straight into the camera again, and again, Carmen felt as though he was looking only at her. *Everyone else in the audience probably feels the same way.* He owned all of them. His charisma and self-confidence were palpable.

Somewhere at the back of the auditorium, wolves howled again, and this time Carmen could tell they were not a recording. Various dancers, mostly young, performed several different sets, each group coming onto the stage in constantly changing but always colorful regalia. Colter himself was the center of many of the performances, his dances made mesmerizing by his very male presence. He perfectly fit the picture of a warrior out of the past, a man Carmen could picture hunting buffalo with bow and arrow while riding a horse bareback ... or wielding a tomahawk or a spear in battle. Could he really do those things?

One dance depicted courting between a Native American man and woman. The dance included beautiful flute music and provocative embraces that made Carmen long for such lovely romance in her own life. She supposed the woman involved was the lead dancer's wife.

"I can't take much more of this," Val said softly as she fanned her face with the program brochure. "This guy is too much. Talk about sexy."

Carmen covered her face and shook her head, laughing softly.

"Don't tell me you aren't turned on," Val added.

"I am not even going to answer that," Carmen said.

"Besides, Jerry did a good job of destroying any needs I might have had in that department."

The sexy dance ended, and the stage went dark. When it lit up again, Ben Colter stood there alone wearing a beautifully beaded buckskin shirt and fringed leggings that fully covered him this time. His hair hung long and straight, decorated with beaded ornaments and feathers. Long, silver earrings flickered when stage lights hit them. He spoke sincerely about wolves and how they were an endangered species.

"Although there are no wolves in South Dakota's Badlands, and lately just a few noticed moving into the Black Hills, I have always felt a personal connection to the magnificent wolf. These beautiful creatures are connected to humans spiritually. All you need is to look into their eyes. I feel as one with them, and my middle name is Red Wolf, given to me after a dream quest. I have slept with wolves, shared food with wolves, and I share ancient stories with them. Look into the eyes of a wolf and he will know you. Wolves helped me through the lowest point in my life. They helped me be strong when I was weak and full of sorrow."

Carmen put a hand to her chest. The lowest point in his life? Weak and full of sorrow? She wanted to know more.

"Help us keep new and more aggressive wolf hunt laws from going into effect by supporting groups that work hard defending this wild, beautiful creature."

The lights dimmed a little more.

"And now," Colter continued, "I ask you to be as quiet as possible while you observe these beautiful creatures." He put a whistle to his lips, the kind only dogs and a few other animals could hear.

Carmen swallowed nervously, at once keenly aware that she sat in a center-aisle seat. She heard the hard patter of feet, then felt a rush of air and heard panting as a wolf ran past her. "Oh, my gosh!" she whispered. A dog attacked her when she was young, and she had been afraid of them ever since. To her, a wolf was bigger, meaner, more unpredictable animal than the common dog.

Another wolf ran past and onto the stage to sit at Colter's feet. Then a third wolf rushed onto the stage. Then came a fourth. It ran past, then slowed down ... turned ... and trotted right up to where Carmen sat. The beautiful, thick-coated animal sat down and looked straight at Carmen.

Carmen felt every nerve and muscle come alive. Her neck stiffened, and she gripped the arms of her seat. Colter blew the whistle again, but the wolf did not budge. It just sat and stared at Carmen, its glowing, golden eyes making it impossible for her to look away.

CHAPTER TWO

"Carmen!" Val whispered. "Don't move!"

As though she needed someone to tell her to be still. Carmen was too petrified even to answer.

"Caesar! Come!" Colter calmly told the wolf that stayed in the aisle.

The animal would not budge. After a few more attempts to get him to the stage, Colter told the audience to please remain still and take no pictures. "And I ask those in charge of lighting to please not turn up the house lights. The sudden change might confuse the wolves." He adjusted his headset and leaned down to quickly pet the three wolves on stage reassuringly. "The white wolf up here with me is called Maggie. This one with red in his gray fur is Sage, and the black one is Rocky. I am asking our trainer, Sammy Thunder, to call these three wolves back to their cages now," he told the audience. "You need not fear them as they run past you."

Easy for you to say, Carmen thought.

The wolves' ears suddenly perked up, and all three charged down the center runway and leaped off it without using the steps. They ran back up the aisle, right past where the wolf called Caesar still sat staring at Carmen. Colter ordered the drummers to keep drumming softly and asked a flutist to play something. "The music will help keep Caesar calm," he told spectators as he walked to the end of the runway and down the steps to the seating area. Tiny tin bells woven into the fringe of his clothing tinkled softly with his every move. He had earlier explained that bells held spiritual value, but sometimes men wore them in their fancier dress to attract women, which brought a ripple of laughter from the audience. Right now, as Colter walked toward her, they were having an odd calming effect on Carmen, as though to say, *A strong man is here. He will protect you.* Was she losing her mind?

"Lord, he's coming here," Val whispered. "We get to see this guy up close!"

I'm more concerned about seeing that wolf up close, Carmen thought to answer, but she still couldn't find her voice.

"Miss, just sit very still, and please do not be afraid," Colter told Carmen as he walked to where she sat. "I assure you, Caesar does not mean you any harm. He would not stop to sit near you if he did not sense something special about you—perhaps a spiritual connection."

I don't want any connection, spiritual or otherwise! Was this a trick? Part of the act? If it was, Carmen didn't like it one bit.

"Again, I ask that all of you in the audience make sure your phones are off until we get Caesar back to his cage," Colter reminded everyone. He knelt beside Carmen's seat. "What is your name?"

Carmen squeaked out her name, so overcome with terror that she couldn't stop a tear from slipping down her cheek. She kept her eyes on the wolf, sure he would pounce any minute.

"My name is Ben," Colter said softly. "And the wolf's name is Caesar. Please do not cry or be afraid."

Carmen swallowed. "I was attacked by a dog when I was seven," she choked out, her throat dry as sand. Finally, she managed to take her gaze from Caesar and looked down at her left arm, showing Ben the scar there from the attack. He touched it gently, and Carmen thought she might pass out. Something moved through her like fire.

"Look at me," Ben told her.

In that moment, Carmen felt as though no one else was in the theater but her, the wolf, and Ben Colter. *What is happening to me?* She dared to meet Ben's gaze, and something unexplainable swept through her. The only comparison she could make was that this must be how it felt when a bomb went off somewhere and its shock waves shot through everyone and everything nearby.

Ben pressed her arm. "Carmen, I want you to get up and walk with me to the back of the theater. I think it might be the only way to get Caesar to his cage. He wants you to come with him."

"Really? I didn't hear that wolf say anything." *What?* Did she just make a sarcastic remark? Several in the audience laughed quietly, and Ben smiled, sending another shock wave through Carmen. His smile was wide and bright and reassuring.

"I know Caesar," he told Carmen. "And I think we can get him back to his cage and relieve this audience of their own fears if you walk with us. It is better than me trying to force him. I promise to stay between you and Caesar."

Carmen tried to move, but nothing worked. "You will

have to help me up. I'm terrified and not sure I can even straighten my legs."

Ben rose and took hold of her hand, pulling gently as Carmen managed to get to her feet. He squeezed her hand reassuringly, then carefully moved an arm around her protectively, holding her tight against his side. "Caesar, come," he told the wolf.

They started walking, and Caesar got up and followed on the other side of Ben. Carmen could barely feel her legs. "Are you sure he won't turn on me?" she asked.

"I am sure. Even if he did, I would die before I let him harm you. Don't be afraid."

What was this feeling? Jerry had never, *ever* made her feel like this. Safe. It was a feeling of pure safety. *I would die before I let him harm you.* Something told her he really meant it. After Jerry's abuse, she wasn't used to being close to a man other than her own father without being afraid.

"Tommy, bring on the next act and keep the music and dancing going for our audience," Ben said through his headset, obviously talking to someone on stage. "I apologize to the audience for this unexpected interruption, but as soon as I get Caesar settled and this beautiful young lady back to her seat, we will finish our show. For now, I am turning off my microphone."

The aisle seemed a mile long to Carmen, but with every step she felt more relaxed and less afraid. One of the other wolves howled as they approached open lobby doors that led into an area walled off by heavy partitions. The mournful howl seemed eerie inside a modern-day theater, but also lonely, beautiful, causing a tug at Carmen's heart she couldn't even explain. The other three wolves were in their cages, and the fourth cage sat open. An older Native American man stood beside it. He nodded to Carmen.

"You do not need to be afraid," he said. "My name is Sammy Thunder, and I am these wolves' trainer. Caesar has never done this before. There must be something special about you, which is why he would never hurt you."

Ben kept her close as he turned with her to face Caesar. The wolf looked at the cage, then back at Carmen.

"Stay still," Ben told her. He let go of Carmen and knelt in front of Caesar, petting the wolf's head and neck vigorously. "What is it, my friend?" he asked the animal. "What do you want to tell us?"

Caesar whined and looked at Ben as though he truly did wish he could speak. An usher on the theater side of the lobby doors quickly closed them, and Caesar walked up to Carmen. She backed away.

"Let him get your scent," Ben told her. He remained kneeling beside the wolf as Caesar sniffed at Carmen's hand, then licked it.

"Don't let him bite me!"

"He is just getting to know you, saying hello. He likes you very much," Ben told her. "He wants you to be his friend."

Carmen noticed he spoke in that oddly stoic Native American way, very deliberate, no contractions.

Smiling, he looked up at Carmen, and all she could think of was that he was even more handsome in regular daylight. "I think he wants you to be *my* friend, too," he told her. "I just wish I knew exactly why he stopped near you and would not obey us." He gently ran a hand from Caesar's head down his back. "Go ahead and pet him, Carmen, but keep your hand in a fist at first. Petting him will help you get over your fear."

Carmen swallowed and reached out with a fist. She trembled everywhere when Caesar licked the back of her fingers, but then he began sniffing at her crotch. She stepped back more, this time in embarrassment.

Ben urged the wolf away. "I am sorry. He is not being rude. It's just a wolf thing, as well as most other animals. It is how he finds and remembers your scent, and it is how all males of any species pick up the female scent."

Is that so? Was the man flirting with her? She should be offended, but he'd spoken the words matter-of-factly, which somehow did not offend her at all. "Please tell me this isn't all a trick you use to find women when you travel," Carmen said.

Ben and Sammy both laughed as Ben kept petting Caesar. He finally managed to get the wolf into his cage, then rose, looking down at Carmen. The aura of masculine power filled the space around him, space that included Carmen.

"I am not the kind of man who lies and uses tricks," he said. "Ask anyone who knows me." He studied Carmen intently. "This has never happened before. I apologize for making you so uncomfortable. Let me make it up to you by at least buying you dinner after the show."

"That's okay. I'm here with a girlfriend. We already have reservations for Three Feathers restaurant."

"Then let me pay for your meal. I will send someone there as soon as I go back and have them tell the maître d' to put your meals on my room bill."

"Oh, you don't need to do that. It's a really expensive restaurant."

"I can afford it. How many will there be? Is your husband with you?"

Carmen folded her arms self-consciously. "I don't have a husband."

Ben glanced at her left hand. 'You wear a wedding ring."

Carmen stepped back a little yet again. "I'm divorced."

"And you wear the ring to keep other men away?"

"No. I'm not sure why I still wear it. I guess I'm still getting used to being single."

Ben's all-knowing gaze made her feel he knew her every thought. She looked away, pretending to watch the wolves in their cages. The drumming and music from the show outside the doors only accented the male prowess of the man who stood a good six feet or more tall in front of her. She cleared her throat nervously. "At any rate, I'm sure you have something planned with your own wife after the show."

A dark tension filled the small area as Ben turned and knelt in front of Caesar's cage, putting his hand against it so the wolf could lick his fingers. "I have no wife," he said flatly. "She ... died."

Carmen looked at Sammy, who frowned and shook his head, as though to tell her not to ask any questions. "I'm sorry. What about that beautiful woman you danced with earlier?"

Ben seemed to brighten a little as he rose. "That beautiful woman is my brother's wife, Sasha. My brother is the main flute player you saw on stage, the slightly older man. We are ten years apart and had different fathers." He folded his own arms, muscles bulging when he did so. "Believe me, even if Sasha *were* available, I would not be interested. She is a prankster, very independent, single-minded, bossy, fun, wild but also a sassy handful."

Sammy chuckled and nodded his head.

"Sasha and I are exceptionally good friends," Ben added. "She was my wife's older cousin and looks very much like my Talia. She is a talented singer and dancer and has had professional training in both. She and Tommy have seven sons, from twenty years old to four."

Carmen's eyes widened. "But she's so young and tiny and beautiful!"

Ben chuckled. "Sasha is older than you think. Her oldest son is in the marines, another in college. The rest are part of this dance troupe. The youngest is four, and he will take part in a dance you will see in the next segment of our show. I promise you he will win your heart and the hearts of the entire audience. His name is also Benjamin. Tommy and Sasha named him after me." He sobered a little again, as though some dark memory had suddenly rushed through his thoughts. "In some ways, I owe my life to my brother and to Sasha." He turned away. "I should get back to the show. Those people in there paid a lot of money to see it."

Carmen nodded. "Thank you for offering to buy dinner, but it isn't necessary."

Ben turned and looked her over in a way that made her feel undressed. He had a way of observing her so keenly that she felt self-conscious of the fact that her hair was damp from a nervous sweat. She pulled it behind her shoulders and wondered how wrinkled her cotton capris were after sitting so long. She wrapped her sweater around her shoulders, realizing her pale green sleeveless top dipped low enough to show ample cleavage.

"That green shirt matches your very green and very pretty eyes," Ben told her. He put up his hands as though to fend something off. "And no, I am not flirting. I am just making an observation because I have never seen eyes so green. You are an exceptionally beautiful woman."

Carmen glanced at the cages again. Why did she feel

like a silly teenager? Jerry had never once called her beautiful. It was always hot chick or great tits or my personal whore. Ben had offered the compliment with honest respect, as though to honor her. She had never heard a man say it the way he did. *And I've never seen a more handsome man in my life*, she wanted to answer. Too forward. Much too forward!

"Well ... thank you," she answered. "Right now, I feel a bit of a mess."

There came his brilliant smile again. "I just realized that I never even asked your last name," he said.

"It's ..." Carmen realized the irony of what she was about to say. "My last name is Wolfe."

Ben looked startled. "You are serious?"

"I most certainly am. It's my maiden name. I took it back when I divorced. I'm German and Scandinavian."

"That explains your natural blond hair. It, too, is beautiful."

Carmen pushed another strand of hair behind her ears. "I'm thinking of getting it cut." *What a stupid remark! What does he care?*

"You should not," Ben told her. "Beautiful hair like yours is a blessing."

Every time Ben Colter opened his mouth, she became even more aware of what an ass Jerry was. Was this guy for real? Was there an ordinary man under all that paint and those feathers and behind all that education, intelligence, and talent? Maybe, but ordinary didn't seem quite the right word. "My ancestors go all the way back to the pilgrims who first landed at Plymouth Rock," she told him. "I'm sure that doesn't impress you, of all people." She'd done it again! Said something stupid. Why on earth was she telling him so much?

Ben snickered. "You mean the famous first landing that was the beginning of the end for my People?"

"Something like that, in *your* mind, at least."

"You might be surprised at the things that are on my mind right now. I am still wondering why Caesar caused all this trouble." He reached out to her. "Come on. I will walk you back to your seat." He opened a theater door, and Carmen took his hand. She liked the reassuring way he gripped hers with a strength that said he could throw her across a room if he chose, something Jerry had done more than once, but Ben's grip was warm and gentle. He led her down the dark aisle and to her seat. Carmen sat down, and before he left, Ben knelt beside her.

"I would like to talk to you again," he told her quietly. "Caesar's attention to you means something. If you are willing, email your address and phone number to me. The website and email addresses for Sunrise Reservation are in the brochure. Promise me you will think about it."

"I will."

"Again, I apologize." Ben reached past Carmen to shake Val's hand. "See? I returned your friend all in one piece." He rose then and left, fringes dancing, bells tinkling.

Val leaned back and sighed deeply. "My God, he's beautiful."

The audience clapped and cheered when the short intermission ended and Ben went up the steps to the runway and announced that everything was fine.

Val leaned close to Carmen. "Did I just hear what I *think* I heard? He wants your phone number?"

"He's just being friendly," Carmen told her. She wasn't in any mood to go into details—or to voice the fact that Ben Colter's presence had hit her like a wave of pleasant desire washing over her. "Besides, by tomorrow night he will be a thousand miles away and living in a world I don't know a thing about and don't *want* to know," Carmen added. "So, it doesn't matter."

"Well, just in case you've been totally taken by your painted warrior, read this." Val handed her phone to Carmen. "I Googled the guy. What I found out will help you make up your mind if he's worth sending your phone number to."

"Are you my mother now?" Carmen asked teasingly as she took the phone.

"Just a good friend who doesn't want to see you hurt again."

Carmen shook her head as she leaned over to shield the bright phone light from others. She scanned down through the information.

Ben Colter. Thirty-two years old. Native American entertainer and activist. Has done modeling and acting. An attempted assassination left him wounded and took the life of his wife and their unborn baby. Carmen scanned to find the date of the assassination. "More than three years ago," she muttered. *The FBI and BIA are still investigating,* she read. *The shooter still at large.* That meant that Ben Colter could still be in danger.

Carmen handed Val her phone. "Interesting, but *I* am *not* interested," she lied. There was too much to consider before she talked to Val or anyone else about what had just happened to her. She wasn't even sure what that was, but rather than being alarmed by what she read, she found herself feeling sorry for Ben. How awful to see his wife gunned down before his very eyes! No wonder he'd reacted the way he did when she'd asked about a wife.

"Not interested? Get real, Carmen," Val scoffed. "How can you spend ten minutes with a guy like that and *not* be interested? But after what you went through with Jerry, somebody in this guy's situation is the *last* thing you need."

After a few minutes, Ben returned to the stage. This time he whirled to wild drumming and glared fiercely into a camera during a fiery war dance. The look was intimidating, black paint around his eyes, flames painted on his cheeks. The drums boomed, and the male dancers shouted war cries.

They haven't found the shooter, Carmen thought. She had a feeling it wasn't just the FBI and BIA who were searching for the culprit, and from the warlike way Ben looked right now, woe to whoever killed his wife.

One more reason to not be interested, she told herself. *The man still grieves for his wife.* But her resolve to ignore any future interest was eroded when Ben brought out his adorable four-year-old nephew, who was dressed in full regalia. Ben danced some of the war dance, and the little boy followed. It was the cutest thing Carmen had ever seen. Anyone could see the love between man and boy. Ben had been right that the child would win their hearts.

The woman named Sasha urged the boy to keep dancing, and the child and his uncle spoke back and forth in the Lakota tongue as Ben showed certain moves and let little Ben copy him. The audience laughed and clapped with each movement.

"Someday he will outdance you, Little Brother," Sasha joked.

The audience laughed and clapped again, then cheered more when Ben grabbed the boy and held him high. "The future of the Lakota People!" he announced.

Roaring applause filled the theater. Then the room darkened, and after a few minutes of soft drumming and flute playing, the stage lights came on. Ben stood there alone on stage. He wore simple white jeans, a beaded belt, and a white collared shirt. His hair was pulled back into a simple tail, and he wore no paint on his handsome face. Silver and feathered earrings decorated his ears, and he wore a turtle shell necklace at his throat.

"The guy looks damn good in jeans," a woman behind Carmen commented. Carmen had to agree.

Then it happened. Ben sang a closing song, and his voice caused peoples' mouths to fall open. Absolutely *no* one expected what they heard. The audience sat enraptured as he belted out the song "Anthem" from the stage play *Chess,* his voice an operatic tenor. Through the song's heartfelt words, the screens on each side of the stage showed Native American men dressed in warrior clothing riding horses bareback across open plains, buffalo and wild horses running among them. It was gloriously beautiful, as was the leader of the warriors, Ben Colter, his long hair flying in the wind, his muscular body bare but for the apron he wore.

As the song continued its words of love for the land, the riders charged up a steep embankment only skilled riders could master. More warriors waited at the top, and the camera filming the scene by helicopter panned outward to show a beautiful plateau surrounded by a vast landscape of mountains and deep green pine trees. Everyone knew it had to be the Black Hills of South Dakota, homeland of the Lakota.

Then came the closing line of the song, about his land having no borders but around his heart. As he sang the words, the warriors on screen held up a huge sign that read THE BLACK HILLS ARE NOT FOR SALE!

The entire audience broke into vigorous applause that lasted a good five minutes, maybe longer. The screens changed back to those on stage, and Ben and his entire youth group, as well as Tommy and Sasha, politely bowed their farewell. Ben held up his little nephew again, and the audience went wild. Carmen and Val joined them in cheers and hoots and whistles. Ben looked in her direction.

"Why do I get the feeling he is looking for *you?*" Val commented.

"Don't be silly," Carmen told her.

Both women continued cheering and clapping with the others, even after the dance troupe stepped back and Ben shouted, "Wakan-Tanka *nici un!*" The words were shown on the screens in English, "May the Great Spirit go with you."

"And with you!" several shouted in unison.

The curtains closed, and Carmen suddenly felt like crying at knowing she would likely never see Ben Colter again. The man was way out of her range in so many ways, let alone the fact that he lived a good thousand miles away. It was silly to even consider contacting him.

But damned if those dark eyes hadn't spotted her and given her that "I want you" look again. Desire she'd never felt with Jerry moved through her almost sinfully. She should not have promised to send the man her phone number. She would have to break that promise and get out of this strange situation while she still could.

"Let's get out of here," Carmen told Val, hurrying away without even waiting. Maybe if she walked outside for a bit, she could shake off this strange spell Ben Colter had put on her. Maybe it wasn't some magic spell at all. Maybe it was a curse.

CHAPTER THREE

"Forget her, Little Brother," Tommy advised, using his personal nickname for Ben.

Ben used bottled water to swallow three Tylenol. "That is impossible."

"Let me see that Tylenol container."

Ben handed his older brother the container. "It is really Tylenol. You must quit worrying, Tommy."

Tommy looked inside at the blue and red pills. "I want to, but I know how much pain you are usually in after a full performance. The last thing I ever want to do is drag my skeleton of a brother out of a back alley again. How is your back?"

"I just took three Tylenol. That should tell you."

Tommy handed back the pills. "I am proud of you, Little Brother, I know how hard it is for you not to take something stronger. If the audience knew what you go through to put on these shows, they would probably donate even more money to the Rez."

"Maybe, but I am not about to explain the ugly mess of

the past three years of my life with a few thousand strangers who don't know the whole story. They would only see a drug addict, and they would pull their money, figuring I am using it to put something up my nose instead of helping those kids back there. It would hurt our fundraising."

"You were shot and lost a kidney," Tommy reminded Ben. "And now you carry shrapnel in your back. Everyone in the audience would understand."

"I am not taking that risk." Ben pushed a button to tilt back his airplane seat. He and Tommy sat in a curtained-off section at the front of the thirty-passenger Plures Air jet, paid for by the government—another perk Ben had fought Congress to be allowed. The youth group could book the jet for up to ten concerts and fancy dance shows a year. For closer venues, they usually traveled by bus.

Laughter and screams came from the main compartment behind Ben and Tommy, where Sasha played trivia games and sang songs with twenty-four young people whose energy knew no bounds.

Tommy put his own seat back. "And now you are worried that if that beautiful woman in Michigan finds out the whole truth about you, she will shut you down so fast you will not know what hit you," he told Ben.

"Something like that." Ben closed his eyes and winced slightly from the sudden pain that often stabbed at his lower back like a knife. He shifted slightly, and it went away.

"And if she is worth her salt, she will understand," Tommy told Ben. "But I still think you should not pursue an impossible relationship. You are not ready for that. You still have not closed the book on Talia, and even if this new woman managed to understand the reason for the opioid problem, she will run as fast as she can when she finds out you deliberately overdosed once and that you also put a gun to your head another time. God knows what it would do to you if you fell in love with some new woman and she shut you down."

"I absolutely do not want to talk about it, Tommy."

"You *need* to talk about it, Little Brother, and often, just to remind yourself how far you have come. You look damn good now. You are happier and healthier than you have ever been, since even before the shooting—except for that shrapnel in your back. And speaking of another woman, you have to be careful whether the one you are thinking about is really into you for *you* or if she just sees you as a dark, handsome warrior from some romance novel. Women in the audience salivate over you for one reason only—and so, probably, do some of the men."

They both laughed hard at the remark. "I will not judge that," Ben answered. "As far as the women, there is only one woman I want, and she is dead."

"But not buried, not in your heart. And now you are thinking of letting in some woman who knows nothing about your life or your background or the history of our people—a woman who lives a thousand miles from the Rez and who you talked to all of five or ten minutes."

"I am a big boy, Tommy. Let me deal with this. Besides, you are the one who keeps saying I should go on with life."

Tommy smiled. "Just remember that you can talk to me or Sasha any time. We love you, and we only want the best for you. You are a man blessed with great intelligence and talents. Do not ever waste either one."

Ben grinned when the kids in back broke into the upbeat song, "Love Can Move Mountains," one of those they sometimes sang when they performed musicals instead of Pow-Wow dancing.

"Come sing with us, Ben!"

Ben recognized Debra Black Kettle's voice. "I used up my voice and my energy last night," Ben yelled back to her. "You kids have more energy than I do. Let me sleep!"

"Old man wants to sleep!" one of the teenage boys shouted in reply.

All the kids laughed. Then came a "One. Two. Three. WE LOVE YOU, BEN!" The youth group shouted the words in unison before breaking into song again.

Tommy laughed. "And they mean it, Little Brother. Whenever you are down, you just think about those kids and how much they need you. Do not ever let them down again. You are their best chance of staying away from drugs and alcohol and keeping that hope for the future. Let the wolf spirit, and your faith in the power of Wakan-Tanka guide you."

Ben smiled but felt a little sad thinking about the words the kids sang—*love can move mountains*. If he pursued a relationship with one Carmen Wolfe, it would take a *lot* of love and understanding to get over the mountains of emotional and cultural differences that would come between them once she found out all the tiny truths about him. A woman like Carmen likely did not know a damn thing about the kind of life he led, or about life on the Rez or his customs and beliefs ... or the hell he'd been through with opioids because of the pain he still suffered from being shot. It wasn't easy going without something stronger than Tylenol, but Native dancing helped keep him in a spirit world where a man could rise above pain.

Trouble was, it did not always help his emotional pain. It did not erase the memory of holding Talia's bloody body in his arms, seeing the hole in her swollen belly from the large-caliber bullet that killed her and their baby. Why was he thinking about a shy, freshly divorced white woman from Michigan when he was not even over his dead wife yet?

He closed his eyes, feeling like he needed to sleep or die.

"She does not belong in your world," Tommy again reminded Ben, "and you do not belong in hers."

"How do you always know what I am thinking?" Ben asked him.

"Because you wear your heart on your sleeve. And do not forget that you are still trying to find out who shot you. There is such a thing as having too much on your plate, Little Brother, and your plate is not big enough to add a new relationship."

"You did not see her up close," Ben said sleepily, keeping his eyes closed. "My God, that hair, those green eyes, that body. Long legs that lead up to a round butt. And she wore a sleeveless top that showed beautiful, perfect cleavage. Plus, she exudes sweetness. A goodness. But something is wrong emotionally that touched my heart. I think maybe her ex-husband abused her. I cannot imagine why any man would, but she just makes you want to grab her and put your arms around her and tell her she is safe, that everything will be okay."

"And you want to do a lot more than just hold her." Tommy sighed.

Ben felt a great need move through him. "Damn it, Tommy, when that tear ran down her cheek, I just wanted to grab her up and make love to her, right then and there, tell her I will always protect her. That tear was for more than being afraid of Caesar and dogs in general. She is afraid of a lot more than that."

Tommy rubbed his eyes. "Good God, Ben, it has just been too long since you had sex."

Both men laughed softly. "I will grant you that one," Ben admitted.

"Yeah, well, you are walking into dangerous territory. Do not do a thing unless she does contact you like you think she will. Even then, just send her information on how she can support Sunrise Reservation and your programs. Send her a picture of Caesar or something like that. Just do not take it any further."

All Ben could see was Carmen's green eyes. "Easier said than done. And quit treating me like I am sixteen years old." He winced at another sudden pain.

Tommy straightened a little to glance out the window at quilt-like farm fields below ... white men's farms that had eaten up plains and prairies where once the Lakota rode free and wild. "I wish I could change it all for you, Ben, but I cannot. It is what it is, and Sasha and I pulled you through it with prayer and the sweat lodge and your spirit search." He leaned back again. "You are strong now, beautiful in your heart—a man who fights for what is right for the People and teaches our youth to be proud and to act on their talents. Do not risk losing everything you have worked for over a woman who will likely tear your heart to pieces."

"You do not know that. You did not meet her. And Caesar sitting there staring at her like that, as if to point her out to me, has to mean something. You cannot deny that. And right now, I just need to sleep. We can talk about this when we get back to the Rez."

Sleep finally took control. Ben's last thought was of Carmen Wolfe. He wanted to look into those beautiful eyes again, grasp that sexy butt, kiss that cleavage. He figured she was five foot six or seven, and she had a lovely tan. Had she ever modeled? What did she do for a living? What had happened to her marriage? Would she call him? Email him? Bother to contact him in any way?

Probably not. Damned if that did not make him sad ... and make him want her more. He could not let this go. Caesar had made that impossible.

CHAPTER FOUR

"I CAN'T BELIEVE I am actually meeting you at your lake house." Val walked into Carmen's sprawling home on Reeds Lake. "It's been so long since I've been here, I forgot how beautiful this place is." She threw her purse onto a slate blue, Maiden Home couch made of rich mohair. "Remember when I joked with you about ordering this couch in mink? Maiden Home *is* available that way, you know."

"Get real, Val," Carmen scoffed. "Jerry is the one who wanted that couch. It could be studded with pure diamonds and I still wouldn't want it. This house and everything in it remind me of him, so I don't miss any of it."

Val looked around. "I'll say one thing, your ex knows how to design and build spectacular homes." She walked across plush carpet to the huge windows on the lake side of the house.

"Well, since Jerry is off doing drugs and screwing whores most of the time, all he has to do is draw up blue-prints and hand them over to the exceptionally talented men who work for him," Carmen answered bitterly. She closed the laptop she'd been working with when Val walked in. "I don't know why his men put up with him. It's probably because he pays them so well. At any rate, he has enough talented builders that they can take Jerry's plans and create more million-dollar homes for him while he chills out on a joint or smokes crack or whatever it is he does. I don't know that much about drugs, and I don't *want* to know. The extent of my knowledge is to know they can turn a perfectly nice, successful person into a monster. Jerry is part of the walking dead now as far as I'm concerned."

The front door drifted open. "You didn't close the door all the way," Carmen told Val. She walked over and closed it against the hot, early-July air outside, thinking how cool the slate entranceway felt against her feet ... the same slate on which she'd fractured her skull when Jerry picked her up and slammed her to the floor months ago. "I don't know how Jerry manages to still design beautiful homes when he's high most of the time."

Val shook her head and turned to face Carmen. "It's such a waste, this place sitting here empty," she commented.

"Want to buy it? I'll give you and Sid a good price."

Val smiled, studying the open layout, a kitchen so beautiful it blended right in with the living room and gave a person the feeling of being outdoors. An elevator led down to Jerry's man cave and upstairs to four bedrooms. The master bedroom was as big as the great room, the master bath just about the same size as the kitchen. "Sid and I would *love* to buy this house, but you know Sid has to live closer to Grand Rapids so he can get to the hospital quicker when he needs to. We can't even use it as a vacation home. Sid is too much in demand. I doubt we will take a vacation before he finally retires, and then we will be too old to care."

"You exaggerate. And, after all, that mansion you own

in Heartside is beautiful—right downtown and probably more expensive than this house."

Val shrugged and turned to watch a gaggle of geese swimming near the pier in front of the house. "Yes, but we can't walk out our back door and sit on a quiet lake."

Carmen walked over to check on a pot of coffee she'd just made. "Val, this place doesn't hold that kind of memories for me. I loved it at first, but now everywhere I look, I remember a beating. If I didn't know you'd keep your promise to meet me here, I wouldn't have come at all. Jerry would never try anything when someone else is around." She ran her fingers through the back of her hair. The gesture reminded her of Ben Colter's remark about how beautiful her hair was. "Anyway, I had to pick up some things from my tax files for a court case I'm working on for some clients," she told Val. "I just didn't want to come over here alone, for obvious reasons."

Val walked over and hugged her. "At least you're back in business. I don't know why you like accounting and math so much, but I'm glad you are working again. How are the headaches?"

"Much better, thanks to Sid's good care." Carmen let go of her friend and turned to pour herself a cup of coffee. "And at least my work is something I can do from home ... or I guess I should say from Dad's house for now." She set her coffee on the kitchen table and thumbed through a pile of papers. "And my staying there has helped Dad get out a little more often and have a few drinks with friends. He needs that. I keep hoping he'll meet a nice woman who can end up helping him take care of the house and look after Grandma and Grandpa."

"Has Grandma Lettie's Alzheimer's gotten worse?"

"Every day. It's a bit humorous sometimes, but so sad.

She was always such a bright, interesting lady." Carmen sighed wistfully. "It's hard to tell how Grandpa is doing. Most of the time he just sits and watches old Westerns all day. He hardly ever talks. It's not the greatest atmosphere over there, but the old home is lovely and has plenty of room. At least I'm safe there, and I'm closer to the city as far as having to visit some of the businesses I work for." She rearranged some papers into different, smaller stacks. "Pour yourself some coffee, Val. I won't be long. I thought we could go back to the city when I'm done and have lunch in Gaslight Village."

"Ooh, sounds fun, but it won't help my diet. How do you stay so skinny when you always eat whatever you want?"

"I suppose it's metabolism. Everybody is different, but in my case, it's a matter of recovering from what I was going through with Jerry. Living with him had a way of ruining my appetite." Carmen studied Val's full but nicely formed figure. She wore her dark, wavy hair in a ponytail today. "You don't need to diet, Val," she added. "You always look good."

Val pursed her lips. "I'm four inches shorter than you and twenty pounds heavier. You don't know how lucky you are to have those long legs."

"*You're* the lucky one," Carmen answered absently. She stared at her cup of coffee. "You have Sid, and he's so good to you. I wouldn't know what it's like to be loved and pampered by a man."

Val sipped some coffee. "Yeah, I know. When that bastard of a husband fractured your skull, I thought we would lose you."

"Thank God Sid was on duty that night. He saved my life."

"Leaving *Jerry* is what saved your life, girlfriend. Sid and I were so happy when you divorced that no-good."

"He wasn't no good when I married him. I don't know how or why he started experimenting with cocaine, but I don't think he will ever change now."

"Well, he's out of your life now, and good riddance. Have you tried to contact that gorgeous fancy dancer you met at that show we went to?"

Carmen smiled softly and shook her head. "No."

"But I'll bet you looked him up and read more about him, didn't you?"

"I forced myself not to. He is out there in South Dakota working on some court case or maybe already back in DC arguing some cause for the Lakota or whatever. The man is busy and brilliant and probably on the go a lot. He's likely forgotten all about me by now. It's been two weeks and I haven't heard a thing. And two weeks is long enough for me to forget about him, too."

Val laughed. "You are the worst liar in all of Grand Rapids! I'm guessing you think about him all the time. Remember who you are talking to, Carmen Wolfe. Hell, *I* think about him, and I'm *married*!"

Carmen removed combs from the sides of her hair and pulled it back to catch some loose strands, smiling as she did so. "Okay. You got me." She secured the combs and got up. "Listen to this." She walked over to the controls for the room's surround-sound system and turned it on. Out came a man's rich voice singing "The Reason," using the Prince Royce version from a 2016 TV original special called *The Passion-New Orleans*. The words were so beautiful, Ben's voice so powerful, that it brought tears to a listener's eye.

When the song ended, Carmen turned to Val, who sat there with her mouth open. "That was him?"

Carmen nodded. "I found it on iTunes and downloaded it. The guy has CDs and albums on Bluetooth. I downloaded a ton of his songs because they are all so beautiful. I couldn't help myself. It's mostly Native American music with some spiritual words but listen to this." She played "My Heart Will Go On," the theme song from *Titanic*.

"Holy cow," Val said, tears in her eyes.

"The guy can sing anything, and that one tells me he isn't over his dead wife. I cry every time I play it. I've been listening to his music as often as I can—on my phone, in my car, in my room at Dad's house. It's ridiculous. If nothing else, I'll keep buying his music because the proceeds go to his youth group. And there is something in his voice ... something so sincere. I'm addicted."

Val folded her arms and knitted her eyebrows. "To the music? Or to the *man?*"

Carmen walked back over to the table to start putting papers into a briefcase. "Both, maybe."

"Yeah, well, that kind of addiction can be as destructive as the other kind if it's the wrong man you are addicted to."

"Well, I didn't lie when I said I haven't contacted him. If anything is supposed to come of it, let *him* make the first move. There are a lot of negatives there, Val: cultural differences, the fact that somebody wants him dead, distance. I have a feeling he wouldn't leave South Dakota and his people if his life depended on it, especially not after all his work for government help and with the young people there." She hooked the latch on her briefcase. "Besides, I suspect that Ben Colter is nowhere near ready for a new relationship, most certainly not with an outsider who is about as far removed from the kind of life he leads as a person can get."

"Maybe. And I suppose he could have his pick of any of

a number of pretty, young Native American women on his reservation. I'm betting he doesn't sleep alone very often."

"And you have a dirty mind, Val Ruben." Carmen snickered. "I don't think he's that kind of man. I think he is still in mourning, and he is very devoted to the causes he fights for and too busy to be messing around with frivolous affairs. The man seems really deep—an all-or-nothing kind of guy. Very spiritual. I love his singing, and yes, he's easy to look at, but that's as far as it goes." She picked up her brief-case. "Let's go. Mrs. Remerez came yesterday to clean and check everything out, so I can lock up and leave the house again for a while. I'm going to talk to a Realtor about selling it." She unplugged the coffee and headed for the door. "Come on. Let's go eat."

Val followed. "I hope I can keep up with that hot Camaro you bought to celebrate your divorce," she joked.

"I am not celebrating something that painful. I just decided to get the car I've always wanted and Jerry wouldn't let me buy because he was jealous that it might attract other men. And yes, I got plenty of money out of the divorce, but that was the court's decision. I can manage just fine with running my own accounting business."

"Honey, I know that. And I didn't mean to hurt your feelings about celebrating a divorce. I just run off at the mouth sometimes."

Carmen laughed as she stopped and gave Val a quick hug. "I know that. It's just still hard for me to joke about splitting with Jerry. In the meantime, no, you won't be able to keep up with me. I suppose you're still driving that big Mercedes."

"I *love* my Mercedes. Why does an overweight married woman need a hot car?"

Both women laughed again. "I told you, you are *not*

overweight," Carmen said. She opened the door to leave but then froze in place.

"Holy cow! I hope that's not Jerry," Val commented.

A clean, black, short-bed Dodge Ram pickup truck pulled into the driveway. It was the kind of truck a person sometimes found intimidating when it was behind them because of its size—high enough to need a ladder to climb into it, a stainless-steel grille guard across the front. Chrome gleamed everywhere—the wheels, the trim. It was difficult to see the driver because of dark-tinted windows that were not even legal in Michigan. A sticker showing an eagle with its wings spread decorated the very top of the windshield, and an emblem on the door was of a Native American dream catcher in beautiful red, white, and yellow colors, white feathers hanging from it. As the truck turned side-ways into the parking area of the driveway, the words THE BLACK HILLS ARE NOT FOR SALE were painted on the side of the bed, and under that, Sunrise Rez, SD

"My God, it's *him!*" Val exclaimed. "The warrior! How did he find you?"

Carmen swallowed. "You can find anything on Google." *God, help me! What is he doing here?"*

The driver side door opened, and a tall man with long, black hair stepped around the truck. He wore a black T-shirt with the letters YESS printed down the front. The left side of his hair was pulled straight back and pinned with a silver hair ornament, a feather somehow wound into it and hanging over his left shoulder. The rest of his hair was swept sideways and hung over his right shoulder. The black shirt and his black low-rise jeans fit snugly over a grand physique, made sexier by a wide, beaded belt and a second skinny belt that hung across an area Carmen felt she shouldn't stare at too long. The second belt was silver with very tiny bells that jingled softly as he walked toward the door.

Those bells. Damned if it wasn't true that they were a sexual attraction.

"Is there a man alive any better looking than that?" Val whispered. "And those are Dior sunglasses. The damn things make him even *better* looking."

It was Ben Colter. He stopped when he saw her, and those dark eyes captured her gaze. A thousand alarms went off in Carmen's head. If she didn't take a breath soon, she would pass out.

CHAPTER FIVE

CARMEN SET down her briefcase as Ben stepped a little closer, neither of them taking his or her eyes of the other. He stopped about five feet from her and put his hands on his hips.

"No, I am not stalking you," he told her with that brilliant smile that kind of washed over her like an ocean wave.

"I didn't think you were," Carmen answered.

"Yes, you did. I can see it in your eyes. I promise I have all kinds of reasons for being in Michigan, and I could not imagine coming here without looking you up."

"How exactly did you find me? Everybody in the neighborhood knows me by my married name, but I never gave it to you."

Ben glanced at Val and nodded. "Nice to see you again."

Val folded her arms. "It's nice to see you, too, Mr. Colter, believe me. You are absolute eye candy," she added in the blatant way she had of voicing her feelings honestly. "But you didn't answer Carmen's question. You must admit this visit is quite a surprise."

Ben turned his attention to Carmen again. "Lawyers have ways of finding out what they need to know, and I have connections with the FBI. And there is that handy app called Google. I am sure you used that to look me up as well. They have a lot more information on me than on you."

Carmen smiled. "I'm too boring for Google. And yes, I looked you up. I read just enough to realize you lead a life I could never keep up with."

Ben looked her over appreciatively with those hand-some, sagacious eyes. "I did not get too personal with you. I only know you are twenty-eight, and your married name was Peterson, and this is your address. I put it in my GPS, and here I am." He turned and waved to someone in the truck. Because of the tinted windows, it was the first time Carmen realized there was someone else there. "My nephew is with me," Ben explained. "He is the main reason I am in Michigan. Remember when I told you about my brother and Sasha's seven sons?"

"I remember."

A tall, good-looking teenager wearing a white YESS T-shirt and ripped jeans stepped out of the truck, his black hair waist-length like Ben's. Ben motioned for the boy to join him. "This is Matthew, son number three," Ben explained. "He is seventeen and graduated high school this year and wants to go to Hope College, which you know is in Holland, just an hour or so from here. I am taking him there myself for an interview. He wants to major in geology, figure out ways we can save this messed up, dying planet." He squeezed Matthew's shoulder. "We have a couple of hours before we have to be in Holland, so I thought we would come here first, take a chance on finding you home."

"I see." Carmen folded her arms. "Good timing. I am not normally here. This is my home but only in title. I don't stay here much. I only came here this morning to pick up some business files I had stored in my old office."

"And now you know I did not go beyond my right to find out everything about you. If I had, I would have known you no longer live here."

Val reached out and shook both men's hands. "I usually say it like it is, guys," she said teasingly, "so tell me, is there anybody in your family who *isn't* good-looking?"

Ben and Matthew both laughed. "Thank you, but that is not a fair question," Ben answered. "I could not answer that without offending someone. Besides, looks do not mean much anyway." He sobered a little. "Like the old saying goes, beauty is only skin deep." He turned those dark eyes to Carmen again. "And if you will allow me, I would like to talk a few minutes." He put up his hands defensively. "Totally your decision. If you tell me to go away and never come back, I will. I was just hoping to hear from you first, but I never did. If that means you have no interest, I understand."

Carmen glanced at Val, who shrugged. "It can't hurt to talk to him," she told Carmen. "After all, you *did* Google the guy," she mockingly added.

Carmen turned to Ben, frustrated that his looks and build made it difficult to think straight. "I guess it's okay." She noticed something suddenly move through Ben's eyes— something that wiped away his smile. Was that pain? He reached out and grasped a railing along the brick steps where Carmen stood, then bent over a little.

"Oh, my gosh! Are you all right?" Carmen asked, noticing a few beads of sweat on his forehead.

"Uncle Ben, do you want me to get the Tylenol?" Matthew asked.

"Sure," Ben answered. He glanced at Carmen as

Matthew ran back to the truck. "I am sorry. I have a back problem that flares up after one of my performances, and also when I sit too long. We left Chicago about seven this morning, so I have been on the road several hours."

"Well, not just that," Carmen said in concern. "Driving all the way here from South Dakota certainly didn't help any, even if you stopped overnight in a few places." She touched his arm. "And I apologize. I've been very rude making you stand here and explain yourself. Please come inside where it's cooler. I leave the air on so things don't get damp in the house. It's so humid in Michigan this time of year."

Ben shook his head. "I do not want to put you out."

"It's okay."

"No. I should have found a way to get hold of you first, but this trip was sort of last-minute, so I just took my chances."

"Here, Uncle Ben!" Matthew interrupted upon returning. He handed out a bottle of Tylenol.

"Come in and I will get you some water," Carmen told Ben. "I insist. Do you need help?"

"No. I am fine now. The pain comes quickly and usually ends quickly if I move a little." He walked into the house behind Carmen, and Val and Matthew followed.

"Wow, this is some house!" Matthew exclaimed.

Carmen led Ben to the mohair sofa. "I'll get you a bottled water. I don't keep much else in the refrigerator because, like I said, I don't live here now. I stay with my dad until I can decide just where I *will* live. I'm putting the house up for sale."

"*Why?*" Matthew asked. "This place is really nice, and it is on a lake! There aren't many like this on the Rez."

Carmen hurried back over to Ben with the water. "This

place holds only bad memories for me," she answered Matthew. "My husband built it. He's a great designer, but he wasn't a great husband. He left me this house and a lot of money, but I would give all of it up to erase the last three years I lived with him."

"That is too bad," Matthew answered, walking to the big windows. "What is his name? Was he mean or something? There are some men on the Rez who beat their wives. I don't understand—"

"Matthew!" Ben interrupted him with obvious irritation. "You should not ask nosy questions of someone you hardly know or offer information they do not care to hear."

"Yes, sir," Matthew answered. He looked at Carmen sheepishly. "I am sorry."

"It's okay. That kind of things goes on everywhere, no matter who the people are or what the conditions are." Carmen watched Ben chug down three Tylenol and drink about half the water out of the bottle. "I have a small bottle of unopened orange juice in the fridge if that might help," she told Ben.

"Water is fine."

"Uncle Ben has shrapnel in his back from a gunshot wound when Aunt Talia was killed," Matthew told Carmen and Val. "And he has only one kidney, so he drinks a lot of water."

"Matthew Dancing Horse Colter, I think you should go outside," Ben told him. "I noticed a pier out there. Go and look at the lake and the boaters."

"Sure!" Matt hurried over to French doors off the great room. "May I unlock these?" he asked Carmen.

"Yes."

Matthew walked out, and Carmen watched him bound over the huge redwood deck and take several steps at a time as he went down a wooden stairway to the pier below.

Ben downed more water. "I am deeply sorry. He is a kid, and he blurts out things that he does not understand might be hurtful. He has not felt that hurt himself, and I hope he never does."

"Ben, it's okay." Carmen glanced at Val, who got the message in her pleading eyes.

"I'm going to sit on the patio until you two finish whatever it is you need to talk about," Val said. She walked out, and Carmen sat down across from Ben in a plush chair that matched the Maiden Home sofa. "Are you really okay now?"

He nodded and set the water bottle on a glass coffee table, along with his sunglasses and the bottle of Tylenol. "I am fine. It comes and goes."

Carmen noticed a long scar on the inside of his left forearm. "Oh dear. How did you get that scar, Ben?"

He looked away from her, in that way some people had of avoiding another's eyes. "It's nothing. Just another leftover from the shooting. I have other scars."

Carmen suspected there was more to the story when it came to his arm. She wanted to ask, to know more about the shooting, but this was not the time. Ben apparently did not want to talk about it, and she didn't know him well enough to pry more deeply. "Why do you drive such long distances if it bothers your back?" she asked.

Ben winced and shifted his seating. "Sometimes when I have several places to be that are in line with a straight-shot drive, I get in my truck and hit them in one trip. I should not say *my* truck. It belongs to the reservation. Either way, it is a good way to be alone, and sometimes I need that."

He leaned back, every move making those bells tinkle

and reminding Carmen the bells were a tool some Native American men used to attract women. They definitely worked.

"I brought Matt along because I knew I would be in the same vicinity as Hope College," Ben continued. "I had legal business first in Chicago." He pushed a loose strand of hair behind his left ear. "After we visit the college, we are going down to a small town called Dowagiac."

"I know where that is."

"It is headquarters for the Potawatomi. They hold their *Kee-Boon-Mein-Kaa* Pow-Wow there on Labor Day weekend, and they want the youth group from Sunrise to go there and put on a show, but I do not think we can make it this year. We have too many other engagements. I spoke with the president of the Pokagon Band when we were in Grand Rapids, but I feel I should visit him in person. We will stay the night there and then head for Detroit tomorrow, where I have more court business to take care of."

He shifted again, and again those tiny bells tinkled softly. He looked her over in a way that made Carmen feel self-conscious of her too-short denim shorts and her pink halter top, which she suddenly thought too revealing. Thank goodness she wore a white linen shirt over it. She pulled it closed enough to hide her cleavage.

"You are far more beautiful than I remembered," Ben told her. "We saw each other for such a short time, and I could not get you off my mind." He looked around the house. "This truly is a beautiful home. It is too bad you cannot live here." He met Carmen's gaze again and shook his head, appearing to be a little embarrassed. "This turned out all wrong, and I apologize. I certainly did not plan on having a sudden bout of back pain, but it is unpredictable. I think maybe I should leave and come back another time.

You and Val were headed somewhere, and I interrupted your plans."

"It's okay. Really. None of our plans were set in stone. I just came here to pick up some paperwork I need for some clients who pay their taxes quarterly. I'm an accountant."

Ben grinned. "You do not look like any accountant I ever knew."

Carmen felt herself blushing again. "I think you meant that as a compliment."

"I sure did."

"Well, thank you. At any rate, Val came over because I don't like to be here alone. My ex is prone to stalking me, which is where my thoughts went when you pulled into the driveway. Jerry used to beat me so bad that I am still terrified he will show up to end my life, which he has promised to do more than once."

Ben frowned, leaning forward to rest his elbows on his knees. "I hope I never run into your ex, because it might not be pretty. He deserves some of his own medicine."

A darkness moved into his eyes that told Carmen he meant exactly what he said. "I don't think I want to know what those ways are, but I assure you, Jerry isn't worth the trouble that would bring you."

"Some things *are* worth the trouble. You do not even know what I have in mind for whoever killed my wife, but that is a subject for another conversation." He rubbed at tired eyes. "Right now, I am thinking how badly I have botched this visit. It has been years since I was interested in a woman other than my own wife, so I guess I have forgotten how it all works."

Why on earth would a man who looks like you have any trouble knowing how to handle a woman? He was not the womanizer he could be. "Join the crowd," she answered. "I am no better than you are at meeting someone new, and I have a lot of trouble trusting *any* man, let alone one who lives a thousand miles away in a whole different world from mine."

Ben glanced around the room again. "Yeah, well, you might *continue* to have trouble trusting me when you learn about all my faults."

"You are too beautiful a man to have faults."

They studied each other as Ben picked up the water again and finished it all at once before setting down the empty bottle. "We all have faults, Carmen. Mine are pretty big, and we do not have time for going into any of that now. At the moment, I only know one thing." He captured her gaze in a way that made it impossible for her to look away. "Caesar saw something in you. Someone from your world might think that is nonsense, but I take it very seriously. I have been living in hell the last three years, putting all my time and energy into causes for my People and into our dancing and concerts and my work as a lawyer—all because those things keep me sane and keep me from not wanting to live at all. And then you came along, and for some reason, I saw a glimmer of hope that maybe, just maybe, I have found someone who can make it all better."

"Ben."

"Hear me out. I meant it when I said that you can tell me to leave and not come back. I promise I will abide by your wishes. But I am hoping you will first give us a chance to get to know each other better and find out why Caesar chose you as someone special. Will you allow that much?"

Carmen was struck by his manners. He was surprisingly humble and so respectful. "Well, since you are so open and sincere," she told him, "I will be the same with you. To tell you the truth, you are the most beautiful man I have ever met, in looks and in your mannerisms, but you can understand why I have a lot of trouble trusting any man or trusting my own feelings. My husband was sweet and great looking and successful and everything a woman would want, until he got into alcohol and drugs. I, too, have lived in hell the last few years, so it looks like we both carry a lot of emotional baggage." She noticed he glanced away when she mentioned drugs. "Ben? What is it?"

He rubbed at his eyes again. "We do not have time to talk about all the things we need to know about each other. Just please answer my question. I will handle it however you want. If we see each other again, we do not have to be alone together if you think you cannot trust me. Someone you know can be nearby."

"It's not that. I just ... this whole matter is so unexpected, and you are so different from anyone I have ever met. You *have* to admit that we are as different as night and day."

Ben nodded. "My brother has told me the same thing." He held her gaze again. "I can say only that I am not perfect, Carmen, but I believe Caesar is trying to tell me something about you. From Detroit I am flying to DC for three days, then back to Detroit. I want your permission to stop here on my drive back and take you to wherever your favorite place is to eat, and then talk more."

"Do you ever slow down?"

He shrugged. "As I said, I need to keep busy, and my main goal in life is to keep the dance and the language and our customs alive forever. Yes, I am a busy man, so think about what being a part of my life might involve if things go that far. I am a lawyer for indigent people and a legal representative for the Lakota. I travel a lot, from the Rez to DC to AIM headquarters, the Native Nations festival in New

York, the Morongo Thunder and Lightning Pow-Wow, the Mendota Annual *Wacipi* in Minnesota, and other Pow-Wows all over the country. Sometimes I take part in protests in South Dakota for the preservation of our land. I worship Wakan-Tanka, and I believe in spiritual guides. Mine is the wolf, and the wolf has told me I should get to know you better."

Carmen could not help a little gasp of wonder. "I am getting worn out just *listening* to you."

He held her gaze pleadingly. "Please do not let any of it discourage you. I am always busy because it keeps me from thinking about my dead wife and child and what I would like to do to whoever shot them and left me with one kidney. And believe it or not, dancing helps my pain. I get lost in the spirit world and forget the desire to take something stronger to make the pain go away."

Was this really happening? Those all-knowing eyes made a woman want to jump into this man's arms and let him do more than just hold her. Jerry had never made her feel that way. What must it be like to be held in strong arms and not be afraid? Could she trust this very unusual man who, she suspected, had only touched the surface of what she needed to know about him?

"I might remind you that besides the different worlds we live in, Ben, you are Harvard and Julliard, extraordinarily intelligent and talented. I went to Michigan State and have a master's in accounting. Period. How dull and simple is that? Oh, and I am a member of DAR, almost an enemy of AIM in your world. And I am far from spiritual. What faith I used to have dwindled when my husband turned into a monster who broke my arm, fractured my skull, and caused me to spend weeks with my jaw wired shut. And there you are, strong enough to throw me through those windows and clear out to the lake if you wanted to. And you don't want to know how much I *don't* know about Native Americans or some of the preconceived notions I have about them that would probably make you laugh."

Ben broke into a grin. "I have a fairly good idea what those notions are. Allow me the chance to prove them wrong. And I could not care less about comparing educations or talents. Everyone is born with different gifts. I have a photographic memory, which is what helped me graduate summa cum laude. As far as throwing you through that window, I have never hurt a woman in my life. I worshipped my wife and never laid a hand on her."

"And there is the final issue. I can tell you still mourn your wife, which means maybe you aren't ready for *any* kind of relationship. And we haven't even touched on the fact that someone apparently wants you dead. How safe would I be with you?"

"Very safe. I would not have Matthew with me if I were worried about that."

"I am talking about your safety at *home*," Carmen told him. "The shooting happened in Rapid City."

Pain shot through Ben's eyes ... emotional pain rather than his physical pain. "There is no commitment right now, so there is no danger in just finding out where this could go. That is all I ask of you. I will give you my cell phone number and the numbers for Tommy and Sasha, in case you wish to talk to them first." Ben stood and took his cell phone from a pocket on the side of his jeans. He handed it to her. "Will you put your phone number and the address of your father in my phone?"

Carmen sighed in resignation. "Yes, but I left my own phone in my briefcase on the front stoop. Just text your number to me—and Sasha's, too." Carmen tapped her phone number into his contact list.

"You do not mention your mother," he told her.

"My mother died of cancer a couple of years ago." Carmen handed back the phone, and Ben captured her with his eyes again as he sat down.

"You miss her," he said.

"Of course."

"I never knew my mother *or* my father. My mother died when I was little, and my father ...." He hesitated. "I do not even know who he is."

"I'm so sorry!"

Ben shook his head. "Do not be. It is what it is. Tommy raised me like a son. We lived with our maternal grand-mother most of our growing-up years. I would like you to meet her. Among my People, it is common for the old ones to raise the young ones, even in days of old. But I know your people turn to their parents, and I am thinking you must have been going through all those bad times with your ex-husband at the same time your mother was dying. It must have been so sad for you. I am thinking you are a strong woman."

Carmen was taken back by his innate understanding. "My father and friends tell me I am, but I can't really say. I only know that letting you come back to get to know each other better could be the worst decision of my life, but I agree to one more meeting."

"Thank you," Ben told her sincerely. "I am grateful. And I am sorry I interrupted your plans for today."

"You didn't. All you did was turn Val's and my brunch into a lunch. Let me know when you are on your way back from Detroit. What about Matthew?"

"He is going to fly back to South Dakota when I fly to DC"

"And you are going to drive all the way back to South Dakota alone?"

"I do it all the time. We have a plane the government pays for, but it is being used this week for something else, so I drove. After being around a bunch of active teens most of the time back at the Rez, I sometimes look forward to being alone for a while. I practice singing while I am driving." He chuckled. "People who pass me probably think I am a crazy man."

Carmen laughed with him. "You have a wonderful voice. I have to admit that I bought a couple of your CDs. My God, Ben, you could give Josh Groban a run for his money."

Ben cast her a sad smile. "Thank you for the compliment. It is my wife who urged me to go to Julliard." He winced a little again. "But that is in the past, and now, here you are, walking into my life like a fresh spring flower after a bad winter."

What a lovely way to put it, but the look in your eyes tells me how much you ache for your wife. Was she headed for a shattered heart? Maybe they both were.

Ben rose and walked around the coffee table. He reached out to her, and Carmen took his hand. He pulled her up, then stepped closer to grasp her face in his hands. She stiffened and grabbed his wrists, pushing at them. Ben frowned, letting go. "I am sorry. That was forward of me."

"No! No, no, no. It's not you." Tears suddenly welled in Carmen's eyes. "It was just a reflex. Jerry used to grab my face in his hands and squeeze my jaw and then toss me around by my head." She brushed at a tear. "I'm so sorry.

Really! You didn't do anything wrong. I'm embarrassed that I did that."

Ben carefully took her hand. "Look up here."

The words were a command, yet so gentle. Carmen sniffed and managed to meet his gaze, and there was that wise old man look again, as though someone else's spirit was in there somewhere. He held up his left hand. "See this hand? Look at it."

Carmen swallowed, thinking of the damage that hand could do. She glanced at it, then back into Ben's dark eyes.

"This hand will never touch you wrongly," he told her. "This body will never force you to do something you do not want. And these lips will never be used to yell or call you names or to touch your lips with anything but worship."

Why didn't she pull away when he leaned closer?

"You can trust me, Carmen. If I touch you wrongly, the wolves will have me for their next meal."

Why didn't she stop him when he cautiously grasped her face again or when his soft, full lips brushed hers lightly without kissing her? He trailed those lips to her eyes and kissed each eye gently, his presence spellbinding, his power overwhelming. His long hair brushed her cheek. "I will remember your scent," he told her.

She remembered the remark he'd made when Caesar sniffed at her. *It is how all males of any species pick up the female scent.* Good Lord, this man was the supreme alpha male. Maybe he was part wolf. She could see him as a black wolf with yellow eyes, running through a forest to find her.

"Not all men are like your ex-husband," he told her. "Trust that." He brushed at a tear on her cheek and kissed her hair, then gave her a smile as he let go of her and walked to the French doors. He called to Matthew. The boy and Val both came inside and said their goodbyes.

Minutes later, Ben and his nephew drove off in the black truck with its Native American emblems, its gleaming chrome and tinted windows.

Carmen turned to Val. "He's coming back in a few days to take me out," she told her.

Val shook her head. "Gear up, girlfriend. This is going to be an exciting ride. I truly want you to find love again, but Ben Colter could be a real handful emotionally."

Carmen watched the truck disappear around a corner. "I have no choice. The man has a way of pulling you in, even if you are kicking and screaming all the way. I think I am already a lost cause."

CHAPTER SIX

"HE IS COMING TOMORROW, and I have to find just the right outfit," Carmen told Val.

"A combination of sexy and demure," Val advised. "I think this guy is already smitten, so you don't need to drive him crazy with want. Just make his mouth water a little."

"Val Ruben, how does Sid put up with you?"

Both women got out of Carmen's white Camaro.

"Sid loves my healthy appetite for sex," Val joked. "After hours of tending to horrible accident injuries and trying to keep patients' brains inside their skulls, he is ready for anything that takes his mind away from blood and sobbing relatives by the time he gets home from the hospital. It can be pretty depressing some days."

"Sid has a big heart," Carmen answered as they headed into Rivertown Crossings Mall in Grandville. "Right now, I'd rather think about which stores to hit. I'm thinking The Buckle—something simple. I hardly think Ben is a fancy Francesca's or Chico's kind of man."

"Versona isn't bad—kind of in between. Of course, once

things get intimate, you're going to want to shop at Victoria's Secret."

"Get serious, Val."

"I *am* serious. And, by the way, with your money, you could have flown to Detroit or New York and shopped Milano or Karen Kane or Valentino."

"And spend two thousand dollars on one shirt? I don't think Ben is looking for a woman who blows her money on bling and shirts that probably cost enough to buy a bus for those young people. I am very sure he's more interested in the quality of strength and character."

"Mm-hmm. How about those Dior sunglasses?" Val put a hand to her heart. "My *God,* he looked good in those things!"

"He *is* a lawyer, you know. As hard as he works, he deserves to blow a little money on himself. You can't hold that against him. He suffers pain just to put on those shows to raise money for those kids."

They walked through the mall entrance and past Chico's Boutique before Val touched Carmen's arm to stop her before they went any farther. She led Carmen to a bench and sat down with her.

"Carmen, I know I shouldn't talk about Ben's hot looks or how you should dress for him. I'm just joking. I want my old, fun-loving friend back. You know I love you, and I know you miss your mom, so I want you to remember you can talk to me if you need to share something with another woman. Putting up with your grandmother's craziness and your lingering fears over Jerry, and now, this very new and challenging thing with Ben Colter—I'm sure you're going through a lot of doubts and confusion, but you need to lighten up and let things happen the way they are *supposed* to happen. I just want you to be happy again, Carmen. So

I'm a little confused about how to feel about it, what to tell you to do."

Carmen shrugged. "Ben is so far from what I expected if I took an interest in someone else. I mean, this whole thing came out of the blue. I feel like I've been hit by a fly ball I never saw coming."

"It would probably be easier if you would look at Ben as just a man," Val suggested. "I'll grant you he's so damn good-looking that it's hard to see past that, but don't lose your perspective. Ben Colter is human, and he's going to have faults, so be ready for that, but have fun while you're finding out. You sure can't judge all men by Jerry. Look at Sid. Men don't come much better than him. And you obviously don't need to worry about impressing Ben. Something tells me you could wear a potato sack on this date, and he wouldn't notice."

Carmen sighed and watched a mother and five little ones walk by, the kids jumping around and asking for ice cream. "I guess you're right. I'm just so damn nervous, Val. I want everything to go exactly right. I want to pick out just the right jeans and top and sandals and whatever. I got my nails done yesterday, and I got my hair layered a little. What do you think?" She turned around and fluffed her blond tresses.

"I think Ben Colter would like to get his hands tangled in that for all the right reasons," Val answered.

Carmen let out a little growl. "You are hopeless!" She got up and started walking again. "Where do you want to eat later?"

Val caught up. "Let's decide after we have shopped for a while. There are about fifteen restaurants here, and I'm not sure yet what I'm in the mood for. Maybe Charlie's."

They spent the next two hours trying on clothes, laughing, imagining what a date with Ben might be like, trying to decide what to eat. Carmen spent a third hour buying shoes, a handbag, and a tiny gold necklace. By the time she finished, she was loaded down with bags from several different stores. "There is Charlie's, just a couple of doors down," she told Val. "Go get us a booth. I'm taking these bags out to the car so I don't have to wrestle with them while we eat. Do you want me to take yours?"

"I didn't get that much. I'm okay. Hurry back."

"I will." Carmen took an escalator to the main floor, then hurried out, grunting a little as she maneuvered all the bags in the long walk to her Camaro. When she reached the car, she set a couple of bags down and took her key fob from her jeans pocket. The car beeped when she unlocked the doors. She managed to toss all the bags inside, then locked the door again and turned.

And there stood Jerry!!

Carmen's heart raced as she pushed the key fob back into her jeans pocket. She adjusted her handbag's skinny strap on her shoulder and swallowed. "What are you doing here, Jerry? I could have you arrested just for standing within ten feet of me."

Jerry flashed the wicked smile she well recognized—the smile that once was charming but now meant he'd been drinking and had probably popped some pill that made him feel cocky and mean.

"An *Indian?*" he sneered. "You're seeing a fucking *Indian?*"

Carmen wanted to run, but she was already backed up against her car. "Who told you that lie?"

"I have friends who know friends who report to me," Jerry told her, bracing his hands on either side of her against the Camaro. A gentle breeze ruffled his golden hair, and his eyes looked bluer in the bright sun. But there was no gentleness in those eyes. They were cold and hard.

"It's none of your business who I see!" Carmen reminded him. "We are *divorced,* remember? And I have a restraining order against you! Now get away from me!"

He grabbed her left arm painfully. "Do you really think a restraining order can keep me from killing you? How many times has your warrior hero already banged you?"

"I still barely know him, and it's none of your business anyway! Now, let go of me before I scream! We are in a public parking lot. There are other people around!"

Jerry kept hold of her arm as he glanced past her then looked to both sides. "I don't see anybody but you and me, *bitch!*"

"Jerry, don't do this! You'll go to jail."

"It will be *worth* it!"

Before Carmen could scream, Jerry's fist slammed into her left eye. It was the last thing she remembered before waking up in an ambulance.

"You'll be okay, honey." The voice was that of an older man. "Let me see your pupils." Someone held open her eyelids one at a time. She could tell something bright shined into her eyes, but she couldn't make out any details.

"I don't think she has a concussion," the man said.

Carmen tried to move but was strapped to something. *Must be a gurney.* She was familiar with the routine.

For some reason, Ben came to mind—his gentle touch, his promise when he held up a big hand and said, *This hand will never hurt you.* She knew in her heart he meant that. How strange that, in spite of hardly knowing him, she wished he was here. That's when she remembered she was supposed to see him tomorrow.

Tomorrow! It was all ruined now. She'd been through

this too many times, knew her face was a swollen mess. She couldn't let Ben see her this way.

"Carmen." She recognized Val's voice, but things were going black again. "When you took so long to come back, I ran out to check on you. By then there was a crowd and sirens and ... I'm so sorry, Carmen! I should have walked out with you."

"Can't ... see," Carmen answered. "Can't think ... remember ..." It was hard to talk. She realized her lower lip was swollen.

Someone took hold of her hand and squeezed it. "It's okay, sweetie. Sid will take care of you. He's waiting at Spectrum."

Again, blackness enveloped Carmen. She welcomed it.

BEN RANG the doorbell of the brick, ranch-style home that was similar to most of the other homes in the subdivision. He moved his sunglasses to the top of his head and waited, a little nervous at meeting Carmen Wolfe's father. He well knew the kind of reaction he might get. He'd grown immune to prejudgments.

It took a couple of minutes for someone to come to the door. He glanced at a light blue Mercedes that sat in the driveway, as well as a white Camaro. Both were cars that didn't quite fit the house or the neighborhood. Why did something feel amiss?

He rang the doorbell again, hoping his white collared shirt and Tommy Bahama jeans were good enough for wherever Carmen wanted to go. His hair was pulled straight back and held at the crown with silver hair orna-ments, and he wore long, feather-shaped silver earrings and a silver and turquoise necklace at his throat. He glanced at his watch to see it was three p.m., which gave him and Carmen plenty of time to talk, go to a nice restaurant, talk some more.

The door finally opened, and there stood a little old lady with gray hair that stuck out every which way because of an old perm. Her clouded eyes widened, and she screamed. "Indians! Indians!" She turned and shuffled into the living room, where a white-haired man sat in an easy chair watching an old black-and-white fifties Western. Indians were attacking a wagon train.

"Carson! Carson!" the old lady carried on. "Get in here! Indians are attacking us!"

Ben realized the screaming old woman must be Carmen's grandmother, who had Alzheimer's. He shook his head and stepped inside, closing the door behind him. He leaned against the wall of the small entranceway, folding his arms to wait for Carmen.

"Mother, it's okay." A man spoke the words. "Come into your room and close the door. I'll handle this."

"Get your rifle!" the old woman yelled.

"Okay, I promise I will."

Ben hoped the man didn't mean it and was just trying to appease his mother. He carried a .45 himself but had left it in the truck.

"You stay in your room," the man told the old woman. "You'll be safe, I promise."

A door closed, and a balding man with a pot belly emerged from a hallway to the right of the living room. Thankfully, he carried no rifle. He stopped for a moment when he spotted Ben standing there, then smoothed back what hair he still had and came closer, rubbing his hands on the sides of his pants. He eyed Ben up and down, then put out his hand. "I guess you would have to be Ben Colter. It would be pretty hard to figure you were anybody else."

"Yes, sir, I am Ben." Ben shook his hand.

"I'm Carson Wolfe, Carmen's father," the man explained. "I was in the bathroom when the doorbell rang and couldn't get here before my mother. I apologize for her reaction. She has Alzheimer's and hardly knows her own name."

"I understand." Ben let go of Carson's hand. "I hope it is okay that I stepped inside and closed the door. This time of year, bugs find a way into your house uninvited. A man could get rich if he had a nickel for every time a mother yelled *shut the door!*"

Carson laughed. "You're right."

"It is a little worse where I come from," Ben added, hoping to keep things friendly with Carmen's father. "Where I live, everybody has horses, which means more flies."

"Oh, I see what you mean!" Carson laughed, but he seemed uneasy, as though there was something more he wanted to say but was afraid to say it. "I don't know much about, you know, reservation life and all of that," Carson added, looking Ben over again. "I *do* know all about your accomplishments, and I've even heard your music. It's impressive."

"Thank you." *Where is Carmen?*

"Kill the sons of bitches!" the old man suddenly yelled from the easy chair. Soldiers in the black-and-white movie were riding after the attacking Natives.

"Oh my God," Carmen's father mumbled. He looked back at Ben and shook his head. "Look, I'm really, really sorry about my mother's outburst when she saw you. And now I am doubly embarrassed. That's my father over there in the easy chair. He sits and watches old Westerns all day, and you know what goes on in those."

"I am keenly aware, sir. Maybe someday you and I can sit down and talk about all those mistakes in old Westerns."

Carson nodded. "Maybe so. But still, I truly am sorry. I'm not ... I mean ... I don't judge like that. This is the twenty-first century, and it's time ... well ... "

"You do not have to explain, Mr. Wolfe." *Where in heck is Carmen?*

"Look, uh, oh, by the way, you can drop the mister. Just call me Carson." The man folded his arms over his belly self-consciously. "Look, there's a problem."

"A problem? Carmen is not here?"

"Oh, yes, she's here, but," Carson scratched at a ruddy cheek. "Something happened. She doesn't want to see you."

Ben's first thought was that Carmen had learned something about his past that had changed her mind about him. "I do not understand."

Carson glanced toward the hallway and back to Ben. "She'd really like you to honor her wishes. Val texted you, but apparently you didn't see her text. Carmen is not in very good shape right now and wants to wait to see you after she is healed."

"*Healed?* Healed from what?"

Carson sighed with concern. "She said she told you about her ex, which is why you can surely understand why I would be concerned about *any* new man she might be interested in. My first job as her father is to protect her, so if I seemed to scrutinize you a little too closely, that's the only reason. It's got nothing to do with the fact that you're Native American. You could be Chinese or Puerto Rican or anything else."

"Healed from *what?*" Ben interrupted, his alarm building.

Carson glanced toward the hallway again. "Look, Mr. Colter – "

"Ben."

"Look, Ben, she had a little run-in with her ex in a mall parking lot."

"Where is she?" Ben demanded. "Let me talk to her."

"She's really embarrassed. She doesn't like people to see her this way, especially you. I mean, she was so excited about your coming back. She went shopping just to find the right clothes."

"Where *is* she?" Ben asked again. "Please let me see her!"

Carson rubbed at the back of his neck. "She will be really upset with me, but if you can do anything to lift her spirits, I sure would be grateful." He looked toward the hallway again. "At the end of that hallway, there is a door to a small apartment added on to the back of the house."

Ben charged past him.

"We built it for my parents a few years ago," Carson called out as Ben disappeared down the hallway.

Ben couldn't care less if the addition was a tent. Carmen was there and hurting. Once he talked to her, he would damn well find out where this ex-husband of hers lived and make sure this never happened again!

CHAPTER SEVEN

BEN CHARGED through the apartment door without knocking, and three people looked his way. One of them, lying on a couch, pulled a blanket over her head so quickly he didn't see her face, but he damn well knew who it was. The other two were Val and a tall, graying man standing beside her.

"Ben!" Val spoke up. "I texted you not to come!" She looked at the man next to her. "That's Ben, as if you can't tell. We should have left the door open so we knew he was out there. When it's closed, you can't hear a thing going on in the rest of the house."

Ben stepped closer. "I received no text, but it is probably because my phone did not recognize your number. I get a hundred or more texts a day from DC, FBI, texts from home, all over, and I have been on the road. I could have easily overlooked a text from an unknown number." He stepped even closer. "What is going on here?"

The man with Val touched Ben's arm. "It's obvious Carmen's father told you what happened. Give this a minute, Ben." He put out his hand. "I am Dr. Sid Ruben, Val's husband."

"And the best damn neurosurgeon in the country," Val added proudly. "He works at Spectrum in Grand Rapids, and he's here to check on Carmen. He saved her life once when Jerry hit her so hard that she fractured her skull when she fell."

Ben glanced at the hidden form under the blanket again, then paused and shook Sid's hand. "I am sorry for how I barged in, but Carmen's father said enough for me to know she is badly hurt."

Sid let go of his hand and folded his arms. "She'll be all right in time. It will be hard for her to talk straight for a while because of a swollen bottom lip, and her left eye is black and nearly swollen shut, but there is no damage to the eye. She has a couple of very painful bruised ribs, so it hurts to move around. I think the rib injuries are from how she fell after Jerry hit her. She ended up lying unnoticed between two cars for a while before someone finally spotted her and called an ambulance. It all happened yesterday."

"Witnesses?"

"None," Val answered. "Jerry caught her alone when she went out to put some packages in her Camaro." Her eyes teared. "I should have gone with her. But I figured a parking lot is such a public place, Jerry would never pull something like this." She sniffed. "This is what she meant when she told you she doesn't like to stay alone at the lake house."

Sid moved an arm around his wife's shoulders. "It's not your fault, honey. If Jerry was high enough on cocaine, he might have hit you, too."

"And is her ex in jail?" Ben asked.

Sid closed his eyes and sighed. "He has a lot of money

and good lawyers, so no, he's out on bail and likely will find a way to get out of this. He's done it before."

"He gets away with everything." Val scowled.

Ben turned and paced, feeling ready to explode. He heard a little whimper come from Carmen as she bent one leg and kept the blanket over her face. Ben stepped closer to Sid and Val, turning his attention to Val. "This time, money and good lawyers are not going to help Jerry Peterson! I *also* happen to be a good lawyer. And I have connections Carmen's drug-infested ex does *not* have. When I am through with him, he will no longer be a threat. I will put fear into Jerry Peterson's heart like he has never known!"

"No. Ben." The words came from under the blanket over Carmen's face. "You will ... get in trouble."

"I will not!" Ben glanced from Carmen back to Sid. "I am sorry for how we have met. I hold much respect for your treatment of Carmen and your good standing. But do not try to keep me from her. I can help her." He took his cell phone from his pocket and handed it to Val. "Put Jerry Peterson's home address in the notes on this phone."

"Ben, no!" Val protested.

"*Trust* me! I will make sure this man never hurts or even threatens Carmen again, and I will not get into trouble for it."

Val looked at Sid, who frowned. "Ben, think about it first and allow yourself time to calm down," he warned.

"I have handled men like Carmen's ex before," Ben told him. "I volunteer for the Rez police when I am home, and I am well trained. I have seen a lot of this thing, and it sickens me. My own wife and my unborn son were shot and *killed* by such a coward as this man is! I was left with one kidney. If this man keeps going, he will kill Carmen, and I will *not* let that happen! It is simply a matter of right and wrong, and I cannot go back to South Dakota knowing this could happen again."

"Let the courts take care of this," Sid warned. "It's happened before, so maybe this time Jerry will go to jail for it."

Ben grinned, but it was more of a dark, almost evil grin. "And you think that will stop him from ever doing this again? It will not! I *know* men like this Jerry. It takes more than jail to stop them."

"Ben, I don't know the laws in South Dakota," Val told him. "But you are in *Michigan,* and let's face it: you would be judged differently here than maybe in South Dakota."

Ben stepped back. "I know the law, Val. But there is something in my world called Lakota justice, and it can be very effective." He turned away and carefully sat down on the edge of the couch while Sid and Val looked at each other.

"I *told* you he's not like anybody you've ever met," Val told her husband.

Ben started to pull the blanket from Carmen's face, but she hung on to it. "Please go, Ben," she begged, her words not coming out quite right. "Go home. We should not have agreed to see each other."

"When I leave here, it will not be to the Black Hills," Ben told her. "Not yet. First, I will pay your ex-husband a visit."

"No!"

"Do not worry." He looked up at Sid and Val. "None of you should worry. I know what I am doing." He turned back to Carmen and tugged at the blanket again, finally prying her fingers away so he could pull it off her face. Carmen turned her head to the left and covered her face with her right hand.

Ben gently took hold of her right wrist and pulled her hand away. "Look at me, Carmen."

"I can't."

"Remember when Caesar was staring at you and you were afraid? I told you to look at me, and when you did, some of your fear went away. I told you the last time I saw you that I believe you are strong. Are you going to let this man who is not a man at all make you cower and be afraid? You have survived incredible injuries to your body and your heart. So, too, have I. I know what that is like, Carmen, but I refuse to let it break me. It almost did, and that is something we still need to talk about. I will not leave until we have had that chance."

Carmen kept her head turned. Ben leaned down and kissed her right temple and a tiny cut on her right cheek. "I have seen it all, Carmen. There is nothing that shocks me and nothing that puts fear in my heart. Please look at me and let me see no shame in your beautiful green eyes."

"They aren't so ... beautiful right now."

"It does not matter. *Look* at me, Carmen," Ben repeated.

Carmen turned hesitantly, and Ben felt rage move through is veins again at the sight of her blackened, swollen left eye. The bruising had moved all the way down her cheekbone to below her left jaw, and her bottom lip was twice its normal size. "Everything ... hurts," she said, tears in her eyes. "I am eating ... through a straw again ... and it hurts to laugh or even breathe."

"I know pain." Ben leaned closer and kissed her good eye, then stroked a strand of hair off her forehead. He looked up at Sid. "What are you giving her?"

Sid ran a hand through his thick, curly hair. "Well, her injuries aren't bad enough for strong pain pills, so I am just recommending extra-strength Tylenol every four hours, more often if necessary. It won't hurt her any."

"Good. No one should take the stronger opioids unless they are dying. Doctors give out opioids too easily. That is something else I am familiar with." He turned back to Carmen, taking hold of her hand and kissing it.

"Ben, I know a lot of high-profile doctors," Sid told him. "When Val told me about the shooting, I looked it up. It happened in Rapid City, so obviously I figured that's where they took you. I thought maybe I could find a doctor who could do something about your back once I learned more details about your injuries. I, uh, I found the doctor who treated you, and I learned something I didn't expect."

Ben closed his eyes and kissed the back of Carmen's hand. "I know what Dr. Yates probably told you, but I am well now." He looked up at Sid. "Carmen has my brother Tommy's number in her phone. You are welcome to call him and ask him anything you want. I have since found other ways to manage my pain. He will tell you."

"I was only concerned for Carmen's sake."

"Of course you were. I do not blame you. You are a doctor and her friend." Ben squeezed Carmen's hand as he turned back to her. "Look at me," he told her softly.

Carmen could only meet his gaze with her good eye.

"I do not know what things you have already heard, but I made you promises the last time we were together. I promised to never hurt you. That includes not hurting your heart the way your husband has done with his use of drugs. I am nothing like him in that way, understand? I do not take bad drugs and never have. I had a problem with opioids after the shooting because the pain I was in is indescribable. But now I take nothing I cannot buy over the counter. Do you believe me?"

Carmen squeezed his hand in return. "You would not have accomplished so much for the youth and the Lakota if you were in the mess Jerry is in. I don't quickly judge people, Ben." She let go of his hand and touched the turquoise necklace at his throat. "Look at you ... a white collared shirt and all. You look ... so nice. Like a business-man." A tear slipped down the side of her face.

Ben smiled for her. "I *am* a businessman. I just came from speaking before Congress. Do you think I could have done that if I had a drug problem? And by the way, I got something from the government I petitioned for. They are going to furnish two new buses for the youth group."

Carmen tried to smile but winced with pain. "I'm glad for you." Another tear slipped out. "Ben, I wanted to look ... nice for you. It's why ... I went shopping. I was so happy when I ... threw those packages into my car. But then I turned, and there was Jerry. He said ugly things about you, and then he slugged me so fast there wasn't time to duck."

Ben kissed her forehead. "It only matters that you are alive and the injuries are not devastating. We can still talk when I come back later. I have so much to tell you, and so many questions for you in return. But first I need to make sure something like this does not happen again. I will not go back home knowing your ex might hurt you again, or worse."

"How can you make sure of that? Jerry gets away with everything."

Ben smiled wickedly again. "Not this time, and not ever again." He kissed her forehead once more and rose, pulling the silver clips from his hair and letting it fall. "I will not be long."

"Ben, don't!" Carmen protested.

"What the heck are you doing?" Val asked.

Ben shook his hair loose. "A warrior does not allow another man to bring harm to a woman. Even if Carmen is never anything more than a friend, she does not deserve to live in fear. I will make sure this man never hurts her again." He dropped the clips onto the coffee table, facing Sid and Val. "Trust me."

Val handed back his phone. "I put Jerry's address in your notes."

Ben took the phone and shoved it into his jeans pocket. "Do not worry. I will not kill him. I will just make him *wish* he was dead!" He headed for the door. "He is probably home celebrating what he did to Carmen. I will wipe the grin off his face!" He stopped and turned his attention to Sid. "Come with me, Dr. Ruben," Ben told him. "I have something to give to you."

"What's going on?" Carmen's father asked as Ben headed for the front door.

"I am taking care of things for Carmen," he answered, not bothering to explain. He made sure Sid was following as he walked outside and to the driver's side of his truck. He reached under the seat, took hold of Sid's right wrist, and slapped his .45 into Sid's hand.

"What the hell?" Sid asked.

"That is mine," Ben told him, "and it is legal. I have a permit to carry it anywhere. I am giving it to you so that I am not tempted to shoot him and cannot be accused of using it to threaten anyone." He ripped off his shirt, then removed a small jar from the truck door and unscrewed the lid. He dipped two fingers into the jar and quickly painted two red stripes down one side of his face, from his bottom eyelid to his jawbone, then put back the face paint. He used what was left on his fingers to paint two more stripes crosswise over the first two, then wiped the rest of the paint down over his other cheek.

"Is that some kind of *war* paint?" Sid asked.

Ben climbed into the truck without answering. "I intend to give Jerry Peterson only a taste of Lakota justice." He started the truck. "Do not call the police. It is not necessary." He sped off.

CHAPTER EIGHT

"This is Tommy. Speak."

"Tommy? Tommy Colter?"

"Who is this?"

"My name is Carmen Wolfe here in Michigan."

"Carmen! Little Brother talks about you often. In fact, he was on his way from Detroit this morning to meet with you. Is everything okay?"

"Well, actually, no. And if my speech sounds a little odd, it's because I have a swollen lip." Carmen struggled against tears of worry for Ben. "Listen, Ben just now took off after my ex-husband! He said something about Lakota justice. Can you call him? Stop him?"

"Wait! Slow down! I do not understand."

"Give me the phone," Sid said.

"Just a minute," Carmen said to Tommy as she handed Sid the phone. Sid sat down beside her on the couch, and Carmen glanced at Val, who sat in a chair opposite her.

"Stay calm, girlfriend," Val told her, giving Carmen a smile.

Sid left the phone on speaker so they all could hear.

"Tommy, it's hard for Carmen to talk right now," Sid relayed. "She's been hurt. My name is Sid Ruben, a good friend and a neurosurgeon here in Grand Rapids. Carmen's ex-husband caught up with her yesterday and beat her. When Ben got here and found out what happened, he kind of lost it. He took off his shirt and painted his face, then sped away in his truck. He gave me his gun first, told me he didn't want to be accused of using it, so I don't know what he has in mind. He's really upset. I felt like I'd just witnessed someone headed for the Custer massacre. Can you stop him?"

There came a pause. Voices. "Little Brother went after Carmen's husband?" Those words came from a woman. "Oh boy, somebody is in for it now," the woman said.

They could hear the woman and Tommy both snickering.

"That was my wife, Sasha," Tommy explained. "She loves seeing Ben in action." He paused again. "Look, if I call Ben, he will know why I am calling, and he will not answer. But do not worry. It is good that he left his gun with you. If he called his intentions Lakota justice, I know what he will do. Ben is a very smart man, too smart to go to jail over this. You can trust this will turn out okay."

"Carmen's ex will be very sorry that he hurt her," Sasha spoke up. "When Ben is done with him, Carmen's ex will never want to run into Little Brother again. You should see him in court. He has outsmarted some of the best government lawyers at times. Congressmen and senators dread seeing him at hearings."

"I am sorry for what happened to Miss Wolfe," Tommy spoke up then. "How bad are her injuries?"

"Bad enough to put her down for a few days," Sid told

Tommy, "but she will heal. Her ex has injured her much worse than this in the past."

"Oh, that is too bad." Tommy sounded sincere. "We will pray for her."

"Pray for Ben, too," Val said. "He's in Michigan, not on a reservation. The rules aren't the same here."

"Ben knows the law," Tommy told them, "and he knows police tactics. He and I volunteer to help the Rez police when we are not traveling."

The woman in the background made a shrill trilling sound. "Little Brother is on the warpath!" she yelled.

"My wild and energetic wife gets carried away," Tommy said. "But she is right. If my brother had lived two hundred years ago, he would have been a leader like Crazy Horse."

"And look how Crazy Horse died," Sid reminded him.

"*Howah!* You know our history. I honor you."

"You really aren't worried?" Carmen spoke up.

"No. I trust Little Brother to do the right thing. I am sorry for the commotion he has caused, and Ben will be, too, once he calms down. He is a very passionate man with much conviction. Miss Wolfe, I am sorry this is how we meet for the first time. If you are interested in Ben, you have much to learn about him. His wife's death affected him deeply. The way he reacted to you being hurt tells you how deeply he feels about right and wrong. He has been on an emotional roller-coaster since the shooting."

"I just feel so bad that this happened at all," Carmen told Tommy. "I was looking forward to our visit."

"Ben works hard here on the Rez to stop spousal abuse," Sasha spoke up. "He gives free legal help to battered wives on the Rez. We are not surprised at how he reacted to this."

"Right or not, I will feel a lot better if and when Ben comes back unhurt," Carmen answered.

"And without ten police cars on his ass," Sid added. "I hope he gets here soon, because I could get a call anytime from the hospital for an emergency. I just hope the emergency isn't Ben ... or Jerry, for that matter, much as he deserves to get a taste of his own medicine."

"Ben will take care of that for you. I have no doubt he will call me when this is over. I will let you know when I hear from him. Watch your texts."

"Thank you," Carmen answered.

"Yes, thank you," Sid told Tommy. He hit the cancel call button and handed Val's phone back to her, then wilted against the back of the couch. "Good God," he muttered.

"I sure would love to see what Ben meant by Lakota justice," Val added.

Carmen pressed an ice pack to her lip. Some of the swelling had already gone down. "I didn't want any of this to happen," she lamented. "Thank you both for being here. I'm so scared for Ben."

"Oh, believe me, from what I witnessed when Ben left, you don't need to worry about him," Sid told her. "And doctor or not, I have to say that the thought of that no-good ex of yours getting his just rewards makes me smile." He rubbed his eyes. "I still wonder if I should call the police and send them to Jerry's house."

"No!" Carmen protested. "Tommy said Ben knows what he is doing, so let it go. Getting the police over there could cause unnecessary trouble or get Ben shot. With all the cocaine and other drugs I'm sure are in that house, they might think Ben is part of the whole mess."

Val snickered. "It's good to know you're worried about

Ben rather than that rotten ex of yours. You should have dumped Jerry long before you finally did."

"Shit," Sid muttered under his breath. He put his head in his hands.

The apartment door was open, and out in the hallway Grandma Florence was carrying on about "that Indian who ran out of here." She thanked Carmen's father for chasing him away "before he kidnapped our Carmen!"

Carmen, Sid, and Val all grinned. "I've already *been* kidnapped," Carmen said. "Even if I wanted to, how in heck could I turn Ben away now that he has run off to defend my honor? I mean, how many men do that nowadays?"

"Apparently, Ben does," Val answered. "Holy cow, Carmen, he really *is* a warrior! I thought what he did on that stage a couple of weeks ago was mostly an act, but the guy is for real."

Carmen closed her eyes. "Maybe too real for his own good. This reaction has something to do with his frustration over his own wife's death. Tommy seems to think so. I don't think Ben is even close to being over what happened. I'm not sure I can handle all that emotional baggage. I have enough of my own."

"I'm sure there is *plenty* of emotional baggage," Sid answered. "When he took off his shirt, I noticed the name Talia tattooed in a half circle right over his heart. And I almost expected to hear a war cry when he peeled out of here. Carmen, something tells me this whole thing has opened Pandora's Box. In this case, it's Ben Colter's box, and it's full of all kinds of pain and sorrow."

BEN DROVE up to the magnificent brick home Jerry Peterson owned. No one could argue the man had a talent for designing homes. This one even had turrets on each front corner. The house sat on several wooded acres, and he guessed the driveway getting here to be a good half mile long. From what he could tell, the back side overlooked a huge ravine where no doubt deer and other wild animals could be spotted.

He noticed four cars in the circular driveway, one of them a Lamborghini Urus he figured belonged to Jerry. The others were average, a Jeep Cherokee, an older Lexus, and a plain white Ford Taurus. He climbed out of the truck and charged up to the beautifully embossed wood front door. He tried the knob. It was unlocked.

He turned the knob and kicked in the door. The strong, skunky smell of pot hit his nostrils when he walked in. Two naked young women crawling all over a naked man lying on the couch looked up at him while the man just lay there. Another man sat at a table a few feet away. He was leaned over the table snorting cocaine and seemed unconcerned about who'd just come inside.

One of the women, with long, red hair, jumped up from the couch and walked up to Ben. "Well, well, well. Join the party, Tonto! I didn't know this would turn into a costume ball." She eyed him up and down. "Damn! You sure fill out those Tommy Bahamas. You're going to be a mouth full! Did you bring the stuff?"

Ben shoved her away. "Which one is Jerry Peterson?"

"Jerry is over there at the table," the second woman told him. She got off the man on the couch. "He'll pay you with cash, but Linda and I can pay you a better way if you take off those jeans." She went to her knees. "Come to mama, honey."

Ben charged past the women while Jerry, wearing only his underwear, remained bent over the lines of cocaine. It wasn't until Ben reached him that he looked up. Before he could say a word, Ben lit into him with a quirt, lashing Jerry across the left side of his face and down over his bare chest. Jerry screamed in pain and fell over backward in his chair. "What the fuck?"

Ben jerked him up by his thick, blond hair and lashed him again, this time the right side of his face, then once more across his chest.

"Stop! Stop it!" Jerry yelled. He put his hands to his face, then pulled them away to gawk at blood on his fingers. He bent over to protect his face, but Ben proceeded to whip his back several times while Jerry tried to crawl away from him. Ben picked him up then and threw him across the table, sending the contents of a bag full of cocaine flying everywhere.

"God damn, you sonofabitch!" Jerry cried. "What the fuck is this about?"

Ben picked him up again and slammed him against a huge front window, cracking it. Again came the stinging lashes. Jerry tried to fend him off, but although Jerry was a decent-sized man, Ben was half again bigger, and anger made him stronger than normal. He shoved Jerry to the floor and put a knee in his groin, then held the small whip over him.

"This is called a quirt," Ben snarled. "It is normally used with just two falls of rawhide to gently urge a horse or cattle to go faster, but mine is not used for animals. It is used for men like *you*, which is why it has many falls, with tiny stones tied into the ends of the rawhide. See how they sting?"

"You ... *bastard!*" Jerry practically sobbed the words

through bloody lips. "You're that fucking Indian who's been banging Carmen, aren't you! I'll get you for this. You'll never make it back to your ... happy hunting grounds, Geronimo!"

"Wrong tribe!" Ben snarled. He lashed the rawhide across Jerry's face again. "I will tell you this only once," he sneered. "If you hurt Carmen Wolfe again or even go near her, I will be *back*! And I will use this quirt in ways that will make you beg me to *kill* you! This time you will heal, but the next time you will *not*! Do you understand me?"

"You can't—"

"I will not just use this whip on you," Ben interrupted. "I know people who can put you out of business and send you to Jackson Prison for *life*! Do you understand *that*? I will have your business investigated by the FBI, the state police, and the IRS! They will not like to know half the money you make goes unreported, but it *does* go *somewhere*! It goes up your *nose*! I can have this house raided, your business office raided, your records confiscated. If you do not want to feel this whip again, tell me you understand!"

"*Fuck* you!"

Ben lashed his face again.

"All right! All right! I understand." Jerry answered.

"Tell me you will never go near Carmen Wolfe again! If you do, within thirty days from then you will have no business, no bank accounts, no Lamborghini, and no *cocaine*! Have I made myself clear?"

Jerry swallowed blood. "God damn you," he sobbed.

Ben raised up and lashed him across the chest again, sending little splatters of blood flying. "Carmen is no longer your *wife*, so you will stay away from her. Tell me again that you understand, or I will stay here and lash you until you can no longer *speak*. I know every law in the book when it comes to men like you. Say the words Say you will stay away from Carmen!"

Panting, Jerry promised through tears, "I'll stay away from her," he choked before spitting blood against Ben's chest.

Ben jerked him all the way to his feet again and lashed at Jerry three more times, until Jerry collapsed to his knees. "Remember this moment, *Wasicus*, or I will ruin you."

"I could call the police on you!'

"*Try* it. With all the drugs in this house and the shape you are in, who do you think would go to jail?" Ben stepped away and turned to see the other man still passed out naked on the couch. The women had apparently fled. He looked backed at a still-sobbing Jerry, who was on hands and knees and gasping for breath. Ben spotted a large glass containing a drink on the table that had somehow survived the battle without spilling. He picked it up and splashed its contents across the table, rinsing off what was left of the cocaine. "If you need more of the devil's white powder, you will have to lick it up off the floor!" He smashed the glass onto the slate floor beside Jerry, and a shard of glass flew up and cut Ben's right cheek.

"Do you know how much that shit was worth?" Jerry cried out.

"Believe me, I know *exactly* what it is worth."

"Damn you! You just cost me a fortune."

Ben turned and left, wincing with renewed pain in his lower back. Jerry kept yelling about how much money the cocaine was worth as Ben walked outside. He grinned wickedly. How ironic it was that there was probably a lot more cocaine in that house. He could easily have ransacked the place looking for enough to kill the pain in his back, but just having that thought angered him. He whacked at a shrub with the quirt, sending leaves and tiny twigs flying. "You are stronger than that, Red Wolf!" he told himself. He jumped into the truck and reached for the bottle of Tylenol in a cup holder. He swallowed three of them, then called Tommy via the Bluetooth connection in his truck.

"Ben? That you, Little Brother?"

"It is."

"You okay? I got a call from Carmen Wolfe's friends. What did you do?"

"The usual, only probably more than I should have. Carmen's ex will not bother her again, but the whole time ... I was wishing he was the man who killed Talia. I wanted to kill him. It was hard not to."

"You stay strong, Little Brother. Are you in pain?"

"Just the Tylenol kind. I took three of them."

"Ben, get yourself a motel room or go to a truck stop and take a shower. Clean up and let the Tylenol settle in. Change your clothes and calm down before you go back to Carmen."

"I will."

"And I don't want you driving all the way back home alone. I am going to fly to Chicago tomorrow. I will text you when I get there and let you know where I am staying. If I have to wait a couple of extra days while you spend time with Carmen, that is okay. Just promise me you will meet me when you leave and not drive all the way back to the Rez alone."

"Sure." Ben sighed deeply and swallowed at a lump that formed in his throat. "Tommy, I miss Talia. This whole thing just stirred things up."

"I know. I can tell this took something out of you, and that worries me. You just remember your strength through

Wakan-Tanka, Little Brother, and the wolf spirit within you. You need to get back here to the Rez."

Ben fought tears. "Why did I live, Tommy? Those bullets were meant for me. Why did I live and Talia and my son died?"

"Do not go there, Ben. You hear me? Do not go there. Go get cleaned up and then see Carmen. Otherwise, you start home right now! I will get the next flight to Chicago and meet you tomorrow morning."

"I promise you, I will be fine. I just … when I am that angry, it all comes out of me … all that frustration over not finding Talia's killer."

"You just think about those young people who need you and all you accomplished on this trip. We have two new buses coming! And you got a letter today, Ben. You are now a member of the National Congress of American Indians, plus you won that case in Detroit. You are on a roll, Little Brother. You remember that there is a reason for everything, and you believe there is a reason Caesar picked out that woman for you, so keep your mind on that. She, too, needs you right now. She is very worried, so go to her and show her you are all right. You are not in any trouble, are you?"

Ben stopped for a red light, and a state police cruiser pulled up beside his truck, waiting for the light. "Not so far, but I am betting there was enough cocaine in that house to supply a lot of users," Ben told Tommy. "I could bury this guy, and he knows it. He will not be calling the police. I doubt he will even call his fancy lawyers, but they do not worry me."

"You did not touch that white powder, did you?"

"I could have. There was enough there to calm my sorrow and get rid of all my pain, but I did not touch it. I would not betray Carmen with the very thing for which she hates her ex."

"You did the right thing. Now go get a room somewhere and clean up," Tommy told him. "I will text Carmen for you and tell her you will see her in a couple of hours."

"Thanks, Tommy." The light changed, and Ben took off. To his relief, the police car turned left.

"Let your soul dance, Little Brother," Sasha called to him from the background. "Let your heart sing. Let the wolf spirit lead you. We love you."

"Wakan-Tanka *nici un,* brother," Tommy added.

"*Ayee.* And you."

Ben closed the call and glanced at a small dream catcher tied to his rearview mirror. Talia had made it to hang over their son's crib ... the son who never lived to see it. He quickly wiped at another unwanted tear, noticing that his fingers had smeared the war paint on his cheek but were also covered in blood.

"Shit," he muttered. He pulled to the curb and wiped at the paint and the blood with a tissue. Why in heck did such a small cut on a person's face bleed like a stuck pig? He kept pressing on the cut until the bleeding finally slowed. All the while he took deep breaths to calm down. He couldn't go back to Carmen's when he was this upset. It might frighten her.

There is a reason Caesar picked out that woman for you, so keep your mind on that. Tommy's words helped him shake off some of the deep depression that often tried to claim his strength when he thought about Talia and his baby boy. Sometimes, he could hear the baby crying. It was torture not being able to pick him up, hold him, comfort him —even worse torture knowing he would never look into his son's eyes. When he held his nephew, little Benjamin, high in the air after a performance, it haunted him. It should be his own son he held high.

The future of the Lakota.

He reached for his phone, which he'd left on the front passenger seat. He used it to look up a list of florists, finding one that could deliver flowers yet today. He ordered a dozen red roses, giving the florist his credit card number and Carmen's name and address. It cost ten dollars extra to have the flowers delivered on such short notice, but that was fine with him. The woman taking his call asked what the card should read.

"Just write *I am okay. May Wakan-Tanka bless you.* Sign it *Ben.*" He had to spell Wakan-Tanka for her.

"What is that, if I may ask?" the woman inquired.

"It is what the Lakota people call God."

"Lakota? You mean Indians? Native Americans? I don't know what you call yourselves now. Are *you* an Indian? We don't have many of those in Michigan."

Ben was in no mood for such ignorant comments. "Yes, you do," he answered, forcing himself not to say something hurtful. "They are mostly Potawatomi here, but there are many others. You just do not notice them. Please send the roses as soon as possible." He closed the call before he might explode with mean words. He reminded himself the woman had no idea how hurtful her comments were, but there were days when such ignorance made him weary.

Yes, we do exist. Everywhere! Our ancestors are dancing beneath you. Carmen probably did not know much more about Native Americans than the woman he just spoke with, but he could tell she wanted to learn. She had a good heart.

CHAPTER NINE

CARMEN PULLED her damp hair back on the sides and secured it with combs. Val had helped her shower and dress so she would not still be in pajamas if and when Ben returned.

"It's almost five o'clock, Val, nearly three hours since Ben left." She winced as she applied tinted lip balm in spite of a cut on her bottom lip. The swelling had gone down surprisingly fast, and she wanted to look as decent as possible when she saw Ben again, *if* she saw him again.

"He'll be here," Val assured her. "Tommy texted us that he talked to Ben, and he sounded all right. Besides, Ben wouldn't have sent those roses if things had not gone well."

"Aren't they gorgeous? I can't believe he thought to send flowers amid all this chaos."

"Well, I sure hope Jerry got what's coming to him," Val declared.

Carmen set down the lip balm and faced her friend in the bathroom mirror. "Ben really is something, isn't he? Talk about defending a woman's honor."

"Mm-hmm. And now Sid knows what I was talking

about when I told him Ben was not like any man he'd ever met," Val answered. "I can tell Sid is really worried about how this will turn out. My very practical-minded husband always pictures the worst."

"He's just being the good man that he is," Carmen reminded her. "Sometimes your husband treats me more like a father than a friend."

"Well, he *is* fifteen years older than us," Val reminded her. "I love teasing him about that and doing things to keep him young at heart ... and young in bed."

"Oh, God, the poor man," Carmen joked. She pulled a black T-shirt farther down over the waist of her denim shorts. "I wish my ribs weren't too sore for a bra. If Ben realizes I'm not wearing one—"

Val snickered. "You don't really think he won't notice those babies, do you?"

"Oh, give me my pajama top!" Carmen told her, yanking a button-front top out of Val's hands. "I'll put it over my T-shirt."

"I don't think you should. Keep it interesting, girl."

"Poor Sid. I don't know how he keeps up with you."

"He loves my teasing." Val sobered. "Sid is the best husband a woman could ask for. And the reason he's more like a father than a friend sometimes is because you are too soft-hearted to know what's good for you, and he knows your dad is no help. Carson is too wrapped up in work and taking care of Grandma and Grandpa to know how to help you, especially since your mom died. And his answer to Jerry's abuse was always to call the police, which never does any good."

"Dad does what he can," Carmen told her. "He is just a very passive man."

"And you are just like him, which is why you took too

much shit from Jerry." Val grinned. "I wonder what Ben did to that jerk."

Carmen shook her head as both women exited the bathroom. Sid was awake and stretching from a quick nap in an easy chair.

"You should still be resting, Carmen," he told her.

"I wanted to clean up before Ben gets back." Carmen sat down gingerly, her ribs still hurting with every move she made.

"You take it easy a few more days," Sid told her. He walked over and studied Carmen's pupils while he took her pulse. "Val, get her some more ice for that pack, would you, honey?. The more she keeps ice on her eye, the better."

Carmen leaned against a pillow. "What a strange couple of days this has been," she told Sid.

Sid relaxed on the other end of the couch and rubbed at tired eyes. "Carmen, it's pretty clear that Ben Colter is deep into his culture and the Lakota religion and beliefs. If you two build a relationship, it's likely you are the one who will have to adjust to his way of life rather than the other way around. You need to be ready for that."

"Sid, we are nowhere near a relationship that makes any difference right now. I still barely know the man."

Sid frowned shook his head. "This is *me,* remember? Don't tell me you aren't completely infatuated."

Val handed Carmen the ice pack.

"There is another thing to consider, Carmen," Sid told her. "I'm not so sure your cultural differences are the bigger problem."

Carmen laid the ice pack against her eye. "What do you mean?"

Sid rubbed at the back of his neck. "Honey, anyone can see Ben is good at being strong for *others.* But how strong is he on the inside? His rather volatile emotional state tells me he is still dealing with a lot of trauma. Soldiers call it PTSD, and I'm betting Ben Colter is going through the same thing. Tommy called him an emotional roller-coaster. That shooting had to be a tremendous shock that is still having its aftereffects. I'd hate to see your heart get broken by a man who doesn't know exactly where his own heart belongs right now."

"Sid, I *told* you, we are just friends," Carmen balked.

"For now, maybe. But you are looking for a hero, and along comes this warrior who's willing to risk his life and reputation to make sure your ex doesn't give you any more trouble."

Carmen moved the ice pack over her lip. "Sid, I don't live in fantasyland. Jerry smashed reality right into my face more than once. I'm not exactly ready to jump into giving my heart and soul and body to some other man."

Sid groaned with frustration. "I just want to make sure you think about *you* this time, *your* needs, not just Ben's or any other man's. I know how big your heart is, *too* big sometimes. It's why you stayed with Jerry a lot longer than you should have. Don't repeat the same thing with this guy."

"You need to stop worrying. Jerry taught me a very painful lesson."

The doorbell rang, and Carmen sat up straighter. "That must be him!" She winced as she got to her feet and turned to Val. "How do I look?"

"It's not possible for you to look bad," Val teased. "Even when you're all beat up. My God, if you and Ben Colter do get together, you're bound to have the most beautiful children on the planet."

"Oh, Great Jehovah and David and all the angels," Sid

grumped as he stood up. "Everything I just said went right out the window with that remark, Val."

Carmen touched his arm and looked into his gentle, gray eyes. "I love you, Sid. I know you want what's best for me. I promise to keep in mind everything you just told me."

Sid scowled. "I'm just trying to stop a disaster *before* it happens. It's so much harder to clean up the mess *afterward*."

Maybe Sid was right. She'd been hit by a shock wave when she first looked into Ben Colter's eyes. Maybe she *should* run from this. She breathed deeply to calm her fluttering heart as they heard voices at the front door.

"Carmen will be very relieved," Carson was saying. Carmen had deliberately left the apartment door open to the hallway so she could hear Ben coming. "She and Sid and Val are waiting in the back apartment," her father told Ben.

"The way Dad is talking, Ben must be all right," Carmen said absently.

Things grew quiet for the next couple of seconds, until Grandma Florence started screaming. "Carson, he's back! He's back!"

"Mother, it's okay," Carson protested.

"You get out of here!" They heard a strange slapping sound. "Don't you hurt my Carmen!"

"Mother, stop it!" they heard Carmen's father order.

"Oh Lord, Grandma is on the rampage again," Carmen lamented. She started out the door, but then she heard them —those tiny bells that seemed to represent protection and safety. A second later, Ben showed up in the doorway, holding a tray with two large Styrofoam cups, straws sticking out of them. His gaze locked on to Carmen, and there it was again, the shock wave, that rush of magnetism that took away her senses.

He looked magnificent and, surprisingly, none the worse for the wear except for a cut on his right cheek. His hair was pulled back at the sides, revealing several tiny silver earrings. He wore a beautifully designed deep gold shirt over black jeans that had beaded designs down the sides. The shirt was more of a dress shirt, with collar and cuffs and a snap front. It was decorated with various circular symbols and feathers made out of quills and beads of many colors. Ribbons were sewn across the front and down the outside of the sleeves, with more ribbons hanging freely down the front.

"Are you all right?" Carmen asked. Why did she want to run to him? She self-consciously pulled her black T-shirt farther down over the waist of her shorts.

"I am fine," he told her, "but your grandmother beat me with a flyswatter as I hurried down the hall."

Sid and Val broke into laughter, and Carmen covered her face, her laughter turning into tears. *Damn* it! Why was she crying? She sniffed and fanned her face. "Oh, I'm sorry. I was just ... so worried. I want to hug you. Can I hug you?"

Ben grinned. "Do you honestly think any man would object to that?"

"Well, no, but ... I don't want to cry on that beautiful shirt."

Ben set the drinks down on a lamp table and walked over to pull her into his arms, being careful of her ribs.

"Why did you do that?" Carmen wept as she wrapped her arms around his middle. "You didn't have to." God, he smelled good.

"Jerry Peterson will not bother you again," Ben told her, keeping her close.

There it is, that wonderful safety I felt when he walked me back to the wolf cages.

"And I am probably hurting you," Ben told her. Those little bells jingled softly as he urged her to the couch and helped her sit back down.

"I'm so happy to see you are all right," Carmen told him. "But you have a cut on your cheek."

Ben handed her a box of tissues from the coffee table. "A minor accident," he told her. "No more talk of your ex. I brought a couple of chocolate shakes. Since it is hard for you to chew, I thought maybe you would like something you could just drink."

Carmen sniffed and nodded. "I'd *love* a shake. Thank you so much! And the roses! I can't believe you thought of all of that after whatever it is you've been up to. It couldn't have been pleasant. Are you sure you are okay?"

"As well as can be expected." Ben walked over to pick up the shakes and carried them over to the coffee table, handing one to Carmen before he turned to face Sid and Val.

"I apologize for how I left here." He put his hand out to Sid, and Sid shook hands with him. "This is not how I usually behave when I meet someone for the first time," Ben added. "I am a normally a man of peace."

"Yes, well, so were your ancestors before Europe discovered America."

Both men laughed, and Sid turned Ben's hand to look at the back of it.

"Your hand looks fine," he said with an inquisitive frown. "Usually when a man slugs someone, his hands and knuckles are bruised or even bleeding. Sometimes bones get broken."

"I do not go around slugging people, Dr. Ruben."

Sid let go of his hand. "What the heck did you do?"

"Sometimes the weapons of old work *better* than guns or fists. Jerry Peterson is licking his wounds and maybe also licking soda-soaked cocaine off the floor right now, still crying over how much the cocaine I destroyed cost him. He will be no trouble after this. I can ruin him and his business, and he knows it."

Sid smiled. "I am no fan of violence, but as far as Jerry goes, I must admit I like the idea of him suffering some of his own abuse." He faced Ben squarely. "And call me Sid, not Dr. Ruben."

Ben nodded. "I hope the four of us can get together again under better circumstances," he told the man.

Sid ran fingers through thick hair that was graying too soon. "Are you really okay? I *am* a doctor, you know. Can I do anything for you?"

Ben smiled sadly. "The only way you can help me is if you can find a doctor who can remove the bone chips and shrapnel from my back without paralyzing me or leaving me in worse pain."

Sid folded his arms and nodded. "No spinal damage from that shooting?"

"Luckily, no, but my insides were a mess for months, and I lost my right kidney."

Carmen noticed a dark anger move into Ben's eyes.

"My spine is fine," Ben continued. "The problem is, shards of rib bone and tiny particles of the bullet that exploded inside of me are still lurking in my back, all scattered and some too close to my spine and other organs to mess with. They did manage to remove shrapnel from my lungs and even a piece of bone from my heart. They said it was a miracle that one did not kill me."

Sid shook his head. "Ben. I'm sorry for what you went

through in that shooting. But that also means you shouldn't be getting into physical confrontations. My specialty is brain surgery, but I will do some investigating into doctors who might be able to help you."

"Sid is the best in his field," Val bragged. "He's famous in the medical world."

Sid shook his head. "Don't pay any attention to my wife. She's a bit prejudiced. What I was getting around to is that I also work on spines, fusions and things of that sort. If you give me permission to see your records and X-rays, I'll take a look at them, maybe find a specialist who could do a better job than I could with your particular problem."

Ben frowned. "You are serious?"

"Of course I am. We doctors love a challenge, just like you lawyers do."

Ben grinned. "My favorite challenge is going up against the Feds and reminding them of the importance of sticking to treaties and not speaking out of both sides of their mouths. I hope you speak with a straight tongue about seeing what you can do for me."

"Sid is the most honest and caring man I ever knew," Val told Ben. She put an arm around her husband. "It's part of the reason I married him."

Sid looked Ben over. "You are in more pain than you are admitting. I see it in your eyes. Throwing a man the size of Jerry around did a number on you, didn't it?"

Ben shrugged. "It was worth it."

Sid nodded. "That's a fact." He sighed deeply. "Val and I are going home to freshen up and give you and Carmen some time to talk. It's too bad how things worked out today, but Carmen knows how to reach us, so if you suddenly need help because of that back or if Carmen has a problem or acts like she's kind of floating away from reality, you call me. Keep an eye on her alertness."

"I will do that. I know what to look for. I have helped abused women too many times on the Rez."

Sid walked over at Carmen. "You remember the things I told you, all right? Be wise, Carmen. Do you want Val to come back later and spend the night?"

"I'll be fine. You two have done enough."

"Either way, I am definitely coming back in the morning," Val told her. She walked over to give Carmen a quick cheek-to-cheek. "I'll spend the day with you tomorrow, make you soup or something. And I'll want a full report on what you two talk about." She grinned. "And anything *else* that happens," she whispered.

Carmen hit her with a pillow. "Get out of here!"

Val turned and looked Ben over. "Take good care of her. She's pretty special, you know, and as delicate as fine china right now."

"She is in good hands."

Val picked up her handbag. "I'm not even going to answer that one!" She chuckled and turned to Sid, who put an arm around her. "I made coffee earlier, but I remember that you prefer plain water," she told Ben. "There is some in the fridge." She glanced back at Carmen. "Don't do anything I wouldn't do, girl."

Carmen blushed and closed her eyes in exasperation. "We know how much leeway *that* gives me," she teased.

Sid just shook his head and pulled Val closer. "My wife has a vivid imagination and usually ends up embarrassing people—*deliberately*," he told Ben. "But after a long day of working on peoples' brains and dealing with a patient's distraught relatives, she is a refreshing change when I get home."

Ben chuckled. "She reminds me of my brother's wife. Sasha teases me unmercifully and makes me laugh. She understands that sometimes laughter is the best medicine." Carmen noticed a touching sadness move into Ben's eyes.

"That it is," Sid answered. "And by the way, I will email you some forms you can sign online. They will give me permission to get your medical records if you agree. No matter what happens between you and Carmen, I would still like to look into your situation."

"I appreciate your concern."

Sid glanced at Carmen. "You get your rest, understand?"

"I will." Carmen managed a smile for him. "And if Ben gets fresh, I'll sic Grandma on him. She wields a mean flyswatter."

They all laughed. Sid and Val headed for the door.

"Wait," Ben told him. He took a key fob from his jeans pocket and pushed a button, then picked up his.45 from the coffee table and handed it to Sid. "I just unlocked my truck. Take my gun with you and put it under my seat. I would feel better if it was not in the house. Grandma might find it, and we all know how that could end up. I know what a bullet feels like, and I do not wish to feel that kind of pain again."

Sid took the gun. "Have you ever had to use this on the reservation?"

"A couple of times, but I have not killed with it. However, if I ever find my wife's killer, it would be best for him if that gun is not in my possession at the time."

Sid glanced at Carmen as though to say *I told you so.* He turned his gaze to Ben. "You are a smart man, Ben. And I believe you truly are a man of peace, but when it comes to whoever killed your wife, I hope you realize that would be a matter for the *law*, right?"

Ben drew a deep breath and did not answer directly. "Just hit the door lock on the truck before you leave," he told Sid.

Sid sighed deeply. "Use your knowledge of the law to get your revenge, Ben. You're smart enough to do that." He turned and walked out, and Ben turned his attention to Carmen.

"We are finally alone," he told her.

Carmen swallowed, her old instincts of not trusting a man kicking in. Ben Colter was not just dangerous in size and strength. It was his *looks* that could kill.

CHAPTER TEN

"THOSE ARE some very good friends you have there," Ben told Carmen.

"They mean well."

"Mm-hmm." Ben walked to the small refrigerator in the kitchenette and took out a bottle of water. "I drink a lot of water to keep my kidney healthy," he told Carmen. He broke the cap and drank about half of it as he came back to sit down on the couch. "I like Sid very much, but what did he mean when he said to remember what he told you?"

"He thinks there is a lot going on behind that handsome face and body," Carmen answered, pointing at him. "He advised me to learn about all that before I fall under your spiritual spell. "

Ben snickered. "You already know there is much to learn about me, which is why this day was supposed to be for talking, asking questions, maybe even sharing dreams. And it is not all just about me. I also have much to learn about you. I was going to take you to your favorite restaurant today, maybe find a club where we could dance, and then—"

"Dance? *Dance?* Are you kidding me? After seeing you *perform?* I wouldn't be caught *dead* on a dance floor with you. I would be shamed right down through the cracks in the floor. I have trouble with a plain old slow waltz."

Ben leaned closer. "I am a good leader, and if you dance slow enough and *close* enough and you get into the rhythm, you soon forget you are dancing at all. The dance turns into something much nicer."

Carmen studied those dark eyes that were already pulling her into his world. She could swear she heard drums somewhere in the distance. "You just move back to your end of the couch, Ben Colter. We aren't dancing yet."

Ben feigned great disappointment and moved to his end of the couch. "I am trying to decide whether you are a woman of great honor and virtue or if you are just afraid of me."

Carmen smiled. "A little of both."

Ben shook his head. "Do not ever be afraid of me. Ever. Did I not prove to you today how much I honor you?"

"Yes, but you might have some of what I think your people call the Coyote spirit inside of you. Don't they believe coyotes are tricksters or something like that? Maybe you have clever ways of tricking me because you are so smart and so handsome, and you damn well know it."

Ben broke into full laughter. "You make me feel good on the inside," he told her. "I like your humor—the way you reacted in that theater when I said Caesar wanted us to walk to the wolf cages together. You said you didn't hear him say a thing, and everyone laughed." He reached over and picked up Carmen's shake, handing it to her. "You should finish this."

Carmen took the Styrofoam cup from him. "I said that

because I was wondering if that entire incident was a come-on. I *still* wonder." She took a sip of the shake.

Ben shook his head. "I swear on my honor that I do not play such games." He sobered. "And I am impressed that you know a little something about what my People believe. How did you know that thing about coyotes?"

Carmen shrugged. "I really am not sure. I read it some-where, I suppose." She handed him his shake. "You should drink yours, too. I'm so sorry about the problems left from that shooting. Whatever you did earlier today, it must have taken a lot out of you."

There was a hint of sadness in his smile. "It *did* take a lot out of me," he answered, "and not just physically. But when I look at what that man did to you, I am glad I paid him a visit." He looked her over in a way that made her grasp her pajama top and pull it farther closed. "You look much better," he told her.

"Thank you, but I feel like the bad guy in *Phantom of the Opera*," she joked. If she kept things light, she could fight the man's animal attraction. "Like I should wear a mask over half my face."

Ben broke into a wider grin. "Ah, you mean Erik!" He leaned closer, again, great desire in his eyes. "Christine! Why do you turn me away?"

Carmen leaned back and put a hand over her mouth. "You did that so well!"

Ben chuckled. "Who does not know such a famous story? I sang some of the songs from the Broadway version when I was at Julliard. They put on the play while I was there. I played the role of Erik."

"Oh my gosh, of *course* you did! You'd make the *perfect* villain!"

Ben frowned. "I am not sure how to take that remark."

Carmen laughed lightly. "You know what I mean. You're tall and dark. With your hair worn slicked back and wearing a tuxedo and cape and that white mask over one side of your face ... Lord, you *are* Erik! I'll bet you really belted out those songs, too."

Ben shrugged. "I did all right, but I wanted to play Raoul." He put on an arrogant mystique. "The lover!"

They both laughed.

"I wanted his role because he got to sing better songs." Ben leaned closer again and set his shake back on the coffee table. "I'm here. Nothing can harm you," he sang softly. "Your fears are all behind you."

Carmen frowned. "Are you trying to seduce me with that song? Because it's working."

Ben chuckled. "Then by all means, let me finish it."

"I think not! And I might remind you that you have moved from your end of the couch again. "

Ben sobered. "Only because you are so beautiful, and I feel that if I can touch your face and kiss those bruises, I can make it all better. I *want* to make it all better. And did I not prove today that I can live up to the words in that song? I'm here. Nothing can harm you."

Carmen sipped a little more of her shake and leaned over to set it back on the coffee table. "I'm afraid it's hard for me to believe words like that. Jerry would probably sing *I'm here to do you harm.*"

Ben shook his head. "Never."

I would die before I let him hurt you. His words about Caesar the night of the concert kept coming back to Carmen.

"I would love for you to come and visit the reservation," Ben told her, "our School for the Arts. I could show you the

Black Hills, the Badlands. We would ride free across the plains."

"I've never ridden a horse in my life."

He smiled softly. "You do not need to know how to ride. You would be safe with me on *my* horse." He leaned closer again. "How do you think my ancestors were able to capture women and ride off with them? Those women knew nothing about riding bareback at a fast pace, but the warriors hung onto them and kept them from falling." Ben shifted slightly, and those tiny bells jingled softly. "Come to South Dakota, and I will show you the most beautiful place on earth—the Black Hills. You will not want to leave."

Their gazes held fast. *He means it!* "You are a hard man to say no to," Carmen answered.

There came the devastating smile. "Then maybe I should be asking for much more."

"Maybe you should not press your luck," Carmen warned.

Ben sighed as though disappointed. "Then I will have to settle for answering your questions and doubts."

Carmen struggled to think clearly. "You won't be offended?"

"I have heard it all, believe me. And after what you have been through, I do not blame you for having questions before possibly giving your heart to another man."

"Oh, hold on there. We are nowhere close to something like that." Carmen took a deep breath. "Anyway, here goes. Sid said something else that does have me wondering." She kept studying his eyes, looking for that flicker that said Sid was right. "Sid noticed that your wife's name is tattooed over your heart." *Wow! There was that first flinch!* "He thinks you still mourn her and that you still suffer trauma from that shooting, kind of like what they call PTSD, which can make a person do crazy things sometimes ... like try suicide or—"

He flinched again and drew in his breath.

"My God, I'm sorry!" Carmen told him sincerely. "I shouldn't have said anything about any of that yet. It's none of my business."

"No, it's okay." Ben scooted farther back again. "I told you we have a lot to talk about, that there is much to know about what is inside all of this." He scanned his body with his hand. "But today is not a good day to talk about my wife or the shooting. And I do not think we should talk about your ex-husband or the things he did to you that make you afraid to love, because I can feel you pull away when I even touch you or try to kiss you. I am not a fool, Carmen. I know by what I saw in that house, and by the way you yanked my hands away when I touched your face the last time we met that your ex made things ugly for you. You are too beautiful and delicate and good-hearted for such treatment."

Carmen closed her eyes and reached for him. "Come closer again," she asked.

Ben took her hand and scooted closer.

"I guess I've botched things up, haven't I?"

He held her hand tighter. "I guess we *both* have. I should not have brought up your ex's filthy life either. It's just that ... what I found in that house—"

"I know." Carmen met his gaze. "Ben, I'm not a prude or frigid or ignorant of how ugly some things can get. We have both seen the ugly, haven't we? I'm willing to learn the beautiful. I knew beautiful when Jerry and I first married. It wasn't until he got hooked on cocaine that things turned ugly. I lost him the same as if he'd died. It broke my heart." She reached out with her other hand and toyed with a ribbon on the front of his shirt. "I guess I'm simply scared we might get serious and then something could happen that breaks my heart all over again. I'm scared of what could be happening here."

"You think I am not?" He reached over and fondled a piece of her hair. "I am scared out of my mind, Carmen Wolfe, because Sid was right about some of what he said. Yes, I mourn my wife, but there *is* something between us, something worth exploring. Tell me you do not feel the same way."

"Truth?" she asked with a smile.

"Truth."

"The truth is, I need to make sure I'm falling for *you*, the man beneath all this, as you said." She waved her hand over him again. "Your looks, your build, your smarts, your talents, that warrior spirit, those little bells you always wear —*any* woman would fall for all of that. I need to know more about what's inside. And what if I find out something that means I have to give you up to your world? To the Lakota? What if there is something about me and my world you are unwilling or unable to accept?"

"There is only one way to know. Come to the Dakotas with me as I asked. Come to the Rez. I promise you would be completely safe, and I would never expect you to believe and accept every small thing about me and my life. You need to free your soul and your dreams and rid yourself of fear. Let me show you beautiful things and see real joy in your smile."

Carmen could hardly believe the magnificent warrior who'd risen from that stage a few weeks ago was sitting here on her couch telling her these things, and after avenging what Jerry had done to her. Was she living in a movie? That was the hard part. Keeping this real. "I will consider visiting," she answered, "but let's do this gradually, Ben." She toyed with another ribbon. "Like this shirt. It's so beautiful. And knowing you, you don't wear anything that doesn't have meaning in your Lakota world. So, do all the designs in this shirt mean something?"

Ben smiled softly. "Every color and every bead and quill. It warms my heart that you asked."

"Tell me. I want to learn."

Ben leaned back and stretched out his arms to give her a full view of his shirt. "The color of this shirt, yellow gold, represents the East. We honor and worship the four directions, the four paths a man can choose in life. East is represented by the sacred tobacco plant. The black in the quilled feathers across the front represents black sage, the plant for West. The white in the feathers is for sweet grass and the North. South is shown in the red in the feathers and around the beaded circles. It represents red cedar. The turquoise color within the beaded circles symbolizes Mother Earth, and the more solid blue is the sky. The white beaded crosses within the circles represent the Lakota medicine wheel, which can have many meanings, and the circles themselves represent the circle of life. The ribbons sewn into the shirt make it a war shirt, representing the war shirts of old that were made of deerskin. Now the ribbons represent a link between the days of the buffalo and today."

"Do you have a *real* war shirt? The kind that would have been made of deerskin?"

"I do. It is an original war shirt and valuable. The ribbons in it are faded now. It is made of deerskin that is growing dark with age. It has many fringes along the sleeves and around the bottom. I wear it sometimes in the war dance. In the old days, my People believed war shirts could protect them from soldiers' bullets. We found out, of course, that was not the case, and it all ended at Wounded Knee, the most sorrowful event in the history of my People."

Carmen studied him lovingly. She was beginning to see the real Ben Red Wolf Colter, not as the drop-dead gorgeous lawyer and fancy dancer, but as the man who genuinely believed everything he told her. "You said *we*," she told him. "*We* found out the shirts did not protect against bullets ... as though you were there at Wounded Knee."

"I *was* there." He put a hand to his heart. "In here. Some warrior's soul lives here inside of me, and that warrior was at Wounded Knee. It is he who rises up from the stage representing the People. He gives me strength when I need it, and wisdom when it is necessary for me to think clearly."

Carmen frowned, completely fascinated by his explanations. "Do you talk like this when you go before Congress to ask for money or special programs for your People?"

"I am not sure what you mean."

"Well, with such simple honesty. I mean, you really believe these things."

"I *do* believe these things, because it is what I know to be true." He touched his chest again. "In here. In my blood. In my mind. In my heart. When I am blatantly honest with the men in Washington, I see their eyes, and I can tell they are a bit speechless. That is because often I make so much sense that they can come up with no argument, so I get what I want."

Carmen smiled. "You are a clever man, like singing that romantic song for me. Do you ever play fair?"

"I *always* play fair, because everything I say is sincere. I sincerely meant those words. I'm here. Nothing can harm you. Did I not prove that to you today?"

Carmen could not stop watching his eyes. "What did you do to Jerry?"

Vengeance shot through his dark gaze. "You need not know. He realizes I was serious and that I can find ways to ruin him, and he knows I can do it. But you said we should speak of nothing serious, remember? Ask me something else."

"All right. How many different dances are there?"

"We showed most of them at the show in Grand Rapids. The women perform the Jingle Dress dance, the Fancy Shawl dance, the Cloth dance, and the Buckskin dance. The men perform the Grass dance, the Gourd dance, the Northern Traditional dance, and the most beautiful of all, the Fancy dance. Each dance requires different designs, colors, and regalia. Some of the things we wear are hand-made from original materials and are expensive." He flashed that bright smile that was winning Carmen's heart. "You would be so beautiful in the Fancy Shawl dance. Sometimes the women throw their shawls over the man they choose to share intimacies with. It can also be called the Blanket dance." He leaned even closer. "What happens under the blanket is their secret."

Carmen pushed at him. "How much time have we spent together, Mr. Colter? Probably a total of under two hours. That does not warrant me sitting under a blanket with you."

"Then I will have to find a way to make you change your mind." Ben reached for his bottle of water and finished it. Before he could say anything more, his phone rang. He took it from a pocket on the side of his jeans and checked it.

"It is my brother." He answered the phone, and after a few words from Tommy that Carmen couldn't hear, the joy left Ben's eyes. "*What?*" He rose from the couch and started pacing. "When? How?" He glanced at Carmen, then walked over to look out the back sliding door. "She is only *fifteen!*" he said, true agony in his voice. He listened a moment longer. "Yes, I will meet you in Chicago. My God, Tommy! Linda was happy and one of my best students! Who would do such a thing?" Another pause as Ben seemed to wilt onto a barstool. "The same caliber?"

Carmen could see him getting very worked up.

"Where was her body?" Another pause. "The Badlands? How would she get there? It makes no sense!" More words. "This has to have something to do with Talia!" There came another pause as Ben listened. "Of course I am upset!" He got up and paced again. "Yes, I will be all right, but I am going to drive to Chicago yet tonight. This could be the break we need. And I should be there for Linda's parents—and for the youth group. Those kids will be really upset and confused, Tommy."

Another pause. "I told you, I will be all right. I will head straight for O'Hare and get a room at the Marriott yet tonight. I will meet you in the lobby whenever your plane lands and we can drive back to the Rez together." He leaned against a wall and bent over as though in pain. "My God, Tommy, maybe we should have seen this coming. She must have been going through something we did not know about, but this does not fit the Linda Two Fists I know. She never talked about any problems or that she might be afraid of someone." They exchanged more words that told Carmen Tommy was telling Ben not to blame himself and urging him to be careful driving to Chicago.

Ben hung up and shoved his phone back into his jean side pocket. He faced Carmen, rubbing his stomach as though it hurt. "I am so sorry. I must leave."

Carmen got to her feet. "What happened?"

"One of the young girls in the youth group has been shot in the back. I know this girl's parents well. I should go to them. And the other young people will need me."

Carmen walked over to touch his arm. "I don't know what to say, Ben. Please keep in touch with me after you go. Call me or text me."

Ben faced her with obvious tears in his eyes. "Tommy said she was shot with the same type of gun as Talia and my son. Maybe we will find new clues, but this girl, Linda Two Fists, was so young and sweet. It makes no sense that someone wanted to kill her." He reached out and touched her hair. "I am so sorry. We have left so much unsaid. I was going to stay and order more food." He turned away. "Nothing turned out right, and now I am needed at the Rez. Tommy will meet me in Chicago, and we will drive back together."

"Good. I'm glad you are doing that much. But I hate the idea of you driving to Chicago yet tonight. Stay here, Ben. Stay here and leave in the morning. It's okay. You're too tired and upset to be driving late at night on Interstate 94 in Chicago traffic."

He shook his head. "I have to be in Chicago and ready to leave when Tommy arrives." He threw back his head and took a deep breath. "You have much to think about. I will understand if you tell me all this must end. This has not gone well at all."

"Ben, I'm not the type who gives up on something right away. And I'm going to worry about you, with so much on your mind and driving through Chicago traffic."

"I will be fine." Ben walked closer and put a hand to the side of her face. "I want to kiss you."

Don't let him, a little voice told Carmen. She ignored it. She reached up and threw her arms around his neck. He reached under her bottom and lifted her, meeting her lips in a deep, delicious kiss, then moved his lips to her throat. "Did I hurt your mouth?" he asked as he kissed his way to one ear.

"No. I mean, yes, but I don't care. I'm scared for you, Ben. Please don't leave yet."

"I have to." He gripped her bottom in big hands as he found her mouth again in a near-desperate kiss neither of them had planned. It was one of those things that simply needed doing.

"Promise me you will be careful, that you will pull over if you get tired," Carmen groaned through another kiss.

"I promise."

"I'm so sorry about what happened to that girl, Ben." Another kiss. Ben moved one hand under the back of her T-shirt, massaging her bare skin. Carmen felt lost in a torrent of muscle and maleness and power – things that should frighten her, but she felt no fear. Finally, Ben lowered her until her feet touched the floor, but he kept her close.

"I have to go." He kissed her hair. "Thank you for agreeing to see me again. I will miss you greatly. I would come back sooner, but there is so much to do now, and I have missed several rehearsals. The youth group has a concert coming up in November in Omaha. I do all the programming and choose all the songs."

"Ben, it's okay." Carmen pulled away. "I'm just sorry for the *reason* you have to go. And I—" She stepped back a little more. "I can't believe I threw myself at you like that." *My God, you're a good kisser.*

Ben grinned, reaching out and grasping one side of her face. "You can throw yourself at me any time you want. Do you really think I mind?"

Carmen felt herself blushing. "I just ... I felt like you needed a hug. I didn't plan on the other."

"I *did* need a hug. The other just seemed necessary." He leaned down and kissed her cheek. "Thank you. Now I am even *more* anxious to see you again." He sighed and moved an arm around her shoulders, leading her to the inside door of the apartment.

"I still think you should wait until morning, Ben."

Ben pulled her close again. "The state I am in right now, it would not be a good idea to stay. You bring me much comfort." He kissed the top of her head again, and they stood there in an embrace for several seconds. "Thank you for caring." He let go and abruptly left.

Carmen felt numb, confused, on fire. What had possessed her to let him kiss her like that? *You bring me much comfort.* Lord, she felt so sorry for him. He was probably right. He needed to leave for more reasons than what happened to that girl, but she felt so bad for him. She realized he was wise enough to know that feeling sorry for someone you hardly knew was one of the worst reasons for falling into bed with them, and that could easily have happened. It almost startled her to realize she might have let him do whatever he wanted, but Sid was right. The Lakota would always come first for a man like Ben. He'd just proved it. She glanced at the beautiful roses, then at her chocolate shake. Ben's sat beside it. He'd never even touched it.

"God, protect him," she whispered.

CHAPTER ELEVEN

"WHAT DO YOU THINK, LITTLE BROTHER?"

Ben felt his stomach seize up at the thought of what young Linda Two Fists must have suffered. "I do not know what to think about *anything* anymore, Tommy. Seeing blood still in the clay means that when the body fell here, or was dumped, Linda was still alive and bleeding. Only Mother Earth knows for how long."

"The coroner says she lived another hour or so."

"My God," Ben hung his head.

"They told me it looks like she was dead about three days before she was found." Tommy sighed and stood. "I thought you should know as soon as I heard, but I hated the thought of you coming out here. I especially hated having to tell you that the bullet that killed Linda came from the same gun that killed Talia."

Ben got to his feet and scanned the endless landscape that was the Badlands. Everything was deathly quiet out here, so quiet that it almost hurt a man's ears. From where he stood, the moon-like geological formations of a thousand different colors and a thousand different rock, clay, and grassland formations meandered north and east for endless miles of chimney rocks, high buttes, prairie, and deep canyons that once were home to ancient species of horses, rhinos, and dinosaurs.

The official park, close to Pine Ridge, Rapid City, and Ben's new Sunrise Reservation, spanned nearly 245,000 acres. Buffalo, ferrets, bighorn sheep, eagles, pronghorn, rattlesnakes, and all kinds of birds and amphibians abounded, and only those who knew this land well knew where to find water.

"Was she pregnant?" Ben asked Tommy. "She had a boyfriend."

"Coroner says no. And she was not raped. They already talked to the boyfriend, that white boy, Lee Clay. He cried like a baby. And the kid does not have access to guns. It looks more like an execution than anything else, although why a fifteen-year-old girl with everything going for her would deserve something like that makes no sense. The coroner says it also was not close range. He thinks she might have been running when she was shot, which means—" He sighed with sadness.

"Which means she was shot with a long-range rifle," Ben finished for him, "just like the sonofabitch who shot me and Talia." Ben walked a few feet away, pausing to pet his horse's nose. After the long drive home, and because of the remoteness of where Linda Two Fists's body had been found, he and Tommy had decided to leave the truck at the stables near a tourist attraction about ten miles away and ride out here by horseback this morning. "I will always wonder, if I had not stepped away from Talia in that last second to shake hands with Henry Trueblood, maybe I would have been the only one to take a bullet."

"Ben, do not start blaming yourself again. With a high-powered rifle, the bullet would still have gone through you and into Talia."

"But our son might have lived. The angle would have been different."

"Do not go there, Little Brother. This is not about Talia."

"It is *always* about Talia!" Ben shot back. "You said yourself the same gun was used on Linda."

"I only meant—"

"I know what you meant." Ben patted the horse's neck and stepped farther away, still studying the spectacular view all around. "I understand that this is a completely different situation, Tommy, but the fact remains that the same gun was used. I am sorry I yelled, but none of this makes sense, especially if you *do* try to connect it to me and Talia." He faced his older brother. "And this time of year, the Badlands are so hot and barren. Few people, Native or not, could be left out here and find their way out without succumbing to the elements. Out of all the people we know, who the hell besides you and me could find their way out here in the first place and then find their way back?"

Tommy shrugged. "Lakota trackers. The Rez police. Probably a few Feds. Park rangers."

"Yeah, well, that does not narrow it down much, does it?" Ben paced, still looking around. "If those hikers had not strayed from the designated trail into places they did not belong, Linda's body might never have been found. And you said the coroner told you she was drugged first. He found chloroform in her blood and lungs." He walked back to the little bloodstained indention in the gravel where the body once lay. "He must have brought her out here after drugging her so that he could shoot her someplace remote and there would be no witnesses or anyone to hear the gunshot, and from the evidence we were given, he probably let her start running first, just for sport."

Tommy thought a moment as he, too, studied the numerous places from which someone could aim a long-range rifle in this direction. "My theory is that he did it that way so that no bullet casings would be found nearby. None were left behind in the room from where that shooter killed Talia, either. And in a place as big as the Badlands, if she was shot from a distance, any casings he might have missed will never be found."

Ben nodded. "And the heavy storm we had just before her body was found has washed away all tracks, so we do not have footprints and no tracks to know if he used a horse or maybe an ATV or a side-by-side or a motorcycle ... whatever. Who would have expected a hard rain out here in the Badlands in August? It is as though the sonofabitch had help from some evil Being," Ben grumbled. He removed his T-shirt and threw his head back, letting the hot sun penetrate his skin. He opened his arms as he turned in a circle. "And in all this time since Talia's death, no one has found the gun that was used."

"Stolen, most likely," Tommy groused, "or bought from an illegal trader, probably in some town miles away. The home of every single possible suspect has been searched. Sammy Little is still threatening to sue us. He says just because he once sold liquor to underage kids doesn't make him a murderer, even though he knew you were going to rat him out and have him arrested."

"I hope he *does* sue. I will enjoy tearing him apart in court and having him sent to prison for illegal liquor sales."

"Well, he is gone now. We accomplished that much. But he owned no guns. They did not even find *illegal* firearms in his house." Tommy sighed deeply. "And now this. The same gun. That means Talia's killer is still around."

Ben let out a high, piercing war cry. "He has to *die*, Tommy! What am I going to do if we never find him?"

"If they *do* find him, you must let the law handle it, Ben. We have been over this too many times."

"And what if it had been *Sasha* who was killed? Would *you* be able to let that go? The mother of your seven sons?"

Tommy turned away, pausing a moment before answering. "It would be because of my seven sons that I would have to let the law handle it. They need their father."

"Yes, they do. But I *have* no sons, Tommy. My son was blown right out of his mother's belly! How do I let *that* go?"

Tommy shook his head. "I should not have brought you out here, Little Brother."

Ben grasped his stomach again and bent over. "Give me a *reason*, Tommy. Give me a reason to handle this the right way."

Tommy swallowed back his own need to weep. "Those kids, Ben. You might not have any of your own, but that youth group who attends your School for the Arts on that reservation you fought so hard to get through government grants are your reason for living. And Talia herself. What would she think if you threw away everything *she* helped you fight for?" He rubbed at the back of his neck and sighed.

"And now this new woman. How do you think she will feel if she finds out you might be going to prison for the rest of your life? Some people might understand, but you are in South Dakota and you are *Lakota*. No judge is going to let you off if you do what you would like to do. And sending you to prison would be the biggest waste of a human life I can think of. Do you want to deny the gifts Wakan-Tanka has given you? Talia would weep forever in the Great

Beyond if she saw you give up on life and on all that is right."

Ben straightened and took a rubber band from his jeans pocket. He pulled his hair back, tying it into a tail at the back of his neck. "I am sorry. I should not have said that about Sasha. She is your wife and like a sister to me. She is as much a reason as you are that I am alive."

"I know your frustration. Sometimes, things boil up inside a man to where he has to explode or die." Tommy grinned in an effort to change the mood. "Hey, it is what led to the Custer massacre, is it not?"

Ben wiped at a tear that trailed down his dusty cheek. "Can you imagine being there?"

"You and I would have led the charge," Tommy answered.

Ben grinned, giving his brother a shove. "My God, that had to be a glorious moment. If not for that golden-haired, pompous ass, we would not still be fighting so hard for the Black Hills. I guess that is part of the problem. We can no longer fight the way we once did."

"We fight through the *courts*, Little Brother, and in that respect, you are just as much a warrior as Crazy Horse. Do you understand that?"

Ben looked up at an eagle circling overhead. "I understand. But sometimes I think of how good it would feel to bury a hatchet into whoever would do something like what happened to my wife ... and now to Linda Two Fists." He kept studying his surroundings. "Maybe he brought her out by helicopter," he suggested. "Did anybody check flight records for the last several days?"

"Yes. All recorded and verified. A government helicopter picked up some suits going from Kyle to Rapid City. The other flights were reservation helicopters, emergency medical flights. Police and Feds flew out here by government helicopter after the fact, and to pick up the body, of course. By then the scene was badly infected with those hikers' footprints, and of course the helicopter down-draft sent rocks and dirt flying all over the place and ruined whatever was left that might have helped."

"Yeah, well, the Feds are good at that. They do not care about one dead little Lakota girl, so if they do not find her killer, it will be no big deal. They do not care if we ever find Talia's killer either. They pretend they do, but I know better. I can even think of a couple of suits who would like to have *me* out of the picture, which is why I know that bullet was meant for me, not Talia." Ben stretched his back a little. Pain was setting in again. "Who was the coroner? Our own Lakota man or a federal officer?"

"Federal."

"Figures." Ben sneered the word, then picked up a stone and threw it as far as he could. It made a pinging sound at the bottom of the cliff—the only sound amid the vast, silent maze of rocks. "Do you think this could have been set up between some federal agent and somebody on the Rez? Maybe to hide something?" Ben rose and threw another rock.

"Calm down, Ben." Tommy also took a moment to scan the horizon. "I know what this is doing to you. I came awfully close to not calling you at all. I am sorry I interrupted your chance to finally get to know that woman back in Michigan. Get your mind off these shootings and think about Carmen."

Ben shook his head. "Yeah, well, God knows what *she* is thinking right now. This is not a good way to convince her to come out here. Knowing about Talia and now this ... she is probably scared shitless to be around me at all." He kept his T-shirt wadded up in his hand and let the sun bake his already-dark skin as he bent over the body site again. "Heaven knows what things Carmen has heard about what goes on out here."

Tommy adjusted his floppy leather hat and knelt beside his brother. "Ben, if this woman is worth her salt and she genuinely cares about you, these things will not stop her from wanting to be with you. I am no fan of you falling for a white woman, but if she learns to love you, her heart will belong to the Lakota, and that is all that matters. I cannot imagine any woman falling in love with you without also falling in love with our People. And the fact that Caesar seemed to choose her for you is no small matter. I do not think you should give up on her yet."

"I am not giving up. It was just embarrassing to have to tell her why I had to leave so fast. I had already invited her out here and told her how safe she would be. And then she finds out some innocent little fifteen-year-old girl was shot and left for dead in a remote area of the Badlands." Ben scrutinized the scene yet again, squinting as he scanned everything within ten feet of the area. It was then he thought he saw something glitter in the sunlight.

"What is that?" he said aloud.

"What?"

Ben pointed. "Something glittered over there." Ben handed his shirt to Tommy and walked around the scene to where he was sure he saw the object. The glitter disappeared as he moved to a different angle, but he knelt close to where he was sure he had seen it and dug into the gravel and clay. He felt it then ... something that didn't belong with the stones. He dug more, then pulled at a small chain.

"Tommy, there is something here!"

Tommy joined him at his side just when Ben pulled out

a small necklace. Though clogged with clay, the chain was obviously gold. There was some kind of lettering attached to it. Ben held it up to study the lettering, then let out another piercing war cry, followed by a heartrending death chant. The necklace was Talia's! *Talia's!* How did it get here? Did someone want the necklace found? Was it only to bring him more torturous heartache? Maybe the necklace had been purposely left in the open. but the rains created the mud that had covered it.

He clung to the necklace and bent over, rocking back and forth and continuing to chant the Lakota death song. Tommy remained beside him, not insulting him by interrupting with questions and risking the heavenly journey of the dead.

But Ben knew the other reason Tommy stayed close. His devoted brother was making sure he did not pull out a pocketknife and slit his arm to let it bleed out in mourning. He'd done it before, at Talia's grave. It left the scar Carmen had asked him about that day at the lake house, but he'd been reticent to tell her the truth. She might not understand his way of mourning.

CHAPTER TWELVE

CARMEN SET a plate of eggs and bacon in front of her father, then poured some coffee and sat down at the kitchen table in the main house.

"Thanks, honey," Carson told her. "What do you hear from that man you met a few weeks ago? Did they solve what happened to that young girl?"

"I don't think so. I can tell Ben is still very upset over it. I think there is something about it he's not telling me." Carmen paused to drink some of her coffee. "I wish he wasn't so far away, but he's so busy that it's hard for him to get back here. He just finished defending a Cheyenne man in some little town in Wyoming. It had something to do with signing false papers that gave away the man's son to some couple who came and took him. Ben proved the father never signed the papers. I guess he could barely sign his own name and would not have known what he was signing. Ben says that happens a lot out there, people coming and taking children out of homes on the reservation."

"I've read about it somewhere. It's a real different life out there, Carmen, so if you are thinking of going there instead of Ben coming here, give it some serious thought. I will say, from what little I know of Ben so far, I really like him. He is apparently smart and talented and successful. I believe he is all around a good man, but you have to remember that he is Lakota and you aren't."

"Now you sound like Sid," Carmen answered with a patient smile. "Ben has also been spending a lot of time with the youth group, so that takes up a lot of the time that he has back on the reservation. They managed to raise enough money to build a theater so the kids can practice dances and songs on a real stage. I guess they are giving a concert at the Orpheum in Omaha in November."

"No wonder he doesn't have time to get back here."

"I know. I miss him. And you are right. I am thinking of going to South Dakota if Ben can't make it here any time soon. Right now, I've been busy getting the lake house ready to sell and finishing up some accounting jobs I got behind on." Carmen could not forget that kiss before Ben left. How could she so deeply miss someone she hardly knew? She swallowed some eggs.

"You care for that man a *lot*, don't you?" her father asked.

Carmen stirred some cream into her coffee. "Very much." She pushed her eggs around with a fork, not really all that hungry. "Dad, I want you to know that once I sell the lake house, I promise to find an apartment or a town house for myself and move out. You never planned on me being here so long."

"That was because you worried Jerry would come after you. He never did bother you again after Ben paid him that visit, did he?"

Carmen smiled. "No. And Jerry's alimony checks have been regularly deposited into my checking account." She touched her father's arm. "Still, since I've been here, I've been able to help with Grandma and Grandpa and save you some money on having help come in, so I'm not sure how you feel about me moving out."

Carson waved her off. "Don't worry about that. Actually, I've been wanting to talk to you about it." He leaned back in his chair. "I've loved having you here, but, Carmen, you're still young and beautiful and now you're single and ... hell, I know what it's like for young people today. Whether it's this Lakota man or some other man, you're bound to end up finding someone else, and I'm not stupid. Some man is going to end up spending the night with you. You might end up living with some guy until you know if you want to marry again, and living here will be awkward. Or maybe some guy will have his own home and you'll want to live there. Either way, you're better off with your own place. I know that."

"Dad, I am nowhere close to getting into a serious relationship anytime soon."

Carson put up his hand. "You don't know today what tomorrow will bring. Either way, I have to think about what to do with the apartment and with your grandparents when you leave. I've been talking to your aunt Mary. You know Uncle Joe died a couple of years ago, and your mom's sister can't keep up with that big house of theirs anymore. She wants to sell it, but Joe didn't leave her very well off financially. She's been hinting at living here in the apartment and helping me with my folks. Even at that, I might end up having to put Mother in a home. I don't want to do it, but I never know what crazy thing she will do next, and she doesn't take care of herself in a sanitary way. It's hard for a man to help with something like that. "

"I understand," Carmen told him. "And I don't blame

you. That apartment is perfect for Aunt Mary. Living here will save her a lot of money and help you with Grandma and Grandpa. You are five years from retirement, and I know you want to work till then so you get your full benefits." She sipped more coffee. "You tell Aunt Mary to go ahead and sell and that she can live here. The way real estate is today, that lake house will probably sell really fast, so I'll go ahead and start looking for a new place. I was putting it off because I thought you needed me here, but if Aunt Mary can live here instead, that's great. She's a wonderful cook, too. She's certainly a better cook than I am."

Carson chuckled. "You do okay." His eyes teared a little. "I'm so glad you are finally rid of Jerry. It's a terrible thing what happened there. I know the sorrow you have been through, sweetheart. I'm glad you've had Sid and Val to help out. And I don't know what Ben did to make Jerry back off, but I'm glad for it. He came along at just the right time."

"I guess so." *Ben thinks we belong together,* Carmen wanted to explain, but her father didn't believe in such romantic notions. She only knew she missed Ben so much that her whole body ached for him sometimes. Was he any closer to finding his wife's killer? She could tell when they talked that he was holding back. She wanted to hug him and tell him everything would be okay.

Her cell phone rang then. She looked at the screen..

Sasha Colter! She'd not talked to Sasha since the day Ben went after Jerry. Even then, they had not spoken directly to each other. She'd only heard Sasha talking in the background.

Carmen looked at her father. "Finish your breakfast, Dad. And go ahead and call Aunt Mary. I have to take this call." She got up and headed down the hallway to her apartment, closing the door. She hit the green button to answer her phone. "Sasha?"

"Hello. This is Carmen, right?"

"Yes! I'm so glad you called I was just talking with my dad about Ben. I haven't heard from him the last several days. Is everything okay?"

"Well ... yes and no. I am hoping perhaps you can help. Little Brother thinks so much of you. His eyes brighten when he tells us about you, and he needs that right now ... to be uplifted, I mean."

"But he can call me any time. He knows that."

"That is different from you being here. I do not know what your life is like, but if you could come out here for a while and surprise Ben ... "

"Does he *want* me to come out there? He hasn't asked lately, and he's been gone a lot."

"Oh, he desperately wants to see you. He *needs* to see you. He has not asked because he thinks, well, he thinks you are afraid to come out here because of Linda Two Fists's shooting. He works so hard to keep honor and respectfulness for our People, to erase the rumors people hear about life out here."

"My gosh, Sasha, murder happens everywhere. I don't know the statistics, but Grand Rapids certainly has its share. I'm no more afraid to come out there than I would be to walk down the street alone here."

"Can you come, then?"

"When? And what happened to make you call me?"

Sasha sighed. "Look, Ben went out to where they found Linda Two Fists's body, and he found something that sent him reeling back to his wife's death. He has been a little messed up ever since. Tommy and I think if he sees you again, it will help. I found a flight out of Grand Rapids to

Rapid City for Thursday. I would pick you up so your arrival would be a surprise for Ben. Tommy will buy your ticket."

"That's not necessary. I mean, go ahead and get the ticket, but I will most certainly pay you back when I get there."

"Then you will come?"

"Well, wait. Go back a little. What did Ben find at that place where they found Linda's body?"

Sasha hesitated, letting out a little gasp. "This is so hard," she answered. "Do not tell Ben that I told you. He might not want me to."

"Of course, but I need to know, Sasha. What am I getting myself into?"

Sasha cleared her throat. "Ben found a gold necklace he bought for Talia years ago. It has Talia's name on it in gold letters."

"Oh my God!"

"Ben really fell apart when he found it. It makes no sense, Carmen. Linda Two Fists was only fifteen, and she came to the School for the Arts only two years ago, *after* Talia was killed. She never met Talia in her life. Why was Talia's necklace there, deep in the Badlands? It is like the killer left it there on purpose to upset Ben. It took Tommy hours to get him to leave that place afterward. Ben just sat there clinging to that necklace and singing a death chant. My Tommy sat there with him the whole time."

Tears welled in Carmen's eyes. "Poor Ben."

"Tommy finally managed to get him to understand that he had to stop, and that he had to drink some water. It was extremely hot, and Ben was sweating in the sun. He needs to drink a lot of water for his healthy kidney. Tommy finally got him home, and Ben actually made it to that trial in

Wyoming and won his case. He has been working with the young people ever since. He tries so hard to keep them confident and upbeat, but I know that deep inside, he is hurting really bad, Carmen. His birthday is Friday, and if you could take that flight, you could be here for a surprise party the kids want to have for him. And for him to see you walk in ... *ayeee!* That would bring happiness to his heart."

Carmen wiped at her eyes. "I know about the opioids, Sasha. He didn't go back to that, did he?"

"No! Never! Truly. It breaks our hearts to see his pain, but what happened with the opioids was so awful, Ben will never do that again."

"But you said Tommy stayed with him for several hours out in the Badlands. If it wasn't to make sure Ben didn't turn to drugs—"

"Please do not worry about that. Tommy only stayed with him because he understood Ben's deep grief. Tommy wanted to make sure Ben did not ..." Sasha paused. "How do I say this?" She paused again. "When Ben first visited Talia's grave after her death, it was many, many months later because he was so severely injured himself that he could not leave the hospital. When he finally was able to visit her grave, he ..." Another pause. "He cut his arm. He lost a lot of blood. It is sometimes a custom among our people to let blood in grief for a loved one."

"I noticed that scar the first time Ben visited. He told me it was from the shooting."

"He was probably afraid that if he told you the real reason, you would not understand, and it might scare you off."

"Sasha, I am stronger and more understanding than that."

"I am glad to hear you say it. Tommy and I told him that

we believe the same. But what happened—that is the reason Tommy stayed close. He wanted to be sure Ben would not try something like that again. My husband is like a father to Ben, so Ben usually listens to him and respects Tommy's advice."

Carmen could tell Sasha was crying.

"You really can trust Ben," she continued. "He has been through so much, Carmen, but he has learned how to be strong again. That shooting left him in such darkness, but when he talks about you, I see new light come into his eyes. If you come out here and surprise him, he will be so happy."

Carmen felt her heart pounding. Should she talk to Sid and Val about this first?

"Please come," Sasha pressed. "I promise you will love it out here, and you will be safe. We will show you the beautiful Black Hills. You can meet the youth group. They will be so excited to meet the woman Ben has told them about ... the woman who interrupted that performance in Michigan when Caesar sat down beside you. They are telling all kinds of stories about that. You will be so welcome."

"Are you sure? I mean, I'll be surrounded by people who probably think it's wrong for Ben to be interested in someone like me."

"Most do not care. Those who might be wary will soon learn to love you. I can tell from how Ben talks about you. I cannot wait to see the look on his face if you show up. Please say yes."

Carmen smiled through tears. "You drive a hard bargain, but it so happens I just had a talk with my father about my aunt moving into this apartment. I need to find a new place of my own, and I can bring my computer and catch up on my work online. I run my own accounting business." She let out a long sigh. Sid would probably be upset that she didn't talk to him first. "Yes, I'll come. Just text me the flight information. I'll print out my ticket at the airport kiosk. What should I bring? Is it as hot there as it is here?"

"Hotter! Have you ever heard of Wall Drug? It was started for people who were trying to get from one side of South Dakota to the other without dying from heat and thirst."

Both women laughed. "Everybody has heard of Wall Drug," Carmen told her.

"I promise to have plenty of water with me when I pick you up, and my car does have air-conditioning. So do our houses. Some of the poorer residents do not have that luxury, but they are used to it. And yes, there is a lot of poverty here, Carmen."

"I already know that. I'm not the kind of person who wouldn't understand, nor do I need people to try to impress me. It is what it is, and I admire Ben for all he has done to get more government help, especially the hard work he puts in for those kids. I agree that he deserves a surprise, but are you *sure* he wants me out there?"

"Oh, he does! Believe me, he does. He has just been afraid to ask because of Linda's murder. Thank you so much for agreeing to come. Tommy will be happy to know. It will be hard for us to keep this secret. We will not even be able to tell the youth group because kids that age cannot keep secrets."

"Ben will be thirty-three, right? Should I bring a gift?"

Sasha laughed. "*You* are the gift! That is all Ben will need. Thank you again. I will send you the information. I must go now. One of the boys is coming inside, and I do not want him to know who I am talking to. Bye for now."

"Bye."

The call ended, and Carmen sat there staring at her

phone. "What am I getting myself into?" She dialed Val's number. "Val? You won't believe this."

"What have you done now, girl? Is Ben coming to visit again?"

"No. *I'm* going to *him*."

Val screamed so loud that Carmen had to hold the phone away from her ear.

Carmen explained Sasha's phone call.

"Oh, how I would love to be there to see the warrior's reaction! You had better be prepared for some lovin', girl."

"You are getting ahead of things, as usual."

"I think I'm right. You go out there and do whatever your too-soft heart wants you to do. It's been too long since you had any gentleness and romance in your life, and anyone can tell that man is capable of both."

"And I do not intend to jump right into something serious," Carmen told her.

"You mean like jump right into bed?"

"Oh, please!"

"Hey, I've *seen* the guy, remember? And he seems so kind and caring. He's the kind of man who is hard to resist. You keep me posted, okay?"

"I won't need to. You will be calling me every five minutes."

They said their goodbyes, and Carmen stared at the dried-up roses from the bouquet Ben had sent her weeks ago. She'd never had the heart to throw them out.

CHAPTER THIRTEEN

"Are you there yet?"

"Val, you sound like a kid asking his folks that question. Yes, I'm here. I'm in the baggage area." Carmen spoke to her friend through her phone's Bluetooth headset. She set down her carry-on and waited for her luggage to show up.

"Tell me when Sasha gets there."

Carmen smiled and shook her head. "I never have seen Sasha up close," she answered, "but I have a feeling she will be easy to recognize." Carmen saw her suitcase coming around the carousel, easy to spot because it was white with red poppies on it. "Here comes my bag. I hope I brought enough stuff. The fact that I have no idea how long I will be here doesn't help."

"Girl, once Ben gets hold of you, you might *never* come back."

"We will see. Hang on." Carmen pulled her bag off the carousel. She rolled it and her carry-on over to some chairs and looked around again. "Oh my God," she told Val.

"What is it?"

"There is a Native American woman walking toward

me. She's a little taller than I thought she would be, but I'm pretty darn sure it's Sasha, and if you think she was sexy up on that stage, you should see her in person. She's wearing sunglasses and has hair all the way down to her butt. And she's wearing the cutest, form-fitting, rose-pink dress. She's smiling and waving."

"I'll hang up for now. I just wanted to be sure someone was there to meet you. Call me later tonight."

Carmen ended the call and took the earpiece from her ear. She shoved it into her purse as she waited for Sasha to reach her. The woman was as beautiful as Ben was handsome. A slightly older Native American man wearing jeans, a floppy leather hat, and a white T-shirt accompanied her. He was a well-built man for his age, not as tall as Ben but with a solid chest and arms and dark skin that looked great against the white shirt. Carmen figured he had to be Tommy. Both greeted her with big smiles.

"You have to be Carmen!" the Native woman exclaimed. "You said your bags would have red poppies on them."

"Yes, it's me."

"I am Sasha." Sasha opened her arms and gave Carmen a hug, then turned to the man with her. "And this is my huggy bear, Tommy." She grabbed Tommy's arm. "Isn't she as beautiful as Ben described her?"

Tommy reached out and shook Carmen's hand. "You are *more* beautiful than Little Brother described," he told Carmen. "Ben called you a blond Cindy Crawford and said you did not look like any CPA he ever knew."

Carmen smiled and shook her head. "That sounds more like a lonely man's exaggerated description," she answered, blushing.

Tommy took her bags. "No, I think he described you just right," he told her.

"Well, thank you."

"Follow me," Sasha told Carmen as she led her toward an escalator going down. At the bottom, Carmen followed the couple down a long hallway to doors that led outside. She found it hard to believe that the shapely, energetic Sasha was over forty years old and had seven sons. But by the way the woman talked nonstop and carried on about "Little Brother" with joking remarks, she could tell that Sasha was exactly the teasing, troublemaking but loving sister-in-law Ben made her out to be. Her personality reminded Carmen very much of Val. The woman rattled off information about which highway they would take to a cabin at a visitor's center in Badlands National Park.

Badlands? Isn't that where they found that girl?

"You will see a little of the Black Hills when we leave, but most of that country is way to the south and west," Sasha told her. "On the way to Kyle, which is where we and Ben live, we will go right through the middle of the Badlands. If you stay there tonight, it will be mostly tourists, so our own people will not know you are here yet. We have to keep it a secret, so I will have to come back and get you tomorrow. Have your bags packed because you will stay with us in Kyle tomorrow night, or maybe you will stay with Ben."

With Ben? Alone? Carmen decided she would face that situation when and if she had to. Tommy led them to a dusty black late model Jeep Grand Cherokee and opened the back gate to throw Carmen's bags inside.

"Ben said you have a Camaro," Sasha continued babbling. "Out here nobody drives fancy little cars. The roads are not the best. Many of them are still gravel, and it is a long way between towns. Everybody drives pickups or SUVs. Remote does not begin to describe South Dakota and Pine Ridge. Most of our relatives are at Rosebud Rez, but Ben and Talia wanted their School for the Arts to be closer to Oglala Lakota College, which is in Kyle."

Tommy got in behind the steering wheel, and Sasha indicated Carmen should get in the back seat with her. She closed her door and clapped her hands. "Ben will *die* when he sees you. He will be so surprised! Won't he, Tommy?"

"*Very* surprised."

Carmen noticed Tommy wasn't much of a talker. Sasha made up for that as she continued pointing out various places outside of Rapid City. "The city itself is west of the airport, so you will not see much of it for now." She touched Carmen's arm. "I am not going to sleep tonight. I am so excited about you being here! When Ben sees you, he will let out a war whoop like you never heard, and the kids will all be just as excited. They will love meeting the woman Ben talks about all the time. They want so much for him to be genuinely happy again. When we pick you up tomorrow, we will go straight to the art school. Ben will be there rehearsing with the kids, who plan to surprise him with a birthday cake. But even *they* do not know *you* will be showing up. This will be so good for Ben. It will lift his spirits."

"Sasha!" Tommy interrupted.

Sasha glanced at her husband in the rearview mirror.

"Baby, you have not stopped talking since we picked Carmen up. Maybe she is tired and would like to rest and have some quiet time while we drive."

"I'm fine," Carmen told them. "To be honest, before I see Ben tomorrow, I'd like to know what I am dealing with. Sasha just said my being here would lift Ben's spirits. I have talked to him often, but getting him to talk about his wife's death is like pulling teeth. I know there is a reason behind you two asking me to come out here, so please tell me what's really going on. Does this have something to do with Ben relapsing? Is he okay?"

They all sat silent for a few long seconds as Tommy drove along a highway that Carmen could see meandered through wide-open country. A herd of buffalo grazed in the distance.

"Carmen, Ben is fine," Tommy assured her. "You do not have to worry about drugs or anything like that. I know Little Brother better than he knows himself, and he will not let himself get that bad again. But finding that young girl in the Badlands and Ben finding Talia's necklace there, that cut very deep. We just know that he is hurting inside, and we hate to see that. He is still pretty vulnerable emotionally. He has been wanting to ask you to our homeland, but he feared that because of this new murder, you would be afraid to come and that maybe you have already lost interest."

"I'm not that kind of person, Tommy. What I have been through with my ex has toughened me up, I guess, but I also don't want to have my heart shattered all over again. You both know Ben well enough to realize how easy it would be for a lonely woman to fall in love with him. The man is like a hero out of a romance novel, especially after what he did to settle that score with my ex, but I don't want to see him with unrealistic eyes, you know? My ex was also an extremely attractive and accomplished man, and personable. Everybody liked him. But it all ended in disaster when he got hooked on drugs. I've seen the beautiful side of Ben, but I also need to know the ugly. I want to know about that shooting three years ago."

Tommy glanced at her in the rearview mirror and

nodded. "I understand, but the ugly might be more than you can handle, Carmen."

"Even more reason for me to know *everything*. You might be surprised what I *can* handle." Carmen could hardly believe she was saying these things to people she'd just met. They were being so kind, but being out here in this world so foreign to her brought up all her defenses. "I'm very sorry," she spoke up. "I don't mean to sound rude or selfish, but I can't help Ben or allow myself to care too much for him if I don't know all the facts."

"That is fair," Tommy said with a nod, "and you are a wise woman. I respect you for that, but this is not something we intended to talk about." He turned off some Native music that was playing softly through the radio. "Still, it is a long drive to where we are going." He rubbed at his eyes. "Go ahead and tell her about the shooting, Sasha."

Sasha leaned her head against the back of the seat. "Do you have a strong stomach, Carmen?"

"I'll manage," Carmen told her.

"It was about three and a half years ago. It was winter." Sasha sighed deeply and looked out the side window. "To help you understand, Ben and Talia grew up together and married right after Ben graduated from Harvard. And by the way, he started college at seventeen. He is so smart, he sailed right through high school and then got his law degree in only five years. He worked extra hard at it because he missed home and Talia and wanted to get back here as soon as he could. They got married right away. It was Talia's dream to help Lakota youth through teaching the arts, so she and Ben attended Julliard together for the extra training they would need to apply for grants and to teach at the school. They waited to have children because they wanted to get the school going first."

"Well, they certainly were trained well," Carmen answered. "That show in Grand Rapids was as professional as any other show I've ever seen."

Sasha sat up a little straighter. "It helped that they were both very talented to begin with. But yes, Ben knows how to bring the best out of those kids. And you saw how he likes to mix Native dancing and drumming with modern music, kind of like Native rock." She laughed softly. "That keeps it interesting and exciting for the young people. A couple of our graduates have already moved on into professional entertainment. Ben could, too, with his voice and those looks, but he will not go that far because he continues to commit his time to teaching, and to traveling to raise money, all to keep Talia's dream going. And then, of course, there is Ben's legal work. He is a real bear in the courtroom or when he speaks before Congress. Most judges and congressmen and opposing lawyers hate seeing him walk in."

"Sasha, you are getting off track again." Tommy slowed down for a group of teens riding horses. They smiled and waved as the Jeep slowly passed them. Carmen turned to watch the beautiful horses. Other than the fact that they wore jeans and T-shirts, the riders could have been Native American youth from out of the past, all of them riding bareback and guiding their horses with rope bridles. She turned to Sasha, waiting for her to continue.

"Sasha, honey, Carmen does not need a history lesson on Ben. She needs to know about the shooting," Tommy told his wife.

Sasha rubbed her forehead and paused for several long seconds. "Tommy, I can't."

More silence.

"All right," Tommy said quietly. "I should not have asked you, baby. I will tell her." He put the Jeep in cruise, and Carmen wondered if there were any other cars around for miles. They had passed only two so far. "By the way, Sasha looks very much like Talia," Tommy continued, "so that gives you an idea how beautiful Talia was."

Sasha leaned forward and tugged at her husband's long hair. "Thank you."

Tommy smiled sadly as he shifted in his seat. "Carmen, I just want you to imagine what the shooting had to be like for Ben." He turned down the air a little. "I think it is important that you understand. It happened in Rapid City. Ben went there to do some editing on a new recording we'd made. I told him to go ahead on his own because I trust his judgment on things like that. He took Talia and a couple of our experienced drummers with him.

"They were all leaving the recording studio when—well, what happened next is what we have put together from witnesses, from the EMTs, the police, and some video footage that recorded Ben and Talia ... going down."

The vision tore at Carmen's heart "It already sounds awful," she said quietly.

"It *was* awful," Tommy said. "From what we figure, Ben turned to shake hands with one of the drummers just as shots rang out. Talia went down instantly, and, of course, screams and running and chaos followed. Ben looked at Talia in horror and threw himself over her. Two more shots rang out from someplace up high and across the street. A search later turned up nothing. The second shots ripped through Ben while he lay on top of Talia. The bullets tore open a main artery on Ben's insides and destroyed his right kidney. The worst part is something Ben remembers just before he passed out."

Sasha let out a tiny whimper, and Tommy cleared his throat in that way a person did when they are about to cry and don't want to. "Little Brother remembers the look of terror in Talia's beautiful hazel eyes, like she was begging him to not let her die. He must have been in shock and didn't even realize he'd been shot because he tried to pull her into his arms, and that's when he saw that the first bullets had ripped open Talia's belly. She was due any day, which means their son was fully developed. Ben saw—" He paused and cleared his throat again. "He saw one of the baby's legs sticking out of Talia's belly. It moved."

Sasha sniffed and wiped at tears. Carmen rubbed at her stomach. "My God," she murmured.

"To this day, Ben would gladly die a thousand deaths if it meant that Talia and his son would live," Tommy said, his voice breaking a little. "Seeing his son move will haunt him forever, but the bullets also tore through the baby's head. There was no saving the child. A few days later, Sasha and I visited the place where it happened, and the city was still trying to scrub the blood from the cement. They said they would probably need to break up and remove that section of sidewalk and replace it because they could not get out the stain. What makes it worse for Ben is his being sure that he was the one meant to die that night. Not his wife and son."

Tommy drove on silently for a few minutes, then wiped at his eyes. "Ben passed out before the ambulances arrived," he finally continued. "By the time Sasha and I got to the hospital, he was in surgery. He came out full of tubes and needles and patches and machines to monitor his blood pressure and heartbeat and a hundred other bodily functions, including his kidneys, of course. He did not look like Ben at all. He did not wake up for two weeks because he had lost so much blood. When he did wake up, he found out his wife and baby were dead and that he had lost a kidney. He could not walk because of shrapnel and bone shards in his back. They managed to remove a lot of that with later surgeries, but you know the rest. He still has a lot of pain."

Tommy paused again to clear his throat. Sasha took a tissue from her bag and wiped at her eyes. "Ben got hooked on opioids because of so much pain," she told Carmen. "And then he turned to them just to keep himself only half conscious so that he could handle the pain in his heart. After months of rehab, he was released. He visited Talia's grave. The baby is, of course, also buried there. He slashed open his arm in grief and again lost a lot of blood."

"Things got worse after that," Tommy continued for her. "Ben left the Rez, and when I found him months later, he weighed about a hundred thirty pounds and was lying in an alley. He hardly knew his name. We have pictures that you will claim cannot possibly be Ben, but it is him. I managed to get him home, and Sasha and I worked with him twenty-four-seven. We even had men come in and tie him down sometimes. Twice he tried to kill himself, once by getting hold of pain pills and overdosing, once by holding his .45 to his head."

That's why he flinched when I mentioned suicide, Carmen thought.

"I managed to talk him out of it," Tommy continued. "We took him to a sweat lodge, where a traditional healer sang healing songs and waved sacred smoke over him. We got him well enough that I took him to the Black Hills on a vision quest. That is when he claims he was visited by a pack of wolves and that he slept with them. There are no wolves in the Black Hills. I believe it was truly just a vision, but Ben insists it really happened. I will not argue the point with him because it was his vision, and visions have deep meaning. And because of Little Brother's closeness to wolves, he is sincere that when Caesar sat down by you that night in Michigan, the wolf spirit was telling Ben that you are the woman who will bring him love again, joy again, help make him whole again. I know that is a lot for an outsider to accept as real, but to Ben it is very real."

As Carmen had suspected, Ben was deeply immersed in his spiritual beliefs.

"I constantly remind him now that he must never give up again like he did when he was hooked on the opioids and tried to die," Tommy said. "I remind him that if he gives up and loses the school, he will destroy the hope in those kids' hearts and destroy Talia's dream."

Carmen wilted against the back of the seat. "Wow," she said softly. "I knew it had to be bad, but ... wow."

Sasha wiped at more tears. "They have yet to find any good clues as to who did the shooting," she told Carmen. "A lot of people knew where he would be that night, even the FBI. They keep track of him because of his AIM connections. The suits still live in the past, the Wounded Knee thing in '76 and all of that."

"Am I safe when I am with Ben?" Carmen asked.

"I am sure you are," Tommy answered. "If whoever it was still wanted Ben dead, he would have tried again by now. I believe that for some sick reason, the shooter now just enjoys teasing Ben with clues and making him suffer. So it has to be someone who truly hates him, which could be a couple of FBI suits. There are forces out there that have been trying to catch Ben at something that would make him look bad. You can imagine how hard it would be to prove anything against the FBI, and out here, everybody on the Rez loves Ben and his work. Of course, some disagree on some of Ben's causes for political reasons, but I cannot think of one person who would fit the description of a local who would want Ben dead. He does too much for the young people. Either way, whoever did this would not be interested in hurting you, just as I do not believe they meant to kill Talia. I would not have let Sasha ask you out here if I thought you would be in danger."

Carmen sighed and closed her eyes, feeling sick at the horror Ben must have suffered seeing his unborn son blown half out of his mother's belly, watching that tiny leg move. *My God, Ben, how am I supposed to help you?* Part of her wanted to go to him right this instant and grab him and hold on tight and tell him everything would be okay. But another part of her wanted to run away from all of this.

CHAPTER FOURTEEN

CARMEN DRANK some free coffee she'd taken from the visitor's center. She squiggled her nose at the smell and taste of cardboard that detracted from what otherwise was not bad coffee. She needed the pick-me-up, so she drank it anyway as she studied the massive brown, white, and red cliffs and buttes of the Badlands surrounding the Center and the cabins where she'd stayed.

A map inside the visitor's center showed the extent of this wild, rugged country, and she couldn't imagine how a fifteen-year-old girl ended up shot dead in such a forsaken place. A woman who worked in the visitor's center had gladly filled her in on all the gossip about the murder, how the girl's body would never have been found if not for some hikers who strayed off the beaten path. How awful it must have been for Ben to find a necklace there that had belonged to Talia. Carmen had not mentioned that to the woman in the visitor's center. Maybe Ben had not told the authorities, for whatever reason. That was his business.

She waited out in front of the center for Tommy's black Jeep to show up, which she hoped would be soon because, although it was only nine a.m., the day was already growing hot. She didn't want to be sweaty and have flattened hair when she saw Ben for the first time after so many weeks. She wore the white jeans Val always told her looked great on her, a tiny silver belt, and a mint green sleeveless T-shirt with a draped scoop neck. It was going to be too warm for much jewelry, so she wore only a very tiny gold chain necklace and small gold drop earrings.

The familiar Jeep finally showed, veering off the highway and up the entrance drive to the visitor's center. Sasha was driving, and, as always, smiling that big, excited smile. Carmen still could not get over the woman's open kindness, her always-friendly attitude, and her moving beauty. She had truly expected some unwillingness on Tommy and Sasha's part to accept her as Ben's new interest. After all, she did not have a drop of Lakota blood in her, and she still knew little about what she was in for. Surely, they expected Ben to fall for a Lakota woman if and when he finally got over Talia. But so far, Carmen felt no resentment at all, which was a big help in trying to feel at home here. Then again, acceptance might not be so easy from others. Ben's friends, coworkers, and the general population of Pine Ridge and Sunrise had not even met her yet.

Sasha stopped the Jeep beside her and popped open the back gate. Carmen walked around and put her two bags inside, then climbed into the front seat next to Sasha.

"Did you sleep well? Sasha asked.

"Not really. I mean, the cabin was wonderful. It was nice having it all to myself. But I couldn't shut off my thoughts and my nervousness at seeing Ben."

"Oh, do not be nervous," Sasha soothed. "Have fun today. You look beautiful, by the way. So sexy. Ben will be knocked over to see you."

Carmen put on her seat belt. "Thank you, but I just ... I feel *so* out of my element."

"You will feel right at home in no time. Ben will make sure of that."

"You and Tommy have been so kind."

"We love Ben. Anything and anyone who makes him happy makes *us* happy. If you had seen him at his worst, you would know why we are so glad to know he is interested in someone new. You make him smile."

Sasha drove off at a high speed, turning down a paved, two-lane road. Carmen couldn't help thinking that the woman drove like she walked and talked: fast and energetic.

"Tell me true, Sasha. Ben doesn't have any girlfriends right here among his own? I don't want to find out some gorgeous Lakota woman like you has already laid claim to him. I have a feeling competing with his dead wife will be a big enough challenge." She set her cup of coffee into a cupholder.

Sasha laughed. "Little Brother has no girlfriends, but there are plenty of our women who would like to be his chosen, and some have tried to cozy up to him. But until you came along, he has showed no interest. He has been too full of Talia." She put the Jeep in cruise. Carmen noticed it was set at eighty-five. Then again, they were driving out of the Badlands and into such wide-open spaces, there was nothing to run into even if they left the road.

"Besides," Sasha continued, "his first year after the shooting was spent just recovering, and the second year consisted of Ben's battle with opioids. This last year and a half have been the first time Ben has lived a fairly normal life, but he has spent most of his time working with the youth group and traveling. I think he keeps himself busy on purpose. In the times when we know he is extra sad, we try to get him to come and stay with us. We worry about him when he is alone." She brightened. "But now *you* are here! Knowing Caesar chose you for him gives him hope for love again."

Carmen looked out at rugged cliffs and mesas that seemed to go on forever. "I'm not sure I like the word *chosen*, Sasha. The man has to fall in love with me naturally, and I'm not sure any of that has happened yet, even on my part. You have to understand that this spiritual choosing is not how things happen in my world."

"Of course we understand. So does Ben, but he told us that what Caesar did does not matter. As soon as he put his arm around you and walked you back to those cages, he felt something warm and good. Ben is particularly good at judging people, reading their eyes, feeling what is in their hearts. He felt only goodness with you. He says there is nothing fake about you. That means a lot, especially to a man who has to deal with powerful, false-tongued people quite a bit. The fact that you told us yesterday that you want to know the real Ben meant a lot to Tommy. That is what Ben needs. Women fall all over Ben at those shows, and some of our own women do the same thing, but they do not know or care what is going on inside the man. Ben sees that you *do* care."

"Well, thank you. That makes me feel a little better." She watched the hills again. The road had curved back into more white cliffs and gullies. "How well does Ben know the Badlands?"

"Very well. So does Tommy. They used horses to get to the site of where Linda's body was found. But there are parts of the Badlands so extremely remote, even Ben and trackers would have trouble finding their way out. That is why they are called Badlands. The soil is not good, and no one wants to live there. They are also extremely dangerous to anyone who is not familiar with them. And some believe the Badlands are haunted."

"By what? Or whom?"

Sasha shrugged. "Spirits of good and evil, monsters no one can actually see. It is just a myth, Tommy says, but I get shivers when we go horseback riding there. Tommy thinks it is funny."

"Where is Tommy now?"

"At rehearsal. He told Ben I was not feeling well and would come later. I have to stop in Kyle and pick up the cake. You will have to wait in the car so no one sees you." She honked at an old man who passed them in a pickup. "That was Lou Many Horses. He is a shaman—the traditional healer who prayed over Ben when he was recovering from drugs. He lives in a rundown old trailer near Kyle and works part-time cleaning up the grounds at the visitor's center." Sasha turned down the air a little. "You will see much poverty, Carmen, as we get closer to Kyle, but there are nice homes and businesses, too, and of course, the Oglala Lakota College. We do have our own newspaper and schools and a health clinic, Kyle Health Center. We have a helicopter that can take serious cases to Rapid City."

"Where did Ben grow up? Near Kyle?"

"No. We all grew up farther east on the Rosebud Reservation. That is where most of the Lakota band lives. I am sure Ben will take you there to meet Old Grandmother. She lives in a broken-down old trailer with a round, sloped roof. When you see it, you will understand the kind of poverty Ben grew up in. He and Tommy have both tried to get Grandmother to move in with them, but she likes that old trailer. One thing you need to understand about our People is, they can be very stubborn, very rooted in the old ways, and often very silent. As an outsider, you will not find it easy getting anything personal out of them or anything to do with our ways. Ben and Tommy offered to buy their grandmother a new trailer, but she refuses, so they keep putting an extra weather coating on the roof so it does not leak in a rainstorm. She even has a real tepee in her yard, and she stays in that sometimes in summer. She likes it better – says it is cooler."

Sasha answered her phone then over her car's Bluetooth speaker. "Hey, Tommy."

"Everything okay, baby?"

"Perfect. We are on our way. Make up an excuse to come out when we get there. I'll need help with the cake."

"I will watch for you."

Carmen could hear group singing and drumming in the background. "Sounds noisy in there," Sasha said with a grin.

"You know how rehearsals get. Ben has not even mentioned his birthday," Tommy answered. "Maybe he does not even remember what day this is."

"He remembers, all right. He is just too humble to bring it up. Wait till those kids embarrass him with what we have planned."

"You are a crazy woman. That is what I love about you," Tommy joked. "Drive careful."

"I always do."

"Liar."

Sasha laughed and hung up, driving silently for a few minutes before sobering a little with her next conversation. "When you see where Ben grew up, you will see what it took for Ben and Tommy—and me and Talia, too—to get out of this and go to college and work hard to bring something back here to help other youth. Ben could have achieved great things in the outside world, but he will not give up on

Talia's dream of helping young people right here. Pine Ridge is a little more central for talented Native American youth who live outside the reservation."

"I don't mean to sound nosey, but how do you and Tommy and Ben, in fact, make money? You seem to do pretty well."

"Oh, making money here is complicated. There are very few jobs. Many get checks from the government, which Ben hates, but it is what it is. We have two casinos, but there are arguments over the bookkeeping. No one makes much from them. Ben makes good money on his own from his legal work. He represents Natives from many other tribes besides our own with domestic problems or criminal charges if he feels they have been wrongly accused or mistreated by the government or outside officials. And he works on official government treaties and such. He helped me and Tommy once when the government tried to take away three of our sons. They do that sometimes. They just come into the home and drag children away. They believe no indigenous person is able to support so many children as Tommy and I have."

Sasha shook her head. "That was a terrible time, but you should have seen Ben when we went to court. He can be a real steam engine. Ben will not tolerate our People being abused or intimidated by the government. He loves our sons like they are his own. You saw how he reacted to your ex beating you. He was pretty much that mad when they tried to take some of my babies away from me. Tommy and I will always love him for getting them back for us. We will always be there for him, as he was there for us. We took care of Ben in our home for about four months after he was finally released from the hospital."

Carmen smiled inwardly at what a talking machine Sasha could be.

"Ben has taken a couple of cases all the way to the Supreme Court," the woman rattled on. "Anyway, I think he charges $250 an hour, but he donates a lot of that to the School for the Arts, and he does a lot of pro bono work."

Sasha stopped talking for a moment, and Carmen suspected it was only to get a second wind.

"When you have known poverty, you do not forget it," Sasha continued. "And you want to help others. Besides that, Native Americans have always lived in a communal atmosphere. One does not stock his freezer while his neighbor or relatives starve. Everything is shared, just like in the old days. When a hunter would kill two or three buffalo, he would share the meat with others who did not make a kill. Of course, because of outside influences, there are those who have become more selfish, and that is a matter of contention for Ben."

So, he does make enemies.

They moved into wide-open country again. "Oh, I have to tell you," Sasha spoke up again, this time with a big smile. "At the end of rehearsal, Ben has this thing where he asks the kids if any of them is smarter or more talented than the others. They have to say no. They are all the same and each is expected to help the others. It is Ben's way of teaching equality and helping them work together as a team. And then he asks, *Who is the smartest and most talented among you?* They answer, *I am!* which means they are all the same. But when he asks that question today, they will point at him and say, *you are!* Ben will melt right down." She laughed again. "He could be so arrogant about his smarts and talent, but he is so humble and easy to embarrass. I *love* to embarrass him. I told him once that during one of our sexy dances,

I plan to have one of those, what do you call it? Costume malfunctions?"

Both women laughed.

"Ben would pass out. He gets nervous every time we do that dance now. He knows me, and he thinks I really will do it and he won't see it coming. He would just *die* if my tunic came undone. Of course, I would not really let it happen, but he knows I like to play tricks on him, and he does not totally trust that I would not do it." She sobered a little. "I do things like that to keep him laughing and to keep him occupied with something other than wondering who shot Talia."

"And what is your theory about that, Sasha?"

Sasha shook her head. "My guess is, an inside job, maybe a disgruntled member of the council who is upset with Ben over the casino thing. He also defends battered women, so it could be an angry husband who went after him. But it could also be some suit who hates being assigned out here or resents the help we get from the government and hates Ben because he is so good at *getting* that help. It could be some outsider who can't get the land or mineral rights he wants. Ben keeps getting in the way, stopping the desecration of the land when outsiders dig into Mother Earth for the valuables She holds deep inside. There are so many causes we constantly fight for, including clean water, more jobs, better schools. The list is long, including arguments over the casinos, and Ben ends up getting involved in all of it. Talia did, too, so for all we know, the shooter *did* intend to kill Talia and Ben both, or maybe he thought killing Talia would destroy Ben. It almost did."

Carmen sighed and took another sip of her coffee. "My gosh, it's a little unnerving to realize how many different people might want Ben dead."

"Don't be afraid of it. Men would never stand up for others if they worried about that. Ben will never give up the fight."

And I will right be in the middle of it all if I fall in love with him. "There is so much to think about," Carmen said aloud. "Ben has to be incredibly busy. I don't know how he keeps up with all of it and still has time for the youth group."

"It is all for Talia, but Tommy and I help with rehearsals when Ben can't be there. I know all the different songs and dances. Our drummers love to be there because at Pow-Wows we have drumming contests, so when they are at rehearsal they can constantly practice. Tommy is particularly good with the flute, and he can play electric guitar like a professional. Ben also plays guitar. Once in a while they just jam with those guitars—Native rock." She laughed. "They are pretty darn good. And Tommy also has a good voice. He just does not have Ben's range."

"I heard him at that concert in Grand Rapids. The whole group does such a fantastic job."

"They do their best because they all love Ben and want to impress him. They are so excited about surprising him today. Just wait until they see *you* there!"

After about an hour, homes, trailers, restaurants, gas stations, and other businesses came in sight. "We are just outside Kyle now." Sasha slowed down. They passed some nicer homes and some not so nice, yards with trash and abandoned cars in them, children running barefoot in dry grass, a few children and adults on horseback, parked cars. Sasha honked, and a few people waved.

"There is our school and high school," Sasha pointed out. "Oh, and out there in the distance is Oglala Lakota College. You can get a four-year degree there. It has grown a lot. They have a library and bookstore, new dormitories, a gymnasium, faculty offices, a historical center, and math and science building. It is as good as any college in South Dakota."

Three small children took turns pushing an old tire down the street. Sasha had to slow down for them.

"We will be at Sunrise soon," she continued in her proud descriptions of Kyle and the schools. "Sunrise also has dorms now where young people can live while attending because so many of them live far away. We are getting increased attendance from other reservations and even talented outsiders who do not live on reservations at all. Our campus is growing. Some of the students live at Oglala Lakota College and come over to Sunrise for extra credits. There is the school itself, and now a theater with a real stage and all the things the students need to be familiar with for when they perform at other venues. Ben named the theater Talia's Theater of Dreams"

Of course, Carmen thought. Again, she realized that in spite of all she needed to learn about life here, about Lakota ways, about the school and Old Grandmother and the Badlands and the Black Hills and Ben's work, none of it would compare as a challenge more than a dead woman named Talia or a tiny unborn baby boy.

"Did Ben name his son?" she asked Sasha.

Sasha slowed down for two women crossing the main street of Kyle. "Yes," she answered. "He named him E-Maha-Nemeneo-O. It means They Are All Singing. To him, it stands for all the angels singing with joy at holding his little son in their arms. It comforts him to picture his baby boy being cared for that way. For the records, the boy's English name is Thomas Singing Boy Colter. He wanted to name him after Tommy."

Carmen looked out the side window, fighting tears. How was she supposed to reasonably decide if she was falling in love with Ben the man or Ben the *lonely* man, when everything she learned about him just made him more loveable?

Sasha stopped in front of a bakery and popped open the back gate again. "I'll be right back." She hurried inside, then returned a couple of minutes later carrying a large cake box. She set the cake into the back of the Jeep and closed the gate.

"I sure hope that thing doesn't melt before we can get it inside the theater," she said absently. "I'll turn the air up." She did just that and took off again. They drove for another several minutes in silence before reaching what looked like a small college campus.

"We are here," Sasha told Carmen. "This is Sunrise School for the Arts. There is Ben's truck."

Carmen felt her heart pounding. There was that big, fancy, almost mean-looking black truck with those letters painted on the side. THE BLACK HILLS ARE NOT FOR SALE. She remembered the first time she saw it back in Michigan and how her heart nearly stopped when Ben got out and walked up to her. She put down her window for a moment and heard loud drumming coming from inside the newest-looking campus building where Sasha had parked. The entranceway was shaped like a gigantic tepee, and a large sign in front that was bordered by stones read, TALIA'S THEATER OF DREAMS. In the top right corner of the sign was a large picture of a beautiful woman with long, black hair, strands of it draped over one eye. She looked very much like Sasha.

"Do not get out yet. Wait here," Sasha told her. "I will

leave the car running so you and the cake stay cool." She closed the door and left.

Carmen stared at the picture. It seemed those exotic, hazel eyes were looking right at her, as though to say, *Will you love my husband as much as I did?*

She closed her window, but she could still hear the drumming. None of this seemed real. Just four days ago, she was cooking breakfast at her dad's house in Michigan. It was as though a rocket ship had landed, taken her hostage, and zoomed her to another planet where she was now an alien. She quickly texted Val.

Can't talk right now. Will see Ben soon. I'll call later tonight.

She sent the text and wished she wasn't so nervous.

CHAPTER FIFTEEN

CARMEN GLANCED at another huge portrait of Talia that hung over the theater doors inside the tepee-shaped entrance. That one read, In Memory of Talia Gentle Deer Sage-Colter. This picture was full front. She wore a white buckskin dress that accented her satiny dark skin. The dress was draped in front just enough to reveal lovely cleavage. She wore a turquoise necklace, and her dark hair hung past her waist on either side of her face—a face that would be hard to forget with its even, white teeth, full lips, sparkling hazel eyes, a smile that showed kindness.

Two more pictures were lit up in the lobby area when Carmen walked inside. To the left of the theater doors was a picture of Ben and Talia together, so beautiful it seemed unreal. Their smiles were infectious. To the right was another picture of the couple, this time from the side. Talia wore a white, tight-fitting dress that revealed her very pregnant belly, and Ben wore a white fringed buckskin shirt. He stood behind Talia with his arms wrapped around her and his hands under her belly in a pose that made it look like he was supporting the baby.

Carmen felt surrounded by a ghost. She waited in the lobby as instructed until Sasha came to let her into the theater itself. She'd led her to a partition where a ticket-taker would normally stand, and where Carmen could watch rehearsal through a window without being spotted.

"I will raise my hand and signal you to come down the main aisle when the time is right," she told Carmen excitedly. She quickly disappeared.

The youth group sang a very upbeat song Carmen was sure she'd heard somewhere but couldn't remember. The main lyric was "when love takes over," and Ben was walking back and forth on a stage that extended into the audience area of the theater, pointing to each young person whose turn it was to sing a line. The whole group danced in a side-step around the stage as they sang, a routine that meant each one would get a turn front and center. The song made Carmen sway and bounce to the beat, and Ben whirled and danced in supportive gestures to encourage the singers to belt out their best and keep the beat going. He grabbed Sasha and they danced a fast step together.

Carmen had almost forgotten how captivating Ben could be to watch, but he looked tired. He stopped mid-song to pull his hair into a tail at the base of his neck and tie it, then grabbed a bottle of water and drank half of it down in several long gulps. He took something from his jeans pocket and swallowed whatever it was.

Tylenol. Rehearsal was bringing on the pain. He finished the water. *You do too much, Ben. You're still trying to forget Linda Two Fists, which only leads to thoughts of Talia.*

More songs. They were rehearsing for a big show in Omaha, Talia had told her, and this one would be mostly singing a mixture of Native song and modern music. The only Native dancing would be at the end of the show—one big, colorful, whirling, fancy dance with loud drumming and ending with Ben and little Benjamin again dancing together.

Right now, the little boy was just jumping around and trying to keep up with the singers. Ben picked him up once and held him in one arm as he again whirled to another fast tune, "Love Can Move Mountains." Just before the song, Ben had mentioned music from a television special from New Orleans several years ago called *The Passion.* Now she remembered where she'd heard some of the songs.

Some of the music came from their own live Native drummers, Tommy on guitar, and several others in a band that was pretty darn good. Some of it was the real instrumental music from the original song, piped in via loudspeakers. The youth group added the words karaoke style, but they were far from Friday-night amateurs. Their professionalism was astounding. Ben definitely knew what he was doing, and he kept stressing self-confidence to the students.

"How many of you belt out a song in front of a mirror using a hairbrush?" he asked.

Most of them laughed and raised their hands.

"Then sing like that here," Ben told them. "You are Carrie Underwood. You are Josh Groban. You are Lady Gaga. You are Celine Dion or Chris Daughtry. A good share of their performances consists of self-confidence. The number one thing to do is win over your audience. Do not be bashful. Do not hold back. If you are out of tune, I can work with you. So can Sasha or Tommy." He walked up to a heavyset young woman who looked about eighteen. "Amy here had trouble with always being a little off key when she first came here. My wife, Talia, worked with her, and now she is graduating this summer with an offer from a record company."

The whole group clapped and whistled, and Ben hugged the young woman, who looked ready to cry. Her headset was still turned on, and Carmen heard her tell Ben, "I still miss Talia."

"We all do, sweetheart," Ben told her. "None more than I do."

More songs.

"Remember that every one of you gets a turn stage front," Ben told them, "because no one here is better than the next. You are all professionals, and you all need practice in being right out front."

The students sang an upbeat version of "What Doesn't Kill You Makes You Stronger."

"Believe that!" Ben told them. "I know it for a fact. Do not let anything in life defeat you!" He made them sing the song again, louder and with even more confidence, joining them as the group moved to different stage positions, their harmony pitch-perfect.

They sang a couple more modern songs, using Ben's renditions that meshed Native tunes and beats with contemporary music in a way only someone truly profes-sional could come up with. Native rock, Sasha had called it.

At one point, Ben came down into the theater seats and removed his shirt. There was that great body that made it hard for Carmen to think straight. He toweled off perspira-tion and took a clean white T-shirt with a picture of a wolf on the front from a duffle bag. The white shirt only accented his dark skin. He drank yet another bottle of water and told the kids on stage not to get too relaxed. They all groaned and whined and said they were tired, then started giggling. Carmen could tell the kids were excited about the surprise cake they knew was coming and were getting anxious.

Ben walked back onto the stage and said the very words Sasha had told Carmen he would say about equality. When he got to the last line, "And who is the most talented, most valuable person on this stage," the students all pointed to Ben and yelled at the top of their lungs, "YOU ARE!!!"

Ben just stood there a moment, then put his hands on his hips and turned away. The kids all jumped up and down and laughed and broke into the happy birthday song. Ben just shook his head and looked at Sasha. He pointed at her.

"*You* did this!"

"Of course I did!" Sasha walked closer. "And Tommy and I want you to take the rest of the day off, Little Brother."

Ben shook his head again. "You know I cannot do that, you vixen."

"Sure you can!" Sasha put an arm around Ben's waist as Tommy walked down the center aisle pushing a cart with the huge birthday cake on it. A pile of paper plates, forks, paper cups, and a jug of juice were stashed on a shelf underneath. Ben just grinned and turned to the kids with an arm around Sasha's shoulders. "Do not ever do that to me again," he ordered. "You know what you are supposed to say!"

"Mom told us to say it," one good-looking young Native man told him. "But we really mean it!" He looked about fourteen, and Carmen figured he was another one of Sasha's sons.

Ben kept shaking his head as Tommy came closer with the cake. "I absolutely forgot today was my birthday," Ben told the group.

"You are really old now," one young girl shouted.

"Okay! Okay!" Sasha yelled. She told Ben to get down

off the stage and stand behind the cake with his back to the theater entrance so they could get pictures.

"You should not have done this," Ben told her.

Sasha held up her cell phone and motioned for Carmen to come down the aisle while Tommy walked in front of the kids with a finger to his lips. A few of them squealed and giggled as Carmen headed down the aisle, her heart pounding with a mixture of anticipation and dread that Ben would not like this at all.

"I want you to know that I baked this cake myself, Little Brother," Sasha told him.

"And I am president of the United States," Ben answered. "You do not have a domestic bone in your body."

"I beg your pardon! I can bake and I can cook."

"You suck at both," Ben answered.

More giggles.

"Well, why would *you* care?" Sasha joked. "You told me that your new girlfriend back in Michigan cannot cook either."

Carmen nearly laughed out loud.

"She told me so. I have never tasted her cooking yet, but it does not matter," Ben said. "With a body like hers, I could not care less if she cannot even boil water."

Carmen's eyes widened at the remark.

"She should know that, Little Brother," Sasha told him. "You should tell her. In fact, I *dare* you to tell her."

Ben folded his arms. "All right. Call her."

Sasha walked closer with a sassy look on her face. "You should just turn around and tell her."

"What?"

"Turn around and tell her," Sasha repeated.

Ben turned.

"Happy birthday," Carmen told him.

Ben just stood there, dumbfounded. He looked Carmen over as though it took a moment for him to realize she was really standing there. "My God," he said quietly before walking up to Carmen and grabbing her close. He lifted her and swung her around, and the kids on stage began screaming and laughing and jumping up and down.

Carmen moved her arms around Ben's neck as he continued clinging to her and turning in circles, her feet off the floor.

"It's her!" the kids were shouting.

"It's his new girlfriend!"

"It's that lady from Michigan!"

"Look! He's kissing her!"

Indeed, he was.

"How?" Ben asked between kisses.

"Plane." Another kiss.

"What made you decide to come?"

"Sasha said you needed me, and I was going crazy missing you."

"How long can you stay?" He kissed her yet again.

"However long you want me here."

"That would be for the rest of your life."

Ben's answer surprised her. "I can't guarantee *that* long," she told him with a smile and another kiss. They laughed again amid more kisses. "Ben, I was so scared you would be upset that I showed up unannounced."

"Are you kidding? You are all I think about. But with everything going on out here, I did not think you would want to come."

Carmen put her head on his shoulder as he continued holding her close with her feet off the floor. "I felt so out of place till now. Ben, I am so out of my element here, but as soon as you put your arms around me, I felt like I belonged.

I hated the way you left that night in Michigan. I've worried about you ever since."

More kisses. *I'm done for,* Carmen thought. All her plans to take this slowly flew right out the window the minute Ben Colter's strong arms came around her. *Slow down! Slow down!* she told herself. But he was still holding her close, still turning with her, still kissing her—delicious lips that finally moved to her neck, her throat. He lowered her but kept a tight arm around her as he led her closer to the stage, where the kids quieted a little.

"Kids, this is Carmen," Ben announced. "Carmen, these are the kids."

They all jumped up and down again, laughing and clapping and making comments about how pretty Ben's new girlfriend was. Chaos ensued. The school's language and spiritual teachers joined them, all of them greeting Carmen kindly. Then more adults who'd been told about the celebration showed up. Ben introduced his office workers, secretaries, accountants, event planners, his law clerk—too many names to remember. To Carmen's relief, they all made her feel welcome.

Sasha introduced her five sons who were there, then started cutting the cake. The next hour was spent eating cake and handing out glasses of juice. Ben announced rehearsal was over for the day, and the kids all cheered.

"And for the next four or five days, your other teachers and Tommy and Sasha will handle classes and rehearsals," Ben told them. He looked at a middle-aged woman standing nearby. "Alice, cancel all my appointments for the next few days," he told her. "I am spending all my time with this woman."

The party wound down. People went back to work. Ben kept an arm around Carmen through nearly all the partying. "Where are your bags?" he asked when everyone left.

"In Sasha's Jeep."

"It is unlocked," Sasha told Ben.

Ben leaned down and kissed Sasha's forehead. "Thank you." He let go of Carmen long enough to give his brother a hug. "Thanks for thinking of this, Tommy."

"I thought it would lift your spirits, Little Brother. Happy birthday."

Ben turned back to Carmen and put his arm around her again. "*Skoden!*"

"What?"

"That is Lakota slang for let's go."

"Where?"

"To my place. That is where you are staying."

"I am?" *Wait! Wait!* Carmen remembered thinking she would figure this out if and when the time arrived. And now, here it was. Ben seemed so happy, she didn't have the heart to tell him no, and for the most part, she didn't *want* to say no, but she wasn't sure what to make of any of this. Did he expect something she wasn't ready for?

Ben grabbed his towel and duffle bag, then put his arm around Carmen yet again and led her out of the theater. She noticed him glance at the picture of him with a pregnant Talia. He suddenly stopped and set down the duffle bag. "Just a minute." He walked over to stand under the picture, then reached up and touched it, saying something in the Lakota tongue. He walked back to Carmen.

"Ben?"

He picked up his bag and pulled her close again. "I always pay my respects to my wife and son before leaving the theater." He led her outside to his truck, which sat so high he had to help her climb into it. "I am so damn glad to see you," he told her before closing her door. He threw his duffle bag into the back, then walked over to the Jeep to get Carmen's bags.

Carmen looked around the inside of his truck. The seats were covered with deerskin painted with various Native American symbols. A small dream catcher hung over the rearview mirror, along with a chain and a little framed picture. Carmen grasped hold of it and looked at it. Talia, of course. *What am I doing here? What does he expect of me?* She sat back when Ben came around and climbed up behind the steering wheel.

"Sasha told me she arranged for my cleaning lady, Rosa, to clean things up at my house," he told her, "and make sure the beds had clean sheets and blankets, clean towels in the bathrooms. "

Clean sheets?

"I guess a neighbor lady supposedly put some food in the fridge. I hope Rosa left some of her buffalo chili. It is the best on the entire reservation. If there is some in the fridge, we are all set."

All set for what?

"Put your seat belt on." Ben put his on and paused, looking at Carmen. He frowned. "Why do you look like a scared rabbit?"

Carmen blinked. "Well, I—I'm so happy to be here, Ben, but, I mean, will we be *alone*?"

He broke into that brilliant smile that left her confused. "Yes." He leaned closer and kissed her cheek. "We will be alone." He grasped her hand. "Do not tell me you are afraid to be alone with me."

"I'm not sure. I mean, I guess not, but still—"

"Carmen, I am not your ex. What did I tell you at the lake house? I should say, what did I *promise* you?"

"That you would never hurt me."

"And who made sure your ex will never hurt you again?"

"You did."

"A Lakota man does not break his promises, Carmen. You have to know me well enough by now to know you are safe with me." He started the truck and pulled away. "I need to take a shower when we get there. Rehearsal can be a real workout. I will give you something to drink, and you can enjoy the cool air in the house and walk around and snoop at pictures and steal from the fridge—whatever you want to do. You must be tired. I know I am. It has been a long, crazy day."

Carmen glanced at the dangling picture of Talia. Would she approve? "Have you ... I mean, have you done this before? I hope you don't make a habit of taking women back to your house."

Ben snickered and shook his head. "I guess you do not know me as well as I thought you did. No, ma'am, I do not take women to my house. Sasha and Tommy will tell you that. You are the first. I swear on the sacredness of Wakan-Tanka." He pointed out a few things as he drove and talked about taking her camping in the Black Hills, horseback riding in the Badlands, showing her his offices, an endless string of things he wanted to show her. "We are holding a Pow-Wow right here in September. I will not be able to make the one in Dowagiac, Michigan, so I hope you can stay for ours."

"We'll see. Right now, I need a couple of days to adjust to being here," Carmen told him.

"Of course you do. I understand that. I did not mean that come morning we would jump on horses and go chase down buffalo." He slowed down and pulled over, putting the truck in park. He faced her and took her hand again. "Would you rather stay at Sasha and Tommy's tonight?"

"No. It's just that—" Carmen laughed in a gasp. "To be honest, I feel like I've just been captured by a Lakota warrior and he's taking me to his tepee to do God knows what to me."

Ben kissed her gently, then grinned. "Baby, this warrior is too damn tired to get into a wrestling match with an unwilling woman. Besides that, I am out of practice."

"Yes, well, some things are like riding a bike. You never forget how to do it."

Ben laughed hard then, putting the truck into drive and pulling it back onto the road. "That is one of the things I love about you, Carmen Wolfe. You make me laugh." He grasped her hand and squeezed it reassuringly. "Do not worry. All we will do the next couple of days is finally have that talk we never got to have yet. Does that please you?"

"That sounds just fine." Carmen kept hold of his hand. *Am I nuts for trusting this man? He's lonely and hurting.* Still, the way he pressed her hand only brought forth feelings of honor and reassurance, things she'd never felt with Jerry.

CHAPTER SIXTEEN

"Val, you should see this house." Carmen sank into a white leather couch. "Ben said the design was Talia's idea. She could give Jerry a run for his money, I'll say that."

"Is it as beautiful as your lake house?"

"It depends on what you like. It's beautiful for a house in a desolate location rather than a house on a lake. It's made of stucco, and it's round, with a cathedral ceiling that goes up to one central skylight, like a tepee! I've never seen anything like it. The bedrooms and bathrooms have their own walls and regular ceiling on the inside for privacy, but they are on two sides of the house and the tepee ceiling goes up above them. The center of the house is nothing but living room with white leather furniture and a beautiful kitchen with a big island. The walls for the central area are round, and it's completely open, even where the cathedral ceiling rises above the bedrooms. You look straight up at the central skylight. Cedar beams support it all. The floors are slate and cool."

"Tell me again. You are there *alone* with him?"

"Don't get ideas. He is being a complete gentleman."

"Yeah? Well, it's not dark out, and you haven't gone to bed yet. What's he doing now?"

"Taking a shower. Rehearsal makes him work up a sweat."

"Well, he just might work up a sweat again later tonight, and you will *both* need a shower."

"You know me better."

"I know you have never been with a man like Ben."

"There are no other men like Ben." Carmen told Val about everything she had seen earlier, what the landscape was like, the Badlands, Sasha, the theater, the pictures of Talia. "The birthday surprise was better than I expected," she added. "Ben was so happy to see me, which was a great relief. He swept me right up into his arms and kissed me."

"Oh, that is so romantic!" Val said. "Was there more than one kiss?"

"We could hardly *stop* kissing. It felt so right, Val. But I'm still afraid all of this is moving way too fast. Something is going to burst this bubble."

"Like heck. Take advantage of it and have fun. You're a grown woman, Carmen, and Ben is a lonely man who needs a woman in his life again. And in his *bed!*"

Carmen sighed and put her head back against the leather couch. "Val, I just got here. Please talk to me in terms of reality. If you totaled it up, I've known the man for maybe five hours."

"Well, sometimes you just know when it's right."

"He's been through hell, Val. When I have more time, I'll tell you about the shooting. It's more horrible than I realized. The man has a lot of personal problems to overcome, and I am still dealing with the trauma of how Jerry turned on me, which brings me to my current situation. I am very frustrated that I'm getting one of those headaches again. I'm too embarrassed to tell Ben. He's so excited I'm here, and he wants me to try some buffalo chili a neighbor brought over. We are supposed to just chill out tonight and talk. But you know how bad my headaches get. If I take one of those pills Sid prescribed, I'll fall right to sleep. I can't do that on my first night here."

"Yes, you can if you have to. Tell him how you are feeling. I'm betting he would understand."

"It's just, I don't know, kind of humiliating. It seems like every time the man has big plans for us, something goes wrong. I'm going to try to stick it out. I'll feel better come morning."

"And I know how bad those headaches get, Carmen. You can't ignore it, and Sid said it's important you take those pills. They lower your blood pressure and open the blood vessels at the base of your skull. You're supposed to put ice on the back of your neck. You know that."

"I can't tell him that." Carmen heard the water shut off. "I have to go. I think he finished his shower."

"Carmen Wolfe, you take care of yourself. If you end up staying very long, Sid and I plan to come out there and see what it's all about."

"They are holding a big Pow-Wow here in mid-September. Maybe you could come out for that, although it isn't likely I'll stay here until then. But I could come back with you guys."

"Girl, you will still be there. I am betting on it. Just text me the exact dates."

"I will. I'd love to see both of you and for you to see the School for the Arts and watch a rehearsal, especially since Sid missed the show in Grand Rapids. And wait till you see pictures of Talia. I can't help feeling like I'm infringing on what belongs to her. This whole house speaks of a woman totally into her culture. I *so* don't fit in."

"You will if that's how this is supposed to be. Right now, you take care of yourself. Tell Ben how you feel. You have had a wild, rushed two or three days, and now you feel like you're in a foreign country. Your headache is probably stress-related. Either way, you have to take care of it."

"I'll manage." Carmen sat up straighter. "I hear drawers opening and closing. He's out of the shower. I have to hang up." Carmen hit the red button on her phone to end the call and slipped her phone into a side pocket on her white jeans. She stood and looked around at Ben's beautiful home again. When they'd driven up to the house, she'd noticed the outside stucco walls were painted with various Native signs. Inside, where the ceiling thrust upward, more Native American symbols were painted between the cedar beams. Every lamp, every couch throw, every rug, every knickknack was of Native America design. Because of the round walls, electrical outlets were in the floor so that no cords trailed from the walls to the fixtures.

She recognized the drumming and flute music Ben had set for his ringtone. He was getting a call. She heard his muffled voice but couldn't make out what he was saying. She noticed yet another picture of Talia hanging above the fireplace, a touching pose of her sniffing a wildflower. The picture caused Carmen to glance at a closed door that, according to Ben, led to the master bedroom.

I have not gone into that room since the shooting, Ben had told her. *Only the housekeeper goes in there, and only when I am not here. There is a smaller bedroom next to this one with a door between. It is the nursery."*

He'd immediately cleared his throat and changed the subject before she could comment either way, but Carmen got the message. She should not go into the master bedroom. Ghosts lived there.

We do have a lot to talk about, Ben Colter. The man needed closure, but she wasn't deep enough into this to get serious about competing with spirits. Somehow, she had to make Ben face the truth. Talia was dead. Yes, he was trying to move on, but he was far from free of that shooting. Maybe finally finding the shooter and why the man did what he did would give Ben the closure he needed.

She walked across the central great room and kitchen to the guest bedroom on the other side of the house. Ben had her put her bags there. To the left of that was another bedroom, but Ben used it as a workout room. His weight bench, a treadmill, and other workout equipment filled the room, which had big windows that looked across prairie land toward the Badlands.

The guest bedroom had its own bathroom, and on the other side of that was Ben's bathroom and bedroom. So close. But he'd made promises. She had to get rid of this fear he might turn into Jerry and force her into something just because he was stronger, hit her if she didn't obey.

She shook away the ridiculous thought. She was so happy to be with him again, yet so confused on what he expected of her and where this was all going. She opened her carry-on and fished out her headache pills. *Damn it!* If she took one, she'd be in a deep sleep in no time and out most of the night. How could she do that to Ben this first night, and on his birthday, no less? They had so much to talk about. Ben was so excited.

"Hey."

Carmen turned with a little gasp of surprise. Ben was leaning against the doorjamb, arms folded. He wore khaki cargo shorts and a plain white sleeveless T-shirt.

"Hey," she answered.

"I think I told you that you can be completely honest with me. Remember?"

Carmen frowned. "What are you talking about?"

"Val just called me. Why do you think you cannot tell me you have a headache?"

Carmen rolled her eyes and wilted onto the bed. Tears started to come, like they always did when she had one of these headaches. "I don't want to ruin our first chance to really be alone together and talk." She glanced at him warily. "At least I thought that's all you wanted."

Ben walked into the room and knelt in front of her. "For God's sake, Carmen, do you think I would not understand pain from old wounds? Val told me you are supposed to take one of those pills Sid gave you. You suffered a serious head injury a couple of years ago. Do not ignore that."

"But the pills put me to sleep."

"That is what they are *supposed* to do." He took her hands. "It is fine, Carmen." He leaned up and kissed her. "Take a pill. Get into your pajamas and get into bed. I will go and fix you some tea and fish an ice pack from the freezer. Believe me, I often use one myself on my lower back."

"I don't want to put you out."

"I do not mind the downtime. You have had a couple of long, stressful days, and I worked extra hard at rehearsal, so I am tired, too. And Talia used to get migraines. I know what that is like. Tea and crackers always helped, but a lot of sleep helped even more. I intend to make sure you get both." He stood up. "Pajamas."

He walked out. *Pajamas?* How awkward was this? Carmen closed the door and hurriedly undressed. *My God, what if he comes in here and I'm not in my pj's yet!* She threw half her clothes out of her suitcase until she found her pajamas, then quickly pulled them on—simple cotton, knee-length blue pants and a pullover T-shirt type top in a matching blue with a white flowered design in it. She picked up the clothes she'd thrown around and put them back in the suitcase, setting it to the side on the floor, then took her pills and makeup bag into the bathroom.

"Get into bed," Ben yelled from the outer room.

What?! Carmen squeezed one pill into her palm, then walked to the queen-size bed and pulled back the covers. Clean white sheets topped with a pink throw, and on top of that a puffy pink and white, lightweight quilt. She noticed only then that everything in the room was pink, from the curtains to the thick, shaggy throw rugs, the bathroom towels, and shower curtain. Ben had shown her around the house so quickly, hurrying past the master bedroom, that she just now remembered he'd said that Talia had loved pink.

The house was full of her. Carmen looked at the bed, then stepped back. She sat down in a white wicker rocker. Minutes later, Ben was at the door again. He held a tray with a cup of hot tea and some crackers on it.

"Why are you not in that bed?" he asked.

"I ... Ben, I am ruining the evening."

He sighed and set the tray on top of a dresser. "Did you take that pill?"

"Not yet."

"Take it."

"But I—"

"Take it!" he ordered.

Carmen got up and went into the bathroom again, reluctantly swallowing the pill in her hand and taking a drink of water. She stood there hesitantly, the tears wanting to come again. She quickly wiped at them, and before she could turn, Ben was behind her. He moved his arms around her and looked at her in the mirror.

"Carmen." He spoke her name softly. "You have to stop being nervous and afraid. I can have Sasha come over if you want me to."

What in God's name am I doing here with that warrior who was on that stage in Grand Rapids? His hair is still wet from a shower, he looks gorgeous, and I'm standing here in one of his bedrooms in my pajamas!

"You have no idea how unreal all of this is for me," she told him.

He turned her and let her cry against his chest. "I think I do. I have lived in both worlds most of my life, Carmen. You have lived only in one. I am so happy to have you here in *my* world now, and I beg of you to please not think I have ulterior motives. We kissed when you first got here, and you said you were happy to be in my arms, so do not judge me by your ex, all right? I promise I am nothing like him, and all I want right now is for you to feel better. So come get in your bed. Drink some tea and eat something to offset those pills. I know strong pills are hard on the stomach." He reached for some tissues and handed her a handful. "You are safe here. Always. Remember what I sang to you? I'm here. No one can harm you."

Carmen blew her nose and wiped at her eyes, then let him walk her to the bed. "I'm so sorry," she wept as she climbed under the covers. "These headaches make me cry."

Ben grinned and pulled the covers over her. "Everybody cries over something. It is called being human. I have shed enough tears to fill a swimming pool." He leaned down and kissed her tears, then rose to bring over the tea and crackers. He set them on a bedside table and pulled it out a little so she could easily reach them. "Drink the tea and eat something. I will be right back with an ice pack."

He left, and Carmen drank some of the tea and ate a cracker. Ben returned with the ice pack. "I have all kinds of these, left over from months in the hospital." He put a throw pillow behind her bed pillow and laid the ice pack across the top of both pillows. "Scoot back against these and stay sitting upright for a while. I know that used to help Talia. I will put the ice pack under your neck after you eat a little."

"Thank you."

Ben grasped her under the arms and helped her move back against the pillows. He turned to leave. "If you are better tomorrow, I will take you to my office with me and reintroduce you to everybody. I have a few things I need to do there. Maybe we can go riding the next day. I have so much to tell you about our history and what the causes are today that I work to support." He pointed to the crackers on her tray. "For now, I will be in the kitchen, so if you need something more, call out to me." He headed for the door.

"Wait," Carmen said. She blew her nose again and wiped at more tears. "Stay here."

Ben frowned. "You sure?"

"Yes." Carmen couldn't believe her own request. She patted the bed. "You're tired, too. Lie down here beside me. I don't want you to be alone out there, and I'm sorry I act like I'm afraid of you. I'm not really. I'm just all mixed up and tired right now. If you ... if you lie down here until I fall asleep, we can still talk a little, and it will be a good beginning to me trusting you. I mean, I *do* trust you, but, well, you have to admit, you are still a stranger in a lot of ways, but you did defend me back in Michigan."

Ben put a finger to his lips. "Drink that tea and do not say another word. You are so mixed up right now that you are talking in circles and will end up talking yourself into a corner you cannot escape from. We will save the talking for tomorrow. Sid believes you should rest, and that is what I insist you do."

Carmen's eyes widened as he walked around the end of the bed and laid down beside her. His feet were bare, and his hair was still damp. He propped his pillow so that he was half sitting up. All Carmen could think of was that she must be losing her mind from her head injury. He was so big that he filled his whole side of the bed. A man who was nothing but brawn and power and who supposedly had not been with a woman in a long time was lying right beside her. And she'd just taken a pill that would knock her out so deeply that he could have his way with her and she wouldn't know the difference until she woke up. "You ... you'll stay on top of the covers, right?" She blurted out the words without even thinking.

Oh my God! Did I just say that?

Ben broke into laughter and pulled the pillow over his face. "My God, woman, you sure know how to test a man. I love the nutty things you say." He chuckled more as he leaned close and kissed her cheek. "Yes, I will stay on top of the covers. Now, finish that tea and let that pill put you to sleep."

"Just don't think you can take advantage while I'm sleeping. These pills don't make me sleep *that* hard," she lied.

More laughter. "Wakan-Tanka, give me strength!" Ben spoke the words facetiously. "If Sasha and Tommy knew what was going on right now, they would tease me beyond cruelty, especially Sasha." He leaned closer and kissed her cheek again. "Show me a smile."

Carmen drank more tea, then set it aside. She looked at

him and couldn't help obeying his request. "I act like I'm sixteen sometimes, don't I?"

"You just act like a woman who wants to do the right thing and does not want me to think she loves too easily." Ben sat up more and sobered. "Let me tell you something, Carmen, and this is very hard for me."

Carmen watched his eyes. "What is it?"

"You should know that this is just as hard for me as it is for you. Maybe harder. Right now, making love to another woman would feel like cheating on my wife. And you are divorced from a man who abused you, so naturally it is hard to trust any man who is still partly a stranger to you. You feel affection for me, but that defensive side of you is saying you should be careful." He reached out and pushed some of her hair behind her ear. "But *my* defensive side also says to be careful," he continued, "because another woman still lives inside here." He put his hand to his heart. "I am afraid to love again. And it is not easy for a 215-pound warrior to say that."

His left hand was still near her ear, and Carmen glanced at the scar from letting blood at his wife's grave. It was a good eight inches long. She met his wild, dark eyes but decided not to mention she knew how he got the scar. "I think your wife would *want* you to love again, Ben. It's natural for both of us to want that. It's just ... kind of scary."

Ben smiled warmly, then leaned in and kissed her softly. "Yes. Kind of scary." He reached for the ice pack and lifted her slightly to move it under her neck. He put a towel over it so it would not be too directly cold. "Your eyes are starting to droop," he told her.

"It happens pretty quickly when I take these pills."

Ben took the tea out of her hand and set it on the side table, then tucked the blankets around her.

"Stay with me," she said sleepily.

"I am right here."

I'm here. No one can harm you. Carmen tried to keep her eyes open, but it was impossible. She felt his arm move under her pillows, felt his other arm move across her middle, pulling her closer.

"I am glad you are here," Ben told her. His voice sounded far away, as though she were dreaming the words. "This is all either of us needs for now. I stay busy on purpose so that I am almost never home. It is too lonely here." He added something in the Lakota tongue. Carmen didn't understand the words, yet she knew it was something beautiful. She was aware that he reached up and adjusted the ice pack. She relished its coolness.

She sensed his head on the pillow beside her then, and she was not afraid.

CHAPTER SEVENTEEN

CARMEN BLEW her hair partly dry after a shower and pulled on a bra and a yellow T-shirt. She left her pj's bottoms on for now, not sure what Ben's plans were. The problem was, she could think of a hundred reasons why they did NOT belong together, yet Ben was already moving into her heart in ways that made it impossible not to care about him. That was the hell of it. If things did not work out, she wasn't sure she could go back to Michigan and put Ben out of her life and out of her thoughts and dreams. Maybe her confusion was just an aftereffect of the trauma of what Jerry had done to her, and her rude awakening to how cruel life could be. Her experience with Jerry had made it hard to realize that some men actually loved sincerely, gently, respectfully. Ben had been so good to her last night.

She heard some noise in the great room and wondered how long Ben had been up. When she awoke, her tray had disappeared, along with her ice pack and Ben himself. She'd checked herself over to make sure he hadn't taken privileges, then felt like a complete idiot for wondering. Thinking he might do something like that was ridiculous.

She fingered through her hair once more to fluff it a little and help it dry, then hurriedly made the bed before walking into the great room. Ben was in the open kitchen area, pouring water into a blender that already had a cream-colored powder and some frozen strawberries in it.

He wore white sweatpants and no shirt, and she wondered if the man had an ounce of fat on him anywhere. *Well, I give up.* Resisting the man was becoming more difficult than she cared to admit. His abs looked like rocks, his arms like a powerful machine, and those sweatpants were tied below his waist, revealing a few dark hairs that headed south. He put a lid on the blender and turned it on, then looked up to see her moving closer.

"Finally up, huh? How do you feel?" he asked.

"Much better," she answered. "I'm so sorry about last night. I'm really stronger than I behaved. The headache really messed things up."

"I do not doubt your strength. I felt it the first time I met you. And do not be surprised if one of these days you wake up to find me still in bed because sometimes I am practically paralyzed from my back. It has happened before, so once in a while I am not already up and showered." He gave her a smile. "You see? We both have ailments that shut us down once in a while."

"Oh, I'm so sorry about your back."

He shrugged. "It is just part of the joyful aftereffects of being shot."

He held the lid on the blender, and Carmen noticed the scar on his arm again. He turned to reach for a spatula, and there was the scar she hadn't seen yet: a very long one on his right side from his belly around to his back. *The kidney.*

What a horror that must have been, lying unconscious for two weeks from loss of blood, several more weeks of being unable to move at all. She noticed another smaller scar just under his belly button ... and the tattoo TALIA, emblazoned in a half circle over the top of his heart.

"I'm still in my pajama bottoms," she told him. "I wasn't sure what to put on—what you had planned for today."

He poured whatever he'd made into two large glasses, then turned to the sink to rinse the pitcher. "We will go to my office this morning. I told my assistant yesterday to cancel all my appointments, but I still have to check my email and probably return some phone calls and catch up on a few things. While we are there, you can get a better idea of what we do—what *I* do. You can wear jeans. I don't think today will be as hot as yesterday."

Carmen noticed more scars, this time even smaller ones on his lower back. Visions of what the shooting must have been like flashed before her eyes ... lying over his bleeding and dying wife and son.

He left the pitcher in the sink and turned to pick up one of the glasses. "Protein drink with fresh fruit. Want some?"

"You get fresh fruit here?"

He snickered. "Well, I know we are not in Michigan where fruit drips from the trees, but we *do* grow a lot of our own food, and what we do not grow can be delivered. We are not in central Africa, Carmen. We are just off Highway 90, and I am betting they do not grow bananas in Michigan, but you can still buy them. Right?"

Carmen grinned and sat on a barstool at the island counter. "Okay, I get it. I am properly embarrassed." She picked up her glass and drank some of the protein drink. "Wow, this is good," she told him.

Ben raised his glass to her and drank some of his own.

"Let me guess," Carmen told him. "That's breakfast."

"Yes, ma'am."

"And you have already been up for a while, probably already worked out before you showered."

"You bet."

"While I slept like a lazy cat."

He smiled the smile that always unnerved her. "You said it."

Carmen covered her face. "It's the pill. I am normally up sooner than this."

"It does not matter. I called Sid last night after you fell asleep and told him how you were. He appreciated the call —said to let you sleep as long as you needed to."

"You called Sid? That was so thoughtful of you." Carmen put a hand to her chest. "Oh my gosh. Was I sleeping with my mouth open?"

Ben chuckled and rested his arms on the island countertop, leaning toward her. Seeing his tattoo even closer brought a catch to her heart and renewed her doubt about him being able to fully love another woman.

"You don't really know all the little quirks and idiosyncrasies about a person until you sleep with them," he teased.

"Oh my God! I *did* have my mouth open, didn't I?"

He leaned even closer and kissed the corner of her mouth. "Only for a couple of minutes. But I haven't had my turn yet. You need to learn what *I* am like when I sleep. That means you must sleep with me again tonight."

"Oh, that's a fine excuse."

"Sounds like a practical one to me."

"Do you snore?"

"Only one way to find out."

"I think I can stand not knowing for now. Did Talia ever complain?"

Ben chuckled and shook his head. "You sure know how to walk yourself right into trouble."

"What do you mean? Oh! I shouldn't have mentioned Talia. I'm so sorry."

"Carmen, it is okay to mention her. What I meant was that you asked a very personal question." He kissed her again. "And the answer is, Talia never complained about *anything* in bed."

Carmen drew in her breath and leaned back. "You are a devil in disguise! I didn't mean it that way and you know it."

Ben laughed and drank down more of his protein shake. "Drink up," he told her. He flexed his muscles. "It will give you more defined muscles."

"Women don't want defined muscles. They just want to keep their figures."

"And you do a particularly good job of that. Let *me* guess this time." He looked her over. "You are a runner."

Carmen smiled. "Right on. But I take a day or two off after one of these headaches. The jostling movements sometimes bring it back."

"I figured you were a runner. That is how you stay so skinny and keep that very defined butt in shape."

"You've been studying my butt?"

"Every chance I get. I meant it when I told Sasha that with a body like yours, I do not care if you cannot even boil water." He gulped down the rest of his drink. "You are also beautiful in the morning with that slightly tangled hair and no makeup. Your beauty is simple and natural."

"I'm not sure what to think of the butt remark, but thank you for the rest of it. I don't think I need to tell you how *you* look in the morning or any other time."

He shook his head. "I do not give it much thought. I stay

in shape only for the shows." He put his arms out and turned. "I am a warrior, don't you know?"

Carmen felt a catch in her heart. "You *are* a warrior, in courtrooms and in DC and in all the things you do for those young people. You are one of the finest men I have ever met."

Ben rinsed out his glass. "Now you are embarrassing me."

"Sasha told me you embarrass easily. But you do a good job of embarrassing others in return. I am fast learning that it's sometimes hard to tell when you are kidding and when you are serious."

He opened the fridge and took out a bottle of water. "Like if I tell you that the only way I got through last night was by taking a couple of cold showers?"

"Yes! That's what I mean."

They both laughed.

"Do you want more than that shake for breakfast?" Ben asked her.

Carmen watched him drink nearly half the water and realized she could stare at him all day. Perfection did not seem like a good enough word to describe him ... except for those scars that reminded her he was a troubled man inside.

"I guess I could use a piece of toast or something."

He set the water aside. "I have just the right thing." He opened the freezer and took out frozen waffles. He set them on the counter in front of her. "Homemade frozen waffles."

"Homemade frozen? Now there is an antonym if I ever heard one."

Ben smiled with a hint of sadness. "That was Talia's favorite phrase. We used the microwave a lot because we were always so busy. *Do you want some homemade frozen fish sticks?* she would ask. *How about some homemade frozen fries? Do you want some homemade frozen waffles for breakfast?* She considered them homemade because they were toasted in our own toaster." He stared at the waffles for a quiet moment, then drew a deep breath and met Carmen's gaze. "So, do you want a homemade frozen waffle?"

Carmen touched his hand. "I'd love one."

Ben turned away and opened the carton. "Just one? These things are a lot of work, you know. If I make one, I might as well make two."

Carmen suspected that was something else Talia would tell him kiddingly. He was missing their mornings together.

"Two, then."

Ben remained silent for several long seconds as he put the waffles into a toaster and shoved the rest of them back into the freezer. "I usually only drink protein mixes for breakfast, sometimes with an egg, but Talia loved frozen waffles."

Carmen suspected his talk about Talia had given him a sudden stab of sorrow.

"You should know that I don't have much around here in the way of sugar," he added. "Sugar is bad for you. I do have honey though. I buy it from an old man in town who gathers it himself."

"Honey will do. In fact, I could tell that you had put some in that tea last night. You make a good cup of tea."

Ben turned and uncovered a small dish of butter. Carmen glanced at the closed door to the master bedroom while his back was to her. Three years. For three years, he had not gone into that room.

"Thanks," Ben told her in reply to her remark about his tea. "I don't care for tea, but Talia's headaches forced me to learn to make it for her." He set the butter in front of her, then took a jar of honey from a cupboard behind him and gave that to her also. "I hope you do not mind going with me to the office. Since you are an accountant, you might be interested in all the bookkeeping we need to do. We raise money in so many different ways. Things get pretty busy."

"Sounds like a big job, but if I remember right, you also said something about going riding. Don't forget that I have never been on a horse in my life."

"Riding a horse is like breathing to me."

"I know. I've seen the videos. Can you really ride down and kill a buffalo with a bow and arrow while riding bareback, like your ancestors did?"

"Of course I can." He narrowed his eyes and deepened his voice. "I am *Lakota!*"

Carmen grinned. "You could have been in *Dances with Wolves.*"

Ben just grinned and shook his head. "Whatever. By the way, I think we will save the horseback ride until tomorrow or the next day. If running can stir up a headache, bouncing around on a horse might do the same. But once you learn to flow with the rhythm of the horse's gait, you can avoid a lot of the jostling. At any rate, when we ride, we will go to Sammy Thunder's place and visit with the wolves."

"Horses *and* wolves? You sure know how to make a person face things that scare the hell out of them."

"Never fear horses. They are gentle and have a wonderful spirit. Besides, I told you that the first time we ride, you will be with me on my horse. I will hang on to you."

"And after my first terrifying ride, plus going to a mysterious place like the Badlands, you expect me to pet wolves that are not in cages."

"Sure. Caesar will be excited. He will remember you."

"You think so?"

"I *know* so. He will start howling as soon as we draw near. He will sense your presence." The waffles popped up, and Ben put them on a plate and set them in front of her, along with a fork. "There," he told her. "I have made you a homemade breakfast, protein shake and all."

"Thank you, Chef Colter." Carmen put butter and honey on the waffles and cut into them while Ben drank down more water.

"Is that all you drink besides protein shakes?" Carmen asked.

"Yes. I am determined to keep my one and only kidney healthy and hydrated." He tossed the empty water bottle into a container under the island counter. "I keep the plastic separate for a special pickup once a month." He gave her a facetious grin. "We Natives try to protect the environment, you know."

"Well, some of us outsiders believe in doing the same," Carmen told him.

"Good. I am glad you care. We do not have all kinds of fresh water here like you have in Michigan, so we have to protect what we *do* have from those who try to exploit our land with mining and mineral explorations." He wiped down the countertop and stacked things in the sink. "I always use bottled water for drinking to make sure I am not drinking too many contaminants because of my one and only kidney. I have plenty on hand all the time, so feel free to take what you need."

He squeezed out a sponge and set it aside. "Rosa will come over later and clean things up better." He faced Carmen with a sigh. "I am sorry about the remarks I made about only Natives are concerned about our water supply, but the government and outsiders are not exactly deeply concerned about the possibility of our People getting sick from things like gold tailings and uranium in the water."

"You don't need to apologize. I am open to anything you want me to understand."

He smiled with a hint of sadness. "You are very sweet." He tossed his hair behind his back. "And right now, I need to get dressed. I always wear a collared shirt to the office in case some suit or a senator shows up. I have to look the part. People on the outside think you must dress a certain way and cut your hair short, like they made the children do at Carlisle Indian School in Pennsylvania." He hung the towel over the refrigerator door handle. "Do you know about Carlisle?"

"I've heard about it ... read about it somewhere a few years back. It isn't something that is regularly taught in school."

"Of course not. There are *many* things the outside world does not know about their own Native Americans." Ben leaned on the counter directly across from Carmen. "Carlisle Indian School is a horror story we will not talk about now, except to tell you that hundreds of Native children died there. We have managed to bring a few remains back here to bury them with family members on their homeland. By some miracle, Carlisle kept decent records. One of Talia's pet projects was working with a committee to identify these children and bring them home." His eyes teared. "And then she never got to hold her *own* child. Someone took *him* away, too. Now I know how those parents must have felt."

He started to turn, but Carmen grasped his hand. "Ben, wait!"

He paused, then drew in his breath and cleared his throat.

"Ben, don't think I don't empathize with all of this," Carmen told him. "What happened back then and what happened to you breaks my heart, but if you and I are going to last, we need to get something straight."

"Not today, Carmen."

He started to pull away again, but Carmen refused to let go of his hand. "Ben, do you want this thing between you and me to work? If you do, then please let me say this." She took a deep breath for courage, not sure this was the right time. "I have thought about this since before I even came out here. When you brought me that tea, you were helping Carmen Wolfe, but in your heart, you were wishing it was Talia in that bed. You were doting on *Talia*. Do you think I don't know that? Talia is almost the only thing you talk about. You are consumed by her memory and by the way she died."

Ben stiffened, this time jerking his hand away, but he did not leave. The look in his dark eyes forced Carmen to draw on all the courage she could muster. She glanced at the scar on his arm again, then back to those eyes that told her to be careful. "I know what that scar on your arm is from. Tommy and Sasha told me everything, Ben."

"*Everything?*"

"Everything. What you saw at the shooting, what you went through afterward, the opioids, how they found you, how you got that scar, the suicide attempts."

"This is not the time." Ben turned away.

"Please let me finish," Carmen asked. "I want to tell you that it's okay, Ben. It's okay! I decided it is easier to embrace Talia and her memory than to let myself hate her because she keeps getting in the way of what could be a wonderful relationship with a wonderful man who is already moving right into my heart. I don't *want* to hate her, but I know her memory is embedded in your heart like your own blood. Her name is blazed right where I have to look at it when I stand in front of you. I want to bring her into *my* heart, too. I want to be her friend. I want to care about her like I care about Val. Don't let her come between us, Ben. Instead, let her bring us *together*."

Ben faced her, pain in his eyes.

"Did you ever stop to think that maybe it was Talia's spirit working through Caesar that caused that wolf to bring attention to me?" Carmen asked. "Your wife had a beautiful soul, just like you do. I am sure she watches over you and wants you to be happy. If and when you make love to me, you should not think of it as cheating on your wife. Think of it as honoring her wishes for you to go on and love another woman and have more children and continue the wonderful work you do here, in her memory."

Ben closed his eyes and sighed deeply before walking away. "I am going to get dressed," he told her, without an answer to anything she'd just told him. "Do whatever you have to do to finish getting ready. When we leave the office, we will go over to the theater and see the kids again, maybe eat lunch there." He walked into his bedroom and closed the door.

Oh shit. I've made him angry. Carmen wished she had time to call Val. Had she said too much too soon? She hurried to her own room. She brushed and fluffed out her hair more, brushed her teeth again, put on a little mascara and some pale lipstick. After hooking small, gold hoop earrings into her earlobes, she changed out of her pajama bottoms and pulled on the white jeans Val claimed looked sexy on her. Maybe right now she *needed* something like that to distract Ben from his anger with her.

She stepped into a pair of white sandals, wondering

what the hell she should say when Ben came out of his room. Did he understand what she was trying to tell him? She slipped her cell phone, driver's license, and her debit card into a side pocket on her jeans, then put a couple of tissues and a skinny tube of lipstick in another pocket, deciding that was all she needed to take today. She walked into the kitchen area and picked up the paper plate that held what was left of her waffles. She threw that away and put her fork in the sink, then quickly finished what was left of her protein drink and rinsed the glass. She sat down on a barstool and waited, worried she would start perspiring from nervousness.

Ben finally emerged from his bedroom, wearing jeans that did not leave a lot to the imagination. He wore a white collared shirt, a beautifully beaded belt through the loops in his jeans, and the skinny silver belt with the tiny bells on it around his hips. His hair was pulled back at the side and fixed there with beaded combs. A feather was tied into one side. It hung downward and had a notch cut into it. Tiny silver earrings hung at his ears, and a wide, silver and leather cuff bracelet accented his strong, right wrist where the sleeve of his shirt was rolled up. He wore an Apple watch on his left wrist.

Carmen watched those dark eyes as he walked toward her and braced his hands against the countertop on either side of her so that she was basically trapped. She swallowed, not sure what to expect. A "none of your business" tirade? A scolding? Maybe he was going to tell her to go back home. She stiffened, and Ben frowned.

"What is wrong?"

"I ... don't like feeling trapped. Jerry used to trap me against the wall, and if you're angry—"

Ben stepped back. "What did I promise you?"

"That you would never hurt me."

"When are you going to start *believing* that? And how often do I need to repeat it? Did I touch you last night?"

"I ... no, but you weren't mad last night."

"And I am not mad *now*."

"I thought maybe what I said made you angry."

He closed his eyes for a moment and shook his head. "Number one, if it *did* anger me, I would not walk out here and hurt you. And number two, you need to get over the things Jerry did to you, just like I need to get over that shooting. Neither one will be easy for either of us, but we also cannot let either one stop what we feel for each other. My God, Carmen, you are a remarkable woman."

"I am?"

He leaned closer again and kissed her lightly, a trace of tears in his eyes. "I expected you to preach at me to bury Talia in that past. I expected you to resent her memory, not embrace it. You never even knew her. For you to want to let her in rather than shut her out only shows me the beautiful person that you are. And yes, perhaps Talia herself brought us together."

He kissed her again, and Carmen wrapped her arms around his neck and breathed a sigh of relief. "I thought you were going to tell me to go back home, and I don't want to go home. I want to be here with you. And I want you to know it's okay to talk about Talia."

He hugged her close. "Carmen, I walked off a few minutes ago because I needed to think about the things you said." He met her gaze lovingly and touched the feather tied into his hair. "The notch in this feather means I am a warrior who has been wounded. But the wound was not just to my body. It was to my heart and my soul. I have never felt I could completely heal from that wound until now ... until you came along."

He met her lips with his own in a kiss that meant much more than a simple friendship. This one was different. This one was deeper. He pulled her off the stool and turned with her in his arms, keeping her pressed close.

"We will talk about this more later today," he said mid-kisses. "I have to get to the office."

"That's fine."

"In the meantime, I think I am falling in love with you."

"I think I'm falling in love with you, too," Carmen answered. *God, you're a good kisser. Is that why I just said something so reckless?*

Ben moved his lips to her cheek, her neck. "Is this the craziest relationship you have ever been in?"

"Definitely." Did he know what kissing her behind the ear did to her? She suspected he did. She felt his hardness against her groin. "We'd better go before you don't make it to the office at all. You don't have time for another shower."

"I might need to take one anyway. A cold one."

"I'm thinking when we walk out that door, you should walk in front of me," Carmen teased.

"For more reasons than you know."

"My reasoning is that every time I walk in front of you now, you will be staring at my butt."

"Oh, definitely. But right now, you are right. I definitely do *not* need to watch your butt when we walk out of here."

"Then turn around and leave," Carmen warned. "I'll be right behind you eyeing *your* butt, which I am sure looks great in those jeans."

"If you are going to watch my ass, that's sexual harassment."

"Sue me."

Ben laughed through more kisses. "You are talking to a lawyer."

"You don't scare me. *You* are sexually harassing *me* right now."

"Damn! You are right. We need to figure out another way to solve this sexual harassment thing."

"I'm not even going to ask how you think we should do that." Carmen gave him a shove. "*Skoden!*"

Ben laughed and headed out the door. "Turn the lock inside when you pull the door shut. Rosa has a key."

Carmen followed him out, glancing first at the closed door to the master bedroom. Hopefully, she'd made a little headway toward someday getting him to open that door.

CHAPTER EIGHTEEN

"This is a beautiful building," Carmen commented.

Ben pulled his truck to the front of a brick building with a huge, colorful wooden Native dancer design on the bricks. "Brand new," he told her. "Built strictly for Sunrise. You should see the small space we worked in before. This building was built a good 60 percent from donations and from the shows we put on. Government grants cover most of the rest, and I also have a lot of my own money into all of this."

Why was she not surprised?

Above big front windows was the lettering DANCING BENEATH YOU, and under that, SUNRISE PRODUCTIONS.

Ben leaned closer and kissed her, then reached behind Carmen's seat to grab a briefcase he'd left yesterday on the rear seat of the truck's extended cab. He started to open his door, but Carmen hesitated. "You okay?" Ben asked.

"I'm kind of nervous. All those workers are your people and your friends. Some of them are going to resent me. They all knew Talia."

"And everyone in there knows you are special to me or I would not bring you here. And you already met many of them at my birthday party just yesterday." He reached down and pushed the button that released her seat belt, the back of his hand brushing her hip. Their gazes held, and Carmen wondered what it was about being in the small area of a front auto seat that stirred a desire for intimacy. Things were so close and confined. His masculinity filled the cab, and the tiny bells on that silver belt around his hips made him even harder to resist.

"If we stay this close much longer, I won't make it inside," Ben told her. He kissed her lightly, then got out of the truck.

Lord help me. Carmen got out her side, realizing she wanted Ben in ways she shouldn't. Not yet. She followed him inside, where workers sat at eight desks in a big, open room that was full of the sound of clicking computer keyboards. Two workers were on desk phones, two others sorting through money and tapping away on adding machines. Two others were sitting together going over paperwork, another stared intently at a ledger, and one graying woman sat near a big outer office that Carmen suspected belonged to Ben. There were even more separate offices along one side of the main room, three of them empty but obviously used and one where a big Native American man sat counting money. He got up from his desk and walked to the doorway to offer a greeting at the same time several others waved and shouted, "Hi, Ben!" and "Welcome back!"

"How does it feel to be a year older?" one young man shouted.

"You will find out soon enough, Bobby," Ben answered, keeping an arm around Carmen. "Most of you remember

Carmen. She is here to visit while I get some work done, so be gracious."

"It is about time you showed up." The words came from the big man who stood in the doorway to their left.

Ben let go of Carmen and turned to high-five the man. "Hey, Billy! How is Karen? She deliver that baby yet?"

"She is ready to burst." The man looked about the same age as Ben and was just as big but with a hefty build that was more like that of a man who ate too many burgers and fries. He had a nice-looking face that was spoiled a bit by pockmarks. "Sorry I did not make your birthday party," he told Ben. "I was the only one available to take the paperwork Alice gave me to the state offices in Pierre. All of your assistants were already gone taking care of other things."

Ben pulled Carmen closer. "Carmen, this is William Big Bull, my best friend since grade school. He, his wife, Talia, Sasha and Tommy and I all grew up together at Rosebud. Billy and Tommy and I used to ride bareback together and stand up on the backs of the horses while the horses were running."

"Oh my gosh!" Carmen reached out and shook Billy's hand. Her own hand disappeared into his big one as he squeezed hers gently and looked her over appreciatively. "Welcome," he told her. He smiled at Ben. "Now I understand why you were late this morning."

They shared smiles. "Hey, brother, it is not what you think," Ben told Billy. "So, how are things going?"

"Thanks to you and the youth group, we are doing great," Billy answered. "That show in Grand Rapids is still bringing in money." He glanced at Carmen again. "This man does more for the youth and even for some of the rest of us than anyone else here. If you are able to put a smile in his sad heart, you are welcome here. Ben still mourns his wife. We *all* mourn Talia."

"From what I have learned so far, I can understand the loss," Carmen answered.

Ben squeezed her a little closer. He kept an arm around Carmen and walked her away from Billy's office. "Billy has two sons and another one on the way," he told her in an apparent attempt to change the subject. "He keeps track of money from ticket sales." He turned to face a woman who sat at the nearest desk in the outer office. She looked perhaps sixty. "And this is Sheila Feathermaker," he told Carmen. "She keeps track of income from CD and DVD sales."

Carmen did not miss the loving way Sheila looked Ben over before she moved her gaze to Carmen. "Ben is like a son to some of us," she said with a smile. "He has no mother, so we fill in." Carmen felt the "he belongs to us" attitude the woman exuded. She could tell Sheila was trying to be kind but that she was skeptical of an outsider.

"That is kind of you," Carmen told her. "My own mother died three years ago, and I miss her wisdom and affection." Her remark seemed to ease some of the uncertainty in the woman's eyes.

Introductions went all around. Martha Bates, a thirtyish Native woman with bleached hair, a husband, and four children, kept track of mailed donations. Lena Running Horse Tucker, in her twenties and newly married, took all phone calls and directed them to the right persons. Robert Two Bears, who looked to be in his forties and wore his hair short, took care of records on government grants. Nancy Black Tomahawk Pourie kept track of all expenses. She was a stout woman who looked all business and wore dark-rimmed glasses as she spouted off what all those expenses covered.

"Instruments, fuel, school supplies, arts and crafts, books, costumes and regalia, outside musicians, office supplies and computers, office maintenance, school and dorm maintenance—the list is endless," she told Carmen.

Leonard Blue Cloud, only twenty-two, kept the website and Facebook pages updated, as well as posting on Instagram and Pinterest and Twitter and a host of other sites. Marcus Mad Elk took care of payroll for both the teachers and for employees.

Patricia Daisy, a mother of three, took care of mailings to possible new donors and reminder mailings to established donors. Carmen did not miss the way Patricia eyed Ben with open flirtation. She looked roughly his same age and wore a very low-cut ruffled blouse that revealed a generous portion of her voluptuous cleavage.

"It is good to see you again, Ben." She glanced at Carmen. "Welcome," she told her with little sincerity.

After the host of introductions, Ben brought Carmen around to the woman whose desk was just outside his office. She looked roughly in her fifties and greeted Ben and Carmen with a smile. "So, you are here to actually work?" she teased Ben.

"I really am," Ben answered with a light laugh. He kept Carmen close. "Carmen, this is Alice Lone Woman, the best administrative assistant a man could ask for. She has been with me since even before I married Talia, and Alice held all this together after we lost Talia."

Alice rose and reached out to shake Carmen's hand. "Sasha has told us what a kind and lovely young woman you are," she said.

"Thank you!" Carmen answered, touched by the

woman's genuine attitude. Her smile was warm and, like Sheila's, almost motherly.

"I hope you know I was kidding about Ben getting to work," Alice told her. "Actually, he does *too* much. Maybe you can slow him down a little and make him hire more help."

"Alice, I have legal assistants," Ben reminded her.

"For *legal* work, not all the other programs you try to run. And even in the legal department, you do not have enough help. I hate to keep preaching at you about it, Ben, but you can't keep this up. You need to hire at least two more legal assistants, and you need to give some of these other programs over to others. And, by the way, Calvin is in Rapid City today talking to the lawyers who represent that strip of land north of us that Clements Oil claims belongs to them. I think you will end up having to go to court on that one."

Ben frowned. "I will wait until Calvin comes back and see what he has to say. I might be able to settle this on the phone." He led Carmen into his office, a large room with windows that looked out on prairie grass, the Badlands in the distance. The floor was carpeted in soft green, and Native American artifacts sat everywhere. Native American artwork decorated the walls, dream catchers hung at the windows, and soft flute music could be heard over speakers throughout the building.

"I hate going to Rapid City," Ben told Carmen. "Bad memories. The courthouse is only a couple of blocks from where the shooting took place. I usually let my assistants handle things there. Most of my work is in Pierre or DC. And by the way, I would love for you to go with me to DC the next time I have to be there. I am sure you like fancy shopping, and there is plenty of it there. Talia used to—" He hesitated. "I am sorry. I will try not to bring her into every conversation."

"It's all right, Ben."

"No. I need to concentrate on you and me." He leaned down to give her another kiss. "And pay no attention to Pat Daisy. She flirts with every man who walks past her desk, but she is a good worker, so I keep her on."

"Well, I *will* admit that she stirred a little green monster in me when I saw how she looked at you."

"*Really?*" Ben pulled her close and kissed her deeply again.

"Get a room or get to work!" a young man in the outer office shouted.

Everyone laughed and some clapped. Ben and Carmen joined in the laughter. "You had better do as he said," Carmen told him.

"Which one? Get to work? Or get a room?"

Carmen gave him a shove. "Get behind that desk."

"With you around, it will be difficult for me to concentrate." He hesitated. "By the way, I am sorry for Billy's remark. He and his wife, Karen, used to be part of the friends Talia and I did things with—riding, camping, cookouts, things like that. Talia's death was hard on Billy, too, but he had no right making that remark about missing Talia, as though you could never take her place."

"He's your friend and probably wishes everything could be the same. Don't worry about it, Ben."

Ben moved behind his desk. "Do you need anything? I keep a small fridge here filled with bottled water, but there is coffee out there somewhere. I don't drink the stuff. Too hard on my one and only kidney."

"I'll take water."

Ben opened a small refrigerator against the wall, taking

out two bottles of water. "You are welcome to go out there and get to know everyone," he told her, handing out one bottle. "I need to check my emails. God knows how many I have by now. I usually take this laptop home and keep working evenings, but with you here, I did not want to bother."

"Do what you need to do," Carmen told him. "In fact, I have my laptop with me at the house, and I'll need to check my own email when we get back. That headache last night put a stop to everything."

"More than you know," Ben teased. He sat down behind his desk and opened his computer, then muttered something in the Lakota tongue. "Alice!" he called out.

Alice came inside. "What is it?"

"When I am done, I will take this computer home and see what I can catch up on later, but I want to take the next couple of days off to spend more time with Carmen. Please keep checking my emails and get rid of the junk. Go ahead and answer those you are familiar with. You know what I would tell some of them, so answer them for me."

"I will take care of it," Alice obliged.

"You are a savior," Ben told her. "And bring me your log of phone calls I need to make. Where are Toby and Darryl?"

"Toby is in Pierre speaking to the governor about improving the meal program for the school, and Darryl is there presenting your arguments against allowing more exploration for gold in the Black Hills. I'm telling you again, you need more help. Why don't you let me advertise for more legal assistants?"

Ben studied the screen on his computer. "I guess you can. I just do not know when I will have time to interview anyone, but go ahead. I prefer one of our own if you can find one with the right qualifications. Nobody understands what goes on around here better than our own People."

"A lot of people understand, Ben, including outsiders. Let them help. I am sure Miss Wolfe here will agree with me."

"I am already learning a lot," Carmen told her. "And I am a C.P.A., so I could help with some of the bookkeeping around here."

Alice nodded. "Good idea." She glanced at Ben. "You see? Sometimes an outsider can see things with a keener eye. They are not too close to all of it. And I might add, it is good to see you looking happier. It has been a long time since you have smiled like you did when you walked in here with your arm around Carmen." She went back to her desk, and Ben put his elbows on his desk and rubbed at his eyes.

"Alice is right about how much there is to handle," he told Carmen. "Old treaties still get broken whenever some outsider thinks they can get away with it. The government has to constantly be pushed to make good on grants. There is a big problem with battered and murdered women, unsolved cases like Linda Two Fists. The BIA is constantly changing its policies, and we are in a continuing battle against alcohol, drugs, suicide, no jobs." He paused. "God knows I am familiar with drugs and suicide. I try to make time to talk to young people on all the reservations, even out-of-state—"

"Ben," Carmen interrupted, raising her voice a little. "Take one thing at a time. For now, just go through your email and make your phone calls. I'll go out there and get to know the others."

"Some will be hesitant to talk at all."

"I'll be careful and considerate. I've noticed that a lot

that goes on out there has to do with keeping track of income and expenses. That is my specialty, you know."

Ben eyed her lovingly. "Does getting more involved mean you intend to stay longer than a few days?"

Carmen put the cap on her water bottle. "We'll see." She turned away. "Get to work," she called back to him.

"After I watch you walk out."

Carmen turned and deliberately walked out backward.

"Doesn't help," Ben told her with a grin. "Looks good coming and going."

Carmen closed the door and stopped at Alice's desk. "Thanks for trying to get Ben to hire more help," she told the woman. "I can already see how badly he needs it."

"He sure does," Alice told her. The woman whipped something out of her desk drawer. "I've been meaning to show this to Ben to help open his eyes to how *much* he needs that help." She handed a sheet of paper to Carmen. "I made a list of everything Ben oversees around here. You can see why I worry. He always had Talia's help before, but now he takes on all her causes and more. Maybe he will listen to you. The woman a man loves usually has more influence than anyone else. You have tools none of us have, if you know what I mean."

Carmen snickered and shook her head. "Alice, our relationship isn't quite to that point yet."

"I meant no offense, Miss Wolfe, but I want to assure you that you couldn't ask for a better man. You are all Ben has talked about since getting back from Michigan. He stays busy to keep from thinking about Talia. I hope you know that. Maybe you can slow him down."

Carmen folded the note. "I'll look at this and see what I can do, but I'm pretty new to all of this, Alice. Gosh, I've only been here three days."

"But you have known Ben for more than a month. I hope you will stay long enough to learn more about him and life out here. And please don't break his heart. It's already been shattered in a million pieces, and right now it's held together by glue made up of Tommy and Sasha and those kids at the school, and his determination to support Talia's causes. You can strengthen that glue, Miss Wolfe."

Carmen was a bit flabbergasted at realizing how much everyone who knew Ben seemed to genuinely love him and worry about him. She did not doubt that a lot of it was because of how much they had all loved Talia.

"I really should get back to work," Alice told her. "I have to help Ben go through these emails."

"Sure." Carmen rose and folded the note even smaller so she could fit it into her jeans pocket. "And thank you for your support, Alice."

The woman smiled. "You and Ben make a great couple."

Carmen wasn't sure how to answer. Everyone here seemed to think she and Ben were already a permanent item. She wished she could be as sure, but with all the baggage between them, a hundred things could go wrong. If it weren't for Jerry, she wouldn't feel so hesitant about giving her heart to someone new. Hers was not in a whole lot better shape than Ben's.

She looked around the office. Martha Bates gave her a smile, so she headed over to the woman's desk, noticing Martha kept her hair long, held at the sides with combs. She had smooth, very dark skin. She nodded to Carmen, her smile kind.

"You handle mailed donations?" Carmen asked.

Martha nodded. "I handle what comes in, and also send out the thank-you notes with new donation cards. Linda

Two Fists was helping me before she was killed." Her smile faded. "Such a sweet girl she was, and so bright. I have a husband and four children, so sometimes I have to run home for something. Linda did a good job of filling in for me. She was smart with numbers and excelled in accounting at school."

"Do you have any idea who could have killed her?" Carmen asked.

Martha shook her head. "It makes no sense, just like Talia's death makes no sense. Most think Ben was the target on that one, that it was planned by the government or by some wealthy company that wants to grab more of our land. Ben knows how to fight such things. He can brilliantly argue them down in court, so there are wealthy outsiders who would like to see him out of the way. Whoever did it has not tried again, but I think that's because for almost two years Ben was not able to keep up the fight, so they had, in a way, gotten rid of him. But now he is back working hard again and winning the battle, so I worry about that." Martha kept her voice down. "Personally, I think whoever shot Ben could have been a disgruntled husband Ben had thrown in jail, or maybe Ben helped the man's wife get a divorce. Ben is extremely intolerant of men who beat their wives."

How well I know, Carmen thought.

"He needs to let someone else handle things like that and concentrate on the bigger issues." Martha turned to her computer. "I am sorry, but I should get back to work."

"Sure. That's fine." Carmen walked around to speak with a few others. Leonard Blue Cloud kept her occupied for quite a while, showing her the Sunrise website and Facebook page, as well as graphics he'd created for both and for Instagram and other sites. *So many pictures of Talia,*

Carmen thought. Everyone she spoke to so far had mentioned Talia, her beauty, her energy, how she was driven to fight for certain causes. There were pictures of her and Ben taking part in protest marches, and more showing them in the Crazy Horse Memorial Ride, a grueling, twenty-seven-mile journey in honor of the great Lakota warrior.

"Some think Crazy Horse's spirit lives on in Ben," Leonard told Carmen. "He, too, is a great warrior, but in the ways a man must fight in today's times."

Carmen couldn't help struggling a bit with her own worthiness to be here at all. The whole room seemed permeated with Ben and Talia. She reminded herself that Ben believed the Great Spirit had chosen her to help, using Caesar as His connection. The "outsider" in her said that was not possible, but if she was going to learn the Lakota way, she had to be open to such a belief.

She left Leonard and spoke for a while with Nancy Pourie, again about expenses, then headed for Billy Big Bull's office.

"Come on in," Billy greeted her with a smile and nodded toward a chair across from his desk. "Busy place, isn't it?"

"I don't know how Ben handles all of this," Carmen answered.

"I help out as much as I can, but yes, he needs help." Billy grunted a little as he sat down. "It is good to see Ben looking happier lately, and you are the reason. Everybody talks about the woman from Michigan." He sighed. "I am sorry for talking about Talia in front of you like I did. It is just that everybody cares a lot about Ben and hopes he can get over what happened."

Carmen looked around at beautiful Native paintings on

Billy's office walls. "So, you are in charge when Ben is gone?"

Billy shrugged. "I do what I can. When Ben is traveling, I keep him updated by email. I have a degree in accounting from Oglala Lakota College. Ben tells me that you, too, have a degree in accounting."

"A master's in business and accounting from Western Michigan University. I'm a CPA. Are you registered as one?"

"Somehow I never got quite got around to that, but I will."

"With what you do, Billy, it's important. In my case, I never got to use my degree much. My ex-husband has a construction business, but he never let me be a part of it."

Billy smiled and shook his head. "One of those, huh? Thinks only the man can run things."

"Something like that. It's a long story. After we split up, I made a business out of doing peoples' taxes. If you ever need any accounting help here, I can fill in." She glanced toward Ben's office. He was still on the phone. "That is, if I'm still around. I don't know yet where all this is going."

Billy chuckled. "*Ben* seems pretty sure where it is going." He zipped closed the bank bag, then turned and put it into a safe behind his desk. "It is good to finally meet you," he told her, rising.

"And you. Just don't go standing up on the backs of horses anymore. Ben needs you."

Billy laughed. "Look at me! Do I look like I could still stand on the back of a horse?"

Carmen smiled. "I've never been on a horse in my life, so I'm not the person to answer that."

"Ah, Ben will have you riding in no time. He rides like he is part of the animal. He and Talia—" Billy hesitated, a flash of pain moving through his eyes. "Her death was hard on all of us," he told her. "Hers was the biggest funeral I have ever seen. It still bothers Ben deeply that he was not able to be there to tell her goodbye and sing over her. He was still lying unconscious in the hospital." Tears showed in his eyes. "Talia is buried high in the Black Hills. It is a beautiful spot. Maybe someday Ben will show you."

It always comes back to Talia. Carmen looked at a wall clock and realized nearly two hours had passed. "Thank you for talking to me, Billy. I'm going outside to make a phone call to a friend back in Michigan."

"Sure."

Carmen walked out, noticing Ben was still on the phone. He was pacing and talking heatedly, the way a man might behave in court when arguing a case. He did not need her interrupting just now, so she walked outside to call Val.

"It's about time you called!" Val told her without even saying hello. "I'm going crazy here, girl. What's happening with you and that gorgeous man you are staying with? And how's the headache?"

"The headache is gone." Carmen sat down on a wrought iron bench in front of the building. "I miss talking to you, Val. Sid, too. I don't even know where to start. Everything is so different here, but nothing I couldn't live with. It's just that ... I don't know. I'm at Ben's office today, and he has a big staff of employees. So much goes on here, and Ben tries to handle it all himself. He's this ball of energy that bounces from rehearsals to courtrooms to DC to God knows where else. Everybody expects so much of him. He needs help. I might have to stay out here just for that."

"Hey, Sid is right here," Val informed her. "I have you on speaker."

"Carmen, what Ben decides to take on is his problem, not yours," Sid told her. "He's a big boy."

"But it *is* my problem, Sid, because I'm already falling in love with the man. What if I jump into the water here and land on a big rock hidden beneath? That's how I feel about the risk I am taking."

"Well, if it were me, I would go ahead and test those waters, girl," Val teased, "if you know what I mean."

"You can joke, Val, but just testing the waters is too serious with a man like Ben. I can already see he's one of those all-or-nothing types. If things get heavy between us, I'll be involved in this busy life he leads, and I have so much to learn about these people and what goes on here at the office and Ben's faith and rituals."

"Slow down, Carmen," Sid interrupted. "Do you honestly think Ben expects you to know and understand all of it in two or three days?"

"But it's really been about five weeks, Sid, and we both carry so much baggage from our pasts."

"You think about *you,* Carmen," Sid reminded her. "We talked about that. Remember? If Ben really loves you, you won't lose him by telling him everything you feel. If you are going to give a little, he has to do the same."

"I know. I feel better just talking to you guys. If I do stay here a while, I'll have to fly back to Michigan first to get more of my things and see my dad and grandparents. We can talk more then."

"Wow, the warrior got to you really fast, didn't he?" Val asked. "And hey, Sasha sent us a video of his reaction to your surprise visit. He was so happy! You say your relationship might go nowhere, but from the way you two hung on to each other yesterday, things looked pretty damn cozy to me. God, I'll bet that man is a good kisser."

"He is. I've never known anyone like him, Val." A second call popped up on her phone. "Val, Ben is calling me from his office. I'll call you later when I have more time to talk. Love you."

"Love you," Val answered. "If you two do the dance, you call me!"

Carmen smiled at the remark and ended the call to answer Ben.

"Mind going to the school to have lunch with the kids?" he asked.

"Not at all," Carmen answered.

Ben hung up and was already walking through the outside doors. "I might have to come back again for a while," he told Carmen. "But you can stay over at the theater and get to know the kids better."

He got into the truck, and Carmen did the same. "I was arguing with the lawyers for Clements Oil," Ben told her. "I thought of an angle that Clements will have trouble arguing. I think I will write a brief and file it. That will stall things for a while because they will have to answer my brief, and nothing moves fast in court." He paused to meet her gaze. "You have no idea how glad I am that you are here."

Ben, I'm not sure we should spend another night alone together. Carmen thought to say the words but couldn't. Ben leaned close and kissed her deeply, a kiss that destroyed her resolve to slow things down.

CHAPTER NINETEEN

"BEN, those kids at rehearsal were phenomenal," Carmen commented, "but when you walked in and got up on that stage and showed them how to put real feelings into a song, I saw a grand mixture of Josh Groban, John Legend, Luke Bryan, Kane Brown—and then you and Tommy got on those guitars and out came ZZ Top and Bon Jovi, older but damn good rock. I don't know how you do it. I suppose you know that you could make millions with your looks and voice if you stepped out on your own."

Ben smiled and seemed embarrassed as he pulled into his driveway and shut off the truck engine. "You mentioned that once before. I want nothing to do with that world of fake people and backstabbing competition out there, let alone being gone most of the time. I will never leave those kids." He kissed her lightly. "I just happen to love all kinds of music, and the Great Spirit blessed me with a photographic memory, so I do not have any trouble remembering lyrics. You cannot brag about what you are naturally born with." Another kiss. "You, in turn, like working with numbers," Ben added, "although I do not know why. I hate bookkeeping, which is why I have a whole staff who does that for me. I would rather write a brief or sing than balance a checkbook."

"Aha! I finally found a flaw!"

Ben chuckled. "We all have them." He unhooked her seat belt. "I just try to impress on those kids that you can't just sing the words. You have to *feel* them. *Believe* them. If you put your heart into the lyrics, you will sing better. It was easy for me today because, although we were just rehearsing, most of those songs I sang were for you., like "In These Arms" and "Drunk On You.""

"Well, if you were trying to turn me on, it worked." Carmen leaned in and, this time, initiated the kiss herself. "And then you turn around and do those wild Native dances and you are a completely different person. I am never sure which man I am talking to."

"Always Lakota, no matter the situation."

Carmen smiled. "Whichever you are, those kids have the best teacher they could ask for. You really know how to bring out their confidence. Earlier, I just meant that you could be so successful with what you learned at Julliard."

Ben shook his head. "Talia and I went to Julliard to learn how to teach *others* how to develop *their* talents. You have seen the results in how well the youth group performs. We are like *Glee*, which is what I wanted. Great harmony and choreography, full of self-confidence. You have heard me tell them they should belt out those songs as though they were Chris Daughtry or Carrie Underwood. It is all part of keeping them busy and proud and away from drugs and alcohol and suicide. Some will one day strike out on their own. A few already have."

"But not you – at least not in a worldly way." Carmen grasped his hand. "I'm glad. I don't like the idea of women drooling over you and offering to come to your dressing room. I don't doubt you *already* get offers at the shows you put on with the youth group."

Ben grinned. "The only offer I would have liked to hear was from *you* after I took you back to the wolf cages." More kisses. "I am *still* waiting for that offer."

Carmen leaned back a little and studied those dark, hypnotic eyes. "You aren't a one-night stand kind of man. And I am definitely not that kind of woman."

"Thank goodness." Ben turned to his door. "We should check out the buffalo steaks Rosa left in the fridge. She will not share her special recipe, but however she marinates those steaks, they are the best you have ever eaten."

"I have never eaten buffalo meat in my life."

"Or ridden a horse or probably even *seen* a buffalo." He paused and looked her over appreciatively. "You will experience a lot of firsts out here."

Carmen did not miss the meaning in his gaze before he turned away and got out his side of the truck. He opened the back door to grab his briefcase. "I think I have lettuce and tomatoes in the fridge," he told Carmen as he walked around to her side of the truck and helped her jump down. They headed into the house. "Maybe you could make a salad while I take a shower. I did not mean to stay so late at that rehearsal, but those kids have a way of talking me into things. I ended up working up a sweat."

Once inside, Ben went to his room, and Carmen washed her hands in the kitchen sink, then explored the refrigerator. She saw two steaks wrapped in cellophane. They were huge, big enough for four people. She would have to tell Ben to cut off just an end of one for her. She found the lettuce and tomatoes, then searched through the cupboards for a large bowl and salad tongs. She took down some dinner plates and set out some silverware, then started slicing the tomatoes, but she couldn't concentrate. She could hear the shower running in Ben's bathroom and pictured him naked, water beading up on that beautiful brown skin.

Stop it! What had gotten into her? This was absolutely *not* her normal thinking. She'd convinced herself it was too soon for anything deeply serious. Ben himself had said he wasn't ready either, but the look in his eyes a moment ago told her he was changing his mind. And watching him at work today had only made him appear sexier, let alone listening to him sing with those young people who adored him. He had them clapping, singing, stomping their feet in rhythm, choreographing dance routines with the songs.

"What gives you a bigger high than drugs or alcohol?" Ben had asked them.

"Music!" came the answer from most. "Dance!" the rest shouted.

"Right! Remember that and stay away from the other."

Carmen hurriedly finished slicing the tomatoes and tossed the salad, then set it back in the refrigerator. *You should have told him you want to stay with Sasha and Tommy tonight,* she thought. Maybe if they ate a big dinner, they would feel too full for anything else.

She decided she should also wash up a little and change her clothes. It had been a hot day, and she'd been in the same clothes all day. She hurried to her room to freshen up, then stepped into clean bikini underwear, a pair of jean shorts, and a soft halter top. She covered the top with a green, lightweight cotton shirt that was a little too big. It was one of her favorites for just hanging out.

She pulled her hair up into a ponytail and secured it with a scrunchy hair band, then squirted on a little of her favorite perfume before slipping into a pair of flip-flops. She walked back into the kitchen, wanting to keep busy and think straight. Maybe there was more she could do to help with supper.

You should have spoken up and told Ben you can't stay here tonight, she again told herself. *We can't keep living this close when we still have so much to learn about each other. We can't keep kissing the way we kiss without ...*

Why was she suddenly so nervous? She walked to the sliding doors that looked out onto the patio and the Badlands beyond. Something about the Badlands scared her. Maybe it was knowing what had happened there to Linda Two Fists. Or maybe it was what Sasha told her about monsters and the place being haunted.

The view made her understand why she was so nervous. In this short time together, she already wanted to stay here, yet she didn't really belong. How could she take the place of the darkly beautiful, talented Talia, whose name was emblazoned on Ben's magnificent chest? How would she ever learn all she needed to know about this life and Ben's beliefs? What was she doing in Lakota country?

The door to Ben's bedroom opened, and there he stood, shirtless and barefoot, wearing tight, black jeans with no belt, not even the little silver one with bells on it. His abs were like a washboard, and his hair was wet and straight He wore just one pair of silver, feather-shaped earrings, and beaded bands around his rock-hard biceps. He walked toward the kitchen, and again she heard those bells that said *I'm here. No one can harm you.* She realized they were on the leather cuff bracelet he wore on his left wrist.

"You changed," he spoke up.

"I thought I would freshen up a little myself."

"I like your hair pulled back like that. It's cute."

Had Talia worn her hair this way sometimes?

"I made the salad," she told him. "Tell me what else I can do to help. And by the way, those steaks are huge. I won't be able to eat even one-quarter of one. What does buffalo taste like, anyway?"

Ben walked over and opened the fridge. "Not that different from beef when it is cooked right, but it is leaner." He took out a bottle of water and closed the fridge. "You are right. Those things are pretty big. I can cut off part of one for you." He faced her. "I killed that buffalo myself, by the way."

"You did?"

"From horseback with an authentic Lakota bow and arrow. None of those fancy, high-powered bows they use today. You saw the video at that show in Grand Rapids. Those steaks are from what we froze after that hunt. Tommy and Sasha have a huge, restaurant-size freezer in their garage where we store the meat, which we share with other families for free."

He opened the water and drank some. "The reason few of our people are independently wealthy is because in our culture, no one stuffs their freezer while a neighbor starves. We are not brought up that way. In the old times, those who were successful in a hunt shared the meat with those who might starve without it. This is why a lot of the money I make in my practice goes to the different causes I fight for and to the School for the Arts. I do a lot of work pro bono for people here who need the help but can't afford it. Many who make extra money from the casinos, which is not as much as you might think, spread that money around to the poorest among us. Same with money earned over and above government handouts. We have lived in a communal atmosphere since before the white man stepped foot on this land."

Carmen folded her arms and leaned against the island counter. "Which brings me to something I wanted to talk about earlier, Ben, but you were too busy at the office and then with more rehearsal."

Ben scanned her from head to toe, then stepped closer. "Have I told you that you have the most beautiful, satiny legs I have ever seen?"

Carmen gave him a little teasing shove backward. "I've seen pictures of Talia, and I've seen Sasha in shorts. That is not a true statement."

"But yours are longer, and they disappear into places yet unknown to me."

"And it will stay that way until you pay attention, Ben Colter. I am trying to be serious."

"Do we *have* to be? It has been a long day."

"And a day of enlightenment for me."

Ben drank more water and set the bottle aside, then folded his arms. "All right. In what way?"

The way he stood there was a bit intimidating, but Carmen dared to say exactly what she thought. "Ben, a lot of people in that office are handling a *lot* of money, and from what I have observed overall on this reservation, most of them likely came from poverty. That much money can look darn good to someone who has never had much of it. Do you have the books audited very often?"

"We have not needed an audit. We turn in reports every month, and the IRS accepts them and has not complained. And there is always enough for what we need."

"Ben Colter, you are smarter than that. I don't want to offend you or those who work for you. They love you and are loyal to you, and of course they will make sure there is enough for all your expenses, but did you ever stop to think that maybe you are making more than you realize? As long as there is money in the pot, no one notices, but you will always need that much and more, and those who might have figured out a way to take a little off the top sometimes start thinking they can take even more without getting caught. You told me you hate bookkeeping, and they probably know that, which makes it even easier to skim a little cream off the milk."

Ben frowned. "You are talking like outsiders would talk."

"Like a white woman who doesn't know anything about your culture?"

"Something like that."

"And that could be a problem for us, Ben, because you understand that outside world and the treachery and lies that come from there. You know how to fight all of it. But I don't think you take into consideration the fact that others from your own world could behave the same way. I have already picked up on the fact that you are not happy with how money from the casinos is doled out. That means there are those who think they should get more than others and who *don't* share the extra. Why would that be so different from everyone who lives and works at Sunrise?"

Ben put his hands on his hips. "Why are you bringing this up now?"

"I didn't. *You* did when you talked about communal living. I am just being realistic about human nature."

"Everyone in that office is a good friend. They have college educations, and they gave up other jobs just to work for me and Talia."

So, here is something else besides Talia that could come between us. "That does not mean they can all be trusted,

Ben. Surely, you understand that. You're a brilliant man in the courtrooms and when you face senators and congressmen. Why can't you see what I am saying here?" She saw his eyes darken a little; his congenial attitude changed a little.

You are stepping into deep waters, Carmen, she told herself.

Ben turned and walked to the sliding doors and looked out. "They would not betray Talia's memory that way," he told her. "As far as I am concerned, she died for this ... for Sunrise, for those kids. No one who works for us would steal from what she worked so hard to build."

"You are talking from *your* feelings for her, Ben. And your feelings are so strong that you have trouble separating them from how others might feel. Human nature is the same no matter what culture we come from. I saw today how busy you are ... too busy to get involved in the daily business end of things at your office. I have a master's in accounting. I can perform an audit for you, because if something is wrong, the IRS will eventually pick up on it. Do you want to risk future grants because of mistakes made? And if I see where someone is honestly mistaken in their bookkeeping, I can help correct it so that it doesn't happen again."

Ben faced her, frowning. "Are you suggesting *embezzlement?*"

"Ben, I'm not accusing anyone of anything. I am just saying you need to be sure, and no one there is a CPA. Yes, they have degrees in accounting, but from what I garnered in my conversations with them, none of them is state licensed. If the IRS discovers missing money, they will point the finger at *you,* not them. That would sully your reputation and hurt future donations. I know Native Americans and reservations are exempt from most state laws and state taxes, but that doesn't mean mistakes haven't been made or that you might not be losing money badly needed for all the things you fight for." She placed her hands against his chest. "It's better that you order an audit before the IRS decides to do their own."

Ben grasped her shoulders. "I do not believe mistakes are being made, but if it makes you feel better, fine. You can perform an audit, but I will have to talk to them first so there are no hard feelings. And I only agree because it means you will have to stay here longer."

Carmen pressed her forehead against his chest. "If I stay, I'll stay for *you* and no other reason." She leaned her head back to meet his gaze. "Alice gave me a list of all the things you try to take care of on your own. It's too much, Ben. You have *got* to give some of that over to others. I want your promise that you will give it serious thought. If I stay, we need to devote some time to each other, and you need to decide what is most important, which things are most in need of your talents and your legal abilities."

His dark eyes drilled into hers. He was obviously surprised she'd suddenly decided to speak up about what she would want if she stayed. "What else is bothering you?" he asked. "More than anything else, I want you to stay, so get it all out, Carmen. Please do not tell me you are thinking of leaving."

"I'm not. I promise. Just ... don't get angry. I still have flashbacks of Jerry hating it when I told him what I thought. I usually ended up being knocked across the room."

"Never!" His grip tightened on her shoulders. "You know that." He let go of her and stepped back a little. "I can see you have many questions. You want to get everything out in the open, so I will start by telling you *why* I have a soft spot for abused women. I am thinking you want the truth about everything, so you should know that I am the product of rape, which is why I never knew my father, except that he was Native American. My mother thought he was Blackfoot, but he took off and never returned, so we do not know for sure. How is that for a bit of news? I am a bastard. What else do you want to know?"

Her heart went out to him. "You can't shock me, Ben. And don't call yourself that. It's a horrible, unnecessary description of a wonderful man. What I want to know is that you no longer let things like that fester inside you. I want to know you are truly done with opioids. I want to know you understand that you are a beautiful gift to this world, bastard or not. *God*, or Wakan-Tanka as you call Him, knows who your father is, and that is all that matters. And whoever he was, he must have been extremely handsome and extremely smart. I want to know that you accept that. And you need to accept Talia's death and fight the dark thoughts that made you put a gun to your head. That would have been a sinful waste of Wakan-Tanka's gift to the Lakota, which is what I believe *you* are. I also want to see Talia and Thomas Singing Boy's graves. And I don't want you letting blood when we go there. Sing for them all you want, but no letting blood."

Ben stiffened. Carmen could not quite read his eyes, but they seemed to get darker, as though to ask, *How dare you ask that of me!* She stood her ground. If she didn't do it here and now, before she fell into a life and love she could not control, she would never do it. "And I want you to promise me you will someday open the door to that bedroom over there and face reality," she continued. "Talia is gone, and I will never replace her. I don't *want* to replace her. It's impossible. I'll love her and cherish her memory just as you do, but I want you to love me for *me* ... for everything that is Carmen Wolfe, a completely different woman from Talia."

Had she really had the courage to say that?

Ben just quietly studied her, saying nothing at first. "All right," he finally told her, his voice husky and the words seemingly forced. "I will take you to where Talia and my son are buried together in a grave that should have been for *me,* not a beautiful woman and her child." He drew a deep breath. "The opioids were the result of my injuries. You know that. It will not happen again. As far as the incident with the gun—" He turned away, visibly shaking. "Wanting to die came from the effects of the drugs, but mostly from my sorrow. I have managed to put the worst behind me. And now, with you here, this is the happiest I have been since that horrible night in Rapid City. If you knew ... if you saw what I saw ... so much blood."

"Ben, I'm sorry. I went too far."

"No. You have the right to talk about these things." He drew a deep breath and pulled his still-damp hair behind his shoulders as he faced her again. "Perhaps if I had not seen my son moving outside Talia's belly, the loss would not have felt so sickeningly deep. I still have nightmares about it. I want to reach out and pull him free. I want to *save* him! That is what a father does, is it not? In the old times, a warrior helped his wife and children escape from enemy attacks. He put his life on the line for them, stood up to the enemy. Today I do it in court, but that night, that awful, bloody night, I was helpless." He breathed deeply and cleared his throat. "Give me a minute." He opened the slider and walked outside.

Carmen covered her face with her hands, wanting to kick herself for saying too much too soon. She waited. Should she call Tommy? Maybe that would upset Ben even more. Finally, he came back inside, his eyes watery. He closed the slider and stepped a little closer. In spite of his promises, she wondered if he meant to grab her and drag her out of the house and tell her to leave. She wished she could quit thinking about what Jerry would do, and Ben was half again bigger than Jerry. One blow could end her life.

"Do not ever look at me that way," Ben told her.

"What way?"

"You know what way. I never want to have to tell you again that I would never hurt you. Tell me you understand that. When I reach out to you, I do not want to see you flinch."

Carmen swallowed as he put a hand to the side of her face, a touch gentle as a kitten's. "You have a right to ask questions and make demands," he told her. "But why now? What made you say all these things so unexpectedly? I was just ... I thought we would share a meal and talk about riding tomorrow."

"I brought it up because I'm already in love with you." Carmen had trouble holding back her own tears. "I brought it up because I care so much about you. I already know that if you were to ... to fall back into that hell of drugs and suicide or ... what if whoever shot you tries again? I've known you such a short time, but if something happened to you now, Ben, I couldn't bear it. I mean, I love you enough that I want you in every way. I want to learn everything I need to learn. I want you to promise you will get some counseling. My God, we *both* need that. I am scared to death of the fact that I *do* love you. This has all happened so fast, and —"

She was wrapped tightly in his arms before she finished. He kissed her hair, then hoisted her up so that she could wrap her arms around his neck and her legs around his middle. He devoured her mouth with his own. "Now, you answer some things for me," he told her amid kisses. "Can you have babies?"

The question shocked her. "Babies?"

"Babies. Are you able to have children?"

"Well, I ... as far as I know. I've never tried."

"Do you *want* babies? Because I want many."

"Of course I want babies."

He held her close with one arm and ran his other hand inside the leg of her shorts, plying her bottom. "I have no protection," he said amid continued hungry kisses. "I have not needed it. And you should know that because of the opioids and because there are certain things I do not remember. I have been tested in all ways. I am clean."

"Ben, what are you—?"

"Are you on the pill?"

"I ... yes. I stayed on them because I heard it's healthier than going off and then starting back again down the road."

"Your ex did some ugly things. I know by what I saw at his house. Are you okay? Physically?"

"Yes. I asked to be tested before the divorce, in case something was wrong that he would have to pay for." Was she actually talking about something so personal?

Power and masculinity surrounded her with his every touch, the way he held her with no effort, the commanding way he mastered her mouth. Fire moved through her when he moved his hand inside her bikini panties. "Do you truly love me?"

"Hopelessly," she answered.

"And I am hopelessly in love with you. I told you I thought being with another woman would be like cheating on Talia, but I only meant it would be cheating if I bedded a woman just to feel good, not if I was in love with her."

He kissed her, and Carmen could no longer leave the stirrings he'd awakened in her unsatisfied.

"And I am in love with you," he continued, "so this does not feel wrong." He kissed her eyes. "I have known you such a short time, yet I feel like I have known you forever, and I want you in every way a man can want a woman." He swung her up and carried her fully in his arms. "Tell me to stop now if that is what you want."

Carmen put her head on his shoulder. "I don't want you to stop."

"Then those steaks can marinate all night. My hunger is not for food." He carried her across the room to the master bedroom. "Do you still want me to open this door? If I do, there is no going back, Carmen."

Carmen saw the intense emotion in his eyes. "Yes. I still want you to open it."

"Do you trust me?"

Carmen kicked off her flip-flops. "I trust you." She felt him bend a little to turn the knob. He pushed the door open with his foot, then hesitated for just a moment. He held her tighter and whispered something in the Lakota tongue before he carried her to the bed.

CHAPTER TWENTY

BEN MOVED his arm from under Carmen's legs and held her close to his side as he reached out and yanked a pink puffy quilt off the king-size bed. A light blanket and top sheet went with it, leaving the bed bare except for the bottom sheet, which was, of course, pink—Talia's favorite color. *Please don't think about Talia, Ben.* One wrong thought or bad memory could bring all of this to an end.

Maybe it *should* end. Maybe this whole thing was wrong. Carmen's heart pounded with anticipation, combined with dread that she might not please him. This was the first time in a long time for both of them, but Ben did not seem worried. He pulled off the scrunchy that held her ponytail and let her hair fall around her shoulders, then climbed onto the bed and pulled her onto it with him. She nestled her head against a pillow as he straddled her and leaned close, covering her mouth with his own in a kiss so deep it was as though he was already making love to her.

This was it. There was no stopping or going back. Without another word, Ben grasped the hem of her big shirt and pulled it up over her head. She raised her arms and let him pull it all the way off, revealing the sports bra underneath. With no need to unclasp anything, he slipped that off, too, and leaned down to kiss each breast, caressing her nipples with his tongue and lips.

With one hand, he unbuttoned his jeans. Carmen ran her hands over his chest while he pushed down both the jeans and his underwear and tossed the clothing to the floor beside her shirt and sports bra.

He stretched out on top of her and pressed his body against hers. The erection she felt against private places told her all she needed to know. He was a big man in every way. The way he searched her mouth again made her feel wanton, hungry, desperate, madly in love. His long hair fell on either side of her so that it seemed nothing else in the world existed but this beautiful man who had so many needs she wasn't sure she could meet all of them. She felt surrounded by his virility, by strength and protection, guarded by the wolf spirit.

It was far too late now for any doubt. Far too late to worry about how wrong this might be. Far too late to deny the burning passion they had both danced around since Ben walked her back to those wolf cages.

This, too, was like a dance ... an exotic ritual no different from a religious ceremony that meant promise, commitment, and devotion. Like a prayer, this was not just an act they both had neglected for too long nor something to be taken lightly. This was not need or lust or just for the fun of it. This was worship, and that was how Ben made her feel. Worshipped.

He moved his kisses to her neck, her throat, her shoulders, her nipples taut with a desire to please his hunger. He plied each breast to its fullest as he gently tasted their pink fruits. Knowing this was Ben tasting and exploring her nakedness made her lightheaded and bold. She grasped his hair and gasped with pure ecstasy.

He kissed her cleavage, kissed her throat again, whispered into her ear, "I am not going to last long this first time. You are so beautiful, and I am so in need."

"It's all right," Carmen whimpered in reply. "We have all night."

"After you feel my life come into you, let me stay inside you," he told her. "We will do it again ... and perhaps again and again." He moved his kisses back to her breasts, then down over her belly. "Have I told you how beautiful you are?"

"You just did."

"I cannot say it enough." He unsnapped her shorts. Unzipped them. Kissed her belly button. Ran a finger under the waistline of her bikini panties.

Carmen closed her eyes as she felt him slip her shorts and panties down over her thighs. She bent her knees to help him get them all the way off her ankles and feet. She heard the soft little thud of the last of her clothing hitting the floor beside the rest. He ran strong hands along her thighs, and she did not resist when he gently but deliberately pushed her legs apart. He kissed places she never dreamed she could even let him look at, let alone touch ... or taste. He lingered there, arousing her to near painful heights. He moved his lips back over her belly, her breasts, to her mouth, and she could taste her own juices on his lips as he explored her mouth while he slipped his penis inside of her.

Carmen gasped at his size. Yes, it *had* been a long time. She climaxed right away just from the thrill of mating with the grand specimen of man she'd watched on that stage at the casino ... the gorgeous man who'd practically dripped with testosterone when she stood near him at the back of the theater ... the man any woman would want. But he'd chosen her, Carmen Wolfe, just because a wild animal had sat down beside her, sending signals to another wild animal called Ben Colter, who shared the wolf's spirit and believed in things she didn't even know or understand yet.

It didn't matter.

Was it her own voice crying out his name? She was lost beneath his powerful frame, his commanding control over her body, the dark hair that shrouded her face and shut out the rest of the room. Within less than a minute, she felt his life pulsing into her. He continued his rhythmic thrusts, and within seconds, another erection filled her. They rocked in a sweet, slightly slower rhythm, sharing wild kisses. He moved his hands under her bottom and raised up to his knees, pushing deep as he held her hips tight against himself to bury himself as deeply as he could.

Carmen grasped his forearms, hard as rocks. The little bells on the cuff bracelet jingled rhythmically with each thrust. The beaded bands on his upper arms tightly hugged his biceps, strained from hanging on to her hips. And through it all, Carmen could not take her eyes from his gaze. Those dark eyes told her she belonged to him now, and he would never let her go. She in turn would never let *him* go— not to any other woman, not to the ghost who was his wife, and not to that world that kept him too busy to think about what he had lost. He had *her* now. She would help him move on.

Still, she felt that little worry that she might not be enough to fill the void left by the horror of what he'd suffered, or enough to fight the fact that if he found whoever had killed his wife and son, the warrior in him would defi- nitely want to kill that man in revenge. Would his love for her be enough to stop him? She could still lose him to death or prison. And the reason was right there on his chest ... right in front of her as he took her.

Talia.

The thought only brought forth a desperate need to keep him close, even when he climaxed again and relaxed beside her.

"It's my turn," she told him. She pushed him onto his back and worked him into another erection, then guided him inside her and rocked her hips, throwing her head back and enjoying his groans of pleasure. He massaged her breasts, then raised up and pulled her against his chest. He rolled her over and rammed into her deep and hard. Again, she felt his release. If he wanted babies, there was no doubt he could make them.

He relaxed beside her again and pulled her close. "That was beautiful," he told her, "and *you* are beautiful. I love you. It feels good to say it."

Carmen ran a hand over his broad chest and kissed his nipples. "I love you, Ben. I've never felt about a man the way I feel about you." She leaned up and kissed his cheek. "But I was going to wait longer for this."

Ben grinned. "So was I."

"What happened?"

"You got tough with me. That was damn sexy."

"Are you serious?"

"I am. I love your strength. Everyone else treats me like I am going to break any minute, but you stood right up to me. That is the kind of woman I need."

"And I need a man who respects me and my own needs, a real man who stands for what is right and will be strong for me and protect me yet gentle and attentive. You are all those things."

Ben stroked her hair. "I must warn you there are times when I will seem distant. Times when I will want to ride alone or take a day to go someplace high in the Badlands to sing and pray and connect with Wakan-Tanka and a spirit world you might not understand."

"Then I will *try* to understand." Carmen decided not to bring up the subject of the shooting and her fear of his reaction if he found out who pulled the trigger.

"We need to shower and change the sheets," he told her.

"We most certainly do."

Ben got up and reached down to swing her up into her arms. "I love looking at you naked. Come into the shower with me. I will wash you, and you can wash me."

Carmen hugged his neck. "I can't believe we've done this."

"And by Lakota custom, you are now my wife. Did you know that?"

"I read it once – probably in a romance novel."

They both laughed at the remark. "True or not, Ben Colter, I grew up on a different custom. In my world, married people wear rings. We walk down an aisle and are married by a preacher or at least by a justice of the peace."

"I do not need such things."

"You are a lawyer. You know how it works—legally, that is."

Ben chuckled as he set her on her feet and turned on the shower. "Sure I do. Talia and I did all of that, just to satisfy state law."

Carmen saw the slight change in him when he mentioned Talia, as though he realized what he'd just done ... and what room they were in. That bed belonged to him and Talia.

"Ben, look at me."

He met her gaze.

"Who am I?"

He smiled sadly as he reached out and touched her cheek with the back of his hand. "You are Carmen Wolfe, and you are my woman. You have brought joy to my heart again."

She kissed his chest. "And I don't expect a ring and a ceremony and all that legal stuff right now. Please understand that. We've just taken a first step." She looked up at him. "Let's just enjoy the here and now. I don't make any demands. Things will fall into place the way they are supposed to."

"I am not worried about that, because you are already my wife." He touched his chest. "In here." Another kiss. "But you will get your customary wedding. As you said, when the time is right. I am aware there are still things we must take care of first." He reached out to see if the water was the right temperature, then pulled her into the shower with him and slid shut the shower door. He pumped liquid soap into a loofah and had Carmen stand under the shower-head as he scrubbed her down, taking his time in private places. The scrub turned to only his fingers exploring deeply as she and Ben kissed while water flowed between them. He worked her intimately until she cried out and lifted one leg to feel his genitals pressing against her.

Ben hoisted her up in strong arms, and she wrapped her legs around him. He hung on and let her slide down onto his erection, then rocked up into her while the water poured over their bodies. Carmen could not remember when she'd climaxed so many times only minutes apart. She balanced her arms on his shoulders to help him hold her up and met his full lips hungrily, tasting hot water and even a little soap.

With one last, hard thrust, Ben ejaculated inside her

again. Carmen lowered her legs and leaned against his chest. They just stood there saying nothing as they clung to each other for several long seconds while water flowed over them.

"We had better finish washing before I run out of hot water," Ben finally told her.

This time they used the loofah the way it was meant to be used, and Carmen drank in his beautiful nakedness as she gently washed him. They dried off with towels that Ben told her Rosa changed every week per his orders, even though this bathroom had not been used in nearly three years.

So it is all kept up in the way Talia would have wanted. Carmen had no doubt that was the reason, but Ben did not mention Talia's name.

They wrapped themselves in towels, then chased each other across the house to the other two bedrooms to brush their teeth and put on fresh underwear and T-shirts, which was all they wore when they sat at the island counter and ate some toast just because they needed to get something into their stomachs.

Ben walked around the island to get some water out of the fridge. "We will sleep the rest of the night in my bed." He drank down most of the water, then reached across the counter to run a finger over Carmen's lips. "And I should have asked you if you are all right. It has been a long time. Did I hurt you?"

Carmen grasped his hand and kissed it. "No. I'm a little worn out but for a good reason."

"Same here," he told her with a grin. "And you are as beautiful as I knew you would be."

"And you are as ... let's say, fulfilling ... as I thought you would be."

Ben laughed and walked around the island to pick her up in his arms. He carried her into his room. Carmen moved under the blankets and Ben joined her, but as delicious as sleep sounded, it would not come. They lay there staring at the ceiling, dimly lit by a night-light.

"I have neglected my workouts," Ben spoke up. "I had better lift some weights in the morning."

"And I need to go for a run or at least use your treadmill," Carmen answered.

They turned their heads and looked at each other.

"I can think of a better way to keep working out," Ben told her.

"So can I."

The clothes came back off.

CHAPTER TWENTY-ONE

CARMEN AWOKE to the sound of a bird chirping outside the bedroom window. She lay there a moment, letting her brain come fully conscious of the fact that it was morning and she was lying in Ben's bed ... still naked. *Oh my God, I slept with Crazy Horse!* That's how Val would put it.

Did last night really happen? Would things be different this morning? She straightened and rolled onto her back, smiling when a rather delicious ache engulfed her. Jerry had never made love to her in the ways Ben did, and after Jerry changed because of drugs he'd done painful, ugly things to her and enjoyed beating her, sometimes first, sometimes afterward.

Ben had kept it beautiful. She felt like she'd made love all night with the most wonderful, gentle man alive. In some ways he was still a stranger, yet she felt like she'd known him forever.

She drew the covers over her breasts. She had let Ben touch and taste every part of her body, and she'd seen and touched every part of his glorious, oh-so-male body in return. She'd spent the night in the arms of the talented, mystic Lakota man whose powerful presence on that stage in Grand Rapids had permeated the entire theater and captured everyone in the audience.

Yes, she was in love, and Ben loved her in return. That made it right, didn't it? After all, a man like Ben didn't do what he did last night without being deeply serious about it. After almost three years, he'd gone through the door to that master bedroom ... to the bed he'd shared only with Talia.

My God, I think I said something about a ring and walking down the aisle! How stupid and presumptuous was that? Still, Ben had declared she was already his wife. Maybe he would wake up this morning regretting all of it. Maybe he would think she'd plotted to trap him into something he was not ready for. Or maybe all he'd wanted was sex. He was, after all, a man.

She stretched again, turned to face Ben, then pulled the blankets over her head when she saw he was lying on his side watching her.

"It is about time you woke up," he told her. "And by the way, how long are you going to lie there trying to figure out if what we did last night was right?"

"How is it that you always seem to know what I am thinking?" she asked from under the covers.

"I saw how you were staring into space," he answered, "probably wondering what I think of you this morning."

Carmen kept the covers over her face. "What *do* you think of me?"

"I think that in spite of all that sweetness and being unsure that what we did was right, you sure know how to wear a man out,. Which, of course, is fine with me. I cannot think of a better way to get my exercise." Ben reached under the covers and pulled her closer. He ran a hand along the back of her thigh, over her bare bottom. "Do you like morning sex?"

Carmen peeked out from the sheets. "You aren't regretting all the promises we made each other in the throes of passion?" She felt his hand move higher, over her breasts, where his hand lingered to gently ply their fullness. He toyed with one nipple.

"Please do not tell me *you* regret any of it," he answered. "You are my wife now. It will break my heart if you change your mind."

He was serious! She pulled the covers off her face. "No! But sometimes men just say what they think a woman wants to hear so they can have sex with her."

He smiled softly and pushed a piece of hair behind her ear. "I am my *own* man. And last night you said you loved me and could not imagine life without me. You wanted me, and I wanted you. It was that simple. And you did not answer me about morning sex."

He moved on top of her. "While our bodies are still warm."

He pushed the covers away. "And the skin is its softest."

He kissed her breasts, her shoulders. "And the house is its quietest."

He kissed her chin. "And the birds are waking up with the sun."

He moved slightly to her side and searched between her legs. "And you are still warm and moist here."

He nuzzled her throat. "And your hair is all messy and your body relaxed, and you are still too sleepy to think about the right or wrong of it."

His hair fell around her face, and Carmen breathed deeply of the lovely scent of man and sage, the very male, very fetching smell of whatever soap he used and whatever men's cologne he wore. Damned if she wasn't already losing all common sense again. She thought to tell him no, but his fingers worked their magic. There was no more talking as the sheer ecstasy of being taken by this man of power and vision brought on a rippling climax as sweet and lovely as the singing bird outside the window.

She opened her legs eagerly when he moved between them, then sucked in her breath when Ben pushed himself inside of her, his groans of pleasure making her arch up to meet his thrusts.

She tried to remember how many times they had done this last night. Yet every time seemed like the first. She wanted to please him, and she found herself wishing she was not on the pill because, at the moment, she could think of nothing more fulfilling than giving this man a child to replace the son he'd lost, a baby to fill his arms and the empty place in his heart. Was she wrong to wish something so serious this soon?

He moved in sweet rhythm, whispering something in her ear in the Lakota tongue as he grabbed her bottom and kept up the gentle thrusts for several long, exotic minutes before she felt his release. They laid there quietly for a while, listening to the bird that still chirped outside.

"Is this real?" Carmen asked.

Ben raised up on his elbows to look down at her. "As real as it gets. And I have not been this happy in more than three years."

Carmen reached up and pushed some of his damp hair away from his face. "Same here ... since the first time Jerry landed a fist in my face."

He kissed her hair and gently rubbed her back. "Every touch from me will be gentle," he answered. "Last night was beautiful, Carmen. *You* are beautiful, in every way, every kiss, every curve, your golden hair, your incredibly green eyes, your bright smile, the sweetness that radiates from your whole being. Everything that is woman about you is beautiful." He moved his hand over her belly, her breasts again. "Being inside you is like heaven on earth. Why your ex ever let you get away, why he abused you, is beyond my understanding."

Carmen rested her head on his shoulder. "I can't believe I am lying in bed with the beautiful man I saw at a casino in Michigan. Going to that performance was not even something I had planned on doing. Val invited me at the last minute. And now I am a thousand miles from the only home I've ever known."

"You have to stop calling me beautiful."

"But you are."

"Carmen, I am just a man and far from perfect." He kissed her hair. "But I am glad you feel that you belong here. This *is* your home now, and you will learn to love it here." He tugged at her hair and sat up. "And you will learn to love riding. I am going to call Alice and tell her I am taking one more day off. My legal aids can take care of whatever needs doing. This day is just for us. I am going to take you riding, and we will go and see the wolves and get up close and personal with a herd of buffalo."

"*Buffalo?* Ben, I'm nervous enough about getting on a horse, let alone being around those wolves!"

"You will be fine," Ben assured her. "You will be with me. I am here. Nothing can harm you, remember? And I have been riding bareback since I was three years old, so get cleaned up and dressed." He stood, completely naked.

Carmen drank in his build. "I swear, you have an extra pair of abs other men don't have."

He waved her off. "You insist on embarrassing me." He

headed for his bathroom. "And these abs do not come easily. I work extra hard for them, and that is not easy with a bad back." He hesitated at the door. "And just so you feel sorry for me, after last night and this morning, I need some Tylenol."

Carmen grinned. "You were not exactly tied to the bed, Mr. Colter. You could have stopped any time. I would have understood."

"No man with a woman like you in his bed stops for anything short of his life. I am not sure even that would have stopped me." He closed the bathroom door.

"You have to help me pick things up before we leave," Carmen reminded him as she sat up. "We left a mess in the master bedroom, and I've never met Rosa yet. I do not want her to find all those clothes and that torn-up bed in there."

Carmen heard the water start to run in Ben's shower. She got out of bed and ran to the guest bathroom where all her own things were kept. "Oh good Lord," she gasped when she looked in the mirror. Her hair looked like it had been through a hurricane, and there were circles under her eyes. "You claim I wore you out last night, Ben Colter," she muttered, "but it was quite the opposite." She looked for her phone. It lay on a dresser and was plugged in, but she had no memory of when she'd thought to charge it. She grabbed it and ran back into the bathroom, closing the door. She dialed Val.

"Carmen! I was just going to my hairdresser to get some dead ends trimmed off and get my nails done. What are you up to out there?"

"I've been dancing," Carmen answered in a lowered voice.

"Dancing? Did you and Ben go to the city?"

"No! For crying out loud, Val, of all times for you to go

dense on me, this isn't it. I sure wish you were out here to talk to."

"Why are you half whispering?"

"Because Ben is in the bathroom next to mine. We are both showering now, but last night we showered together. *Get* it?"

"Holy cow! You mean you did *the* dance?"

"All night long, and again this morning. Val, it was incredible, almost sacred. I don't know how else to put it. Ben is so beautiful in body and spirit. He's gentle and respectful and everything you would expect a man like him to be. But it was a big step for him. He still isn't over his wife, and they still don't know who shot her. I have so much to tell you about that and the baby they lost and all the possible suspects and—"

Val let out a scream. "Carmen, this is great," Val interrupted. "And I can tell you are totally smitten. I'm so happy for you, but am I ever going to see you again?"

"Of course! I have to come home and get more clothes and some of my tax files and see my dad and settle the lake house, except now I'm thinking of keeping it. Ben works so hard. He needs to take a break once in a while. Our vacations can be in Michigan at the lake house. That would be a great getaway for him and give me a chance to come home and see you and the family occasionally."

"Oh, Carmen, you actually had sex with that gorgeous hunk of man last night?"

"Too many times to count. It just ... I don't know. It just happened. I ache everywhere this morning, but it's the nice kind of ache, and it's so nice to be able to trust a man. There is so much more to tell you, Val, but still so much I don't know about the man and his life out here. And yet I'm not worried about it. I must go for now, but

I'm going to text you with a list of more clothes I need. I want you to go to Dad's house and pack them up for me and send them out here. I'll text you Ben's address. Right now, I have to get cleaned up. We're going horseback riding."

"You? On a horse? I'd love to see that one."

"I know. I'll take some pictures. I just had to tell somebody about last night."

"I knew you wouldn't be able to put it off. Lord, you just look at that man, and common sense and discretion go right out the window. I would have been in his bed the first night I got there."

"And you have no shame whatsoever." They laughed together as Carmen started her shower. "I know this all sounds great, but we have a lot of problems still to solve, Val. This won't be easy, especially since I can tell Ben is still obsessed with finding out who shot him and his wife. And the fact that he *doesn't* know scares me, too. And his wife's presence fills this house, from pictures on the walls to every decoration. Somehow, we both have to learn to deal with that."

It hit Carmen then that even though Ben had finally gone into the master bedroom, he never opened the side door that led to the nursery. "I'd better go," she told Val. "Keep your fingers crossed that I don't fall off a horse and break my neck."

"I saw the videos at that performance in Grand Rapids, remember?" Val answered. "That man rides like he's part of the horse. You'll be fine. Right now, your biggest fall is falling for the man himself. This is crazy, Carmen! Six weeks ago, you'd never even met the guy. The way things have happened, this has to be right, girl. I think I'm going to cry. I'll try to get Sid out there for that Pow-Wow. I want to see the two of you together as a real couple. And when you call back, I want more details about last night."

"You wish! I *can* tell you that I've never seen abs like his on any man. And he's so ... so sweet and romantic. Let's just say I would not kick him out of bed for eating crackers. I wouldn't kick him out even if he was eating *spaghetti*."

Val howled with laughter. "I can't believe this! You and a Lakota fancy dancer from South Dakota. Who would have thought?"

"Certainly not me before you took me to that performance," Carmen answered. "I keep waiting for something to happen to spoil it all. Please tell Sid I'm fine, and tell him to call me if he finds out anything about a doctor who might be able to help Ben with his back trouble."

"I will, but, honey, so far, the news isn't good. You just enjoy yourself, and we'll get back to you. I'm so happy for you. Sid will be, too."

"Thanks for being such a good friend. I have to go. Ben is already done with his shower. I'll call again soon."

Carmen ended the call and jumped into the shower, keeping her hair out of the water. There wasn't time to shampoo, and she'd already washed her hair in the last shower she took. She smiled at the fact that she'd never taken so many showers within just a few hours. And after riding horses, she would probably need another one later today.

Me, riding horses. That's a good one. She realized she'd forgotten to tell Val they were also going to see the wolves. "I've lost my mind," she muttered. "And my heart." She rinsed and dried off.

She hurriedly dressed in blue jeans and a pink T-shirt. She would have to wash some clothes soon. She brushed her hair and pulled it up into a ponytail, then put sunscreen on her face. She grabbed her phone and decided not to take anything else with her.

"Wear tennis shoes, not sandals," Ben yelled from his room. "Some types of tall grass can cut your feet. And since those steaks are only one day old, I am thinking Tommy and Sasha can come over tonight and help us cook and eat them. Buffalo meat lasts well, especially the way Rosa marinates it. Tommy is great at grilling steaks, but you will have to make a fresh salad."

Carmen went into his room to help strip the bed, but Ben already had everything off it. And the way he was dressed, he looked like he'd just stepped out of the past. He was wearing buckskin pants and a beaded, fringed buckskin shirt, his hair long and loose but with a feather tied into it on one side. He wore those feather-shaped silver earrings and the belt with the tiny bells was draped around his hips. "You look ready to ride out and hunt buffalo," Carmen told him. "Maybe even make war."

Ben grinned. "These clothes are cooler and more comfortable for horseback riding." He looked her over. "Those tight jeans are turning me on, but they will not be comfortable for riding. We will go to Tommy and Sasha's house first. Maye you can get some coffee there. Either way, they have seven boys, and three of them are teenagers. Maybe we can find some jeans from Matthew or Zeke that you will be able to wear. Zeke is tall and very slim, still not filled out much."

"You want me to wear boys' jeans?"

"We are going riding, Carmen, not someplace fancy. You want to be comfortable, and you will not be if you spend the day straddling a horse in those very tight, very sexy jeans. I already want you again, but if I take you back to bed, we will end up spending all day right here." Ben bundled the sheets and blankets into his arms. "We can wash these things when we get home," he told her. "Rosa will have some of the wash done by then. We can finish it later."

Home. He'd said it in such a comfortable way, as though he figured that's where she was now. Home.

"You know how to make beds and wash clothes?" Carmen teased.

"Sure I do. I have been alone a long time, and I do not like leaving everything up to Rosa. Besides, I used to help Talia with things like this." He suddenly sobered and walked past her, carrying the bed clothes to the laundry room. "Rosa is a sweet lady. You will like her. We will keep her on because I will still travel a lot, and I will want you to go with me. I am sure you will like the shopping in DC I can also take you to Denver or Pierre any time you want to shop or find a salon or whatever else you need."

Carmen noticed he did not mention Rapid City.

"I already gathered the towels from my bathroom," he told her. "Go ahead and get yours. I will get the sheets from the other bedroom."

Carmen hurriedly bunched up the towels from her bathroom and put them in the laundry room, located behind the back kitchen wall. She walked through the house to the master bedroom. Ben already had the fitted sheet off the mattress. He threw a blanket and the pink ruffled quilt on top of the bed, then straightened them and tucked the quilt under the pillows. "We will make the bed look made for now so Rosa does not notice. We can put clean sheets on the bed ourselves later."

Carmen quietly helped from her side, sensing it was just hitting Ben that he'd made love to another woman in this bed that was almost sacred to him. His attitude had turned somber.

"Ben, are you okay?"

He met her gaze. "Being in here is still hard." He looked her over lovingly. "I feel Talia everywhere, but then I see you, and that is all I need to help me live with the memories."

"I know what I told you, Ben, but I didn't mean you have to deal with all of it at once. I know we joked about second thoughts, but I hope you aren't having them now that we are up and facing reality."

Ben finished straightening the quilt. "No. I just worry that *you* will have second thoughts. You are not dealing just with loving another man, Carmen. You are dealing with your own bad memories and with life-changing events, far from home and from your friends and everything familiar. I want you to know that you are free to go back to Michigan any time you need to. You have a father there. Fathers are important. I should know. And your grandparents and friends are there."

"I will adjust. Having Jerry out of my life and finding a man who knows how to love a woman in all the right ways helps me know where I want to be, and I want to be here. Believe that." Carmen gave him a smile. "Besides, I'm your wife now, and I have no desire to set your moccasins outside the front door."

That brought the brilliant smile that turned her to putty. "You know about the old custom our women once used to get rid of a husband?" Ben asked.

"I read about it once." Carmen laughed lightly. "If only divorcing a man was always that easy. I threw every stitch of Jerry's clothing out on the lawn once at the lake house, but I still had to go through court proceedings to get rid of him."

She sobered. "In the meantime, I got a beating for daring to throw out his things."

"I would not beat you for it."

Carmen faced him; arms folded. "Oh? What *would* you do?"

Ben snickered. "I would take everything back inside and then tell you to try throwing *me* out."

They both laughed. "I would have to hire ten men to do that," Carmen answered. "Even that many might not be enough. Then again, if you smiled at me like you are right now, I wouldn't *want* to throw you out. In fact, I already told Val I wouldn't kick you out of bed for eating spaghetti."

Ben shook his head. "I might have known you have already called Val. I hope I got a glowing report."

"Oh, believe me, it was glowing."

Ben grabbed up the tangled sheets from the floor, then stopped to give her a kiss before he headed out the door. "I am glad that I pleased you. Would you like me to please you again?"

"Yes, but later. We really, really need to leave."

"Catch you later then," Ben told her with a grin.

"Hey," Carmen said as he left. "You didn't say what kind of report you would give someone about me," she teased.

"I would say that the experience was as radiant as the sun, and that you are as hot as a volcano," Ben called back to her. "And I would say that you have the body of a goddess."

Carmen smiled as she picked up the last of the clothing, then sobered when she glanced at the door to the nursery. She would not bring up the subject of that closed door yet. Making love in this room had been only a first step for Ben. Facing the death of Singing Boy might be much more diffi-cult. She did not want to spoil the joy of this moment.

CHAPTER TWENTY-TWO

"You boys get breakfast going. You know what to do." Tommy handed orders to his six sons still at home, while Sasha led Carmen into their bedroom to try on jeans that would be more comfortable for riding. "Come out to the patio with me, Little Brother," Tommy told Ben. "The boys will set the table."

Ben followed Tommy outside his and Sasha's sprawling stucco home and slid the door shut. Both men studied the Badlands in the distance for a moment before Tommy folded his arms and faced Ben. "It did not take you long," he said with a sly grin.

"What do you mean?" Ben pretended he did not know what Tommy was talking about.

"I mean the look on your face when you and Carmen got here so early this morning. I am surprised you did not stay in bed all day instead."

Ben chuckled as he pulled his hair behind his shoulders. "We spent plenty of time in bed last night and again this morning. We are worn out."

Tommy joined him in light laughter and gave Ben a

slight shove. "It is about time you got back to living again," he said. "I am happy for you. Just be sure this is what you want, Little Brother. I suspect she is not the kind to do something like that just to satisfy a need. Do not turn around and break her trust and her heart."

Ben sobered. "You know me better than that. She is everything I could want or need. She is tolerant, understanding, unselfish, smart, and strong."

"And beautiful to boot," Tommy added.

"She knocks me over, but it goes beyond that body." Ben watched the trail of a jet flying high in the bright blue morning sky. "I felt it that first night we met. Some things are just meant to be, Tommy. I always thought that if this happened, it would feel like cheating on Talia, but it was not like that at all. Carmen believes this is what Talia would want for me and that it is her spirit that led Caesar to bring us together. She is so accepting of my love for Talia and the memories I carry. I will always love and honor Talia, but there is nothing wrong with loving again."

"I am glad to hear you say that." Tommy nodded. "I agree. You have to listen to your heart and to what the wolf spirit tells you. I can see Carmen makes you happy. It has been years since you have smiled the way you were when you walked through that door this morning."

Ben took a few steps and continued studying the distant scenery. "Tommy, you should know that the first time was in the master bedroom. You are the only one I would talk about something so private with, but you know what it means that I was able to go into that room."

Silence filled the air for several quiet seconds. Tommy moved beside him and put a hand on his shoulder. "That is exactly what you needed to do. She must be some woman to have encouraged you to go into that room."

Ben faced his brother. "She practically ordered me into that bedroom. I have never met anyone like her. She understands what I need to do to put the past behind me, but she is not pushing me to do everything at once. And she does not expect me to change my ways just for her. And in return, I have told her she does not need to change her own ways and beliefs. We can love each other in spite of our differences."

"Of course you can." Tommy smiled softly. "When she jumped into your arms the day of the birthday party and I saw how you clung to each other, I knew bringing her here was wise."

"It was. Again, you and Sasha have saved my life, Tommy, by bringing Carmen here. Everyone at the office likes her. And more important, the kids like her."

"So does Sasha."

"I am glad. At the office yesterday, Carmen did not seem put off by how busy we all are. In fact, she is going to help out, mainly with accounting. She thinks we should hold an audit, to make sure things are being handled right so we do not get into trouble with the IRS. That could hurt our fundraising. I told her how much I hate bookkeeping."

Tommy chuckled. "You have *never* been good with money. You earn it, and then you allow others to handle it all. I think that is yet another good reason you found this woman. She is good with the one and only thing you are *not* good at."

Ben's smile widened. "She is damn good at a *lot* of things." He sat down at a picnic table. "She is understanding because she, too, has issues to deal with. Because of how her ex treated her, it has been difficult for her to trust me. He abused her so badly."

Tommy sat down beside him. "So, she understands loss

and heartache. And pain. All the things you know well yourself. That only makes her more understanding." He paused. "Tell me, Little Brother. You went into that master bedroom, but did you show her the nursery? Did you open *that* door?"

Ben felt the rush of deep sorrow. *Singing Boy! My son.* "No," he answered. "I could not bring myself to show her the nursery yet or go in there myself." The thought of his baby boy always brought the urge to cry, to scream.

"And she did not ask you to open that door?"

Ben swallowed back tears and stared at an ant crawling across the patio. "No."

Tommy nodded "Then she is even wiser than what you have described. She knows that is something you must decide for yourself. And I think the day is coming sooner than later when you will go into that nursery, Ben, and do what you know you must do."

Ben drew in his breath and rose, wiping away a tear and putting on a smile. "We should go inside now and help the boys. I want their ideas on new songs we should try for Omaha."

"You just want to change the subject," Tommy told him.

"Yes. I do."

"Then we will go inside. It is enough that you have found a good woman and are happy. Take one thing at a time." Tommy moved in front of him and put out his hand. Ben took it and squeezed it.

"It has been a long journey, Little Brother," Tommy told him. "Now a new journey begins."

Their gazes held. "The old journey cannot end until I know who killed Talia and put me through so much pain and loss," Ben declared.

"But you cannot let that keep you from loving again. Do not let your anger and thirst for revenge come between you and Carmen, Ben. The answers will come. Perhaps Carmen coming here is part of that answer. I feel there is a reason for all of this, a reason for so suddenly finding this joy in your life."

Ben squeezed his hand again. "I feel the same way."

Young Luke came to the sliders. "Father, we have scrambled eggs cooking and have set the table," he told Tommy. "And we want Uncle Ben to come inside so we can talk about the coming Pow-Wow and what dances we will do. Mother and Carmen are still in the bedroom."

"Telling their own secrets, I imagine," Tommy said quietly to Ben. "I suspect your new love is just as excited about being in love again as you are. And you know Sasha. She will get all the details out of Carmen."

"Oh Lord," Ben answered, shaking his head.

Luke turned away, and Tommy went inside. Ben glanced at the Badlands again. Carmen had told him she was afraid of them. Was there more to all of this than finding love again? *The spirit of the wolf is strong.* He felt something more was taking place, something yet to come. For today, he would teach Carmen not to fear the elements or nature's creatures or a man's embrace. He would teach her not to fear the Badlands. If they were calling to her, it was for a good reason.

"THIS IS JUST SILLY," Carmen told Sasha. "Wearing a boy's pants."

"At least my Zeke is tall enough for the length to fit, but he is bigger than you in the waist and butt." She handed

Carmen one of her own belts. "Here. This will hold them up."

Sasha went back into a walk-in closet to get some of her own things. Carmen glanced at pictures on a dresser, photos of Tommy and Sasha and Ben and Talia all together, smiles on their faces, Ben's arms around Talia. Outside the bedroom door she heard Sasha and Tommy's boys babbling all at once with their Uncle Ben and with their father, suggesting new songs to sing. Everything was "Uncle Ben" this and "Uncle Ben" that. One of the older boys insisted on Latin music. "Something different and with a beat you love, Uncle Ben. And you know Spanish."

"Ben knows Spanish?" Carmen called to Sasha, who was still in the closet.

"Yes. And French."

Of course. "Is there anything he *doesn't* know?" Carmen joked.

"Yes. Numbers. He hates math. He loves that you are a CPA. He says he did not know accountants could be so fun and beautiful."

Carmen listened to more banter going on outside the bedroom door, some of the boys singing a Latin song by Pitbull. "I'm sorry we barged in on you guys so early," she told Sasha. "This was Ben's idea. I've never even been on a horse. They scare me."

Sasha came out of the closet, holding a pair of her jean shorts and a pink T-shirt. "You will learn to love horses and love riding," she told Carmen. "Ben will make sure of that, but for today, do not be afraid of falling off. Ben is very skilled at riding. You will be in his big, strong arms." The last words were said with a sexy tease. "I do not think you will mind that."

"Not at all." Carmen put a hand to her heart.

Sasha carried her clothes into the master bath. "Oh! You need a hat," she shouted from the bathroom. "With that fair skin, you should not be out in the sun all day without one." She went back into the closet. "The brim of a cowboy hat would be too big for sitting in front of Ben. You should wear a baseball cap." She came back out with a pink ball cap with YESS displayed across the front in glittery rhinestone letters and handed it to Carmen. "This was Talia's. She would not mind you wearing it."

Carmen took the hat hesitantly. "Will Ben mind?"

"No. He will want you to have the protection." Sasha stepped closer, her eyes bright and teasing. "Something happened last night. Am I right?"

Carmen could not help the flush she felt come into her cheeks. "Yes."

"I *knew* it! That is why I teased you about Ben's big, strong arms. He seems so happy today. It is a different kind of happy than just goofing around with the boys out there. It was in his eyes when you two first got here, a look of peace and happiness we have not seen in years."

Carmen sighed and sat down on the end of Tommy and Sasha's still-unmade bed. Sasha was still in her pajamas and was just getting ready to shower and go to the school when Carmen and Ben arrived. The boys had all been in the kitchen drinking orange juice, and Tommy was making coffee.

"I am glad you asked," Carmen admitted. "I didn't know if I should say anything, and I wasn't sure how you and Tommy would feel about it."

"How *we* would feel? It is not even our business, but oh my gosh, Carmen, we have wanted this for Ben for so long."

Carmen met Sasha's gaze. "You should know that we … that it happened in the master bedroom."

Sasha sucked in her breath and sat down beside Carmen. "That is amazing! Such a big step for Little Brother." She put an arm around Carmen's shoulders. "I am happy for both of you. You also have been through some hard times. You deserve a man who truly loves you, and when Ben loves someone, it is with his whole heart. But I thought you were still unsure about a lot of things and were going to wait."

"I was, but, my God, it's Ben, and he's so damn hot."

Both women let out little screams.

Carmen blinked back tears that were a combination of joy and concern. "Ben is such a beautiful man in every way. So easy to love."

"Tommy is going to be so pleased that you are finding a way to bring back the old Ben he grew up with."

Carmen felt relief at knowing this woman so important to Ben, and who had been close to Talia, was happy about the relationship. "You should know that I kind of let loose on Ben last night. He wants me to stay, so I told him I would if he would try harder to let go of what happened. I told him he could start by opening that bedroom door. I said I loved him, but he has to love me for me, not as a replacement for Talia. The next thing I knew, he picked me up and carried me into that room. I could have stopped him, but things quickly went beyond trying. He took away all my common sense, and I think he lost a lot of his own."

Both women laughed, and Carmen felt a warming relationship, someone she could talk to the way she talked with Val back home. "I should tell you that Ben now considers me his wife by Lakota custom," she told Sasha.

Sasha hugged her shoulders. "Of course he does. That is Ben for you. I am not surprised he feels that way. He needed a good, strong woman who would stand up to him, and now you are together. Now you must *stay* strong, Carmen, even when Ben is down. He has to know you mean business. It is the only way *he* will stay strong enough to keep moving on. Everyone who loves Ben will be happy for him." Sasha stood. "I have something you should see." She walked to a bookcase and came back with a picture album. "You need to understand how bad the shooting was and the hell Ben went through, the strength it took for him to even want to live. Look at these pictures while I take a quick shower and get dressed."

Carmen heard more laughter and what sounded like boyish romping outside the bedroom door. Thank God Ben had Tommy and this big family and all the love that came with it. She opened the picture album hesitantly, almost afraid of what she would see. The first pictures were of a very happy Ben and Talia, obviously in love, so much joy in their eyes. Then came some wedding pictures, Ben looking gorgeous in white buckskins, Talia wearing a beautifully beaded white, fringed buckskin dress, flowers in her hair. Her eyes glowed with joy, her dark beauty absolutely radiant.

She turned to pictures of Ben and Talia marching in an obvious protest, carrying a banner that read, "We Have Our Own Lawyers Now." Others carried signs about Native American rights:

"We Are Dancing Beneath You!"

"Save The Black Hills!"

"Crazy Horse Lives!"

It was a huge procession, Ben and Talia in the lead. Carmen wondered if the protests were linked to the shooting, perhaps a disgruntled person who disagreed with Native American rights? Someone hired by Clements Oil? Maybe someone hired by one that company's lawyers?

She thumbed through pictures of a pregnant Talia, pictures of Ben kissing her belly, hugging her from behind while both of them smiled joyously at the camera, beautiful pictures of a very photogenic couple.

She turned the page and drew in her breath. The next pictures were of a horribly bloodstained sidewalk, the area cordoned off with yellow police tape. Newspaper clippings were Scotch taped to the album pages, showing bold headlines with articles about the shooting, pictures of ambulances, and eyewitness reports.

He tried to protect her.

He was shot, but he kept holding his pregnant wife in his arms and screaming her name.

He passed out right there on top of her. There was blood everywhere, just everywhere! It was running into the gutter.

I thought he was dead.

Then came pictures of Ben in a hospital bed, so full of wires and tubes hooked up to all kinds of fluids and machines that a person could hardly tell who was in the bed.

"Oh my God," Carmen said softly.

The bathroom door opened. "I showered really quick so I can make breakfast for you two," Sasha told her. "I did not even let my hair get wet."

Carmen barely heard. She kept staring at the hospital pictures. "Did Ben have any veins left to stick something into?" she asked.

Sasha quickly pulled on a pair of jean shorts. "He was hooked up to so many fluids and machines that one of his veins collapsed," she answered. "His heart stopped more than once. It was awful. Tommy says the bullets were large-caliber hollow points. He said bullets like that do not just make holes. They blow apart inside the body and do terrible damage. Ben is lucky it did not damage his other kidney or split his spine, but it damaged his liver and colon. Besides taking his kidney, they had to remove part of his liver and repair his colon."

"How awful," Carmen muttered, turning more pages.

Sasha pulled on a T-shirt and sat down beside Carmen. "The doctors took as much shrapnel and bone as they could from Ben's lower back, but they could not locate or remove all of it. There is no guarantee that a particle could not still take a wrong turn in his body and paralyze him. The doctors say that the longer the particles are in his back, the more solidly they will be held in place by tissue that grows around them. That is the only hope we have now, except that Ben's immune system could decide to reject the remaining particles at any time, causing new infection. He will be on antibiotics the rest of his life. And the pain is still there, of course. Ben says staying physically active helps him."

Carmen shivered at the pictures. She turned more pages, photos of Ben in a wheelchair, Ben learning to walk again and looking so thin. She put a hand to her heart at the sight of a gaunt, hollow-eyed skeleton of a man in the next group of pictures.

"This isn't Ben! It can't be!"

Sasha studied the picture Carmen pointed out. "That is how Ben looked when we found him in the alley near where the shooting took place. That was after he got hooked on opioids and disappeared. He was living on painkillers and other drugs he is not even sure of and was sleeping in an abandoned building. Tommy and Billy Big Bull and our oldest son managed to get Ben home. The struggle to get him off the drugs was long and painful. That is when Ben tried to kill himself. He had very bad depression."

Carmen found it hard to believe the man in the picture was the same handsome, strong, intelligent man who'd made love to her last night. "I don't know how he managed to come back from the man in this picture."

"Tommy took Ben to pray in the sweat lodge several times, then took him to the Black Hills, where Ben fasted and had the vision of wolves. After that, Ben took part in many of our rituals, rejoined Pow-Wows, found his strength in the blood of his ancestors."

Carmen kept staring at pictures of the bony, destitute man that was once Ben. The difference between that man and the Ben she knew now was phenomenal, and she realized the courage and faith it must have taken for him to be the strong, active man he was now. "Sasha, I feel like I have just touched the surface of helping Ben truly get over this."

Sasha brought her long, black hair around one shoulder and began twisting it into one big braid. "Love can work miracles," she told Carmen. "You are *Ben's* miracle, but as I said, stay strong. Make him face reality. He truly wants to go forward, but he did not have the courage until you came along."

Carmen sighed, turning back to the hospital pictures. "Sasha, he went into that bedroom last night, but he didn't go into the nursery. That is another big hurdle, isn't it?"

"Yes. And it is one you should let Ben decide when to face. It is custom at burials to take a piece of the deceased's hair and toss it to the wind so that his or her spirit can travel on that wind to the Great Beyond. Tommy did that for Talia at her funeral, and it breaks Ben's heart that he was not there to do it himself. That is why he cut himself when he finally visited Talia's gravesite."

She twisted a rubber band around the end of her braid and rose. "You should know that Tommy asked the doctors to save a piece of Singing Boy's hair," she continued. "He put it into a little leather pouch we call a medicine bag and put it under the pillow in the baby's crib. It is there waiting for Ben to release it. If he decides he is ready to go to Talia's grave and release his son's spirit, do not let him go alone. Tommy should go with him for support and to sing over the grave. The ceremony with the baby's hair is deeply sacred."

Carmen blinked back tears. "I can't believe what Ben went through. There have been so many repercussions."

"Are you two ready yet in there?" Ben yelled from outside the door.

Sasha grabbed the album and put it away, then opened the bedroom door. "You two cannot leave until I make you some breakfast, lover boy," she told Ben. She walked past him and headed for the kitchen.

Ben came inside the room, grinning. "Lover boy?" He shook his head. "You cannot keep a secret, can you?" he asked Carmen. "You have already called Val, and now you have told Sasha."

Carmen stood up and put her hands on her hips. "Did you really think she wouldn't figure it out? I didn't need to say a thing. *She* asked *me* about it."

Ben walked closer and leaned down to kiss her. "To be honest, Tommy figured it out, too. He said I seemed abnormally happy ... and I am." Ben looked her over and chuckled. "Nice pants."

Carmen frowned. "Don't you dare make fun of me or I won't go riding."

"I am just thinking what a nice butt lies under that gathered denim. I swear, those boy jeans are sexier on you than the tight ones."

Carmen took the pink ball cap from where she'd been holding it behind her back. "Is it okay if I wear this? Sasha said I should have some kind of shade over my face. This is all she had for me."

Ben took the hat from her, fingering it for a moment. "I remember it well. Talia loved glam. Even her baseball cap had to be pink and had to glitter." He stuck it on Carmen's head. "And you look good in pink."

Carmen removed the hat and leaned up for another kiss. "You're really sure?"

"About the great butt under those pants?"

Carmen gave him a shove. "You know what I mean!"

"I am sure." Ben put an arm around her shoulders and led her out to the kitchen, where Tommy handed Carmen a cup of coffee.

"You are a beautiful and a welcome addition to the family," he told her. He put a hand on her shoulder and offered her a chair at the kitchen table. "I had my doubts about you when Ben first talked about you on our flight home from Grand Rapids, but anyone who brings such a smile to my *sohn-kah's* eyes is Lakota at heart. Just know that Little Brother can be a handful. If something comes up that you cannot handle, give me a call."

"I just let Tommy *think* he can handle me," Ben joked. "And by the way, *sohn-kah* means younger brother. To me, Tommy is *chee-ay* in the Lakota tongue. Older brother."

Carmen took the coffee cup. "Thank you for the support, Tommy. I hope I never have to take you up on your offer to help."

Bedlam followed as Sasha made scrambled eggs and toast. Ben's nephews poked fun at each other, and everybody talked at once. The oldest brother there, Luke, left for Oglala Lakota College on a motorcycle. The others begged Ben to come to the School for the Arts for rehearsal.

"It is always more fun when you are there," Jeremiah complained.

"Tomorrow I will be there," Ben promised, "in the afternoon. I have a lot to do at the office first, and Carmen needs to get situated there so she can keep her accounting business going. I promised she would have an office of her own there."

After a good deal of conversation and laughter, seventeen-year-old Matthew and fourteen-year-old Zeke left for school on horseback. Jeremiah, Tommy Jr., and little Benjamin piled into Tommy and Sasha's Jeep to also head for the School for the Arts.

Ben grabbed a large canteen and a leather sack.

"We call this supply pack a parfleche," he told Carmen, holding up the leather bag. "Today you and I will have a wonderful lunch of baloney sandwiches, peanut butter and jelly sandwiches, carrots, and apples. It is all packed in here. How does that sound?"

"Elegant," Carmen answered. "I'll settle for the peanut butter and jelly." She looked around the kitchen. The table was clean as a whistle. Sasha had made every child clean up his mess before leaving. "Pretty organized," she told Ben.

"With seven boys, you *have* to be organized," Ben answered. "Number one son is still overseas, but he is supposed to come home soon on leave. Sasha and the kids at the school will make sure he gets quite a reception."

"I'm sure they will."

They headed out the door. "Hey," Ben told Carmen as he opened the truck's passenger door for her. "I promise to take you to Pierre next week for a proper fancy meal and maybe dancing. We will stay in a nice hotel and make love all night in a bed fit for a queen. There are some nice stores and restaurants there. And I will dress like a successful lawyer."

Carmen stood on the truck's side rail and faced him, wrapping her arms around his neck. "You *are* a successful lawyer, but that doesn't matter. I like the way you are dressed right now, like the warrior you are."

Ben met her mouth in a deep kiss. "You know, we just might end up naked in the grass out there."

"You wouldn't!"

"Never underestimate a man in love."

"Don't forget I still might set your shoes outside the front door."

"But it is *my* tepee."

"You claim I am your wife now, so according to your own words, it is now *my* tepee, too," Carmen teased. "I wonder if that would hold up in court."

"By Lakota law, maybe. But I would find ways to change your mind about casting me out."

More kisses.

"I'm sure you would," Carmen answered. She got inside the truck, and Ben closed the door. He threw the supply bags and canteen into the back seat.

"We can also go to Denver," he told her. "It is a great city, and the shopping is as good as DC or New York."

"Ben, don't worry about taking me places. There is nothing I need right now, and I am loving it right here."

Ben took a bottle of a special hydration drink from a cooler he'd put in back before leaving the house. He got inside and opened the bottle, drinking down about half of it. "Sorry, but I'll be watering the prairie grass fairly often out there," he told her. "I drink a lot of this stuff."

"I understand."

Ben backed out of Tommy's driveway and headed west.

Carmen watched the landscape, the Badlands looming in the distance. She glanced at the dream catcher that still hung on the rearview mirror, the tiny chain that held a small picture of Talia. She wanted to ask about the little medicine bag under the pillow in Singing Boy's crib.

When are you going to let the boy go? She did not voice the words.

CHAPTER TWENTY-THREE

BEN POINTED to a gray spotted Appaloosa inside a fenced grassy area near the stables. "That is Spirit. He belongs to me and is the horse I rode in the video that showed Tommy and me hunting buffalo. His spirit and mine are like one. The reddish-brown mare with the black mane and tail is also mine. I call her Lacey."

Carmen braced her arms against the top rail of the fence that surrounded the corral. "They all look big to me. I need one of those little ponies kids ride around in a circle at fairs."

Ben snickered and put an arm around her shoulders. "The rest of those horses belong to Henry Whitefeather, the owner of these stables. He uses them for tourists who want to go riding. There is another riding stable way over on the west end of the Badlands. I have a pinto there also. Tommy has three horses there." He gave out a whistle and called Spirit's name. The horse came running. "We will not be riding the designated trail used by visiting riders," Ben told Carmen as he climbed over the fence. "We will ride through that grassland out to the right and into the

Badlands from that direction. It is prettier country and a faster way to get to Sammy's place to see the wolves. And we will be alone, so we will not need to put up with tourists."

He greeted Spirit with words in Lakota Carmen did not understand, then put his forehead against Spirit's forehead as he scratched the horse's ears. In that moment, with Ben wearing buckskins, his hair hanging long and loose, Carmen saw a warrior from 150 years ago. She could picture a village of tepees close by. It was as though everything out here was sacred: the prairie grass, the trees, the animals, the Badlands in the distance, the dark beauty of the Black Hills. In country like this, it seemed today's modern amenities were surrounded by spirits from the past. And here, Ben was in his element. Here was where Carmen sensed he found strength and purpose.

Ben called Lacey to him, and both horses followed him toward the corral barn. "Go around to the front entrance," Ben told Carmen. "I will take these two in through the side. You can get acquainted with them while I saddle Lacey. I ride with only a blanket, so we will tie our supplies onto Lacey's gear."

Carmen studied the jagged rocky spires in the distance. They were mostly gray, but mixed in with them were smooth rock formations with striped layers of multicolored rock. She still felt a hint of danger when she thought about Linda Two Fists's body being found there. Just the name Badlands made her nervous to go there. How many other bodies were hidden there among that endless sprawl of secret nooks and crannies?

She shook off the thought. She was, after all, with Ben. *I am here. Nothing can harm you.* She walked through the wide front wooden barn doors and took a moment to adjust to the odor of horses and hay and manure, none of which seemed to bother Ben.

"You get used to the smell," he told her as he threw blankets on both horses, then began saddling Lacey.

"You read my mind," Carmen answered with a grin.

"It is a good smell, the smell of nature and spirits and the earth." He spoke softly to Lacey in the Lakota tongue.

"Do you know a lot of people from other tribes?"

"Sure, from Pow-Wows, speeches I have given, meetings to share information about how to get along with the government and the FBI and the BIA and the endless list of those who wish we did not exist at all." Ben kept adjusting straps as he spoke. "I even defended an Apache man down in New Mexico once. He was accused of helping rob a convenience store, but he just happened to be there at the same time. Because he was Apache, the law assumed he must have been part of the robbery."

He jerked at the cinch, urging Lacey to suck in her belly. Carmen got the hint. *If you are an indigenous person, you are automatically guilty.* She could feel his sudden anger.

"That is the kind of thing I love to defend," Ben told her, "which reminds me that I need to write that brief in the Clements Oil case and get it filed. I can stop them from drilling for months, which frustrates their lawyers to no end. I am sure they call me some choice names when I am not around."

Maybe they are the ones who want you dead. Carmen kept the words to herself, but the thought brought up those hospital pictures again. It was no wonder he had trouble getting over the trauma of the shooting.

Ben buckled Lacey's harness and named parts of the saddle and gear for her as he pointed them out.

"Ben, I will never remember all this," Carmen told him.

"You will in time, especially when you do it yourself. With Spirit, I use only a blanket and a rope bridle and braided leather bit." He patted Spirit's neck. "I would introduce you to the stable owner, Henry Whitefeather, but he is way out in another corral." He led the horses out of the barn and to the truck, where he began tying the supplies to Lacey's tack. He grabbed a bottle of his hydration drink and uncapped it, drinking down about half of it. He put two more bottles into the parfleche, then took his .45 from under the driver's seat of the truck and shoved it into a holster at his side.

"You are making me nervous, Ben."

"Just a precaution. No one with any common sense goes into the Badlands without plenty of supplies and protection, just in case. You never know what could happen in such wild country, but I have done this many times, so quit worrying. This is home to me, remember?" Ben drank down the rest of his drink and tossed the empty bottle into a trash can labeled plastic. He mounted Spirit in one swift leap, then reached down for Carmen. "Come on up."

Carmen took a deep breath. "That's a big horse."

"He is also smart, sure-footed, and obedient. Come on. Get up here. Just grab Spirit's mane. It's either that or climb up on Lacey and ride her by yourself."

"No!" Carmen closed her eyes and took hold of Spirit's mane, holding on as Ben leaned sideways and grasped hold of her under her breasts. He lifted her as though she weighed nothing and plopped her in front of him. Carmen moved her right leg over Spirit's neck and straddled the horse.

"Ben, we are so high! And no pommel or horn to hold on to. How will *you* stay on?"

He leaned to the left again and grabbed Lacey's reins, handing them to Carmen. "Hold these." He wrapped his left arm tight around her middle. "Did you not watch the video? I rode Spirit this way and did not even hang on while I used bow and arrow to kill a buffalo. When will you learn to trust me?"

"I—" Carmen clung to Lacey's reins with her left hand and grasped Ben's solid forearm with her right. "I'm sorry, but we are sitting so high!" she repeated.

"Carmen, take your sunglasses from that side pocket on Zeke's jeans and put them on."

Carmen let go of his arm and obeyed while Ben slipped on his own sunglasses. She grasped his arm again, holding on tight.

"You do not need to cling so tight," Ben told her. "I am not going to let go of you. By the way, this first time we will ride only about half a day." He reached around her and took hold of Spirit's reins. "You would be surprised how fast that beautiful butt of yours will get sore, but Sammy's place is just a half mile or so into the Badlands. You tell me right away if bouncing around on this horse bothers you. I do not want you to get a headache over it. I understand how old wounds can rise up to remind you they are still there."

"Speaking of old wounds, what about your back? You got quite a workout last night, Mr. Colter."

Ben laughed and hugged her closer. "Believe me, if my back flared up last night, I would not have noticed. The pleasure I was involved in would mask the pain." Ben lightly kicked Spirit's sides. "*Fiyah!*" he said softly.

Carmen jumped a little when the horse shook his mane and started walking.

"To be honest, I am full of Tylenol right now," Ben added. "But I love riding. Connecting with nature always makes me feel better." He led Spirit into grassland, heading into the opposite direction from the normal riding trail.

After close to an hour of riding, Carmen managed to relax against Ben's chest. The awesome grandeur of the Badlands came ever closer, and Carmen felt as though a mysterious Being beckoned her to enter the endless maze of spires and shadows and hidden crevasses.

Ben halted Spirit and waved his arm across the expanse of grassland and wild country. "All of this, from the endless plains south to the bigger mountains in the west and all the way north of the Badlands to Canada, once was ours," he told her. "Our hunting grounds. From Illinois through Minnesota, North Dakota, Montana, and south through Wyoming and Colorado, Nebraska, Kansas ... we roamed and ruled all of that land, moved with the buffalo and the seasons, conquered our enemies, hunted all kinds of game. And now we are confined to just parts of South Dakota. What land that is afforded us is held in trust by the government, but at least it cannot be sold without our permission. But to sell the Black Hills would be like selling our hearts and having them removed from our bodies. We would die."

A gentle breeze swished through the tall grass, and Lacey nickered and shook her mane.

"Tell me about Jerry," Ben asked Carmen. "If he got well and wanted you back, would you go?"

Carmen squeezed his forearm. "Never. It's far too late, and the memories are too ugly. I would never risk going through all that again."

Ben leaned around her and kissed her cheek. "I just want you to be sure. If you want out of this relationship, tell me soon, because I already love you beyond measure. You and you alone are my only addiction."

"I have no thoughts about leaving, Ben. I've never been

in love in the way I love you, and I will always be here for you. I want to learn everything about your life here—the language, the ceremonies. Everything."

"Then for now I will tell you there are seven Lakota rites. *Inipi*, which is the rite of purification. *Hanblecheyapi* is crying for a vision. *Wiwanyang Wachipi* is the sun dance. *Hunkalowanpi* is the making of relatives. *Isnathi Awichalowanpi* is a girl's coming of age. Both Sasha and Talia took part in that one. *Wanagi Yuhapi* is the keeping of the soul, and *Thapa Wankayeyapi* is the throwing of the ball. That one sounds strange, but I will explain each one another time. And I will explain the origin of the Lakota sacred pipe. I should also tell you there are more dialects than just Lakota, and several different tribes among the Sioux Nation."

A hawk floated overhead, and other than the whispering wind, everything was dead quiet, as though they had ridden into a whole new world totally unrelated to daily life.

"What is that ahead of us?" Carmen asked. "It looks like cattle, but they are bigger. Are those buffalo?"

"Yes, ma'am." Ben kicked Spirit into motion. "Let's get up close and personal."

"Ben! They might charge at us!"

Ben laughed. "They are more docile than you think, as long as you do not yell or deliberately goad them." He urged Spirit into a faster lope.

"You're going too fast!"

"You are fine. I will not let you fall." He spoke louder to be heard above Spirit's heavy breathing and the air that rushed past their ears. "Hang on!" He broke Spirit into a gentle run.

"Don't forget how much I love and trust you," Carmen yelled.

Ben let out a war whoop and whistled and yipped as though he was part of a war party, leaning in and keeping Carmen tight against himself.

Carmen screamed as they rode hard toward the grazing buffalo. "Ben, we are going to die!" she declared at the end of her scream.

Ben laughed and rode harder. "Enjoy it," he told her.

Carmen let the wind hit her face and breathed deeply at the scent of grass and horse and wildflowers. Ben finally slowed Spirit to a trot, then a walk, as he led the horse right up beside a huge bull buffalo.

"Ben, he's as tall as Spirit is! And my foot touched his side! You're going to make him mad."

Ben reached out and touched the thick, curly hair at the crown of the buffalo's head. *"Tahtonkah, Tahtayshne,"* he said softly.

The buffalo gave out a deep snort and shook its shaggy hump. Carmen drew up her leg. "Oh my God!" she said in a near whisper.

"Touch him," Ben told her. "It is okay. One day you will think of this moment and understand why these animals were once our lifeblood. You will be even closer to the heart of the Lakota, for *Tahtonkah* is truly our blood and lungs and heart. One day I will explain how our People used every single part of the buffalo for food, shelter, weapons, utensils, clothing, even medicine."

With a shaking hand, Carmen reached out and touched the animal, which simply kept ambling along beside Spirit. Ben finally slowed Spirit and let the buffalo walk away. A flock of birds flew in and perched on the backs of several bison.

"Why do they let those birds ride on their backs?"

"Those are starlings," Ben told her. "Some call them

cowbirds. They eat the seeds and bugs that the buffalo stirs up as he grazes. That keeps parasites out of the animal's fur, relieving them of bites and itching, as well as helping prevent diseases among the bison. The birds also pick bugs off cattle and deer. Mother Earth has a way of letting nature keep her and her creatures clean and organized. Every breed of animal has a purpose." He fell silent for a moment.

"Listen!"

Carmen strained to hear something. After a few seconds she did hear it. A wolf's howl.

"That is Caesar," Ben told her. "The wind is out of the north today. That is why we can hear him. He knows you are near!"

"Ben, that can't be possible. Because of the wind, Caesar can't possibly catch my scent. It's blowing in the wrong direction."

"He does not need to smell you. It is his spirit that knows you are near, just like the wolf spirit told him to sit and point you out to me at that show in Michigan."

"You're making that up."

"You know better. I never lie or joke about something that spiritual. I carry the wolf spirit in me. I would never mock it. Caesar knows you are coming, yet he is at least a half mile away. I told you this would happen. It is why I brought you out here, to show you I am right about you being chosen by the wolf spirit."

Carmen felt chills move through her in spite of the warmth of the day. The bull buffalo that had walked beside them meandered away as the whole herd moved westward. A few strays stayed behind, quietly grazing. "Do you know how crazy this all seems to me?" Carmen commented. "What is this Michigan girl doing out here in Lakota country on a horse and riding among a herd of buffalo?"

"The wolf spirit brought you here, and now you have proof. Look what is coming."

Carmen studied the horizon. Something bigger than an average large dog was moving toward them through the tall grass. "Is that what I think it is?"

Ben smiled. "Yes. It is Caesar."

Ben dismounted, then reached up for Carmen. "Get down. The wolf will make the horses restless. He is a natural predator, so they might bolt. They will settle down when they realize Caesar means them no harm."

Carmen leaned over and let Ben lift her down from Spirit. "I thought their trainer kept the wolves in a special fenced area."

"He does, in a specially built, very strong kennel, because wolves can chew their way out of a chain link fence. I told Sammy that, if Caesar started howling today, he should let him out because it would mean we are close. I wanted to see if he would really find us." Ben grabbed Spirit's reins, then took hold of Lacey's. "We need to be careful around the horses until they get used to the presence of a wolf. Get on your knees now. I will lead the horses a little bit away from you."

"Why my knees?"

"You will see. Trust me."

The few remaining buffalo suddenly took off at a run, heading west. Both horses whinnied and shuffled restlessly. Carmen, too, felt like running. It was unnerving to watch a wolf heading straight for them.

CHAPTER TWENTY-FOUR

LACEY WHINNIED AGAIN and started to rear up, but Ben hung on to her and said something to her in his own language. At the same time, Spirit snorted and shook his mane again.

"*Haynahkinktay.*" Ben said the word firmly but calmly. Whatever it meant, the horses stayed calm. "Put your head down for a minute," Ben told her. "Let Caesar realize your scent. He is happy to find you again."

Carmen covered her face with her hands and bent over. "You had better be right," she told Ben.

"If I was not sure, I would already have shot Caesar to protect you."

In the next moment Carmen felt Caesar sniffing all around her, nosing at her hair, whining the way dogs whined when they were happy. She parted her hands slightly and the wolf licked at her face. "Oh my God!" she exclaimed.

"Go ahead and pet him," Ben told her.

"I can't! Not without you beside me."

Ben let go of the horses, and they both ran off. He knelt beside Carmen and reached out to Caesar. The wolf licked his face, and they began playing like man and dog, rolling in the grass, Ben brushing his fingers into Caesar's thick hair and talking to the wolf in the Lakota tongue while Caesar kept whining and licking at him. Ben moved to sit behind Carmen then and pulled her between his legs to let Caesar sniff and lick at both of them until Carmen felt easier with Caesar and freely petted the animal.

"I can't believe I am doing this," she told Ben.

Ben reached around her and moved on top of her, laying her back and covering her with deep kisses. They laughed when Caesar stuck his nose between their faces. "Come on," Ben said, helping Carmen to her feet. "We will ride to Sammy's place and make sure Caesar is put back where he belongs."

Caesar jumped up and put his paws on Carmen's shoulders. She closed her eyes and pressed her lips together as Caesar licked her face again and knocked off her sunglasses. "Ben, this wolf is so intimidating. He's *huge!*"

"Down, Caesar!" Ben ordered. He ran his hands into the wolf's coat and let Caesar put his paws on his own shoulders. Ben grinned and hugged the wolf. "We are now part of Caesar's wolf pack," he told Carmen.

"I think I prefer belonging to the *human* pack," Carmen answered.

Ben said something to Caesar in the Lakota tongue, and the animal ran several feet away and sat down. "I will get you a towel from Lacey," Ben told Carmen, walking over and wiping at her face with his hand.

"Wolf spit!" Carmen said, shaking her hair. "Do you know how scary that was? That wolf could open his mouth and swallow my whole head." She grabbed Ben around the middle.

He gave her a reassuring hug. "Carmen, Caesar will never hurt you, okay? He just proved it. He still gets overly aggressive at times with humans, but only because he wants to play with them like another wolf. Sammy is doing a good job of teaching him he cannot do that."

"Well, tell Sammy he has a lot more work to do."

"But Caesar did not hurt you, right?"

"No."

"And when you learn the right commands in the Lakota tongue, you will be able to control him just as I did a moment ago." He turned with her to look at the wolf. "See? He is just sitting there waiting for us. A moment ago, he was simply happy to see you again. He had no intentions of hurting you. And without Caesar, whose same spirit lives in me, we would not have found each other." He leaned down and kissed her softly.

"And right now, I see a strange wildness in your eyes that makes me think you are going to start howling right along with the wolves," Carmen told him.

He broke into the mesmerizing smile she loved. "I would like to howl about how much I love you and how last night filled my heart with new joy." He kissed her again. "I only want you to learn to be more free-spirited, Carmen."

He kept an arm around her as he whistled to Spirit. The horse came running but stepped sideways at the sight of Caesar. "Calm down, boy," Ben soothed. He lifted Carmen onto Spirit with ease, then leaped up behind her and hung on when Spirit whinnied and stepped sideways again. He kicked the horse into motion and trotted Spirit over to where Lacey had stopped to graze. He grabbed her reins before the supply horse could bolt, then handed the reins to Carmen as they headed toward the Badlands. Caesar walked and ran beside them the way a plain, happy dog would do. "How are you doing?" Ben asked her. "No headache?"

"No."

Ben urged the horses into the wild maze of rocks. They were instantly surrounded by rugged granite and multicolored clay mounds. They rode in and out of shadows created by oddly shaped spires that loomed hauntingly overhead. In a matter of minutes, Carmen felt completely lost in a wilderness of cliffs and caves and shadows called the Badlands.. A cool darkness enveloped them as they rode deeper into a narrow canyon, leaving the open grassland and the buffalo behind them.

Carmen shivered closer to Ben. Another hawk flew overhead, screeching loudly, and a few small rocks scattered and danced down into their pathway from above. They both looked up to see a bighorn sheep standing high on the side of a gray spire, the sure-footed animal looking as though it were standing on air. The rocks startled Spirit, and the horse reared slightly. Ben hung on tight to Carmen and spoke softly to Spirit in words she did not understand.

"How close are we to Sammy's?" she asked.

"It is just beyond this canyon," Ben told her.

Carmen clung to his arm. "Ben, I feel danger."

"Why? I know this place well. There is nothing to fear here."

"It isn't this particular place. It's just ... I can't help feeling like the answer to who shot you, and maybe Linda Two Fists also, somehow lies right here in the Badlands. Every time I look out at this mysterious land from your back door, I feel like something here is trying to speak to me. And now here we are. All I can think of is that we are in the belly of the beast."

Ben pressed her close. "Maybe the answers *are* here. I have told you there is a reason Caesar stopped beside you that night at the casino. Trust your instincts, Carmen. Let the spirit of the wolf guide you and do not be afraid of where it will lead. That is what you need to learn, to release your own feelings and your own inner spirit and let *that* guide you ... not fear." He led the horses around one last bend and left the canyon behind. "Look. The shadows are gone, and the land is wide open again."

Carmen drank in the sight of a glorious green valley that glowed in the morning sun. Several wooden buildings and corrals were sprawled against green and yellow grass, and the layered colors of the Badlands's rocky spires surrounded the entire area. "Oh, Ben, it's beautiful!"

The air came alive then with the sound of howling wolves.

"That is Sammy's ranch down there," Ben told her. "The other wolves are howling to help Caesar find his way back. He is a father now. When I called Sammy about coming here, he told me that one of the females had pups a few days ago. Maybe going down there and seeing those pups will soothe your troubled spirit."

"I'm sorry I act so spooked by this place. I think it's the name. Badlands." Caesar ran ahead of them as Ben and Carmen rode up to Sammy's lovely but very plain and small wood and stone home. Sammy and a stocky young Lakota woman came out onto the porch to greet them as Ben helped Carmen down from Spirit.

"Ah, the beautiful woman from Michigan!" Sammy

exclaimed, putting out a gnarled hand. "The one Caesar chose for Ben." He laughed as he shook Carmen's hand. Carmen thought he looked old enough to be the young woman's father, but he introduced her as Many Blankets, "wife number three." His dark eyes glittered with genuine friendliness, and when he spoke, his hesitant English revealed a man who would much prefer using his Native tongue.

Many Blankets wore a fringed tunic and looked as though she'd just stepped out of a tepee. She smiled at Carmen and looked her over admiringly but said little as Ben and Sammy visited for nearly an hour. They ate Sasha's peanut butter and jelly sandwiches, and Carmen washed hers down with strong coffee Many Blankets had made. Dessert was frybread coated with cinnamon and sugar. Carmen took all kinds of pictures of everyone there and of the wolf pups. She ached to hold them, but the mother would have nothing to do with it. Ben took a picture of Carmen kneeling beside Caesar with her arm around him.

"Val will never believe this!" she told Ben.

"You and Caesar are one in spirit now," Ben answered. He explained to Sammy about Caesar jumping up on Carmen.

"He needs a little more work," Sammy answered. "He is still a little *wahtohgahlah,* right?" he said with a grin. "Soon he will be *wahwahtaychah.* I will make sure."

"Good," Ben answered whatever it was Sammy had told him. "Someday I want him to live with me and Carmen."

Live with us? Carmen decided not to say anything about that ... yet. They all said their goodbyes, and Carmen was surprised that she actually hated leaving Caesar behind.

But still ... *live* with them?

Ben headed back into the canyon. The sound of horses' hooves echoed against the canyon walls, and an eagle screeched overhead. They both watched above for more big horn sheep that might stir up rocks when a sudden rush of frigid air swept past them. It was so quick and so much colder than one would feel on a muggy day like today that it startled Carmen. She sat up straighter and looked around, sure she'd heard a woman's whisper in the draft that blew her hat off.

Ben halted Spirit and told Carmen to hang on to the reins while he jumped down and retrieved her hat. He climbed back on Spirit in one swift movement and put the hat back on Carmen's head.

"What was that rush of air?" she asked Ben.

Ben kicked Spirit into motion again and did not answer right away. He held Carmen closer when he finally spoke. "Nothing but the wind," he told her.

Carmen sensed that he felt something much deeper than that.

"Strange drafts often rush through these canyons," Ben added. "That's just how it is in the Badlands. This land holds many secrets from the past."

Like who killed Linda Two Fists? Carmen did not voice the words. How often would he keep certain things from her because he felt they could be shared only with blooded Lakota?

Ben kicked Spirit into a lope, and they emerged onto the plains grass through which they had ridden to get here. The buffalo were gone, and the sun was moving into early afternoon. Ben remained strangely silent as they headed for the stables. Several cars were there now. Tourists. A man Carmen figured must work for Henry was walking along a string of saddled horses and adjusting the stirrups for the riders.

"Look, Mommy!" a young girl yelled to the woman behind her. The girl was pointing at Ben. "Is he a real Indian?"

Ben said nothing as they rode past the girl. "Get down," he told Carmen when they reached the front of the line of horses.

Carmen obeyed, clinging to Ben's hands until her feet touched the ground.

"Hand Lacey over to Henry's hired hand over there," Ben told her. "When I start riding right toward you, step out a little."

"Why?"

Ben grinned. "You will see." He kicked Spirit into a much harder run than anything he'd done when Carmen was on the horse with him. He whooped and yipped and screamed war cries as he guided Spirit into twists and turns and shouted words in the Lakota tongue as though he was riding into war. He rode up and down the string of horses, giving out more war cries and performing some trick riding while the tourists watched.

Carmen heard someone behind her chuckle, and she turned to see an older Lakota man standing there.

"I am Henry Whitefeather," he told her. "You must be the woman from Michigan."

"Yes," Carmen answered. She was beginning to wonder if every person on every reservation in South Dakota now spoke of her as "the woman from Michigan."

"I am glad to meet you," Henry told her. "I see Ben is showing off for the tourists." He took Lacey's reins from her. "I heard the little girl ask if Ben was a real Indian. That upsets him. It is not just the use of the word *Indian*, which is a wrong description, but some people think there are no Natives of original blood left in this country. Ben is showing them that we are alive and well."

Henry let out his own war whoop and raised his fist. "Your man is a leader," he told Carmen. "He would have been a great warrior in the old days. His name would be in history books."

"I am Lakota!" Ben shouted, as he continued galloping past the tourists. "The blood of Crazy Horse! My ancestors dance beneath you! One day they will dance on your graves!" He gave out another war cry, then headed for Carmen.

"Now Ben will grab you up like a captive," Henry told her.

"You're kidding!" Carmen said.

"Just relax. He knows what he is doing."

Carmen grimaced and closed her eyes, sure that the oncoming Spirit would run her down. In an instant, a strong arm grabbed her under the arms and flung her onto the horse in front of him. Carmen screamed through the whole thing, then broke into laughter as Ben held her close.

"You brat!" she yelled at him.

Ben trotted Spirit past the tourists.

"Is she okay?" the little girl's mother asked.

"You could have hurt that woman!" a man yelled.

"He would never hurt me!" Carmen yelled amid laughter. She leaned her head back and tilted it so she and Ben could kiss in front of the tourists, some of whom laughed with them and some who just stared in bewilderment.

"That was a great show!" someone yelled. "So, you really *are* Lakota."

Ben yelled a few words in the Lakota tongue.

"Did you just cuss them out?" Carmen asked, laughing against his shoulder.

"They will never know," Ben answered. "What else do I have to do to prove I am a Native American? *Scalp* them?" He rode past them once more, yelling, "The Black Hills are not for sale!" He headed for the stables then, he and Carmen both laughing.

"I do not usually do things like that, I swear," Ben said. "It just gets tiresome knowing a lot of people hardly know we exist, until, of course, they want something that is ours. I am sorry for my behavior. Are you okay?"

"I'm fine. And I loved watching you in action. I am now officially your captive."

Ben grinned and gave her another kiss. "Actually, *I* am *your* captive." He rode into the stables and jumped down from Spirit, then lifted Carmen down. A young man who worked at the stables asked Ben if he could brush down the horses for him.

"You bet," Ben answered. He took ten dollars from his gear and handed it to the boy. "Peter, this woman with me is Carmen. She soon will be living here permanently, I hope."

Peter grinned and nodded eagerly. "Everybody knows that, Ben. They talk about how pretty she is."

Ben began unloading supplies from Lacey. "Peter, you will be at the Pow-Wow next month, right?"

"Yes! I will be with the junior dancers. What will you do this year?"

"I will be announcing the Grand Entrance," Ben told him. He handed a few things to Carmen and gave her a quick kiss.

Carmen sensed something was not quite right. It started after the rush of wind back in the canyon. They carried everything to the truck and loaded it into the back seat. Ben grabbed another bottle of water from the cooler and got inside, waving to Peter as he pulled out and headed home.

He suddenly became quiet. He reached over and took her hand. "We will shower and change when we get to the house," he told her. "I still need to make my protein drink, and we should have time to eat some real food, with time left over to go see if the kids are rehearsing this afternoon. We need to practice a group dance for the Pow-Wow."

Carmen watched the vast expanse of buttes and spires and deep, secret gorges of the Badlands grow smaller as they drove away from them, and she could not help wondering about that cold rush of wind ... and the fact that it seemed to whisper to them.

"Ben?"

"What is it?"

"What happened back there in the canyon?"

Ben remained silent.

"Don't leave me out," Carmen told him. "If this is going to work, I need to understand these things. You told me a while ago to share everything I think and feel with you. You need to do the same for *me,* not just with Tommy. I'm trying to learn, so help me. I damn well felt something in that wind, and these things run a lot deeper in you, so tell me what that was about."

His fists tightened on the steering wheel.

"Not yet," he answered.

The statement seemed more of a command than a request. They said little else on the way home. Ben got out of the truck and walked around to Carmen's side before she could even climb out. He lifted her down.

"Leave our things in the truck for now," he told her. He walked her to the door, stopping just long enough to unlock it. He closed the door, locked it again, then threw his keys on a nearby small table. He lifted Carmen into his arms and carried her into his bathroom. He turned on the shower, then removed his buckskin shirt and took the feather and beaded decorations from his hair.

Carmen stood there in wonder and anticipation as he grasped her T-shirt from the bottom and pulled it up and off her. She watched his dark eyes as he ran his fingers under the straps of her stretchy sports bra and slid it down over her shoulders, over her waist, her hips.

"I want to make love to you," he told her, "to be inside you. To give you pleasure. I need to know that you are here to stay, that I can love and be loved again."

"Ben, I'm not going to leave you. I *love* you."

He put fingers to her lips. "Let me do this." He unbuckled her belt and let her too-big jeans fall to the floor. He pulled down her bikini panties, kissed the patch of hair between her legs, then picked her up in his arms and set her in the shower. He removed his buckskin pants, his moccasins, his briefs, then stepped into the shower with her.

"There is something I must do, but first I want to be sure this is forever."

"It *is*, Ben. How many ways can I tell you? Show you?"

"I need to make the past go away and remind myself there is only you now. My Carmen. Our future."

The water poured over them. It was almost like a cleansing of the past, of her nightmares over her awful abuse, of Ben's trauma over the shooting and the loss of his beloved wife and son. They lathered each other as they let the water pour over their hair and their faces. Ben put liquid soap on his hands and washed Carmen in places that now belonged only to him, working his fingers inside her to Carmen's shuddering climax. Carmen soaped up her own hands and gently washed that part of him she hoped would one day create life in her belly so she could give him a son to replace the one he lost.

They finished showering and toweled off with clean towels Rosa had left earlier in the day. Ben carried her to his bed, ripping back the covers and laying her down. He moved on top of her and devoured her mouth hungrily as she opened herself to him, her juices still slick from her climax. Carmen reached down and stroked his penis until it was hard and hot. Ben grasped her bottom, massaging it enticingly while he thrust himself deeply inside her in an almost desperate need to prove something to her. *Or maybe to himself,* Carmen wondered.

This was crazy. This was wonderful. This was wrong but so right. Carmen did not understand this sudden change in Ben, this burning need to prove to himself she was here to stay. She kissed his broad chest, ran her slender hands over his powerful arms. He pushed into her rhythmically, desperately, as though he had a great need to end all his heartache. And he was the answer to all her fears and disappointments over another man, one who had hurt her deeply, both physically and mentally. She trusted Ben, and trust was something she'd lost along the way ... in another life.

"You are my holy woman, the savior of my heart," Ben told her. "And I will be your protector, the man who creates life in your womb." His ejaculation seemed to suggest a forceful determination to make good on his words. Afterward, he traveled kisses down her body, from her neck to her breasts, her belly, between her legs, on down to her thighs and calves and finally her toes, then kissed his way back to her mouth while he again made love to her, using a hard rhythm, as though to the beat of a drum. He was her warrior, a man so strong in body but a man who needed her for a different kind of strength. Once his life spilled into her, he lay still a moment., then rolled to his side. To Carmen's surprise, tears welled in his eyes. "Talia spoke to me in the canyon," he told her.

So, that's what this is about. Carmen remained calm. "Can you tell me what she said?"

Ben sighed and swallowed, obviously struggling to find his voice and not break down. "She wants me to send our baby boy to her. But he is ..." Ben hesitated, swallowing back tears. "All I have left of Singing Boy is a lock of his hair, tied into a little medicine bag. It is under the pillow in his crib in the nursery. As long as I have that lock of hair, it is like he is still with me. I have never been able to let go of it, but it is not right to keep Singing Boy's spirit hanging between Heaven and Earth. He needs his mother, but when I send him away, he will be gone from me forever. I will have nothing left."

Carmen kissed his chest and wiped at his tears with her fingers. "*I* will be left, Ben, and I am ready to give you more children. You won't be alone. I, too, heard something in that rush of air. Just because I am not Lakota doesn't mean I don't believe there are spirits out there, angels protecting us, loved ones reaching out to us. Talia is telling you that your son needs to be with his mother. Until you send him to her, you will not be able to truly let go of what happened, and that will make you weak. Your strength is in letting go, Ben, not in keeping everything inside.

Carmen felt his agony. She could see him lying in the hospital full of wires and tubes and unable to move, knowing his baby son was dead and he could not even share his sorrow with his wife. To be in so much pain and so alone made her ache for him.

"I did not think I could love another woman," Ben told

her brokenly. "But here you are, so beautiful, so understanding, so generous and kind."

I am here. No one can harm you. This time Carmen felt as though *she* was the one who should say the words. But the fact remained that someone *did* still want to harm Ben, and if that person tried again, she would have no way of stopping them. How would she go on without this man in her life?

CHAPTER TWENTY-FIVE

"Hey, girl, have you forgotten your best friend?" Val said as soon as Carmen answered her phone. "You left six weeks ago and haven't called me since we talked after you and the warrior did the dance—all night long, as I remember. What's happened to you since then?"

"*Ben Colter* happened to me." Carmen said, putting her phone on speaker and leaning back in her office chair. "And we have been incredibly busy. You would not believe all the things Ben is involved in. He is a human dynamo. I'm sorry I haven't called, but I have called my dad several times, and I think about you and Sid every day."

"Did you get that big box of clothes I sent?"

"Yes! Thanks so much. I really needed those, but I've been able to buy everything else I need right here. And you will be happy to know that Ben and I are coming to Michigan in September after the big Pow-Wow here at Sunrise. Sasha said it's okay for us to bring Matthew there for his first semester at Hope College. She knows I really want to come back to Michigan."

"Oh, I'm so glad, because I don't think Sid's schedule

will allow for us to come to that Pow-Wow. By the way, he told me to ask about your health. Any more headaches?"

"Just one more so far. I think I overdid a morning run in high humidity. Ben and I run together every morning now on a quarter-mile track at the school. He lifts weights at home first. There are showers at the school, so we run when we first get here and then shower before we come to the office."

"You shower with that beautiful man?"

"Not at the school!" Carmen laughed. "But as far as home, I'll let you use your imagination."

"Oh Lord, you are killing me. But how is all that going, *really*? Is the warrior still the great guy you figured him to be?"

"Better. We've done a lot of talking, and we both try to be understanding of each other's needs and differences. I've gone with Ben to a couple of court hearings in Pierre and Rapid City, although he hates going there because of bad memories. Honestly, though, I have never seen anyone argue a case better than Ben can. He really is as smart as they say. And by the way, there are some great high-end stores in Denver, and wonderful restaurants. We took a couple of days off and went to a bed and breakfast there. You would love Denver and the scenery out here."

Carmen glanced toward Ben's office. The door was closed, and he was talking with two of his legal assistants. She loved how he looked in his plain white collared shirts. He wore his hair drawn back on the sides today, held with two silver combs.

"Girl, it sounds like you are really adjusting to everything out there."

"I am," Carmen answered. "And Sasha has become a

good friend. She is so accepting of the fact that so much of this is still new to me. I have my own office here at Sunrise headquarters now so I can be sure there are no problems with the government or the IRS. I've been researching South Dakota's tax laws and federal laws for reservation and Native American fund reporting. This whole youth group thing is bigger and more complicated than you would think. Ben's best friend, other than Tommy, of course, oversees the funds, but he doesn't have his CPA license yet. I've convinced Ben it wouldn't hurt for an outsider to audit all of it, just to be safe."

"What does Ben's friend think of that?"

"His name is Billy Big Bull. He seems to be okay with it, but I think he's a little resentful. I've been careful to include him and make sure he realizes this doesn't change anything as far as his job. I don't want him to think Ben doesn't trust him, because that is not the problem. Billy and Ben have been best friends since childhood, so I'm kind of between a rock and a hard place. I don't want to get between them. I have assured Billy that the audit is strictly a third-person look to insure Ben doesn't have any problems with government funding."

"You be careful about stepping on toes," Val told Carmen. "That's a whole different culture out there."

"I know. But I think Billy understands that having an office here is for my own tax and accounting business. I won't be working for Sunrise."

"Sounds like a plan, but that still leaves you out there and me here in Michigan."

"I know. And you are welcome to come out here on your own sometimes if Sid is too busy. I would love for you to see Ben's home and to show you around the school and the theater. And in the meantime, I'm sending you some pictures. Ben and I visited a professional photographer in Denver. The pictures turned out gorgeous!"

"How could they *not* turn out great? I can't wait to see what you send me."

"I've also met Ben's grandmother at the Rosebud Reservation. Her name is Wilma Breadmaker, and she lives in an old house trailer. She likes the familiarity of her old place and even has a tepee in her backyard. She treated me like something to be adored and is so glad that Ben is in love again. On our way back from Rosebud, we visited the Wounded Knee memorial. I'm learning so much, even some of the language. In Lakota, you are *koo-lah*. Friend."

"What about Caesar? Have you seen him since that first time Ben took you there?"

"Yes, but we have to ride through the Badlands to get to the ranch where the wolves are kept. Honestly, Val, there is something ominous and spooky about the Badlands. They give me the shivers, especially this one canyon we ride through. We went again just a few days ago, and believe it or not, I rode my own horse."

"I *don't* believe it."

Both women laughed. "Well, Ben is a good teacher and determined to turn me into an experienced rider, but I'm still scared of the dang horses and afraid to go very fast. Ben says my poor horse doesn't know whether to stop or go, because while I'm kicking her sides, I'm pulling too tight on the reins because I am so tense. But you should see *Ben* on a horse. I swear, he's like the horse whisperer or something."

"That man can whisper in *my* ear any time he wants."

"I'll tell him that. One thing I've learned is that the Lakota have a very subtle sense of humor. Sasha is always finding ways to embarrass Ben. He is a lot shyer and humbler than you'd think a man like him would be. I love him for that. But hey, how are you and Sid doing?"

"Oh, things are about the same. We're fine and happy, and still hot for each other."

Carmen snickered. "Maybe all four of us could spend a couple of nights at the lake house when Ben and I come to Michigan. I'm going to keep it as a vacation getaway for me and Ben."

"Good idea! I can't wait!"

"Is Dad doing as well as he claims when I ask him?"

"He's doing great. Your aunt moving in was a real blessing. But they both miss you. We check on them often, and they both expect a big wedding soon. What's the prospect?"

"The prospect is excellent," Carmen answered, smiling. She watched two men walk into Ben's office. She kept her eye on them as she continued with Val. "For now, we are waiting until after the Pow-Wow to make real plans. Ben expects a good five hundred people to come from all over the country to the Pow-Wow. And the night before opening day, he is planning a performance at the theater. He thinks it will be good practice for the youth group's appearance in Omaha in November."

"Sounds like things are really busy out there."

"That's why I've been working on getting Ben to give up some of his projects so he can concentrate on those that were the most important to Talia. He has finally formed a few committees to take on some of the others."

"And you are probably becoming just as involved as Ben is."

"I am. Ben has a way of pulling you right into his life without even trying."

"Well, *that* I can understand. You just make sure to take care of your *own* health."

"Now you sound like Sid."

"Sid is just concerned for you because we love you, *koo-lah*."

"Has Sid learned anything more about a doctor who might be able to help Ben's back problem?"

"I'm sorry, but it doesn't look hopeful," Val told her with a sigh. "When they read the whole case, every one of them says they can't believe Ben lived at all. His current health is amazing, but none of them is willing to risk more surgery."

"Well, he takes really good care of himself," Carmen told her. "But I feel so sorry for him when his back flares up. Otherwise, he's in great shape."

"Oh, he's in great shape, all right! I'll bet those injuries don't interfere with all the dancing you two have been doing."

Carmen laughed. "You aren't going to get details out of me, Val Ruben. All I can say is, it's as good as you are imagining it is."

"You don't even want to know what I am imagining."

"I do know, because I know *you*."

Both women laughed, and Carmen glanced toward Ben's office again. The legal assistants had left, and the two men who'd come visiting were talking to Ben with the door closed. Ben raised his arm and signaled her to join him.

"Hey, Val, I have a lot to do, and it looks like Ben needs me for something. He just motioned for me to come into his office. Say hi to Sid for me."

"I will."

"Thank you for everything you've done for me so far—the clothes and checking on Dad and all. I really, really miss you and Sid."

Carmen ended the call and kept her phone in her hand as she hurried over to Ben's office. She noticed several in the outer office were glancing that way, wondering who the two men were. FBI? BIA? AIM? Ben either belonged to or was visited by so many diverse groups, she could hardly keep track, let alone conferences with attorneys from those entities, with whom he often ended up in court either fighting or defending. She went inside and closed the door, and the two men stood for her. Ben also rose.

"Carmen, this is Hal Bennett," he told her as she moved to stand next to Ben's chair. Hal nodded. "And Stuart Greenley." Greenley also nodded. "Gentlemen, this is Carmen Wolfe, soon to be Carmen Colter, hopefully," Ben told them. "And since it looks like she will be my wife sooner than later, I think it is only fair that she is a part of this."

Carmen frowned at Ben. "A part of what?"

"Bring that extra office chair over here beside me," Ben told her as he and the other two men sat down.

"Your wife-to-be is beautiful," Stuart told Ben.

"To say the least," Ben answered as Carmen sat down. She smiled bashfully, suddenly self-conscious of the frayed denim shorts she'd worn today with a white, spaghetti-strap tee. "Thank you," she told the two strangers.

Ben reached over and grasped her hand, squeezing it reassuringly. "This woman is more than beautiful in looks. She is quality, in all kinds of ways, and she's smart when it comes to money. She's a CPA and has her own business. She helps me with bookkeeping, the one thing I hate and am no good at. The fact remains that my future is *her* future, so I want her opinion."

"Okay, is someone going to tell me what's going on?" Carmen asked.

Ben squeezed her hand. "These men are from a talent agency." He rubbed the back of her hand with his thumb.

"One of the biggest in the country," he added. "They have just offered me a recording contract, but it includes a huge publicity campaign, which means touring the country and performing live, sometimes four to five different cities each week."

Carmen blinked with surprise. She faced Ben. "You told me once you wouldn't do something like that."

"And I meant it, but when we make things legal between us, this could affect your income in future years, even if I die."

"If you die, I won't give a damn."

Ben smiled affectionately. "Carmen, I just think it is only fair that you be a part of this." He squeezed her hand again. "The offer is five million, with royalties that could keep coming in for years."

Carmen arched her eyebrows, then couldn't help coughing. She remained speechless for a moment. "Five *million?*" she repeated to Ben when she found her voice.

"Five million," he answered, smiling. "You aren't going to choke to death, are you?"

Everyone in the room chuckled.

"No, but I'm just ... I mean, talent-wise, you deserve that much and more. But I'm worried that expanding your career in a public way might not be all that good for you." She kept hold of Ben's hand as she turned to the two talent scouts. "We are talking about Ben constantly on the road for at least a year, right?? People herding him around and forcing him into things he might not even want to do? Making him pretend to be something he isn't? Ben doesn't have a fake bone in his body. He just ... I can't see him living in the world of lies and gossip and people fawning over him just because he's rich and famous."

Stuart frowned. "We think Ben is strong enough to

stand up to such things. Miss Wolfe, we have been quietly watching Ben at his performances. In fact, we were at the one in Grand Rapids, where you two met because of that wolf mishap."

"Really?"

"Yes," Hal added. "We have been to several other performances, listened to Ben's CDs, watched his videos, watched the youth group and the School for the Arts grow. We even know about the shooting and the opioids. That really disappointed us, but we waited it out, and we have to say, Ben's comeback has been nothing short of a miracle, a story that would draw public sympathy and interest, making him even *more* popular. And when Ben is on that stage, he absolutely owns the audience. I mean, *look* at him."

"Oh, I've looked," Carmen answered.

They two scouts laughed, but Ben just rubbed his eyes as he shook his head. "Looks don't mean jack," he said.

"Ben gets embarrassed when people talk about his looks," Carmen told Hal and Stuart.

"He shouldn't," Hal answered. "And in the world of entertainment, looks are everything. Ben, whether it embarrasses you or not, you have it all : the build, the tall, dark and handsome aura, the great smile, a bit of mystery behind your eyes. Women salivate over you, and the fact remains that you could be the next really big star. I've never come across an entertainer who can sing in so many genres and pitches, and the way you mix modern music with Native American drumming and song is just ... I can't even find a word for it. We would have to find a whole new lead line for what you do."

"And we all know that an entertainer won't survive just on looks," Stuart said. "The really big ones have to have real talent, and you do. Plus, you are smart as hell. No recording company or talent agent is going to screw you with a contract. Contracts and treaties are one thing you know better than anyone."

"Most new talent needs coaching and training and to be taught self-confidence," Hal added. "You don't need any of that. Hell, you train *others*. Those kids in the youth group are way ahead of most kids when it comes to belting out songs and showing confidence."

"They are having fun up there," Ben answered. "That is half the battle."

"Well, whatever the secret, you are good at it," Hal said with a smile. "We keep an eye on them, too, but they are all pretty young, and you know as well as anyone, Ben, that walking into the big world out there can be a real challenge, which is another thing we admire and trust about you. You are familiar with the world outside the reservation. You have both feet on the ground, and I doubt success would go to your head."

"Maybe not," Ben answered, "but it can still be a problem in a lot of other ways." He turned to Carmen. "What is your honest opinion?"

Carmen sighed and looked at the strong hand that held hers firmly, the silver rings, the silver and turquoise bracelet that graced his solid wrist. Ben shifted in his chair, and the tiny bells on that silver belt he wore tinkled. All of it was a reminder of where he belonged—in the Badlands. In the Black Hills. He was, above all, Lakota. "I don't have the right to dictate your life, Ben."

"Yes, you do. You *are* my life. Your opinion means everything."

She met those dark eyes, so deeply spiritual. "I will answer with a question. We have talked about this before, and it comes down to the fact that your heart lies in this land and with the People you represent and fight for. Can you really leave your homeland for weeks or months at a time? Leave those kids? Can you leave *me* for long nights apart? Leave your grandmother? You know your weaknesses. You fight them with the strength you get not just from me but from this land."

"The five million would be as much yours as mine," Ben reminded her.

Carmen smiled sadly and shook her head. "I admit I was blown away with the offer, but I don't need that kind of money. I have more than enough for a comfortable life on my own income. I don't need what you make now or what you might make in the future. We have a beautiful home and friends and loved ones right here. What else do we need?"

Ben grinned and squeezed her hand again, raising it to his lips and kissing the back of it. "That is what I was hoping you would say."

"Ben, we know you share what you have with Sunrise and the school, and that you use your own money to help others," Hal reminded him. "Just think what five million dollars will do for all your causes, let alone the millions more you will make in royalties. If we didn't believe this will work, we wouldn't make this offer. Consider the kind of money you could be donating to the school, the needs on the reservation. This could benefit every cause you fight for."

Ben shook his head. "And it could cost me things that are worth more than that to me. You two know I have an addiction problem. Leaving here for months at a time could break me, and you know where that would lead. I could lose this woman sitting beside me. She went through hell with her first husband's drug problem. I will not turn into someone who cannot get out of bed in the morning, with some other woman whose name I do not even know lying beside me. And I will not risk the destruction of the only kidney I have. If things get bad, someone is bound to offer me alcohol or drugs when I am down. After that shooting, I almost destroyed what was left of me. My brother and friends saved my life. But if I do what you are asking, I would eventually be right back down as low as a man can get. I cannot guarantee either of you that drugs or even attempted suicide would not be the result, because I have already tried both."

"We can make sure you get home once in a while," Hal assured. "And we can have a counselor and doctor travel with you."

Ben shook his head. "Those who do not live in my world cannot understand. Once in a while is not enough. I travel a lot, but usually for only two to five days at a time and then I am back home for several days. I have to stay grounded.

"And I will not abandon those kids at the School for the Arts, not for any amount of money. They depend on me and would not do nearly as well without me. When I was missing because of the shooting and then the drugs, we nearly lost everything because of a huge drop in donations. And Carmen and I want children. Being on the road too much would mean she might have to give birth without me there. I would not miss that for anything. And afterward, traveling would make me an absentee father. I won't let that happen. And I have to continue working for the causes my dead wife worked so hard for." He turned and smiled gently at Carmen. "Carmen is right. *She* keeps me strong. This sacred land keeps me strong."

He looked at Hal and Stuart again. "I appreciate your praise and your offer, but the answer is no."

Stuart sighed and shook his head. "Set in stone?"

Ben let go of Carmen's hand. "Set in stone." He leaned back in his chair and studied both men intently. "But I promise to discuss it with my older brother. He has saved my life more than once, and I trust his judgment. He and his wife are very involved in my work and my first wife's causes, so it is only fair that I tell them about this. However, I expect he will agree with me that it is a bad idea. At the same time, *I* will make *you* an offer."

The two men looked at each other and frowned, then leaned back in their own chairs. "Fire away," Hal told Ben.

"CDs and digital music of our song and performances can be purchased online. That helps us broaden our audience. You might be able to expand sales outlets, maybe advertise for us, create even more sales and income. You could have a cut, but I would reserve the right to compose the contracts. And I would require that there be no traveling involved outside of what we already do, and never without me or Tommy along.

"If you see a particularly outstanding talent in any of those kids and want to build a career for them after they are at least eighteen years old, their parents or guardians and I would have to approve. No child could sign a contract that I did not draw up. I know what can happen in the world of entertainment. Even with what little we do when we travel, I have to keep an eye on those kids, let alone the fact that I have had illicit offers from adults.

"So, boy or girl, if I learn that *anyone,* and I mean *anyone,* makes an illicit move toward any of those kids or a child tells me they were abused, touched wrongly, given drugs or alcohol, raped on an agent's couch, or even left alone with strangers, you two will never work again. I will sue you from here to China, and you will be looking over your shoulders for Ben Colter to come after you. I am not talking just in court, if you get my meaning. Help these kids and the school make money the right way, and you will make money, too. I do not want one cent of it. This would be strictly to support the School for the Arts and its needs."

Both men let out long sighs as they glanced at each other. Carmen pictured them as big balloons that had just been popped and were releasing air as they spun around the room. *Good for you, Ben.*

Ben folded his arms and leaned back in his chair.

Stuart let out a long whistle, and Hal fidgeted.

"I think I see why judges don't like seeing you walk into their courtroom," Hal commented.

Ben shrugged. "I just say it like it is, and I do not talk out of both sides of my mouth like a few other people I have dealt with. I intend no insult to either one of you, but these students are like my own children. And I have to answer to their parents for whatever happens to them."

Stuart nodded. "We will consider your suggestion. Send us a sample of the kind of contract we would have to sign and what percentage you would consider fair."

"I will do that, but it would also have to include a better, more professional recording studio than what we can afford to use now. Besides, my wife was killed outside the studio we always used in the past. I cannot bring myself to go back there. We have been recording in our own make-do studio right here. Either way, you claim our music can make a lot of money, so I will let you prove it if you accept my offer."

Hal looked at Carmen. "Have you ever won an argument with this man?"

Carmen smiled. "Women have their own ways of winning arguments."

Hal and Stuart both laughed loudly, and Ben grinned at Carmen. He turned his attention to the agents again. "If you think I am a hard case, try reasoning with this woman beside me. She keeps me in line."

Both men rose.

"We will think about your offer," Hal told Ben. "But our offer to you stays open for a while, just so you can think it over a little longer and talk to your brother about it." He handed Ben a business card. "If you change your mind, for whatever reason, give me a call. We might even go as high as ten million."

"No amount of money would be enough," Ben answered, rising. They all shook hands, and the two men left.

Ben sat back down with a heavy sigh. He put his elbows on his desk and held his head in his hands for a moment.

Carmen scooted closer and rubbed his shoulders.

"Are you really okay with me turning them down?" Ben asked.

"*More* than okay. And I am proud of you for recognizing and admitting to your problems. It only means you are accepting what cannot be changed, and you know what you have to do to go on." She kissed his cheek. "I have always believed that admitting and owning up to our faults is the best way to beat them. And I am proud of the way you turned the tables on those men. That was the coolest thing I have ever witnessed. They were really taken back. I wanted to stand and clap."

Ben snickered. "I just figured maybe there was a way we could still make money off them," he said. He leaned in and kissed her. "I would like to go to rehearsals. Being with those kids always lifts my spirits and will help me know I have done the right thing. Can you get away?"

"Sure."

Ben kissed her again, then stood and pulled her into his arms. "I do not want those kids or the people out there in the office to know about that offer. The kids might feel bad that I did it for them. And others might resent the fact that I could have brought huge money into the system."

Carmen looked up at him. "Ben, you are the engine that keeps all this going. That is more important." They shared a deeper kiss. "And I need you at home in my bed every night," Carmen added. "When you made that remark about waking up with some woman whose name you didn't even know, I felt the claws coming out."

Ben snickered. "I was just thinking of a Bon Jovi song when I made that remark. I think he has a line like that in "Bed of Roses." And right now, I would love to lay *you* down in a bed of roses." Another kiss. "Let me tell Tommy about this. Don't say anything to Sasha yet."

"I understand."

Ben turned and reached for a bunch of bananas on his desk. He broke one off and handed it to Carmen. "Here. Have a Michigan banana."

Carmen broke into laughter, remembering her remark about being surprised Ben had fruit in his fridge that first morning at his house. "You remembered!"

"I remember every word, every smile, how your hair smelled, every touch, the taste of your lips." He kissed her again and ran a hand into her hair. "I remember your scent, the taste of your tears and the feel of your body that first time I held you close before I left your place for Chicago. I *hated* leaving, and I ached for you all the way home. If I took that five million and had to be on the road all the time, I wouldn't be able to stand the pain of being apart."

Carmen kissed him once more, then pulled away.. "If we don't leave right now, we will be putting on a show for everybody in the office out there."

Ben glanced through the large window that separated his office from the outer office. Every single worker was watching them. They all started clapping and cheering.

"I need to get some curtains," Ben joked. "Let's get out of here." He hit Save on his computer and closed it. "And you had better walk in front of me."

"Oh? Why?" Carmen giggled as she grabbed her small purse from his desk, where she'd left it that morning. She put her phone into the purse and drew the strap over her shoulder.

"We are going over to the school," Ben called to the others as they left. They passed Billy Big Bull's office, and Carmen glanced at Billy, whom she'd noticed coming in just minutes before she'd ended her call with Val. The look he gave her made her lose her smile.

Ben put a hand to her back and led her outside to the truck. Carmen climbed inside and set her banana on top of the dashboard. She fastened her seat belt, lost in thought over that look in Billy's eyes. It almost looked like hatred, and that unnerved her.

"Ben? Have you talked to Billy lately?"

Ben fastened his own seat belt. "Not lately. He has been home the last few days helping Karen with their new baby. We need to go see the baby, but I do not know if I can bring myself to hold a tiny newborn." He met her gaze. "Why do you ask?"

"Oh, it's just a look Billy had in his eyes just now when

we passed his office, like he was really upset about something."

"He is just tired from a couple of sleepless nights and probably pissed at me for not coming to see the baby yet. Sometimes he gets his feelings hurt over things like that. And this audit has his nose a little bent out of shape. He thought it meant that I don't trust him. I set him straight on that."

"I've been wanting to ask you to do that, but you're such good friends that I wasn't sure I should stick my nose in. Maybe he thinks the reason you haven't been to see the baby is because I am taking too much of your time. I just felt some animosity in the way he looked at me just now."

"Do you think I need to go back and talk to him again?"

Carmen smiled for him. "No. I'm sure everything will be fine, and you're right. The new baby probably has him stressed out. We really should go see his new son."

Ben looked behind him and pulled out of the parking lot, then headed for the school. "Billy does not know how lucky he is," he said rather absently. "I would give everything I own just to hear my son crying. He could cry 24/7 and I would not care. At least he would be alive."

Carmen immediately felt bad about her comment. "I'm sorry. I wasn't thinking."

"Don't be sorry. I know you meant well. It's just hard for me to hold a newborn."

Carmen reached over to touch his shoulder. He still needed to let go of Singing Boy, but he had not brought up the subject.

CHAPTER TWENTY-SIX

As soon as Ben and Carmen walked into the theater, all the kids on stage cheered and clapped.

"Ben's here!" The comment came from several young people, some of whom jumped up and down.

"Hi, Ben! Hi, Carmen!" Various greetings came from each different young person on stage, and it was obvious they were holding back on something.

"I smell trouble," Ben told Carmen, keeping her close.

"Hey, Ben, Mom and Dad have a special song for you and Carmen!" Zeke yelled over a microphone.

"Oh my God," Ben said. "What is going on? I know Sasha. She is going to embarrass us."

"Get up here," Tommy told him. "Both of you."

"Ben, I am not getting up on any stage," Carmen objected. "That's *your* thing."

"Come on! Come on!" several of the kids shouted, laughing and clapping.

"We might as well do what they ask," Ben told Carmen, grinning.

"Ben, if we have to dance or something, you are out of

luck. I'm lucky to do the Cha-Cha Slide they do at weddings."

Ben laughed as he kept hold of her hand and made her climb the stairs to the stage. As usually happened almost every day, several parents who loved watching rehearsals were sitting in the audience chairs.

"Ben, I'm not good at people watching me on a stage!"

"You have so much to learn, woman." Ben dragged Carmen center stage. "This had better not have anything to do with a bikini," he told Tommy and Sasha.

The kids all screamed with laughter.

"*What!*" Carmen said, trying to pull away.

Ben chuckled and pointed to Sasha. "That crazy woman over there embarrassed me so badly once that I would not dance with her for three weeks afterward. We were practicing that dance we do in full Native regalia, and as she sashayed up to me, she yanked off her tunic and was wearing a bikini underneath."

The kids laughed and woo-hooed. Carmen covered her mouth with her hand. "Are you serious?"

"I told you once that I am glad she is not *my* wife," Ben replied, "although she sometimes would put Talia up to tricks to embarrass me. They both knew how easy it is to embarrass me. Tommy is the only one who can handle that little vixen over there." He pointed to Sasha while the students kept laughing and joking about it.

"You loved it!" Sasha told him. "I look good in a bikini, don't I, Little Brother?"

"Yeah, well, I went to my knees with embarrassment while everybody else had a good laugh!" Ben yelled in reply. "You have no shame, Sasha Colter! You are a full-fledged *weechashasnee!* A troublemaker." He turned and pointed to the students. "And you kids are no better for going along with her."

The kids just kept laughing, obviously enjoying the entire exchange.

"Hey, Ben, Tommy and I have a song for you," Sasha told him. "This one is no joke, Little Brother, but you and Carmen have to dance to it."

"Sasha, I can't dance with this man," Carmen told her. "He's too good."

"Oh, you can dance, all right. According to Val, you have been doing plenty of dancing. Little Brother smiles a lot now."

The remark broke everyone up even more, and Carmen buried her face against Ben's chest. "I will never live this down. When on earth did she talk to Val?"

"Never underestimate Sasha," Ben answered. He hugged her as recorded background music started.

"Tommy and I are going to sing a little Faith and Tim for you," Sasha told them.

Ben pulled Carmen close and grasped her right hand, moving it behind her back as he turned with her to the song, "Let's Make Love."

The young people giggled and whistled and hooted, and some of the parents joined them while Ben and Carmen danced to the romantic Faith Hill/Tim McGraw song. Ben led Carmen through it with ease, and he sang the song himself softly to Carmen as they danced.

"Between embarrassment and what you are doing to me right now, I am going to pass out," Carmen teased.

"Hey, this is not easy for me, either," Ben answered. "I have to let go of you when we are done, and I don't want to."

"Don't you dare play some kind of trick on me."

"I promise I will not." Ben whirled her around again, his

lead forcing her to follow every step. "See?" he told Carmen. "Dancing is not that hard."

"So you say," Carmen answered. "Just don't try something fast or make me dance like Sasha. I would never have the courage."

They laughed and hugged and even kissed through most of the song, and when they finished, the twenty or so people sitting in the audience clapped and whistled, and the youth group joined them in celebrating their new love by raising a banner they had made, which read Ben and Carmen Forever.

"Oh, that's too cute," Carmen said as they finished. She felt the genuine happiness the children exuded. He was so loved, and the joy in the eyes of the students explained why he would not leave them for months at a time just for money. She glanced at a picture of Talia that hung at the base of the balcony over center aisle. Did Ben feel Talia watching them?

"There. See? We did not embarrass you," Sasha told them when the song ended. She raised her hands and clapped, urging the kids and the audience to do more clapping of their own. "We are all happy to see *Ben* so happy," she told Carmen, coming over to give Carmen a hug.

"Thank you for making me feel so welcome," Carmen told her. "And for all you and Tommy have done for Ben."

"Hey! Hey!" Ben told the youngsters. "It is time to get serious! We are going to perform the night before the big Pow-Wow, and that is just a month away. It will be good practice for Omaha, so no more goofing around."

"We feel like *rehearsal* is goofing around, Uncle Ben," Sasha's son, Jeremiah, answered.

"Yeah, it's fun!" some of the others agreed.

"I *want* it to be fun," Ben answered. "Any time you love

what you are doing, you are always going to do it better. Who is the most talented person on this stage?"

"*You* are!" they all answered, laughing.

Ben shook his head. "I do *not* want all of you to continue answering that way," he told them. "That birthday thing should be a one-time event. Now, who is the most talented person on this stage?" he repeated.

"*I* am!" each student answered.

"That's better. And if you want to have fun, we will start with a song you all love. 'When Love Takes Over.'"

They all jumped up and down like someone had just given all of them ice cream and candy. Carmen left the stage and sat in a front-row seat to watch Ben the instructor.

"Drummers, you know how to follow along," Ben told the four Native drummers who sat in an orchestra pit with the huge drum used for Pow-Wows. Also in the pit was a group of musicians, a piano player, regular drummer, three guitarists, and a young Native man there to operate a synthesizer.

"Amy, you do the lead singing like you usually do with this one," Ben told a young Native girl who eagerly rushed up to a center microphone. "The rest of you know what to do. Chime in on background, and dance, dance, dance. Move from one microphone to the next and back around again so every single person up here gets a chance to be front and center. It is only fair that each of you gets audience attention. Besides, I do not want to get attacked by some parent who is upset their kid did not get a turn to show off."

Some of the parents chuckled as Ben came down the steps and told the piano player to open the song. Sasha joined him, and Tommy joined the musicians below, picking up an electric guitar.

"Remember," Ben shouted from center aisle, "you are all professionals. Belt out the song and do not be bashful. Pretend you are on *American Idol* and there are scouts in the audience. Sometimes there *are* scouts in the audience. That is no lie, so do not hold back!"

Carmen couldn't help thinking what Ben had given up for the kids on that stage as they burst into the happy song. They'd barely gotten started when half the parents in the audience were on their feet, clapping and dancing in front of their seats. Amy belted out the song as though she were Carrie Underwood. Every singer held bells that they shook to the beat of the song. And every singer had their eyes on Ben, who was all over the place, encouraging them not to hold back in any way.

They moved into more songs, several that Ben sang, with the students providing background lyrics. One song, "Shouting Grounds," was a modern song of faith and joy with a very Native American feel to it. Some of the parents were standing and moving to the beat, and behind Ben the students stomped their feet and whirled in Native American dance moves. The ending was totally Native singing and drumming, with Ben singing and performing to his own dance, using a spear decorated with beads and feathers and whirling it around almost like a baton, banging the base of it on the stage floor to the beat of the song. It was a grand mixture of modern music and Native American drumming and dance.

Carmen shook her head at a great example Ben was for how someone could recover from tragedy and drugs. The students watched his every move and obeyed his every request. Their performance was like watching *Glee,* and none seemed envious of the other or tried to outdo the other. Their only goal was to be their best, and probably to impress Ben. Sasha and Tommy did their own part in encouraging the students, and half the time Sasha was onstage dancing with the rest of them, encouraging them to be just as confident in their dancing as their singing.

The theater vibrated with song and drumming, and not one person could sit still through any of it. When Ben and Tommy shared "Let Freedom Ring," Carmen came close to tears at the words. Tommy's voice was just as strong as Ben's, but he did not have Ben's range. Yet Carmen was more certain that Ben had made the right decision to turn down the five-million-dollar offer from the talent scouts.

And she could not help but worry about what was going on inside the man she watched guide those students to do their best. *It's still partly for Talia.* Her name was still tattooed over his heart and would be there forever. And a medicine bag with a little boy's hair in it still lay under a pillow in the nursery Ben would not visit.

"I think now we should get back to the song all of you love performing. We always include 'Love Can Move Mountains' in our program."

The students brightened and took their places.

"This one is all yours again," Ben told them. "You do not need me for it. Belt it out because I want you to dedicate it to Carmen. If anybody could move mountains with her love, it is her."

The students' joy returned, and they sang the song enthusiastically, Sasha's sons taking each next line of the song in succession. Young Benjamin hopped and danced around, making the small audience laugh at his antics. The entire musical group sang the background words and practiced moving in succession from one microphone to the next so each got a turn up front. A few more parents came inside to pick up their children, and the entire rehearsal ended up more of a joyful festival than a rehearsal.

A Native woman sitting next to Carmen chuckled. "Ben starts pulling you into all this as you watch, doesn't he?" she told Carmen. "I feel like he is teaching me, too. But when I watch, I think maybe just keeping up with that man takes all your energy."

"Oh my gosh, you are so right," Carmen answered. "He's got me riding horses and rolling in the grass with wolves and traveling all over the place and sitting in court-rooms. I am trying hard to slow him down a little."

"When that man is happy and well, he is dynamic," the woman answered. "It was so sad for us to lose Talia and see what Ben went through after that." She touched Carmen's arm. "I am sorry to talk about Talia to you."

"That is not a problem. Ben and I talk about her often. He *needs* to talk about her."

The woman smiled. "I am Katie Walks With Horses, Amy's mother, and happy to meet you. You saw what Ben has done for my Amy. Her father left us, and that, combined with her thinking she was not pretty enough to perform and being acutely bashful on top of it all, caused my daughter to be low in spirit. I was afraid of drugs or suicide. Ben saw it coming, and he knows about drugs and about unhappiness. He recognized what a good voice Amy has, and he worked with her to build up her confidence. When Ben encouraged her to perform center stage, it completely changed her. She is so confident now. And Sasha helps all the girls with hair and makeup. Amy always looks beautiful up there. It is that kind of beauty that shows in the eyes. I see it in *your* eyes."

Carmen smiled. "Thank you, but it's easy to smile when you are around Ben."

"Ah, I know! And he is easy to look at, yes?"

Katie fanned herself, and they both laughed. Two o'clock turned into five o'clock. Ben finally told all of them it was time to quit for the day. The kids complained that they wanted to keep going.

"You have homework," Ben told them. "And your parents have other things to do, and so do Carmen and I. I will come back tomorrow. While you are home, think about any new dance routines and songs you would like to try, but make sure you first do your regular homework." He started to say something else when someone burst through the inner theater doors.

"Ben, I want to talk to you!" a man yelled.

Everyone turned to look, and there stood Billy Big Bull, stumbling drunk. "Oh my God," Carmen muttered.

"You gotta get rid of that blond bitch over there!" Billy roared.

In half a second, Ben leaped off the stage without using the steps. Tommy did the same, hurrying behind Ben, while Sasha told the kids to stay back.

Ben shoved hard at Billy, forcing him back to the inner doors. "Watch your mouth!" he growled. "You are *drunk!*"

"I am tired of you putting that blond hussy in charge of everything!" Billy yelled. "She ain't *Lakota!* Send your new piece back to—"

Ben rammed him through the doors, and there was no mistaking the sound of a hard fist landing into someone.

"Ben, don't!" Carmen heard Tommy shout. Some of the students screamed and cried, and the four Native drummers charged down the center aisle to help Ben. Carmen hurried behind them, feeling sick at the crashing sounds and grunts coming from the lobby.

"Ben!" Tommy yelled. "Damn it, you're killing him! Think about your back! Think about the kids!"

By the time Carmen reached the lobby, Tommy and two of the drummers were struggling to keep Ben off Billy, and the other two drummers were helping the much heavier but very out of shape Billy get up off the floor. His face was covered with blood, some of which came from the inside of his mouth. His shirt was completely torn, his big belly protruding over the waist of his blue jeans. He stumbled a little and roared for the two men to let go of him.

"What is the matter with you!" Ben shouted to Billy. "We are *friends!*" Ben's lip was bleeding, and his white shirt was ripped, but Billy was in far worse condition.

Billy gripped his belly. "We are no longer friends! You have not been the same since that woman came here," he roared at Ben. "You have not even come to see our new son!"

"You know damn well why I have not," Ben answered, his dark eyes ablaze. "Holding a newborn is hard for me and you know it! *Carmen* is the one who just told me earlier today we should go see the baby, and then you come here and *insult* her? If you say something filthy about her again, I will *kill* you!"

"It is not just the baby," Billy answered. "You know the *real* problem! Being with another woman is a betrayal to Talia. That woman is going to take over *everything* in your life, and you will let her start running the office. That is *my* job!"

"And I told you that will not happen. Carmen has no intention of taking over anything. She has her own business. She is at headquarters only because I gave her an office there."

Sasha came into the lobby to stand beside Carmen.

"This is exactly what I did *not* want to happen!" Carmen told Sasha in a near whisper while Ben and Billy yelled back and forth and some of the other men joined in, supporting Ben.

"I don't want to cause problems like this," Carmen told Sasha. "Maybe I should go home."

"Do not even *consider* such a thing," Sasha said quietly as she urged Carmen farther away from the fray. "It would kill Ben! Billy has always been a troublemaker. He and Ben used to get into fights when they were younger, but Ben always made up with him. Billy goes on drinking sprees. That is all this is."

"You are drunk," One of the drummers repeated to Billy. "Go home! You will feel different tomorrow."

"I will *not* feel different! Ben always gets what he wants. I *loved* Talia!"

Ben jerked away from Tommy.

"Yeah. You never knew that, did you?" Billy sneered. "I loved her, too, but *you* got her. Now she's *dead,* and you are fucking a beautiful blond who does not belong here."

Before anyone could grab him again, Ben landed into Billy, fury in his punches. Carmen screamed, and Tommy took an elbow in the gut when Ben tried to shove him off, but Tommy held on. The two men helping him ducked blows as they again pulled Ben off.

"Ben, *stop* this!" Tommy demanded. "You know how Billy gets when he drinks."

Ben turned away, panting. "He's never turned it on me like this," he told Tommy. "Get him out of here before I kill him. Call the Rez police and throw his ass in jail."

"Let go of me and I will leave," Billy told the two men who held him. "He cannot have me arrested because *he* hit *me* first. All of you witnessed it!"

"And he hit you with good reason!" Tommy answered, enraged. "Just get out of here for now. We will deal with this after both of you have cooled down."

The men holding Billy let go of him, and before anyone realized what he intended, Billy rushed Ben while Ben was still turned around. He charged headfirst like a defensive player in football, forcing Ben forward and to the floor, where he began punching him in the back. Carmen and Sasha both screamed, and it took all four drummers to get Billy off Ben and drag him outside. They landed a few blows of their own as Billy yelled, "I hope he never walks again!"

Ben stayed down. Tommy started to help him to his feet, but Ben literally screamed "No!"

Tommy knelt beside him. "Tell me what to do, Little Brother."

"I can't move," Ben groaned. "Don't try to make me. The pain ..." He lay on his side in a fetal position.

"God help us," Sasha muttered, tears forming in her eyes.

CHAPTER TWENTY-SEVEN

A FEW FROM the youth group had snuck through the inner doors to watch the fight, and some of the girls were crying as their parents finally urged them back into the theater, telling them everything would be fine.

"Is he dead?" one girl asked.

"Maybe he will not ever walk or dance again," another sobbed.

Sasha's sons all came into the lobby, telling their parents they were there to help their uncle Ben however they could.

"Call his doctor and give me the phone on speaker," Tommy told Sasha. "Then run home and get the Percocet."

"No!" Ben screamed. "No painkillers!"

"Ben, it's just for now," Tommy told him. "You haven't been in this much pain since the shooting. I cannot let you suffer like this."

"No! Damn it, Tommy, don't you give me that shit."

It was obvious how bad the pain was. Carmen knew Ben would never use such words around the youngsters.

Tommy looked at his sons. "Go home with your mother when she leaves. Stay there until we come back. Zeke, you watch your younger brothers, and Matthew, you drive home and back with Ben's medicine. I do not want Sasha driving alone when she is upset."

"Yes, *Ahtay*."

Carmen put a hand to her stomach. *Ben!* She walked closer and knelt near his head. "Ben, let Tommy help you."

Ben tried to sit up, then screamed and curled up even more. "Carmen," he said weakly.

Carmen leaned closer and he managed to grab her hand. "Don't let them give me the strong stuff."

"Ben, it won't be like the first time," Carmen tried to soothe him. "You are surrounded by people who will help you through it. Tommy. Sasha. All the kids. And me. No one will let things get out of hand, and no one expects you to handle this without something to kill the pain. We have to get you to the clinic, to a place where you can rest and people can help you."

"Just get ... Tylenol."

"Tylenol will not help this time, Little Brother, and you damn well know it," Tommy told him sternly. "And you are stronger now. You have too much to live for to let yourself go down that old pathway. Do you want to lose Carmen?"

Ben clung to Carmen's hand. "Please do not ... leave."

"Ben Colter, the only thing that could make me leave you would be if you turned to drugs again, understand? *Nothing* else can make me leave you. And you need to prove to those kids you just worked with that you can overcome this without falling back into drugs."

"Do not ... let them see me like this."

"The parents are keeping them inside the theater," Tommy told him.

"They should not have ... seen me go after Billy." He

squeezed Carmen's hand tighter. "I am so sorry, Carmen ... for the ugly things he said."

"He was drunk," Carmen reminded him, "and I am too strong to be affected by remarks like that. I heard a lot worse out of Jerry's mouth, believe me. I can take it."

Sasha finally handed Tommy the phone. "Dr. Yates is on the phone. I will go get the Percocet."

"Not yet!" Ben groaned. "The pain will ... go away. Give it some time ... before you put that poison in me!"

Sasha left the phone on speaker while Tommy explained what happened.

"Can he move at all?" they all heard the doctor ask.

"He can," Tommy answered. "He is not paralyzed. It is just that the pain is too great when he does try to move."

"Give him a half hour or so," the doctor answered. "If he is still in too much pain to move him, give him the Percocet so you can get him to the clinic there."

"No! No painkillers," Ben yelled.

"Ben, it's going to be okay," the doctor said loudly over the phone. "We will manage this. Tommy, let me know if you have to give him a second dose. We have drugs we can give him to help the pain and also bring him down from the Percocet."

"No! I do not want ... anything that strong."

"Ben, trust Tommy," Dr. Yates spoke louder again. "You know how much he cares. He won't let you take the wrong path this time. He has my permission to chain you to a tree if he must."

The remark brought a bit of nervous laughter to the others.

"We really can help you come off this with nonaddictive drugs, understand?" the doctor added. "And Sasha says you have a new woman in your life. I can't think of a better reason to stay off drugs than a beautiful woman who might leave you if you go over the edge again. Can you think of any better reason to let us help you?"

Carmen smiled and leaned down to kiss Ben's cheek, letting her hair fall around his face.

"No," came a quiet reply.

"He says no," Tommy answered for Ben. "His voice is just pretty weak right now."

"Tommy, if he's not better by tomorrow, don't be afraid to give him a second dose of the Percocet. And have the clinic X-ray his kidney and send me the results. His kidney could be bruised, but that should not stop it from working properly. If there is any sign of blood in his urine or if he is suddenly paralyzed, get him here to Rapid City as fast as possible."

Ben groaned again. "No. Carmen, tell Tommy ... not to take me there. I never ... want to go back ... to that place."

Carmen thought about the awful hospital pictures and could understand the black memories and terrible grief going there could stir up again. "We'll see," she told Ben. "But wherever you end up, I will be there, understand? I will be there. It's my turn now. I am here. Nothing can harm you, including strong painkillers. *You* won't let that happen, because you are not going to let those kids down. Agreed?"

Ben didn't answer. He'd passed out.

"Ben?"

His grip on Carmen's hand weakened. She straightened and looked at Tommy. "Tommy, he's not answering!"

Tommy took his pulse. "His heartbeat is weaker. It is probably just the pain."

"We already called for an ambulance," one of the drummers spoke up.

"We cannot let them try to pick him up until Sasha gets back with the Percocet," Tommy told them. "If he wakes up without it and they force him to move, you do not want to know how loud he will scream. It is unnerving, even for a man to hear."

Carmen broke into tears as she smoothed some of Ben's hair away from his face. In spite of his normally dark complexion, he looked pale. The pictures she'd see of him in the hospital haunted her, and she grasped his hand again, bowing her face close to his. "Hang on, Ben. Can you hear me? Hang on."

———

BEN AWOKE to voices outside his room.

"I have not eaten yet, so I am going to the lunchroom."

Sasha's voice.

"Tommy knows where I will be. Did you hear from Ben's doctor in Rapid City?

"Dr. Yates said Ben can go home to heal if he can move when he wakes up," a woman answered. "He has to be able to get up and walk, and his urine tests have to be clean. The ultrasound looks fine, so right now everything looks good except for the bruises on his back. He will need to rest several more days before he gets too active. Dr. Yates also said no more Percocet, as long as Ben's pain level is tolerable."

Percocet? My pain level? Where in hell am I? Ben looked around a room that was like a hospital room, but homier. The voices in the hallway faded. He glanced out a window and saw a view of the Badlands that he recognized from the reservation clinic. He'd been here too many times to count, either for his own tests or to bring in a battered wife he represented.

Thank God I am not in the hospital in Rapid City. He noticed flowers and balloons everywhere and suspected they were from the students at the School for the Arts. He was just there. Wasn't that earlier today? Or was it yesterday? The sun was out, and from the shadows in the distant Badlands, he guessed it was morning. Had he been here all night? He moved slightly, and the pain in his back reminded him why he was here.

The fight! Billy! Did the kids see that? Was Billy in jail where he belonged? And Carmen. Where was Carmen? He turned his head to look out into the hallway. No one in his view. Everything seemed so quiet —maybe he was the only patient here. What day was this? What the heck *time* was it?

He heard a light snore and saw Tommy sleeping in a big leather visitor's chair.

"Tommy?" he said weakly. He bent one knee, glad he could move it.

Tommy stirred awake, rubbed his eyes.. "Hey, Little Brother, how do you feel?" He stood and stretched, then ran his hands through the sides of his long hair and pushed it behind his ears. "I see you are moving your legs."

Ben bent the other leg, then put out his hand. "Help me sit up."

"You sure?"

"Hell yes. I just heard a nurse telling Sasha I could go home today if I could get up and walk and stand the pain. I'll do anything it takes to prove I don't need any more strong pain meds. How much of that crap did they put in me?"

Tommy pulled on his arm and helped him sit up. "Just

two doses," he answered. "They kept checking your urine the first night and all day yesterday. Everything looks good. They took out the catheter last night and have just been letting you sleep off the Percocet. Until now, you woke up a few times but did not seem aware of where you were or what happened. The Percocet left you pretty dazed, but Dr. Yates wanted you in a deep sleep so that you would stay calm and rest a good twenty-four hours. We have to let him know how you are now that most of the Percocet is out of your system."

Ben moved his legs over the side of the bed and winced with the ugly pain he knew all too well. "So, this is my third day here. Enough of this. Tell Yates I am fine."

"I would rather tell him the truth," Tommy answered, arms folded.

Ben knew it was useless to try lying to his very perceptive brother. "Let's just say I can move, and that much is fine with me. I will start taking extra Tylenol till this is better. All I have to do is get up and walk so I can go home."

"Well, the doctor's one requirement is that you stay with me and Sasha the first few days. If you pass out or fall down from pain, Carmen sure as hell cannot pick you up."

"Where *is* Carmen?"

"She will be back soon. She ran home to get some fresh clothes for you because she knew you might be able to go home today. She will feel bad that she was not here when you woke up. She had been right here beside you since you first arrived."

"Help me to my feet. I want to be standing and walking when Carmen gets back."

Tommy grabbed his hands, and Ben put his feet on the floor and stood there a minute, then let go and retied his hospital gown before taking a few steps. "The pain is bearable," he told Tommy.

"Be honest, Little Brother. It is important. Let me know if the pain is more than you can handle or if you see blood in your urine or have pain urinating. And if you feel a need for something you know you should not take, you *admit* it, understand? Dr. Yates can help you. Will you be honest about that?"

Ben ran a hand through his hair and shook it behind his back. "Of course I will. I don't want to lose Carmen." He studied Tommy's eyes. "How is she? Really? Is she upset over that fight?"

"No. She is upset over the vicious, underhanded thing Billy did to you, as all of us are. And she feels responsible. We've tried to convince her she should not feel that way."

"No, she should not. I need to see her and assure her of that. I am worried she will change her mind about staying here."

"She loves you far too much to leave, Ben. And she has handled this well. She is strong, and heaven knows she is used to abuse."

Ben moved his hands into fists. "I still want to kill Billy." He began walking back and forth in the room, forcing himself to pretend the pain was not as bad as it really was. "Did you ever suspect Billy felt this way? That he loved Talia and resented me? Damn, Tommy, he *hates* me!"

"Ben, none of us saw this coming. I do not understand this any more than you do, but Billy has also always been the jealous type. He was always trying to outdo you with games and riding and such when we were kids. He was always challenging you to something physical. I just never thought he felt so strongly about besting you. I thought it was just fun and games. And he has always had a drinking problem. It got worse after you and Talia were shot. Now we know why he mourned her so deeply. He was in love with her."

Ben walked to the window and looked out at the Badlands. "We have to fire Billy, *chee-ay*. We cannot have him at the office or around the kids any longer, not even if he comes back with apologies. I cannot forgive him for this or ever trust him again."

Tommy nodded. "I agree, but it will not go well with him. I only hope he does not take it out on Karen and the kids. She knows what happened, and she is sorry for it. She has taken the kids and the new baby back to Rosebud to live with her mother until she decides what to do about Billy. And Billy has left town."

Ben frowned and faced Tommy. "Left town?"

"That is what Karen said. He got in his truck and took off after he came home all beat up. He told her to do what she wanted. He was leaving for Rapid City to look for work. He did not want to go back to Rosebud. And he said he would not stay here as long as ... as long as Carmen was here, only he did not call her Carmen, if you know what I mean."

Ben's deep anger tightened his chest. "I know what you mean. And good riddance. It saves me the job of firing him. Besides, I am worried what I might do if I see him again."

"You know the laws, Little Brother. You cannot let loose like that again. Let the Rez police or the FBI or whoever finds Billy handle this. Understand?"

"I understand."

"You are the smartest man I have ever known, so be smart about *this*. That fight could have crippled you."

"Ben!" Carmen into the room then, carrying clothes on her arm. "You're standing! How much pain are you in? Can you walk?" She threw the clothes on the bed and met him halfway across the room.

Ben wrapped his arms tightly around her. "One question at a time," he told her. "Yes, I am awake and walking. The pain is still very bad, but I intend to take extra Tylenol and nothing more." He kissed the top of her head.

Sasha walked in at almost the same time. "Hey, Little Brother, you look good to go."

Ben reached out and pulled her close also. "I do not think I could throw you around in a dance yet, but I am walking."

Sasha leaned up and kissed his cheek.

"Hey, why do you get both women?" Tommy joked.

Ben kept Carmen close and gave Sasha one last squeeze. "You can have this one back," he said, letting go of her. "I am going to get dressed and go home with the other one."

Sasha gave him a light shove. "You had better let the PA here take a look at you first."

"Which one is here today?" Ben asked.

"Bethany Morning Star is on duty today," Sasha answered, "and she is anxious to get you out of here, too. She gets off soon and has a party planned for her son, who is going off to college. Leona Fast Elk will give you the proper papers to sign and instructions to take home with you on how to treat the ugly bruises on your lower back. And I hope Tommy told you that you must stay with us a few days first."

"Well, that puts a crimp in my plans for Carmen, but I will do whatever it takes to get out of here," Ben answered.

Carmen rested her head against his chest. "We can go as soon as you get dressed and Bethany checks you over."

"How about if I let *you* check me over?" Ben suggested.

"Now you *know* he is better," Sasha teased. She gave Tommy a kiss. "Let's go see Bethany and tell her Ben wants to go home. Carmen can help him dress."

Tommy and Sasha left, and Carmen pulled the curtains that blocked the view from the hallway and untied Ben's hospital gown.

"You know I am naked under this, right?" he asked with a grin.

Carmen snickered. "Nothing I haven't seen before."

"Yeah, well, be careful helping me dress or it might be difficult getting my underwear on."

"And you are a great liar at times. I know how bad the pain must be." Carmen helped him step into clean underwear, then pulled it up. She met his gaze, sobering. "Ben, I was so scared you would be paralyzed. I'm so sorry about all the misunderstandings over why I have an office at headquarters. I'm sorry I upset Billy and—"

"Stop right there," Ben interrupted. "Do not blame this on you coming here. This was all Billy's doing, and apparently it started long before you were ever a part of the picture. I love you, and nothing and no one is going to change that or make either one of us leave here. Nothing will take you away from me. You are my wife." He put a hand to his chest. "Here. In my heart.

"And even though you have much to learn, you are Lakota." He put a hand between her breasts. "Here. In *your* heart. And in spirit. What happened had to do with Billy holding secrets we knew nothing about and Billy wanting something he could not have. I know now that the only reason he was friendly for so long is because I gave him a job and paid him well. He thought that job was threatened, and that was all he needed to bring up everything else that had been eating at him for years, so do not ever blame yourself."

Carmen leaned up and kissed him, a kiss that turned into something much deeper than Ben first expected. He pressed her close again and ran a hand into her hair. "It is I who worries that you will hold all of this against staying here. I worry you will want to go back home to Michigan."

"Never. I could never live away from you." They kissed again. "I can no longer imagine waking up without you beside me, without you holding me, without the safety I feel in your arms. I will never leave here, Ben, unless we go someplace together."

"You dressed yet?" Sasha's voice came from outside the curtain.

"No!" Ben answered, followed by laughter.

"Hey, Little Brother, after taking care of you for months after that shooting, you've got nothing I haven't seen. Get dressed before I come over there and finish dressing you myself. And hurry up. The PA is waiting to take your blood pressure and all that fun stuff."

Ben smiled and kissed Carmen once more, then stepped into the blue jeans she'd brought him. Carmen helped him pull on a black YESS T-shirt, handed him the silver belt with tiny bells on it. He wrapped it around his hips and hooked it, then saw tears in Carmen's eyes. "It's okay," he told her. "And by the way, Tommy and I have agreed to fire Billy. They say he has left anyway and will be no more trouble. I could have him arrested, but that would only bring him back here, and I do not want that. We will just let this go and be glad Billy is gone."

He saw the relief in Carmen's eyes. God, how he loved her. Finding this woman had lifted his heart and spirits to heights he never thought would be possible after losing

Talia. It sickened him to remember Billy's ugly words. "You sure you are okay with all of this?" he asked.

"Yes. It would do me no good to go back to Michigan anyway, because you would come after me, wouldn't you?"

Ben smiled. "You bet I would." He turned with her and started for the door. "Where is my phone? I have information in the notes I might need for signing papers. Photographic mind or not, I always have trouble with which insurance covers what. And there are some people I need to call."

"Oh my gosh!" Carmen pulled away. "I left my purse on the seat of the truck. It has both our phones in it. I'll go get it. You go on to the office."

Ben gave her one more kiss. "Right now, I hate to leave you even for two minutes."

"I'll be back in *less* than that."

Ben watched her walk to the door. "Nice jeans," he teased. She'd worn the snug white jeans he loved. Carmen wiggled her butt on the way out, and he chuckled as he headed for the office, wondering how he'd been so blessed as to find the perfect woman who could mend his shattered heart.

In the office, Bethany directed him to sit in a chair next to a blood pressure gauge. She started to take his blood pressure when he put up his hand. He listened, as he stared across a desk at Tommy and Sasha.

"Did you hear that?"

"Hear what?" Tommy asked.

Ben frowned. "Tommy, I heard a wolf howl."

Their gazes held. "I heard nothing," Tommy said.

"Nor did I," Sasha added. "Besides, there are no wolves around here except for Sammy's place, and that is much too far away for anyone to hear the wolves."

"Perhaps it is your inner spirit," Tommy suggested, "telling you that you made a good choice by choosing Carmen over a man who betrayed your friendship and trust. Billy wanted you to send Carmen back home, but you sent him away instead."

"And I *wanted* him to leave, but now I am thinking we should have the FBI find Billy. I think maybe what happened runs deeper than Billy wanting Carmen gone. If he became so violent after such a small thing, what other dark things has he done that we do not know about? He needs to be interrogated, Tommy. Linda Two Fists reported directly to Billy. Maybe he knows something about her death that we do not."

Tommy nodded. "I would never have thought of Billy as dangerous, until what he did to you. For now we need to get you checked out so we can go home and talk about it."

Ben held out his arm for Bethany. "Let's get this done, Bethany. Carmen will be right back with my phone so I can check my insurance information. I changed to a different supplemental since the last time I was here. Their address and phone number are in my phone."

Bethany wrapped the blood pressure flap around his upper arm, and Ben met Tommy's eyes again. He knew Tommy sensed the same thing he did.

There was something more to Billy's outrage.

CHAPTER TWENTY-EIGHT

CARMEN WALKED around the side of the building, where she'd left Ben's truck parked in the shade. A small, dark-colored car was parked on the driver's side of the truck. It wasn't there when she'd pulled in. Someone must have come in while she was helping Ben dress, perhaps someone who worked at the clinic.

She opened the truck door and reached inside to grab her purse, but as she pulled the key fob from the dash, someone brutally strong grabbed her from behind. Her abductor put a cloth over her nose and mouth, and she dropped the key fob and her purse.. After only seconds, she was unable to fight whoever had grabbed her. She felt herself being thrown into a car. The center hump pressed against her ribs; she must be on the floor in the back seat. Strong hands pulled her arms behind her back and tied her wrists painfully tight. A door closed. Then the door near her head opened, and someone tied a scarf or piece of cloth around her eyes.

"Now you cannot see where I am taking you, bitch!" a man's voice told her.

It sounded like Billy! The door slammed shut. Then another door. Carmen felt the car bounce a little. Someone heavy must have climbed inside. She heard the engine start, felt the car move. She grimaced when it hit something, a rock or a pothole maybe. Her body banged against the back seat as the vehicle was driven away so fast that she could hear the tires spin against the gravel. She pushed at the door near her feet, then realized she'd lost her left shoe.

I'm wearing only one shoe. What a silly thought.

Her thoughts whirled. Was this a bad dream? She struggled and kicked again, but to no avail. She tried to move her head in a way that she could work the scarf away from her eyes and see something, but she was wedged too tightly between the front and back seats. Whoever was driving must have put his seat all the way back so that there was little floor room.

Ben! He was waiting for her in the clinic. So close! If she'd had a chance to scream, he would have heard. Moments ago, she'd heard those tiny bells that told her she was safe in Ben Colter's arms.

I'm here. No one can harm you.

If only she could hear those bells now.

Ben, I'm here, in this car! Help me! Hear me calling you!

That was her last thought before blacking out completely.

"It's been more than five minutes," Ben complained to Sasha and Tommy. "It should have taken all of two minutes for Carmen to get her purse." He took a deep breath while Bethany listened to his lungs.

"Ben, I am sure she will be right back," Bethany said.

"Sit still and breathe for me again." She listened another moment, then straightened. "I am glad to say that your heartbeat and your lungs sound fine." She patted his shoulder as the office assistant, Leona Fast Elk, came in with a clipboard holding release papers for Ben to sign.

Ben took the clipboard from Leona. "You still planning on going to U of M to become a full-fledged doctor?" he asked Bethany.

"I sure am. I start in January. Imagine that. My son and I both going to college."

They all smiled, and Sasha congratulated the woman for wanting to pursue her dream. Ben glanced through the open doorway and down the hall toward the front doors. "Sasha, go tell Carmen to come inside. I'm betting she called Val to tell her how I am doing."

"That sounds like something she would do," Sasha answered. "I will go get her."

Ben set the clipboard on his lap while Bethany took a needle and a vial from a nearby cabinet. "Dr. Yates said to give you one boost of antibiotics," she told Ben. "Those blows to your back could have stirred up some of the shrapnel and bone shards, which in turn would wake up your body's desire to attack anything foreign. You know the procedure."

"Go ahead and stick me," Ben told her, taking a look at the papers while Bethany stabbed his upper arm.

"Are you in any pain anywhere other than your lower back?" Bethany asked. "Be truthful. I know you want out of here, so don't fib to me, Ben. If there is anything going on with your kidneys or bladder, you do not want to risk letting it get worse."

"No other pain," he answered as he signed the papers. "Just my back, and managing it for the next few days is going to be a real Tylenol challenge, believe me. But I don't want anything stronger."

"Just don't try to be a hero about it," Bethany warned. "Dr. Yates promised he could manage your doses and keep your addiction under control if you honestly need something stronger. There is no shame in asking. Remember that."

"I'll manage."

"Now *Sasha* is taking her time," Tommy complained. "She and Carmen are probably both talking to Val. I will go make sure they get back in here to help carry out all those flowers and balloons. As you probably already guessed, most of that stuff is from the kids at the school."

Ben grinned, handing the papers to Leona.

"Those kids are great," Leona commented.

Tommy left, and Ben stood to stretch and move his legs. He walked gingerly down the hall, then noticed Tommy had stopped at the front doors. Sasha came running inside, a look of terror on her face.

"Sasha, baby, what is wrong?" Tommy asked.

"She's gone!"

"What?"

"Carmen is gone! Her purse, the phones, the key fob, and one of her shoes ... they are all lying beside the truck, but Carmen is gone!" Sasha covered her mouth with her hand and started crying. "Oh my God, Tommy!"

Ben hurried down the hall as best he could, struggling to ignore the pain in his back. He felt a palpable rush of dread move through him. "What's going on?"

"We need to call the Rez police," Sasha answered. "Oh, Ben, I am so sorry, but I cannot find Carmen! She parked around the side of the building in the shade, and her things are out there, but she is gone!"

Ben could not find his voice.

"Stay calm, Ben," Tommy warned. "There might be an explanation."

Ben headed out the door before Tommy could finish. He forced faster steps, caring little at the moment for his condition. It was Carmen who mattered. Tommy and Sasha caught up with him as he made his way past Tommy's parked Jeep and around the corner to the truck.

"I left everything where it was in case I should not touch them," Sasha told both men.

Ben looked down at Carmen's handbag, then studied the ground around it. "Drag marks," he muttered.

Signs said someone had dragged Carmen away, probably into another car. The marks covered only about five feet before they ended. Ben turned to his brother, so full of rage, his head hurt. "*Billy!*" The name came out low in his throat like a bobcat growling.

"Billy is gone," Tommy answered. "He went to Rapid City."

"He has had time to come back." Ben turned away, looking around, pacing. "Good God, Tommy! He would know it was likely I was here. He could have been watching Carmen come and go all along, just waiting for a chance to grab her! And if he is drunk again, who knows what he will do? He weighs twice as much as Carmen. He could kill her easily, and he would not need a gun to do it!"

"We should not think the worst right away, Ben. Come inside. Let's call Ralph Harding at the FBI headquarters in Rapid City right away and explain what happened between you and Billy and what we have found here. He will send help." He turned to Sasha. "Go inside and call the police right away. And call Detective Harding."

"Tommy! What if ... this could turn out like Linda Two Fists. Maybe Billy had something to do with her death."

Tommy put a finger to her lips. "Go."

Sasha burst into more tears as she hurried away.

"She is right," Ben groaned. "Why else was Talia's necklace found with Linda's body? It was someone who knew Talia. And someone who hated me. That is why he left the necklace. It all makes sense." He bent over, grasping his middle. "Carmen! I promised her nothing bad would ever happen to her."

"We will find her, Ben."

Ben shook his head. "Tommy, it is hot as hell out here." He walked farther away, looking around again. "It will probably reach a hundred degrees by this afternoon. You can *feel* it. This weather alone could kill Carmen if Billy leaves her someplace desolate and she is wounded or drugged."

He studied the ground. "Here! Tire tracks in the gravel. He tore out of here, and we do not even know what he is driving or which way he went. Billy probably rented a car." Ben felt dizzy and stumbled backward. Tommy grabbed him before he could fall, then held on to him as Ben's breathing quickened. "I cannot ... do this again, Tommy!" he groaned.

"This is different, Little Brother. It just happened, and we have a couple of clues. We have those drag marks. There might be prints on the truck door or Carmen's purse, maybe on the key fob. We can start an investigation right away. Come inside now. Sasha is calling the FBI."

"What good are *they?*" Ben screamed. "They still do not know who killed Talia, or who killed Linda Two Fists. They are *useless!*"

"But they have all kinds of ways of collecting evidence. And they have helicopters, designed especially for search and rescue. This is *fresh*. If we can find out what car was parked here, we will know what to look for."

"We have to go after her before he kills her," Ben screamed at Tommy. "*Now! We have to go now!*"

"Go *where,* Little Brother? We do not know what kind of car we are looking for or which way it went. You said that yourself. If you drive out of here, which way will you turn, Ben? Which way?"

"To the Badlands!"

"Two hundred and forty-four thousand acres of rocks. Seventy-five million years of canyons, mountains, plateaus, dry riverbeds, sand, clay. Every kind of lifeless landscape known to man. You tell me where to start looking, Little Brother, and I will do it! Do we drive out of here and go left? Or right? Which part of those thousands of acres of uninhabited, endless layers of rock do we start looking in?"

Ben hung on to Tommy's arm, feeling sick at what could happen to Carmen. "I did it again, Tommy. I have failed the woman I love and who trusted me. My God, I promised her if she came out here, she would be safe. I joked with her about a line from a song ... I am here. Nothing can harm you."

"You *are* with her, Ben, in spirit. She will feel you with her, and she will fight to get back to you. Carmen is *tough.* Come back inside with me and we will talk about the possibilities while we wait for the FBI. Let us think about things that might help them know where to start looking."

Ben straightened and tossed his hair behind his back. "We know *exactly* where to start —with Billy Big Bull! You know as well as I do that Billy did this. Maybe Sasha is right. Maybe Billy killed Linda Two Fists, and look where she was found. And Carmen told me once that she felt fear in the Badlands, that she was going to end up lost in the Badlands. She must be terrified."

"And right now you need to think straight," Tommy reminded him. "The police will be here soon, and the FBI right behind them. You believe Billy might have rented a car, so we will ask the FBI to check every car rental business in Rapid City. They have the ability to do it quickly."

Ben headed for the clinic. "When they find Billy, I will *kill* him for this!"

Tommy grabbed his arm to stop him. "Look at me, Little Brother."

Ben met his gaze.

"When we find Carmen, she will need you to be with *her,* not sitting in jail. For now, it is first things first. Let's go inside and see if the clinic's security cameras are working. Maybe we will find footage that shows the car Billy was driving. Maybe we will even see the abduction." He put a hand to Ben's back. "Come on. Come inside. If you get too worked up and do too much pacing out here in this heat, you will only exacerbate your injuries. You cannot do this alone, so let all of us help, and you keep a cool head. I can see you are in more pain than you let on. You told Bethany you would be honest about that."

"I will manage. There is too much to do for me to take anything so strong it would put me to sleep. I will not sleep one bit until we find Carmen."

"Then at least get inside and sit down," Tommy told him.

Sasha met them at the door. "Three men from the FBI are on their way by helicopter," she said amid new tears. "They said it will not be long, and I was happy to know they are responding so quickly. They know Ben and what he has been through. They want to help."

They went inside, where Ben half fell into a chair. He held his head in his hands. All he could think about was Linda Two Fists. Would they also find Carmen dead? Bethany came into the hallway to ask if any of them needed anything while they waited. During her conversation with Tommy and Sasha, Ben heard another voice.

Ben!

He raised his head and looked around, sure Carmen had just spoken to him. Bethany left, and the hallway grew quiet.

Tommy grabbed a nearby plastic chair and sat down in front of Ben.. "I will *not* let you go down the same road as before, Little Brother. Understand? I believe Carmen is alive, and you must believe that, too. She is *alive!* And we will find her. She is strong physically and strong-*willed*. She is not going to let the worst happen. She will fight, and *you* also must fight. Come into the library. We will look at the video from the security camera, and then we will have something to tell the men from the FBI."

Ben understood more than ever how a warrior of old might have felt after soldiers murdered his wife and children. A steely resolve moved through his blood. He straightened, feeling a new strength surge through his very being.

"You told me to keep a cool head, Tommy. I will try. But when I get my hands on Billy Big Bull, I cannot promise that he will not die. I would rather hear him crying and begging me to finish him off. I would rather hang him head-first over a fire and watch him slowly burn."

Tommy drew a deep breath and touched his arm. "You let Talia's spirit guide you, Ben. I believe Talia is with Carmen and will protect her. I believe that when Caesar sat down beside Carmen that night in Michigan, he was guided by Talia, and that can only mean Carmen was meant to come into your life and save you from your grief. Talia will not let Carmen die. Use your own abilities and your own intelligence to find her, and once you do, you must be there for her. You must put Carmen's needs above your own need for vengeance. Tell me you understand that. The warrior in you wants to kill whoever took Carmen. But today you must be a different kind of warrior."

Leona came into the hallway. "We have the security video ready," she told them.

They heard the sound of a helicopter in the distance.

CHAPTER TWENTY-NINE

CARMEN WOKE up in pain from her cramped position on the back seat floor. Her hands remained tied behind her, and the hump in the floor still pressed against her ribs every time the car bounced, which it now was doing repeatedly. She smelled dust, so much that it seemed to seep right up through the floor. There were a lot of dirt roads out here, but most of them were in the Badlands.

The Badlands! The one place that had haunted her since she got here. Her stomach seized at that thought that she might die here. She tried to think straight, but everything was foggy, apparently from whatever her abductor had put over her mouth and nose to temporarily knock her senseless. Something was still tied around her eyes.

She shifted and tried to sit up, but the area she was in was too narrow. She remembered now. The front driver's seat was pushed back so far that it was impossible to change her position, especially with her hands behind her back.

"Who are you?" she called out, her voice weak.

No one answered. He must not have heard her. The car was noisy, like one that needed a new muffler. Combined with the rumble of the dirt road, she would have to talk louder. Bathed in perspiration, and thirsty, she struggled to bring enough saliva to her mouth to speak again. "Who are you? Where are you taking me?"

A man's voice finally answered. "You know who I am, bitch! And you know where I am taking you. But you will not be found as easily as Linda was found. There are no tourist riding trails where we are going. No people. No water. No shade. The grass and stones will cut your feet. The sun will burn your white skin. You will likely run into a rattlesnake or make a meal for a pack of coyotes."

Carmen recognized Billy Big Bull's voice. *Linda? Good God, was it Billy who'd killed Linda? It made no sense. Why would he do that? Was she going to meet the same end?*

"Why are you doing this, Billy? You don't even know me well. I have nothing against you."

"I do not care about you," Billy answered. "I am doing this to show Ben he cannot always have everything he wants, and because I know where your fancy audit will lead."

The audit. Linda was working at the office at the time of her death, learning the bookkeeping. She must have figured out Billy was cheating with donation money. Her own suspicion of possible embezzlement must have been right. "Don't do this, Billy," she begged. Ben will understand and help you. Embezzlement can be forgiven. Murder can't!"

"It is too late. I will be found out, but I am not going to let Ben win again. If I go down, *he* goes down, too. I know that soft heart of his. Losing Talia almost destroyed him. This will finish him off, unless I find a way to kill him myself. He will never get over losing you."

The man was crazy! Carmen's mind raced with possibilities of how she could escape. She felt like she was suffocating from the heat, and she was desperately thirsty. She began kicking at the door nearest her feet. "Get me out of here!" she yelled. "I can't breathe!" She heard the grinding of tires on gravel. The car came to a sudden stop. She heard Billy get out, and the door nearest her head opened. Billy grabbed hold under her arms and yanked her out.

Gravel scraped Carmen's one bare foot as Billy dragged her around the other side of the car and opened the passenger door. He shoved her inside. Carmen fought him, kicking hard, but she couldn't see to kick him in the right places. He grabbed her knees and squeezed so hard she screamed as he forced her legs into the dashboard area so that she was sitting on the front seat, her hands and arms crushed behind her. She smelled the sickening stench of whiskey and sweat. Billy was drunk, and it was hot out. So damn hot. Carmen grunted when something slammed into her face then, twice.

"Now you will not be so beautiful," he told her. "Kick me once more and I will knock those perfect teeth from your mouth! Ben will not care much for you then, will he?"

The door slammed shut, and Carmen heard ringing in her ears from the hard punches. She sensed Billy getting back into the car. He drove away, the tires again tearing into gravel from taking off too fast. "We will be getting out soon," Billy told her. *"Then the fun begins!"*

Yes, it does, Carmen thought. *Because I can outrun your out-of-shape ass.* She was not going to cry. Billy would like that. *You might weigh more than Ben, but he would easily have killed you if Tommy and the others hadn't stopped him. You were no match for Ben, and you are, by God, no match for me if I can start running. Go ahead. Hit me again, you sonofabitch. I've been hit before. I am used to it.* She wanted to shout the words, more angry than scared at the moment.

Ben! Hear me. Feel me. Find me! She tried to concentrate her thoughts, but they were interrupted by another blow to her left jaw.

"That was for ruining my life, you uppity bitch! Why did you have to come here? I wish that wolf had attacked and *killed* you back there at that show in Michigan. You have destroyed all my plans."

Caesar! Caesar could find her, couldn't he? What part of the Badlands would Billy take her to? The west end? That would be too far away. Even Caesar could not find her there. And Billy would likely kill her before *anyone* could find her. If Billy would at least remove the blinder around her eyes, she could think better, see where they were going.

Ben. Oh God, poor Ben. Billy was right when he said her death would destroy him. She had to live for Ben. She scrambled to think straight. "What did you mean about Linda?" she asked Billy, talking awkwardly through swelling lips and terrible pain in her left jawbone. "Did you kill her? Did she catch you taking money?"

"She was too smart for her age."

"How did Talia's necklace end up where Linda was found?"

Billy laughed wickedly. "I took that necklace a long time ago. Talia left it at the office. I remember she was upset when she could not find it. I had something of hers that was all mine. And when I took Linda out to kill her, I gave the necklace to her and told her to give it to Talia in heaven. She cried and cried. I knew when her body was discovered that the necklace would be found, too, and Ben would mourn Talia all over again. I heard he almost did not find it right away. Even the FBI did not find it. It must have flown out of Linda's hand when my bullet smashed into her back. And then it rained, so dirt and clay got washed over it." He chuckled. "Now you have all the answers, but it will do you no good. You will not be alive to tell Ben any of this. You will die like Linda died."

Carmen swallowed back vomit. "You didn't need to kill Linda, Billy. You could have invented a pity story about the money, and Ben would have forgiven you. I know him. He has a big heart, and he trusted you completely."

"Ben never knew how much I hated him growing up. Ben, the good-looking one. Ben, the smart one. Ben, the talented one. Ben, the one who got to marry Talia. I *loved* Talia! I used to dream about fucking her myself. But with Ben around, she never gave me the time of day. She was crazy about him. The only way I ever could have had her was if Ben were out of the picture. She would have leaned on me. She liked me. I was her friend. I mourned her death as much as Ben did, but he should not have been alive to mourn her at all."

The sick feeling in Carmen's gut grew worse. Could it be? No!

"Billy, you didn't ... you couldn't have."

"Did I kill Talia?" He slammed on the brakes, and Carmen fell forward and hit her forehead on the dashboard as the car slid around on the gravel. Billy grabbed her shoulder and slammed her back into her seat.

"YES!" Billy roared the word so loudly that Carmen jumped and put her knees up and her head down, ready for another blow. "It was an ACCIDENT!" Again, the words were roared. "If Ben had not turned away at the same time I fired, HE would be dead. Not Talia! Not my Talia! When I realized I had hit her instead, I shot BEN. He had no right to live instead of Talia, so I decided to kill him, too. I could have handled Talia's death better if Ben had died, but the bastard LIVED!"

My God! It was Billy! How many times did murderers turn out to be the last person anyone would expect? "So, no one suspected you because you were Ben's best friend." Carmen could feel her jaw swelling.

"Right. I even visited Ben in the hospital. I helped Tommy bring him home from that alley in Rapid City. No cops ever questioned me. I was not investigated. No one searched my house to find the rifle that killed Talia. I was not even considered a suspect. Why *would* I be? I was Ben's good friend, and I made sure everyone continued to think so."

So, you decided not to try killing Ben again, because you had already gotten away with murder. You couldn't risk another try, so you decided to steal from Ben instead. It all made sense now. "How much, Billy? How much have you taken these last three years?"

"Thousands. Once I had enough put away, I was going to leave Karen and take off with Pat Daisy. We have been sleeping together. Pat was going to leave *her* kids, too. We were going to Vegas to live. But you would have figured out the money thing, so now I have to get rid of you, too, and that will ruin Ben while Pat and I take his money and leave."

Pat Daisy! The divorced woman who liked to flirt with Ben. Carmen remembered Ben told her he had helped the woman get a divorce from her alcoholic husband. Ben had been good to Pat, probably helped her pro bono. She'd flirted with him and probably offered Ben free sex as payment, but he'd turned her down. This was the thanks he got for helping her. She was going to run off with Billy and have a good time with Ben's money.

So many things made sense now. Carmen had heard it in other murder cases in the news. *They were such good friends. He was such a nice guy. He was well liked. He would never do a thing like that.* Trust turned to betrayal. Even if Billy killed her, Ben would figure it all out. "Billy, you are beyond the point of hiding this. Why add another murder to what you've done? You said Talia was an accident."

"Linda was not. That girl was too damn smart for her age. She knew, and she threatened to tell Ben. And now, because of you, the FBI will figure *all* of it out when they learn about the embezzlement. I have no chance, but I am not going to let Ben get off lightly. I want that charmed man to *suffer,* and I want you dead because you are the one who messed it all up."

Carmen's head began to hurt. Hitting the dashboard, combined with Billy's blows, had awakened the migraines she was prone to getting from too much stress or jostling. "Could you please put a seat belt on me?" she asked. Fear and dread rushed through her veins as she heard the click of a gun, felt something shoved into her ribs.

"Do you think I care that you might get hurt more? Do not say another word or I will splatter your insides all over the door beside you."

"If you are going to kill me, then get it over with!" Carmen shot back.

"Not yet, unless you keep bitching at me. I plan a slower death for you."

"At least ... some water for now?" Carmen asked. "Please?"

"I told you to shut up!" Billy rammed the gun harder into her ribs. "Of *course* you cannot have water! I told you that you will die *slowly.* Thirst is one of the things that will kill you, unless the sun kills you first, or coyotes. Who knows? There are many ways to die in the Badlands."

Carmen kept quiet after that. Her only chance was to obey him for now. If he meant to turn her loose in the Badlands, maybe she had half a chance of living. Maybe she could somehow get the better of him, or at least run. He was taking her deep into the Badlands, the very place she feared most. The very place where she'd felt danger, ghosts, something calling to her in ways she did not understand until now. Ben had told her not to be afraid of this place. He'd taught her not to fear horses or wolves or buffalo ... or the spirit winds of the most rugged country a person could encounter. Ben knew this place, big as it was. He would find her or die trying. She had to keep that hope. Ben was with her. As surely as she was breathing, he was with her.

Billy took a sudden sharp right turn, and Carmen braced herself as best she could to keep from falling into him. She felt the car speed up again, felt it start to weave, probably because of Billy's drunken condition and the fact that he was driving too fast on gravel.

They suddenly came to a severe stop. Carmen flew forward against the dash again, and this time no one pushed her back against the seat. She heard Billy groan. Was he hurt? Had he just had an accident? This could be her chance to flee, but her hopes fell when she heard Billy open his door. Seconds later, the door on her side opened. Billy jerked her out of the car and shoved her, hard. She stumbled over a rock and fell, hitting her head yet again. She heard Billy cussing a blue streak.

"At least we landed down an embankment," he grumbled as he picked her up. "The car is under a big, flat overhang. No one from the air will see it."

Carmen thought she heard the noise of a helicopter far in the distance. Ben? Was he searching in a helicopter?

"Move!" Billy told her. "We need to get through this big

grassy area and get to the rugged peaks ahead ... lots of crevasses and canyons. No one will see us there."

To Carmen's surprise, Billy cut the ties on her wrists and tore off her blindfold. She squeezed her eyes shut for a moment, the shocking brightness of the blazing sun making it hard to see at first. She rubbed at her wrists and realized they were bleeding.

"We need to move fast," Billy told her. "You will have better balance and less chance of falling if you can see what is ahead of you, and we need to make time before that helicopter in the distance sees us. I think it is headed away from us, but I do not want to take chances." He held up a rifle in front of her. "And if you try to run faster than me to get away, you will feel a bullet from *this* in your back. Understand? The gun I held on you in the front seat is a .45. This big guy will do much more damage. I am sure Ben has told you what a bullet from one of these feels like." He grinned. "The insides of someone as skinny as you will be blown all over this prairie grass. Now, move!

Carmen took a quick glance at the direction of the whirling helicopter. It was too far away to spot them and heading in the wrong direction. She started running, her bare left foot soon badly scraped against the rocky gravel she had to run across to reach the grass. She thought the grass would be softer, but the knee-high blades cut into her foot like knives. She stumbled and fell again.

Billy jerked her up. "Keep going!"

"My foot!" she screamed. "The grass is cutting it!"

"Then maybe coyotes will smell the blood and come and chew it off for you." Billy rammed the butt of his rifle into her back and forced her to keep going. Once they reached the edge of the deeper canyons and shadows of the rugged crags and peaks of the Badlands, he stopped her and shoved her into the shadow of an overhanging rock. "Take off your shirt!" he ordered. "And those jeans!"

Carmen backed up.

"Do not worry. I am not a rapist. Even if I were, I would not touch an outsider like you. Screwing you is *Ben's* job. He has betrayed Talia's memory by laying with an outsider. I only want you half naked so that your skin is exposed to the sun and to the bugs and the rocks and gravel as much as possible. I want you to bleed and burn while you die of thirst and exposure. When I am through with you, you will no longer be Ben's beautiful cunt!"

Carmen still hesitated and backed away even more. Billy cocked the rifle and aimed it at her. "Do you want to die quickly, with your guts blown out? Or do you want a chance to run? Take off those clothes!"

Feeling sick inside and already faint from the heat and humidity and the blows to her head and face, Carmen did as he asked, hoping he would leave her clothes right where she dropped them. If someone spotted them, they would have a better chance of tracking her. She stood there in her sports bra and panties, and she deliberately left her one shoe on, hoping he would let her keep it. By some miracle, Billy did not ask her to take it off, but for one quick moment as he looked her over, she feared the worst. His vow not to rape her might not be long-lasting.

"I think I have changed my mind," he told her. "What better way to get back at Ben for stealing Talia from me than to have a piece of his *new* woman?" He walked closer and pushed his mouth against hers, hard enough that a couple of her teeth cut into her lips. His breath reeked of whiskey. He ran a hand into her panties, and all the while Carmen felt behind her for something, anything, to hit him with. She grabbed what felt like a decent-sized rock on a ledge behind her, realizing that in order for Billy to use his hands the way he was now, he must have dropped his rifle.

God, give me strength, she prayed. She landed the rock against the side of Billy's head as hard as she could. It was enough to make him stumble sideways. She hit him again, this time in the face, twice into one eye and once against his lips. She screamed with rage at every blow.

"No man as good as Ben"—another blow—"should have to go through this again!" Another blow. "I won't let you *do* this to him." On the word "do," she hit Billy again, then stumbled backward at the sight of his bloodied face. "I'm not going to let him find me dead!"

She tried to grab the rifle next to Billy, but he had enough of his senses left to grab it first. Before he could get up and use it, she kicked him hard between his legs. He screamed out from pain and curled up, and Carmen started running. There was no time to grab her clothes, and carrying them would only slow her down anyway.

"God, please don't let him shoot me!" Ben had told her that's how Linda had been shot. She was running from her abductor. Right now, Carmen had no choice. Maybe Billy would stay down long enough that he would never catch her.

"Oh God! Oh God! Oh God!" All she could think of was Talia lying dead on a sidewalk, her insides blown out. And those pictures of Ben in the hospital. What he'd been through. And poor Linda Two Fists, found rotting in the Badlands.

The sharp blades of grass cut into her left foot, already bruised and cut and bleeding. She forced herself to ignore he terrible pain in her jaw, the sting of scrapes on her body, the screaming pain in her foot, the raging migraine that was getting so bad that the world around her was turning black.

She headed for rugged red peaks ahead of her, where there might places she could get out of the sun and hide from Billy. If she could stay alive till dark, Billy would lose her. He would not be able to chase her. The sun hit her back and shoulders like flames, and the humidity made it hard to breathe. Her hair was soaked with perspiration. She ached for water and to lie down in shade.

Ben! See me. Feel me. Find me.

A shot rang out. She screamed when something slammed across her lower left ribs. *He shot me!* She stumbled and fell. Strangely, the initial pain from the bullet went away. She didn't even stop to look down at her side. She got up and kept running until she reached a wall of red rock. Every second she ran, she expected another bullet to slam into her. She turned and darted behind the rock wall, stones cutting into her left foot. She could feel blood under her foot with every step. Between her blinding headache and blood that ran into her eyes from too many blows to her forehead, she was close to seeing nothing.

That was when it happened. She ran right over a cliff. She had no idea how deep it was or what was at the bottom, and wearing only her sports bra and her panties, there was nothing to shield her skin from the rocks and gravel on her way down. She grabbed at anything she could, but there was nothing. She screamed all the way down, the sensation of her skin being flayed from her body more than she could bear.

She finally hit bottom, which was surprisingly soft. She tumbled onto her back, screaming again from the ground scraping her skin. She moved just enough to realize she was lying in sand, which had probably saved her life. Everything hurt too much to move. Maybe that was good. Intuition told her to lie still and not move a muscle. She opened her eyes and saw just enough to realize the cliff she'd tumbled down was steep and straight up. Billy could never get down here. And if he saw her down here, he needed to think she was dead.

Struggling not to cry, she lay sprawled in the sand, the hot sun beating her with its fiery heat. She saw movement at the top of the cliff. *Billy!* She tried to not even breathe.

Do not move! Who said that? It was a woman's voice. *Talia?*

She waited in agony, needing to crawl out of the sun, needing to find shelter, needing water. Oh, how she needed water! The thought helped her think of Ben, always drinking his mineral water, joking about "watering the grass" when they went for rides because he needed to keep his kidney healthy. She wondered where she'd been shot. Had she lost a kidney, too? Would she go through what Ben went through?

She closed her eyes, the heat and her headache lulling her into a sleep. She thought maybe she passed out, because when she came more fully alert again, the sun had turned to a red glow above jagged peaks that cast a shadow over the canyon where she'd landed. It had to be very late afternoon now. She opened her eyes and looked up. Billy was gone.

"Ben," she said, her voice barely above a whisper. "I beat him. I'm still alive. You just ... have to find me." The shadow made her feel cold. She groaned with the awful pain in her left side and in her foot, and her head ached fiercely. The sand she lay in actually felt good, soft and warm. She managed to roll to her right and curl up slightly, burrowing a little into the sand. She felt things going black again, and she prayed coyotes would not come and feast on her.

CHAPTER THIRTY

"WE WILL NEVER FIND HER," Ben lamented. "There is too much territory to cover, and we have already been up here for hours." With Tommy and FBI detectives, Ben scanned the Badlands in an FBI helicopter big enough for six passengers and a stretcher. Two agents who sat behind Ben and Tommy were trained medics. In front, FBI Detective Hugh Bannon, a broad-chested, older man with gray hair that was thinning, sat in the passenger seat next to the helicopter pilot.

Bannon had been assigned to Carmen's case and had worked in Rapid City for years. He was now the lead detective for the Pine Ridge area, and he was not exactly one of Ben's favorites, as Ben believed Bannon had mismanaged the investigation over Linda Two Fists. He preferred Ralph Harding, someone he knew better, but Harding was working on a different case and had sent Detective Bannon in his place.

The FBI had at least responded within a half hour of Carmen's abduction. Quick action was always a benefit. An immediate FBI inquiry into car rentals in Rapid City had resulted in the discovery that Billy Big Bull had, indeed, rented a dark blue Chevy Sonic, the same car they'd seen on the clinic security video. It had been the only car available and needed a new muffler, but the clerk at the rental business had told them Billy insisted on taking it. He'd seemed in a hurry.

A hurry to steal Carmen. Ben felt sick to his stomach. They had set out immediately, searching the western Badlands, looking intently for the car and for signs of life.

"It is getting too dark to see anything!" Ben fumed. He struggled to control his fury at watching Carmen's abduction on that video. A stout Native American man whose identity could not be mistaken had grabbed her from behind and put something over her nose and mouth before she'd had a chance to fight back. Ben felt crazy with desperation to find Carmen ... and to kill Billy Big Bull. Seeing Carmen thrown into that car made him crazy with desperation to find her.

"I agree with Ben," Tommy answered. "There are too many places down there where Billy could hide a car, too many holes in some of those rock walls, holes and overhangs big enough to hide a small car. And there are thousands of shadows and canyons. The shadows are getting worse because the sun is setting."

"We will never find her this way," Ben insisted. "Head farther northwest," he told the pilot.

"Ben, that's the biggest part of the Badlands," Bannon answered. "No helicopter carries enough gas to cover all of that. It's peak after peak after peak of striped stone, rugged cliffs, and deep canyons. You couldn't see an *elephant* walking down in there."

"We've got to do something more!" Ben demanded. "Maybe Billy fooled us. He knows about the security cameras. Maybe he wanted us to see him pull out left and then later turned around."

"That would take him to the Sage Creek area," Tommy reminded Ben. "The scenic highway runs through half of it. He would not take her to a place where she might be found by tourists. I think he will stay on the west end. It is much more rugged. And that is where Linda was found."

"Ben, we have combed a lot of area," Bannon added. "Believe me, we want to find Carmen as much as you do, but we can't stay in the air much longer. We have men ready to search some areas on foot tomorrow. We will find her."

"Is that supposed to give me hope?" Ben bit back. "What crimes have you actually solved lately?"

"Hey, listen, Cochise, I -"

"Wrong tribe," Ben seethed. "Cochise was *Apache*. Is that all you know about Native Americans? I wonder if you even *care*. You sure don't try very hard to find any of our own indigenous missing women."

"Ben!" Tommy yelled. "Do not blame this on Detective Bannon. He got to us with a helicopter and the information about that car pretty damn fast."

"This is *Carmen!*" Ben raged. "I cannot have another woman die because of *me!*"

"It is *not* because of you! It is because of someone else's *jealousy*. His alcoholism. His greed and his foolishness."

"What difference does it make? Carmen is ... she could already be dead, or suffering. It got to over a hundred degrees there today. And Billy would know the places where there is no water."

"Ben, calm down." Bannon rubbed his eyes and sighed. "Look, I apologize for the Cochise remark. I know what you went through losing your first wife, and I truly wish we could have found the shooter by now. It has *not* been for lack of trying. You hate the fact that Feds get involved in Native American affairs, but in times like this, we have some pretty damn good tools at hand to help find someone."

Ben looked out the window again. "I am sorry, but in this case, even tools of the FBI cannot help. And now I am wondering if it could have been Billy who killed Talia. He is the *last* one anyone would have suspected. He was a friend. No one questioned him or searched his house. And he owns more than one rifle with a scope." He closed his eyes. "My God, why did I never think of that? He mourned Talia as much as anyone, but now I am wondering if it was because he had a guilty conscience. He would have meant to kill me, but I turned away at just the right time." He fought tears. "I turned away. I turned away."

"Billy is a drunken fool, but I don't think he would do something as awful as kill you," Bannon answered. "He even helped Tommy find you when you were dying from drugs. He helped get you home."

"That could all have been for show, to make sure no one suspected him." Ben glowered at Bannon. "He wants me dead. He as much as said so when we fought. I did not die, so now he wants to hurt me another way. I feel it in my bones. If he is the one who shot me, he knows he got away with murder. He probably felt lucky to have gotten away with it and decided to leave well enough alone and find another way to get back at me. Billy knows what killing Carmen will do to me. And maybe Carmen was right."

"About what?" Bannon asked.

"She thought someone might be skimming money from our school funds," Ben answered. "That is why she wanted to do that audit." He looked at Tommy. "All the funds go through *Billy.* Maybe he got scared. Linda Two Fists was working with him. She was a smart girl. Maybe she figured it out, so he killed her. Whoever did, he left Talia's necklace there just to remind me someone might still be after *me*. Talia was bad about leaving things lying around the office. Maybe Billy found that necklace lying on her desk, and he took it." Ben hesitated. "My God! He told me *he* had loved Talia, too. He probably took that necklace to remind him of her." He turned his gaze to Tommy. "You told me Billy wept openly at Talia's funeral. It all makes sense. He started drinking after that. Maybe that was because he mourned Talia out of remorse for accidentally killing her."

"I do not want to think that could be true, Little Brother," Tommy told him.

Ben looked out the window again. "I do not want to think it either, but you know I am right, Tommy. You feel it the same as I do. Billy started drinking to soothe his own guilty conscience. And he kept pretending to be a good friend to cover up for any suspicion anyone might have. He is the *last* one any of us would have suspected." He faced Bannon. "Get on the radio and have someone go to Billy's house. Look for evidence. Pictures of Talia. Maybe something that belonged to her. And his guns. Maybe they will find the one that matches the one used on Linda and me." He ran a hand into his hair and pulled it behind his shoulders. "My God, we *hunted* together when we were younger, before I got so busy. I wonder how many times he thought about killing me then. My *friend!* My *friend!*"

"I'm sorry, Ben, but I have learned over the years that it often turns out that way," Bannon told him. "So many times, the murderer is a friend or a trusted relative."

"Such a sick betrayal," Tommy said sadly. "All of us were good friends all our lives. My heart breaks to think Billy would do such a thing."

"He will kill Carmen the same way he killed Linda," Ben said, shaking. "I feel it, Tommy. He will beat her and make her run. He likes to shoot at running targets. When we went hunting, he waited until a buffalo or a deer or a bighorn sheep started running before he would shoot it. He said it was a bigger challenge than when they were standing still." He held his head in his hands. "My God! Carmen will be so afraid, and I cannot help her up here. I could not help Talia, and now I cannot help Carmen."

"How else can we search, *sohnkah*? The only thing that makes sense is a helicopter."

"Tomorrow I'll order another one to search the east end," Bannon told them.

The pilot banked the helicopter to the left, over a new area.

"I still don't see a sign of life," one of the men in back told them.

Ben looked at Detective Bannon. "Tell me you can put up two more helicopters tomorrow, and that you can start immediately. At sunup."

"Of course we can."

"As soon as it is dark, take me home. Come back in the morning with this helicopter as soon as the sun is rising. Fly me into the Sage Creek area, to Sammy Thunder's ranch."

"Why?"

Ben turned to Tommy. "Caesar. The first time Carmen and I went riding into the grassland south of Sammy's ranch, Caesar ran to us before we even rode through the canyon to the ranch itself. I told Sammy to let him loose to see if he would come to us."

"He found you because he caught your scent," the detective told Ben. "He knows you from those shows you do."

"No." Ben kept his eyes on Tommy. "The wind was north to south, Tommy. He could not possibly have found us by scent. He found us in *spirit,* and I believed it was because of *Carmen."*

"Ben, you sound like an old traditional Native healer," Bannon scoffed. "Dreams and visions and spiritual connections are part of a past long gone."

Ben glared at him, feelings of warrior vengeance surging through him. "My spiritual connection to the wolf is *real."*

Detective Bannon moved back a little. "Jesus, Ben, you don't even look like yourself right now. I am beginning to feel like George Custer."

"You have no spirit," Ben told him. "The things of today's world *destroy* the spirit. I found mine in a vision, and it is one with the wolf. You would not understand because you do not believe, but I will show you that the old ways are not gone and that they have *power!*" Ben turned to Tommy. "Do you know what I am saying?"

Tommy nodded. "I do, *Lutah Meeyahslaychah.* You believe Caesar can find Carmen. But he is clear over in the Sage Creek area. If Carmen is somewhere in the western maze of endless spires and canyons, we cannot be sure he could sense where she is from so far away."

"We can be sure!" Ben declared. "*I* am sure. I have to believe she is alive, *chee-ay,* or I will go crazy. Sasha is safe in Kyle with friends while she waits for us, so tonight you and I will go home and paint ourselves for war and vengeance. We will make a fire of sage and smoke a pipe and offer our prayers to Wakan-Tanka and ask the Great Spirit to protect Carmen until Caesar can find her."

The detective sighed and turned around. "Oh brother," he muttered.

"You think I am crazy," Ben told him. "But you will

learn the truth about the spiritual power of the Lakota. Be at my home tomorrow as soon as the sky starts turning red with sunrise. Take us to Sammy's ranch and we will pick up Caesar."

"*What!*" Bannon sat up straighter and faced Ben again. "Pick up a *wolf?* Are you saying you want to put a wolf in this helicopter with me and my men?"

"Yes. He will not harm any of you. He will know why he is with us."

"And you *are* crazy. *Crazy Horse!* That's the name I should have used instead of Cochise, isn't it? It fits the look in your eyes right now. Your suggestion could get us all *killed.* What if that wolf attacks one of us? What if he attacks the *pilot?* We will *all* go down."

"I assure you that will not happen. Trust me."

"*Trust* you?"

"Trust the spirit and the power of the wolf," Ben told him calmly. "These are things you need to learn and believe if you are going to keep serving in Lakota country, Detective Bannon. We will fly over the west end again, start at the Plenty Star area of the Badlands. We will watch Caesar, and when he gets restless and starts behaving as though he needs to get out, you will set the helicopter down in any nearby clearing and let us out. Tommy and I will follow Caesar on foot, and you can follow by helicopter. There are canyons and shadowed pathways so deep there that you will not be able to see us, but we will keep in touch by radio. In the meantime, have the local Rez police and state police keep a lookout for Billy's rental car and for Billy himself."

The words were spoken more like an order than a request. Ben turned to Tommy. "Carmen is *alive.* I feel her with me. She is waiting for me to come for her. I cannot let her die, because if *she* dies, *I* die."

Bannon wilted a little and turned around to settle into his seat. "You know, Ben, *I* am supposed to be in charge of this search. Do you realize the trouble I could get into bringing a wolf on board this helicopter?"

"You will not get in trouble. I know Caesar, and he will obey me and be still. And if you get in trouble, I will represent you at any hearing you need to attend. You know the FBI does not like having to deal with me. I will keep you out of trouble."

"Gee, thanks. That helps."

Ben felt suddenly calmer, more hopeful. "I am right, Detective. Caesar can find her."

"Yeah, well, I don't know why I am going to trust you on this, but I have always felt sorry for never finding your wife's killer. If that's what happens, you make sure I get the credit and not a wolf."

Ben looked out the window again. "I will make sure."

Bannon leaned back in his seat. "Good God. A helicopter ride with a *wolf*. God help us."

CHAPTER THIRTY-ONE

BEN SAT by the sacred fire by his Lakota cultural mentor, Yellow Robe, whose name in Lakota was Tashinagi, had built in his backyard. The very old shaman lived in a ramshackle trailer on Pine Ridge, far from most settlements. Sean Bear Killer, whose family Sasha had agreed to stay with until Billy was found, had picked up Tashinagi for Ben and brought him to Ben's house for prayers and rituals meant to help find Carmen.

Ben and Tommy had both stripped to only breech-clouts. They sat outside in the dark now, Ben on his knees and bent over as Tashinagi chanted to Wakan-Tanka, asking that Ben and Tommy and Caesar be blessed with the ability to find the white woman with a Lakota heart. Using a fan made of bundled prairie grass, he fanned smoke over Ben and Tommy as he sang.

After nearly an hour of chanting and prayers, the old shaman stopped his singing and asked Ben to look into his eyes. The dim firelight seemed to enhance the hundreds of wrinkles in the old man's face, but age could not dim Tashinagi's intense gaze, the dark eyes that spoke of wisdom and much knowledge, the eyes of a man deeply connected to a world most people did not and probably would never understand.

"You must do two things," he told Ben. "You must tell your brother about the riches you have refused, so that Wakan-Tanka hears and knows you have a good heart and a sincere love for your People."

Ben turned to Tommy, who frowned. "Riches?" Tommy asked.

"I was going to tell you, but then all this happened and I never got the chance."

"Tell me what?"

Ben glanced at Tashinagi. "How did you know?"

The old man grinned. "I know everything. The spirits talk to me but only of men with pure hearts. You are such a man, and what you did proves it."

He would just have to accept that there was no fooling Yellow Robe. His all-knowing connection to a person's soul was not something that could be explained. And it was the shaman's deep understanding of Ben's heart after losing Talia and becoming an addict and the man's prayers and counseling that had saved Ben from preferring death to life.

He turned to Tommy. "Talent scouts came to my office the morning before I had that fight with Billy. Part of the reason I went to rehearsal that day was to verify to myself that I had made the right decision. Watching those kids, feeling their love and their dependance on me to guide them gave me my answer."

"What kind of talent scouts? What was the offer?"

Ben turned his gaze to the fire. He watched the flames dance around sage and pine, listened to the wood crackle as it split from the heat. "I checked them out on the internet right then and there when they first told me their names and who they worked for. They were legit—two of the biggest scouts in the country. Some of their customers were several big recording companies, *American Idol*, and even several big names in the movie industry." He glanced at Tashinagi, who nodded his head.

"They offered me five million dollars to let them represent me and build me into a big name," Ben told Tommy. "It would have involved at least a year of constant traveling, often a different city every night, but they were certain I could make it big—*really* big. They were certain they would make their money back tenfold or more, and they reminded me that I would be able to donate that money to the kids, the school, all the causes Talia and I worked so hard to help. They talked about how rich and famous I would be."

The air hung silent for several seconds.

"Does Carmen know?" Tommy asked.

"She was right there."

"You turned them down? And Carmen agreed?"

Ben nodded. "She agreed. I reminded her that she would benefit greatly when I marry her, but she is not the kind of woman who would ever marry a man for his money. She knew all the obvious reasons I should not take such an offer. She valued having me with her every day far more than the offer, and she understands how me being gone all the time would affect those kids."

He met Tommy's gaze. "I told the scouts I would talk to you about it. It is only fair that you know, because you also would need to travel with me, probably Sasha, too. Even if you did not, you would have a share of the money because part of the deal was to record our music and market it all over the world, to give us tremendous publicity."

Tommy smiled softly and shook his head. "Such a life would destroy you. You know what that kind of life can bring to someone with addictions, let alone your need to stay in touch with the People, with this land, with those kids, and with your family."

Ben nodded. "I am fully aware of what could happen. I would lose the joy in my heart. I would be an absentee father to whatever children I have with Carmen. And I would likely lose Carmen herself, because I would come home a changed man. But I told Carmen to say nothing until I talked to you. And I do not want the children to ever know, Tommy. They might think I gave up too much for them and feel bad. And others might be upset with me for turning down the chance to bring in a great deal of money for all the things we need here."

"You bring in enough with everything you already do," Tommy said. "You must know what my answer would have been. I am glad you did not hesitate to turn them down, and I respect you for making sure it is all right with me, Little Brother." Tommy sighed and put a hand on Ben's arm. "Wakan-Tanka will bless you for your sacrifice. You could easily become the wealthy entertainer those men predicted, but we both know what is more important. I believe the Great Spirit will help us find Carmen and that we will find her alive because you have put the People above personal riches. I am proud of you, Little Brother."

Ben fought tears at worry over how Carmen might be suffering, a lingering fear that Billy would beat and rape her for revenge against things that needed no vengeance. When Billy drank, all common sense left him.

"It is a bold and wise decision that you made," Tashinagi told him. "But you must vow to do one more thing as soon as possible, before you make the white woman legally your wife."

Ben had a feeling what that thing was. He swallowed

back a lump in his throat and quickly wiped at a tear. "I must send my son to his mother."

Tashinagi nodded. "I am glad I did not have to tell you. Glad that you already know this in your heart. The spirit of your beloved first wife speaks with the wolf spirit, and together they brought you the outsider, who is wiser and more tolerant than most. Already she knows your heart. Already she wants to understand your ways. She does not mock them or think those ways are wrong. She holds to her own beliefs, but she knows your own beliefs are close to hers, that your God and hers are truly the same. Your differences will not come between you, and your union is strong and right. You will find her, because I see her in your future. She will give you many children, and they will be the best of your world and hers.

"And now I want to pray over you once more, pray that you will find the strength and wisdom to perform the wind ceremony for your son and send him where he belongs, in his mother's arms. Together they will watch over you."

He fanned more smoke across the fire while Ben bowed his head and wept.

———

THE SUN WAS BARELY UP when Tommy and Ben climbed into the waiting FBI helicopter at Sammy Thunder's ranch. The engine was off, at Sammy's request, in order to give the wolves time to settle down after their initial commotion over the helicopter's noisy landing.

After their prayers last night, Ben and Tommy had driven the long way around to Sammy's ranch and told him about their plans. Ben spent the rest of the night resting next to the kennel fence, with Caesar beside him. Several of the other wolves had sprawled around them as though to protect both Ben and Caesar. Ben had petted Caesar constantly, talking to him about Carmen, making every effort to instill his thoughts and spiritual needs into the wolf, pulling on all that was Lakota in his own soul. He prayed for Caesar's power and animal instincts to fill him, too, so that together they could find Carmen.

Once inside the helicopter, Ben could feel Detective Bannon's doubts about this mission. The pilot, Dan Hyer, was obviously more nervous than the others.

"I hope you know that I am not crazy about flying this thing with a wolf hovering over my shoulder," Hyer said.

"You will be safe," Ben answered. "This I promise you."

Detective Bannon only frowned as he settled into his seat and tightened his seat belt. "Ben, the way you are painted and dressed, I'm not sure which is more dangerous, the wolf or you. If this were the 1800s, I would be praying that my death be quick."

"The only one who might die today is Billy Big Bull," Ben answered. "And if I have my way, I will make sure his death was anything but quick."

"I would feel the same way if the woman taken was my wife," said one of the medics behind them.

Ben turned to greet them with handshakes, as the two FBI men introduced themselves as replacements for yesterday's medics. "John Buckheimer," the first man told Ben. "My partner here is Steve Lake. We are both family men, and we understand how important this is to you. If we find Carmen and she is still alive, we will do all we can to save her."

"We're experienced with the kind of attention needed for exposure and heat exhaustion and dehydration," Steve added, "as well as wounds, including gunshot wounds. This is only the second day, Ben, so we hold a lot of hope of finding her alive. Maybe not well, but alive. We'll do the rest."

"Thank you. I also have much hope. I spent part of the night with a shaman I trust. He prayed for Carmen and for all of us over a sacred fire."

"Well, while we wait for Sammy over there to keep those wolves settled down, would you tell us the meaning of the paint you and Tommy have on your chests and faces?" Steve asked.

Ben and Tommy both wore only buckskin pants and moccasins. Ben had tucked one of Carmen's unwashed shirts into the waist of his pants to help give Caesar a scent to follow. He also wore a knife and carried the quirt he'd used on Jerry Peterson. His and Tommy's chests were painted with black, white, and red stripes, as were their cheekbones. They wore their hair long and loose, with beads wound into some of the strands. Ben had again tied an upside—down feather into his, and he wore the silver belt with the tiny bells because he knew that if he found Carmen, the sound of those bells would soothe her and assure her she was safe.

I'm here. No one can harm you. He felt sick at realizing he'd been unable to protect her from Billy, and he wrestled again with feeling responsible for what had happened to her, even though Tashinagi had told him he should not blame himself.

This was meant to be, he'd told Ben. *It is a pathway to your future with the outsider. This will teach you to trust. The answers for which you have been searching will come, and you and the white woman will walk together into the future, both of you letting go of the past.*

"The red stripes are for revenge," Ben told the medics.

"The black is for death. There is no need to explain who that is for. The broad white stripe from shoulder to shoulder represents peace and life, in hopes we find Carmen alive and not—" He turned away. "Not horribly abused."

He silently prayed for the wisdom to know how to help Carmen with the trauma she must be suffering. And he would need strength to face the worst that might have happened, other than death itself.

"Stay calm, Little Brother," Tommy warned. "Wakan-Tanka is with you."

Ben nodded and looked out the window to see Sammy leading Caesar toward the helicopter. "The upside—down feather in my hair shows that I have been injured in battle before," he said rather absently to the medics. "I just did not know until now that battle has been with Billy Big Bull." He watched Sammy undo Caesar's leash. Sammy waved to Ben, and Ben put a dog whistle to his lips and blew it.

Caesar charged toward the helicopter and bounded inside, licking Ben and Tommy excitedly. Ben spoke to the wolf calmly in the Lakota tongue, and Caesar sat down between him and Tommy.

"Lord, help us," Detective Bannon muttered.

Ben grinned. "Maybe you should turn around and pet him. Then you would not be afraid of him."

"No thanks."

"He *is* a beautiful animal," Buckheimer commented. "Is it really safe to pet him?"

"Yes. Just do not touch him from the back without saying his name and letting him turn and look at you," Ben warned. He leaned back in his seat and tightened his own belt. "Caesar plays like a dog," he added. "Carmen has hugged him and rolled around in the grass with him, even though he used to terrify her."

Buckheimer cleared his throat and said the wolf's name. Caesar turned.

"Fist first," Ben told the medic.

The fit young man put out his fist, and Caesar licked it. Buckheimer gently rubbed his fist against the wolf's shoulder, then opened his hand and petted Caesar's side and back. "My god, his fur is incredibly thick. What a beautiful animal."

Ben rubbed Caesar's chest vigorously. "You know you are handsome, huh, Caesar?"

Steve Lake joined Buckheimer in petting the wolf briefly, and Caesar growled and huffed, but not in a way that seemed dangerous. It was more a sign of pleasure. He licked Ben's face.

"Detective Bannon and Officer Hyer. Hold up your fists and let Caesar lick them and get your scent," he told them. "That is all he needs."

The pilot and the detective glanced at each other, then rather reluctantly held out their fists. Caesar made a little whining sound and licked the backs of their hands.

"Let's get this thing in the air now," Ben told the pilot. "Now that Caesar has been introduced, we must get going. It is getting light enough to start searching." He took the shirt he'd tucked into waistband and held it to Caesar's nose. "Hey, boy, do you miss Carmen? We are going to look for her. We talked about this last night. You can help us."

Caesar sniffed vigorously at the shirt and whined. Ben moved an arm around him to steady him as the helicopter lifted off and banked to the left, heading across the narrowest part of the Badlands. The scenic highway below was empty. Few tourists were up this early. They took a little time flying over the Sage Creek area, all part of the public national park, but Caesar sat quietly.

"Carmen is not in this area," Ben told them. "Caesar is too calm."

"Yeah? Well, he'd better *stay* that way," Bannon answered.

"He will not be calm once he senses we are near Carmen. But he is no danger to you. Fly southwest and down to the Plenty Star area and Stronghold Table. That is the most rugged part of the Badlands. I believe Billy took her there."

Caesar growled low in his throat.

"Why is he growling?" Detective Bannon asked nervously.

"He feels my anger," Ben answered. "He feels my rage at the thought of Billy hurting Carmen. If Caesar starts getting more anxious and restless, it will mean we are either close to Billy or Carmen or maybe both of them. If it is Billy, you will not have to worry about me killing him. It is Caesar we will have trouble controlling. Do not be afraid for yourselves. It is Billy's throat he will want to plant his fangs into."

"Just so he knows we are the good guys," the pilot told Ben.

"If he did not know that, he would already have growled and bit at you. Or if any of you tried to attack me or Tommy, you would regret it."

"Oh, that's not going to happen, to be sure," Steve said.

They all grew silent as the pilot veered west. All six men began watching the ground below, and Ben sensed the others feared the worst but hoped for the best. The air hung thick with his own anxiety and anger.

"We have a cooling blanket for sunburn and an IV for hydration," Buckheimer spoke up. "If we find her Ben, you had better take some mineral water with you, but give her only a sip, all right? She will want to guzzle it, but that will make her sick."

"I understand." Ben answered. "Believe me, I know all about injuries and pain, and about how to survive the Badlands." He realized they were all making small talk, needing to think positive.

"We had better stop talking about possible injuries," Tommy told them. "Caesar will pick up on Ben's anger and worry."

Ben watched the landscape below. "I am fine. I believe Carmen is alive because she is a fighter and strong—willed." He struggled against a need to scream and lash out. *I love you, Carmen. I will find you. I am so sorry it was my own friend who did this to you.*

———————

CARMEN AWOKE TO A RED SKY. She lay still, taking a few minutes to remember where she was and how she got here. She shifted in the soft sand beneath her, then cried out with pain. There was not one bone or nerve or skin surface that did not hurt.

She looked around, seeing nothing but ragged peaks, gigantic boulders, and smooth rocks with perfectly spaced stripes of red, silver, brown, white, and black, as though a painter had measured each stripe so it would be equal to those on either side.

Sediment left from when this land lay under a sea, Ben had told her.

How many millions of years had it taken to form such perfection? She could not remember. Who knew a couple of million years ago that a young woman from Michigan would be lying here half dead in this ancient bed of sand and clay? Maybe soon she would be *more* than half dead.

Her chest tightened as memories and reality set in. Where was Billy? Was he still up above? Watching? Ready to shoot her? She cried out with a sharp pain in her left side. He *had* already shot her!

She remembered that sometime in the night she had wet herself. She'd had no choice. Sitting up was too difficult. At least her kidneys must be working right. In spite of her condition, she supposed that was something to celebrate.

Was anything broken? Was she dying from some other injury? She groaned with a massive headache. Maybe Billy had injured her head so badly when he kept hitting her that it had reinjured the skull fracture she'd suffered from Jerry's abuse. That was in Michigan. She was so far away from there now, far from the lake house, far from her dad, far from Val and Sid.

The sun peeked higher over the cliffs. She had to get out of the sun. She might lie here all day and burn to death. And she was thirsty. So painfully thirsty. It felt like her mouth was stuck together. She tried hard to bring up some saliva, enough to move her tongue and lips, but it almost felt as though they had melted together.

She noticed a little weed sticking out from a crack in a nearby boulder. Did plants have water in them? Even if they did, this was the Badlands. She didn't know the plants here. This one could be poisonous.

She managed to move one hand to shade her eyes and looked up at the top of the cliff. She did not see Billy anywhere. Maybe he left last night, trying to flee the law ... and Ben. He would be wise to not let Ben find him. Ben's rage would be explosive. She forced herself back onto her right side, crying out again with excruciating pain. It took every effort to get to her knees. Maybe she could withstand the pain and force herself to stand and walk. She grabbed a flat rock that stuck out from the boulder near her and tried to pull herself up, but when she stepped on her left foot, the pain was excruciating.

My foot! She remembered stones and sharp blades of grass cutting into it. She moved to a sitting position and looked at it. Oh my God! Bloody. It was so bloody. How was she going to walk on it? Amazingly, after falling down that high cliff, she still had her right shoe on. If she could cover her left foot with something ...

It was then she realized she had nothing on but her pink sports bra and pink lacy bikini panties. Ben liked the pink ones. She snickered at the silly thought. Who cared now? In fact, she should take them off. They must smell of urine. What an ungodly mess she was, the skin on her legs and arms horribly scraped and bloody, her underwear filthy, her lips and jaw swollen, her eyes probably black. She bent her head to look at her left side as best she could. It, too, was bloody. Did she have a hole there?

She sat there a few minutes and cried like a baby. So much pain. So much blood. And she was lost and had no water. How in God's name could she live much longer without water? Without medical help? She would probably die of thirst or of head injuries, just like Billy had told her she would. He said she would die slowly.

Her heart tightened at the thought that Billy might be right about something else. Coyotes could smell blood. Billy said maybe they would come along and chew her foot off!

She looked around again. How would anyone ever find her down in here, even by helicopter? She remembered hearing a helicopter yesterday. Maybe that was *two* days ago. She had no idea how long she'd lain here. The helicopter she'd seen had flown off in the wrong direction and would likely not come back. She was doomed to a horrible death, just like Billy wanted. And he wanted it because it would destroy Ben emotionally.

She could not let that happen! Surely, Ben was out there looking for her. She had to stay alive until he found her. And right now, she had to get out of the sun. But her foot ...

She got to her knees again, but as she crawled away from the sand, small stones cut into her knees and palms painfully. She had to figure out a way to walk. She had to cover her foot. She looked around, looked down at herself again.

Her sports bra! It was soft and lightly padded. She was already close to naked, so what difference did it make if she took if off? Would the sheep or the rabbits or the birds or the bugs care? Who was there to see except God Himself? She sat down again and pulled the bra over her head, then wept with pain as she bent her leg and managed to lean far enough to wrap the bra around her foot, tying the wide straps into a knot to hold the bra in place. She cried harder, wondering where the tears came from. She felt so dried up. She begged God to bring help, feeling sick from the awful headache. It was more than just a migraine this time, and she feared she was dying from a head injury.

Ben, please find me! Call Sid. He will know what to do about my head injuries.

She wiped at her nose, realizing all she was doing was smearing dirt on her face. Oh, how she longed for water ... for a shower ... for her headache pills ... for cool air—conditioning ... for Lake Michigan ... for Ben's arms around her. *I'm here. No one can harm you.*

I need you here now, Ben. I'll hang on for you. Please come find me.

She could not let herself die. Ben loved and needed her. And she'd never loved anyone as much as she loved him. She let herself think about how wonderful it would be to share a cool shower with him, to feel him holding her, his hands sliding over her body and washing away the blood, the dirt, the awful stench of Billy's whiskey breath. She groaned at the memory of Billy's lips pressing hers painfully, the feel of his hands touching her in places that belonged only to Ben. Why was it so beautiful when Ben touched her there and so filthy ugly when those hands belonged to a man she did not want?

She remembered now. She'd hit Billy with a rock. Over and over. She hoped he would *die* from it. She looked up again. Still no sign of Billy. *I won't let you win, you bastard. I'll live, for Ben. He will win, and he will find you and make you suffer."*

She pressed her hand on a flat rock and used it to help push herself up, managing to stand for a moment. Her left foot screamed with pain, but she did not feel the awful poking of rocks. The bra was working. She noticed a large overhang up ahead. She had to get to that. There would be shade there. She would lie down there and wait for the sound of a helicopter or maybe horses.

That helicopter would come back. Ben would not stop looking. He would not fly over the Badlands just once. He would keep looking, and maybe they would find Billy's car, or Billy himself. If they found his car, they would be able to track her from there. Ben was a hunter. A warrior. He would know how to look for her.

She cried out with every step as she limped and stumbled to the overhang, where she collapsed underneath it. It dawned on her then that her panties were not just pink. They were hot pink. Even in their dirty condition, they might show up from above. She managed to get them off, then crawled out from under the ledge and stood up long enough to lay the panties on top of it. The area all around her was as still as a tomb, and maybe it *would* end up a tomb.

Hers.

She remembered her other clothes then. Her white jeans! Those would show up from the air, too, if a helicopter flew low enough. So would her blue shirt. She prayed Billy had left both items lying out there in the grass. When was that? Yesterday? The day before? It was up on top of that cliff somewhere. Maybe Billy was still up there, too. She went to her knees and crawled back under the overhang, hoping if Billy *was* up there, he would not be able to spot her under here. The trouble was, he would know she had moved, so he would know she was still alive.

She studied the cliff again. So high! And almost straight down. How had she managed to live through the fall? The good thing was, Billy, heavyset and out of shape, could never climb down that cliff. There was nothing to grab onto. She was safe down here. But how in God's name would Ben find her down in these shadows? She had to pray her jeans or her panties would help.

Everything grew black again. Her head felt like it would explode. She could not stand much more of this pain. She sobbed in terror that she truly could be dying. She just needed a little water to survive.

God, please let Ben find me. Don't let me die without seeing him once more.

CHAPTER THIRTY-TWO

"It is one o'clock." Ben strained to see into every nook and cranny below. "She has been out there almost a full twenty—four hours. All this time, and we have covered only about half of the western end of the Badlands. Carmen cannot hang on much longer. Not in this heat."

"Hey, Little Brother, she knows you will come for her. She will do what she can to stay alive," Tommy reminded Ben.

"Talia wanted to live, too. I saw it in her eyes before *death* took over." Ben's voice broke on the words. He unhooked his safety belt.

"You'd best keep that on, Ben," Detective Bannon told him.

"I cannot stand it a moment longer. I am going *crazy* up here."

"You won't get any farther if we take you down there," Bannon reminded him. "You know this is the only way to keep searching. I'm just glad I arranged for that fuel truck to meet us in Kyle. With the auxiliary tanks this thing has, we can last another three hours or so, but this heat makes flying a helicopter dangerous. The hot air affects the lift, and the weight of these extra fuel tanks doesn't help."

"Head toward Red Shirt Table," Ben asked. "Highway 41 goes past there, and there is a dirt road going into the worst of it, more like a rugged path than anything else. Billy would be stupid enough to take it when he is drunk. We took a joy ride through there once in an old beat—up Jeep." He looked at Tommy. "When we were all young and crazy and careless."

Tommy smiled sadly. "When we were all friends."

The pilot banked the helicopter west, over territory still not covered.

"Those were good times," Ben told Tommy. He kept an arm around Caesar, his eyes tearing. "How will I live without her, Tommy, after losing Talia? I cannot do this. I cannot go back to that house without Carmen. And she *trusted* me to keep her safe!"

"Think of all those kids who love and depend on you. And remember that Caesar brought Carmen to you. There had to be a reason, something more than for it to end like this."

They all watched the ground again, peak after peak after endless peak. Another hour passed before Caesar began to growl. His fur bristled, and he perked his ears. He stood up on all fours and growled again, then snorted and whined.

"Caesar is getting restless!" Ben told the pilot. "Circle this area slowly."

They all watched for any sign of life. Another five minutes passed.

"There!" Tommy exclaimed. "The sun reflected on something, like maybe glass. Nothing would reflect the sun in country like this unless it was something that did not belong here."

"Go lower!" Ben demanded.

"I see it." The pilot flew lower. "Looks like a windshield."

"Ben, if we go down there, let me approach whatever it is first," Bannon said. "If Billy is anywhere around, he probably still has a handgun or a rifle with him. Put on the bulletproof vests we brought for you and Tommy."

Bannon and the two medics strapped theirs on, and Tommy and Ben did the same.

"You remember to let Bannon go first," Tommy warned Ben. "The last thing you need is to get shot again, Little Brother. Your insides are likely so full of scar tissue, they would never be able to operate on you. Stay alive and out of jail for *Carmen's* sake."

The pilot flew closer. "I think it might be a car window," he told the others.

"Get down there!" Ben demanded.

"Ben Colter, I am not letting the pilot land this thing until you hand over that .45 on your leather belt," Bannon ordered.

"No! I will not take the chance Billy will get away if he is down there. He knows where Carmen is."

"Give me the fucking gun, Ben. I mean it! I happen to like you, and I don't want to see you go to prison. One of us can legally shoot the sonofabitch, and it's not you. This is a federal case, not a reservation matter."

Reluctantly, Ben yanked out his .45 and handed it over. "There is more than one way to make a man suffer. I do not need a *gun* to do it." he declared.

"This is a matter for the FBI and *only* the FBI," Bannon reminded him.

Caesar was growling and showing his fangs now.

"Go ahead and land this thing before that beast kills us all." Bannon ordered.

"Gladly!" the pilot answered.

He settled down in prairie grass to the east of what they thought was a car window. Ignoring Bannon's order to let him go first, Ben was the first one out, Caesar sprinting ahead of him. Tommy and Detective Bannon followed, hardly able to keep up with Ben and the wolf.

"Ben, damn it!" Tommy yelled. "Let Bannon go first. And remember your back. Don't do something to throw it out again."

"How in hell can he run this fast?" Bannon shouted to Tommy. "I thought you said he was in a lot of pain."

"He *is*. But that means nothing to him right now."

They all reached a dark blue wrecked Chevy smashed against a big boulder and hidden by a huge overhanging shelf of rock. Caesar was already at the door of the car, going crazy trying to get in. He snarled and growled, leaping over and over against the driver side window.

"Get him away! Get him away!" a man inside the car was screaming.

"It is Billy! He is in the car," Ben yelled to Tommy. "Get him out of there!"

"The way that wolf is behaving, I'm not going near him," Bannon told Tommy.

"Caesar! Down! Down!" Ben yelled to the animal. He shouted something in the Lakota tongue and Caesar finally backed off, but the animal ran in circles and kept up the wicked growling.

Ben pulled a quirt from his belt, the one with tiny stones tied into the ends of the rawhide falls. He ripped open the badly dented driver's side door and yanked Billy out by the hair, using one hand. Because of the heat, Billy had stripped down to his underwear. Ben thought the worst. Had he raped Carmen?

"Ben, look out for a gun!" Tommy shouted.

Ben was already whipping the shirtless Billy about the back and shoulders. "Where is she?" he screamed. "Where is Carmen?"

Billy ducked and rolled, trying to get away from the quirt. "I'm not sure, man," he screamed back. "I think she is dead." He screamed more as Ben whipped him even harder. "I did not kill her!" Billy insisted over and over. "She fell! She fell!"

Detective Bannon pulled his 9mm Glock and held it on both men, moving it back and forth, unable to keep it on Billy alone. Caesar kept running around both of men, making a weird sound that was a mixture of howling and barking. Billy rolled away from Ben, and the wolf lit into Billy's bare ankle, biting down fiercely and pulling at Billy while Ben yanked off his own bulletproof vest so he could move around better. Billy managed to reach for his .45, which had fallen out of the vehicle when Ben dragged him out. He tried to aim it at Ben, but before he could get control of the gun, Ben landed into him again, grabbing his wrist and shoving Billy's arm down to the ground as he managed to roll him to his belly and plant a knee into his back.

"Tommy, get his gun," he yelled.

Tommy stomped on Billy's wrist and grabbed the .45 out of his hand, tossing it aside.

By then Steve Lake reached the car and looked around inside. He stepped away with a rifle and held it in the air.

Ben got up and kicked Billy onto his back, while Tommy remained standing on his wrist. Bannon pointed his

Glock close to Billy's face. "Stay down or I can't guarantee Ben or that wolf won't *kill* you before I get the chance!"

"Get him off!" Billy started crying.

"Caesar, down!" Ben yelled, feeling a need for vengeance in every part of his being.

Caesar finally backed off yet again.

"He had a Marlin 336 in the car," Steve shouted. "It has a scope on it!"

"You rotten *murderer,*" Ben growled. "Did you kill Carmen?"

"No! I told you. She fell. I mean ... " He panted and sobbed. "I shot her ... but she kept running. She was not dead. She fell over ... a cliff. I watched her lying at the bottom ... for a long time. She never moved after that. I think the fall ... killed her."

"*Where! When!*" Ben demanded.

"Yesterday, over ... way over there." Billy pointed with his free hand. "Beyond that grassland. She ... ran into the Badlands beyond." He sobbed harder. "I ... followed her ... can't remember when ... I shot at her, but she disappeared ... over a cliff. I was going to follow her down ... but it was too steep ... straight down. She looked dead at the bottom."

Ben let out a cry as though someone had stabbed him in the gut. He began lashing at Billy again, opening more cuts in his shoulders, his arms, his chest, his legs, screaming at him the whole time. "Did you rape her first? You filthy bastard!"

"No! No!" Billy protested.

"God *damn* you Billy Big Bull! You fucked her for vengeance, didn't you? You fucked me over and you fucked my *wife!* And you wanted to fuck Talia!"

Steve put down the rifle, and he and Tommy managed

to pull Ben off Billy, but only because Ben was weakened by the pain in his back.

Ben went to his knees and stayed there a moment. "*Kill* him!" Ben begged. "Someone please kill him!"

Tommy wrapped an arm around his neck from behind and held on. "Stop this, Ben. It will not change anything, and it will only get you in trouble. We have to find Carmen. He has told us where she might be, so calm down. Leave Billy to the feds. He said he did not rape Carmen. I believe him. Promise me that if I let go of you, you will not go after Billy again. We have him. He cannot get away now."

Ben panted with rage and sorrow. "Let go," he told Tommy.

"Not until you promise not to light into Billy again. I will not let you, even if it means getting hurt."

Ben groaned from his own pain. "I would never hurt you. You know that."

Tommy let go, and Ben wilted, lifting his head long enough to study Billy's bloody body and the terrible bruising, cuts, and swelling all around Billy's forehead and cheekbones. "What happened to your face?" he asked.

"That ... bitch of yours ... hit me with a rock. That's how she ... got away."

Ben grinned wickedly. "Good for her. Too bad she didn't kill you." He winced from the deep back pain that plagued him. "You killed ... Talia ... didn't you? And you were trying to kill *me,* you rotten sonofabitch!"

"Killing Talia was an accident!" Billy wept. "An accident!"

"And not killing *me* was an accident." Ben looked away. "My God, Billy! Why? *WHY?*"

"You had everything," Billy answered through sobs. "Including Talia. I ... loved her. I *mourned* her."

"Not as much as I did and still do," Ben answered, wiping at tears. "That's why you started drinking, isn't it?" Ben looked at Detective Bannon. "Are you listening to all of this? You are witnesses to sending this man to prison for the rest of his life. I hope he gets the *death* sentence. I will gladly take the needle myself and put the poison in him and watch him slowly *die*." He reached for Tommy, who helped Ben get to his feet. "Tell me which way to go look for Carmen," Ben asked Billy dejectedly.

Billy pointed again. "Like I said. She is over there." He pointed again. "In the Badlands. I stayed here ... last night and was going to ... go look again today ... see if she was still ... lying there. I wanted to be sure ... she was dead from the fall."

"And you probably have food and water." Ben said. "You let her lie there, maybe still alive, while you came back here and ate and probably got drunk again. Which way should we go once we get inside those rocks?"

"Left. She ran ... left. I don't think I can walk ... or I would show you."

"You *bet* you can't walk." Ben smiled wickedly. "If this were the old days, I would tie you upside down from a tree and build a fire under you and watch you slowly *roast* to death, your brains first. Your screams would be music to my ears."

He turned to Tommy. "Let this man who used to be our friend think about what he has done. We will go and find Carmen." He turned his gaze back to Billy. "And she had better be alive, or by God, prison or not, I *will* come back and kill you!

"Detective Bannon, leave a man with Billy and get another helicopter here to pick him up. If we find Carmen, I do not want her to have to ride in the same helicopter as the sono-fabitch who tried to kill her." He glared at Billy again. "Besides, if he is with us, I cannot promise I will not throw him out as soon as we are high enough to break every bone in his body when he lands. I would wait until we are flying over rocks and canyons."

"Go get a blanket and some water from the helicopter," Bannon told him. "I'll stay here with Billy and radio for help. Take both medics and the helicopter across the open grassland to where the grass ends. You can get out and search from there while the helicopter keeps track of you. He said that Carmen fell over a cliff. She might be in a canyon we can't reach by helicopter. We might need to lower you down from above."

Ben ignored the intense pain in his back and ran to the helicopter, Tommy on his heels. Caesar sprinted beside them. Tommy took off his bulletproof vest, and the two medics climbed inside along with Ben and Tommy. Ben leaned out and rubbed Carmen's shirt over Caesar's face again. "Go find her!" he told the wolf.

Caesar darted away, charging through the grass as though his life depended on it.

"He is on her scent!" Ben told the pilot. "Follow him!"

The pilot flew off, and the medics handed Tommy a light cotton blanket and gave Ben a large bottle of water. "That water also has nutrients in it," Buckheimer told Ben. "As soon as we get her in here, we will start an IV to begin hydrating her."

"If her kidneys have not already stopped functioning," Ben lamented. "They will shut down and poison her body if this has gone too far. Carmen could be beyond saving."

"Stop thinking the worst, *sohnkah*," Tommy told him. "If we find her alive, that is all that matters right now. And she is young and healthy. It has only been about twenty—four hours."

"Twenty—four hours of ungodly heat and sun and no water! And if she is injured ..."

"Look," the pilot exclaimed then. "What is that? There is something white down there." He flew closer and hovered.

"Her jeans!" Ben noticed something blue also. "And her shirt!" He turned his gaze to Tommy. "He said he did not rape her. Why was she wearing no clothes?"

"We can only find and help her for now, Ben, and learn the truth from the doctors." He turned to the pilot. "Let us out here. We will leave the clothes for evidence. Remember this place and send men back later to look around for anything else that might help make sure we know everything that happened. Right now we must follow Caesar."

The pilot landed, and Tommy and Ben jumped out, running into the rocky area nearby, where Caesar ran back and forth, whining and making an odd howling sound, almost like an otherworldly creature. As soon as Tommy and Ben reached the animal, it took off again. Tommy and Ben followed while the copter hovered above them. Minutes later, the pilot called down to them on a loudspeaker.

"I see something pink in that canyon ahead of you," he told them. "It's on top of a rock." He flew ahead of Ben and Tommy and hovered lower. "Right here. Jesus! I think it's a pair of women's panties. Watch out for the ledge. You're almost on it. It's steep and straight down."

Ben and Tommy reached the ledge, and so did Caesar. The wolf ran back and forth wildly, then headed down the cliff, all four paws sinking into mostly sand. He tumbled partway down, then managed to get to his feet again. When he reached the bottom, he stood still a moment and shook his fur wildly, then ran toward the flat rock where Ben and Tommy could also see the panties.

"I'm going down there," Ben said frantically.

"Ben, that could destroy your back. Let the helicopter lower you down."

"You saw Caesar! It's mostly sand. And lowering me might take too long."

"*Ben!*"

Ben went over the cliff, stumbling, tumbling, clawing at anything he could, his long hair flying, one hand holding onto the bottle of water, which he finally let go of and tossed ahead of him.

"Shit!" he heard Tommy swear right before he followed Ben over the edge.

———

THROUGH BLOODSHOT EYES that were just slits because of her agonizing migraine, Carmen watched a small lizard slither up a rock a few feet away. *So, you are under here for the shade, too.* Would the lizard be the last thing she saw before death finally claimed her?

She could no longer open her mouth. It was so dry that everything stuck together. She imagined being found as a curled—up skeleton with blonde hair stuck to its skull. She watched the lizard disappear over the rock, wondering at the strange droning noise she heard then. She became more alert when she felt something licking at her side, where Billy had shot her. The licking moved down her body to her leg, then her left foot.

Coyotes! Billy had said they would come. She whimpered with horror, then saw a big man with long, black hair kneel beside her.

Billy! He'd come to finish her off! She tried as best she could to fight him, made a fist and hit at him. He held her wrists together and kept saying her name, then splashed her face with something cool. He was trying to wake her up so she would be more aware of some awful thing he meant to do to her. She gasped and choked when he poured water between her lips, more into her hair.

"She's alive!" a man's voice said. "My God, Tommy, she's alive! But there is blood everywhere. So many cuts and bruises and scrapes. And she's been shot! Look here. My God, she's been shot."

"Calm down, Little Brother. Look. It is just a flesh wound. She is so skinny, the bullet went right through her side and did not settle anywhere. I do not think it even hit any organs." Someone covered her with a blanket. "Look at her foot. She still has a shoe on her right foot, but left foot is a mess. And look at this hanging off her ankle. It's a bra. She must have wrapped it around her foot to protect it. I told you she is smart and would fight."

Carmen heard a sharp cry, of someone in pain. "Tommy, are you hurt?" the other man asked.

"My shoulder. I think I sprained it coming down that cliff. I'll manage."

Carmen felt someone fidgeting with her foot. She groaned when he touched her ankle. The other person leaned closer. Long, dark hair shrouded her face. Whoever it was kissed her lips so gently it was like a breath of air. He trickled water over her face again, over her lips.

"Carmen," he whispered. "I am here." He smoothed her hair away from her face. "Tommy, so much blood. She could still die."

"You are thinking of Talia. Do not go there, Little Brother. This is Carmen, and she needs our help. Let the medics tend to her. I will go signal them to send down a stretcher."

"Call Sid Ruben," the first man answered. "Ask him what to do. Her face is so beat up, plus she fell. Maybe she broke something. And maybe this made her old head injury worse."

"We will not know much until we get her hydrated. That is the first thing we must do. Give her just a little more water, Ben."

Tommy? Sid? Ben? Little Brother? Familiar names.

"You will be okay now, Carmen. I am here. Hang on!"

Carmen heard the sound of tiny bells. *I am here. No one can harm you.*

"Drink just a little, baby," someone told her. More water trickled into her mouth. She managed to move her lips and tongue. More water fell through her hair, over her neck. Cool. So cool.

"Carmen, talk to me. Tell me what hurts the most so I can tell the medics."

She heard the whining noise again, felt something lick her face. "Coyotes!" she whimpered.

"No, Carmen, that's Caesar. He found you. You are safe. We will take you straight to the hospital. They will clean you up and make everything better. I will be with you. I promise not to leave you for one second."

"Ben?" she managed to choke out.

"It is I. You are safe now."

"Don't ... leave me."

"I am never letting you out of my sight again. And you coming here has brought so many answers. My God! My best friend! I am so sorry, Carmen. So sorry. I should have seen it."

"My ... head. My pills."

"We will take away the pain. I promise."

More voices. Someone grasped her wrist gently.

"Her pulse is strong, but she is obviously severely dehydrated. We will get an IV started right away."

Who was that? The voice was unfamiliar. Someone picked her up and laid her in something and tightened straps.

"Ben!" she cried out.

"I am right here." He had to shout now because of the loud rap-rap-rap of a helicopter. "They are taking you to the hospital, but they will bring me up so I can be with you."

The loud engine. Wind blowing sand everywhere. Whatever she lay in felt like it was swinging around. She looked up and realized she was being raised into a helicopter. Once inside, a man uncovered her left arm and felt for a vein. She was aware of a needle going into her.

"Hang on, sweetheart. We will pump you up like a water balloon and get you hydrated. We will get those kidneys working right. You'll be okay."

Carmen moved in and out of consciousness. "Ben!" she kept calling, starting to cry..

Suddenly, he was there.

"My head!"

"She gets bad migraines," Ben told someone. "Give her something for pain. She suffered a skull fracture not all that long ago." Someone gently wiped her forehead with a cool rag. "Look at the bruises on her face. And her jaw is swollen. Her husband used to beat her, too. How can such a delicate face take so much battering?"

Carmen felt Ben take her hand as someone lifted the blanket for a moment.

"My God, she's covered with cuts and scrapes. Her skin is almost completely scraped off in a couple of places. And what's this? A bullet wound?"

"The fucker shot her," Ben answered.

Ben? He never cusses like that. He must be really mad. Somewhere inside, Carmen found it amusing. She tried to smile, but her lips and tongue still would not work right. It felt like her lips would crack if she smiled. She sensed someone else's presence now.

"I think it is a flesh wound," someone answered. "It looks to me like the bullet went right through her side without hitting any organs."

Tommy?

"Her foot is also badly injured."

That was Ben's voice.

"Looks like you need attention, too," a man said.

"It is my shoulder," Tommy said. "Tend to Carmen first."

"I am more afraid for her head injuries and the bullet wound before worrying about her foot," Ben said. "That is what they should tend to right away when we get to the hospital. Tommy, call Sid."

"If you can't get through up here, we can do it with the radio," another man's voice said.

"Sid Ruben is her neurosurgeon back in Grand Rapids," Ben told someone. "We will try to get him to fly out here. They should take an MRI of her brain and skull right away. Tell the doctors at the hospital. Sid might want to look at her injuries online."

"Don't worry, Ben. They will know what to do. From what I've heard, the doctors in Rapid City saved *your* life once, and you were in far worse condition. Detective Bannon told me you should not have lived at all."

"And I do not look forward to walking back into that hospital, but I have no choice now."

Carmen felt the blanket come over her again. "I'm going to give her something to put her out." The other man was talking again. "She has to be in a lot of pain besides the migraine. And she'll need to be out when they start cleaning up all those wounds. They are full of sand and gravel. It won't be a fun job for the doctors or for Carmen. I have already started an IV that is a combination of antibiotics and a fluid that will help cool her down, including her brain. That might help against inflammation and swelling."

"Thank you."

"What about you? Your back? Do you need something for pain? I see agony in those eyes, Ben."

"I only use Tylenol, if you have any. I have an addiction to opioids."

Carmen felt an odd, cool tingling move through her body. Someone leaned close. She recognized his scent.

"Ben," she said weakly. "Your back."

"Right now you are all that matters. I love you, Carmen. We never stopped looking for you."

Carmen was aware that the helicopter was in the air. Someone kissed a corner of her lips. *"Ohwahzheeahnkah, washtay,"* he whispered near her ear. "Be still and rest. I am with you."

"I love you," Carmen answered weakly. "I knew you would find me."

"And you will never grasp how much I love you," Ben told her. "You are my life and my strength."

"I felt her with me," Carmen told him. "Talia spoke to me. She told me ... to lie still ... so Billy would think ... I was dead." She felt Ben grasp her hand, felt him kiss the back of it. "Don't ... let go."

He squeezed her hand lightly. "Never. I will never let go."

A blessed cooling relief moved through her veins and the pain in her head disappeared. Sweet blackness moved in.

CHAPTER THIRTY-THREE

CARMEN STIRRED AWAKE, taking a moment to look around the room. She was sure she'd been awake before, and vaguely remembered doctors and nurses fussing over her, talking about her kidneys, her skull, something about superficial wounds and keeping her off her foot. She also remembered Ben barking orders at doctors ... Tommy telling Ben to calm down. Other times Ben's voice was close, so close. Promises that he would never leave her alone again, never let someone hurt her again.

Those memories brought her to uglier ones.

Billy. Punching her. The searing pain of a bullet plowing through her side. Was she even really alive? Did everything work right if she was? Could she even move?

She shifted slightly, then groaned. Everything hurt. It was not so much direct pain from wounds. It was more of a deep, deep ache from head to toe. She remembered having a painful, bloody left foot. She tried to move it and was relieved that she could wiggle her toes and bend her ankle, but she felt something constricting full movement. The head of her bed was slightly cranked up, and she was able to look down to see her left foot was heavily bandaged. She shifted in bed, slowly bent her legs, moved her arms. Everything worked, but she felt utterly exhausted, and that deep ache enveloped her again.

She lay her head back and closed her eyes, remembering fuzzy-looking people, doctors asking her questions, nurses sticking needles into her, Ben helping bathe her, putting some kind of lotion on her arms and legs, soft kisses, constant "I love you's," "Please don't die on me," and "I'm so sorry."

Anger rushed through her then. How tragic that one of Ben's best friends was the one who tried to kill him, the one who killed Talia and Ben's precious baby, killed poor Linda Two Fists. *And tried to kill me!* She licked her lips. Her jaw hurt. She remembered the blow to her jaw, the awful heat, and running ... falling ... crawling ... and finally the sound of those tiny bells.

She moved again, relieved that she wore no casts. At least nothing was broken ... except maybe her jaw. She did have pain there every time she licked her lips.

Water! She craved water. She saw a glass of ice water with a straw in it and reached for it, but it was too far away. She noticed she had an IV in her right arm, then realized how bruised and scraped her arms were also. She looked at a clock on the wall. It was 1:30. Bright sunshine peeked through the slats and sides of closed venetian blinds at the window. It must be afternoon, not the middle of the night.

She looked for a call button. She wanted that water, wanted a nurse who could answer her questions, wanted Ben. Poor Ben! This had surely been so hard on him. Her own ordeal, finding out Billy was responsible for all of it. Why wasn't he here? *Oh my God, maybe he killed Billy!*

Maybe he is sitting in jail. He needed her. Ben needed her. She looked again for the call button as someone walked in.

Carmen smiled in spite of her sore jaw and dry lips.

"Val!" She meant to shout the name, but it came out in a hoarse whisper.

"It's about time you recognized me, girlfriend."

Carmen reached out one hand, and Val took it and squeezed it gently. "I'm afraid to touch you or hug you. Are you in pain? Do you want a nurse?"

"No," Carmen answered, realizing her voice didn't quite want to work right. It sounded foreign to her, rough and raspy. "I just want water."

Val grabbed the water and held it for her while Carmen drank through the straw. "Girl, when will men stop using you like a punching bag? Sid and I couldn't believe it when we heard what happened. He rearranged his schedule, and we flew right out here. Sid insisted on being the one to take care of your head injuries."

Carmen took comfort in the knowledge that Sid was here for her. "Oh, I'm so ... grateful," she told Val.

"He kept you in an induced coma and kept your brain cooled down for three days. That's why you haven't been aware of much. He was worried about inflammation. But he said an MRI showed no sign of your old fracture being compromised and no new fractures. Those bright eyes tell me you have no brain damage, but then Sid will have to determine that for sure. They've had the kidney specialist who treated Ben watching your kidney function—something about severe dehydration can cause your kidneys to shut down. Ben about went nuts over that one. He's something of an expert on kidneys, isn't he? Anyway—"

"Stop!" Carmen put a hand up. "Give me a minute."

She put her arms out. "And give me a hug. It's so good to see you, Val."

Val leaned down and lightly hugged her. "Tell me if I'm hurting anything."

"No. I ... feel pretty good except for ... " Carmen rubbed at her throat. "My throat is so dry."

Val straightened and handed her the glass of water again. "I'm so glad it looks like you will be okay. They have been pumping you full of antibiotics and hydration fluids. I bet you're ten pounds heavier with water." She wiped at a sudden tear. "What a crazy adventure you've had since you left Michigan. But when I look at the man you came out here for, and watch how he fusses over you, and hear in his voice how much he loves you, I know you did the right thing. You have found a man who appreciates you the way you deserve to be appreciated."

"Where is he? Where is Ben?"

"He took us to lunch down in the cafeteria. He and Sid are still down there talking. They have become great friends. And Carmen ... oh my God, I have never seen a man so much in love. If you had died, I swear he would have shot himself or something. Actually, I think the doctors might have shot him instead. He has pestered them something awful." Val smiled through more tears. "Constant questions. Constant orders: 'Check this. 'Check that.' 'Are you sure?' 'Shouldn't you take another X-ray?' 'Is she in pain?' 'Don't overdue the pain medication, but I don't want her to suffer either.' 'What about her kidneys? Keep watching her kidney function.' I'm telling you, Carmen, it's been almost hysterical, if not a real irritation for the doctors. Sid had to remind Ben more than once that he's a lawyer, not a doctor. And for the first couple of days, Ben never left, ate, or slept. He was walking around here in those buckskin pants, all dirty from falling down that cliff, still all painted up. I mean to tell you, he was scary-looking, but here's the best part. They made him-"

Carmen waved her hand again. "Falling down that cliff? Ben jumped over that cliff I fell over?" She wished she could speak louder and without this pain.

"He and Tommy both. Tommy dislocated his shoulder, but he'll be okay."

"Oh, no! What about Ben's back? He wasn't even well yet ... from a fight he got into with Billy ... a few days before that."

"Oh, he's been paying for that jump, believe me. He's been chucking the Tylenol like M&Ms. Doctors here offered something stronger, but you know Ben. He won't take it. Anyway, let me tell you the best part." Val grinned wickedly. "Everybody kept telling Ben to go home and change, but he wouldn't leave. So, Sasha—oh, by the way, I *love* that woman—anyway, she went into town and bought new jeans and a shirt and underwear for Ben, and the hospital made him clean up. They let him use the shower in your bathroom here." Val sighed and put a hand over her heart. "Let me tell you, girl, when he stepped back into this room wearing those tight jeans and no shirt, his hair still wet, I thought I'd pass out. It was like watching one of those commercials for men's cologne, where the hot guy rises out of the water. That man isn't just handsome. He is beautiful. He was such a mess those first couple of days, I'd almost forgotten how he looks without all that dirt and paint on his face. I mean to tell you, God definitely broke the mold on that man."

"You should ... walk through a mall with him. Women ... trip over themselves." Carmen laughed, but it came out as more of a squeak. "He *is* beautiful, Val." Carmen suddenly wanted to cry. "And I don't mean his looks. He is beautiful in so many other ways."

Val helped her drink more water as she struggled to keep her voice working.

"I know what is under those ... good looks," Carmen continued. "He's just a man, Val, a warrior in the courtroom. I wish you could see it. When Ben walks in, the judge ... and the opposing attorneys ... get kind of an 'Oh shit!' look on their faces."

"Oh, that is choice."

"But Ben is such a softie otherwise ... so devoted to those he cares about. When I am better ... I'll tell you something that shows you how *much* he cares." *He turned down five million dollars for those kids.* She rubbed at her throat again. "More water."

Val held the glass for her again. "Softie is right," she told Carmen. "Ben walked around here like a warrior ready to kill any doctor who might let you die, and then I walked in here a couple of days ago to find him sitting by you, holding your hand and crying. I just left so he wouldn't know I saw him."

Carmen closed her eyes. "It's not just what happened to me. It's finding out his best friend ... betrayed him in the worst way. And he spent months in this same hospital, going through surgery after surgery ... so much pain and heartache. It must be hard for him to have to be here again."

"I can see you haven't changed," Val told her. "It's just like you to be more worried about Ben than about yourself." She handed Carmen more tissues. "Girl, let me tell you something. Those nurses out there have made Ben's stay here more bearable just by how much they all love him. They stumble all over him when he walks down the hallway, and they wait on him hand and foot."

Carmen managed a smile. "Val, you are just what I needed. But how did you get in? Hospitals allow only one visitor at a time."

"Have you forgotten who my husband is?" Val snickered. "Sid used his powers as a top surgeon, *your* surgeon to boot, and Ben used plain old emotional heartstrings to get his doctor to step in and allow all of us to be here at the same time. I was allowed in because I'm Sid's wife and your best friend. Sid claimed I was as good medicine for you as the real thing."

"You *are*." Carmen squeezed her hand, breaking into tears again.

"They told us when we're here in the room, we don't need to wear masks," Val added, "as long as we have all had the dreaded vaccine and cases of the virus are low where we came from, which they are. Ben has been putting a special salve on your wounds, but he has to wash clear to his elbows first, just like the doctors do. They have been watching for infection, and of course watching your brain and your kidneys. So far, so good. You might even get to go home soon."

"Oh, Val, you look so good. I like that shoulder-length haircut ... and you've lost weight."

"Fifteen pounds." Val stood and sashayed in a circle.

"You look wonderful! Can you stay a while? How long have you been here?"

"Four days. We flew right out here the day after Ben called us. We are staying in a nearby hotel. Sid has to go back tomorrow, but I'm staying here with you for a couple of weeks. I'm going to look after you while Ben goes back to the office to catch up and gets back to rehearsals for the program he has planned for the Pow-Wow. Sid is going to fly back for the show."

"Oh, I'm so glad. I hope I'll be able to go too."

"Oh, you will, girl. Ben is planning on it. I think he has something special planned, but he won't tell us about it."

Carmen put a hand to her sore jaw. "I doubt I will be … completely healed by then. How badly bruised am I?"

Val pursed her lips mockingly as she studied Carmen's face. "Honey, it ain't pretty, but you have two weeks to lose the swelling and a lot of the bruising before the concert."

"Oh, so I'll be … all green instead of black and blue. That's almost worse."

Val laughed. "It's not as bad as you think, but maybe you should wait a few days before you look in the mirror."

Carmen dabbed at her eyes again. "How bad was it? Ben and Billy I mean. I was afraid I would wake up … to find out Ben was in jail for murdering Billy."

"Well, according to Tommy, if an FBI man hadn't taken Ben's gun away from him before they found Billy, I think Ben *would* be in jail right now. They found Billy holed up in a wrecked car. I guess Ben dragged him out and beat him near to death with one of those warrior weapons, a quirt, I think they call it. Ben said later that's what he used on Jerry, but not nearly as bad. With Jerry, it was just a warning. With Billy, he wanted the man to bleed to death. As it is, Billy is already dead."

"*What?* How?"

"The FBI guy shot him. I guess Billy landed into the guy and knocked him over. He grabbed the man's gun and took off running. The FBI guy pulled a second gun he carried and ordered him to stop. He didn't, so the FBI guy shot him dead. Tommy thinks Billy ran on purpose. What do they call it? Suicide by cop or something like that. Tommy thinks Billy couldn't live with what he'd done, so he decided he would rather be shot down than face the death sentence ... or ever have to face Ben again."

"Oh dear," Carmen whispered, more tears coming. "I never dreamed me suggesting an audit would lead to all of this. It's all so sad." She blew her nose, and even *that* hurt. "You never know how life will turn out, Val."

"Life turns out the way it is *supposed* to turn out, which is why God made it so Sid couldn't go to that show at the Indian casino. I invited you instead, and look what happened. It changed your life, probably forever."

"What about ... Caesar? I think he was there ... when they found me."

"That wolf is *how* they found you. They took Caesar with them in the helicopter. Ben figured he would sense when they were near you. I'm sure Ben can tell you more details. Caesar stayed right where they found you, and they flew in his trainer to pick him up. Now Ben wants him trained so you can keep him at home as a guard dog. How's *that* for protection? I'd say a yellow-eyed, fierce-looking wolf is better than carrying a gun. Wouldn't you?"

Carmen smiled softly and wiped at her eyes again. "Ben is being *too* cautious now."

"That's not how Ben sees it. I have a feeling he is going to mother you and watch out for you so much that you'll get sick of him, although I can't imagine that. If you *do* get sick of him, send him my way."

Both women snickered. "Same old Val, I see," Carmen commented.

"Well, we haven't really been apart all that long. It just *seems* like a long time because so much happened after you left." Val patted her hand. "It's been crazy, but we've gotten to know Ben so much better. We're so happy for you, Carmen. You have finally found a man who totally respects you for who you are. It's like he already knows every little thing about you, and he's okay with you two being different. All he wants from you is your love ... and ten kids." Val giggled at the suggestion. "*You,* with ten kids."

"He's still talking numbers? I told him ... I have to think about it."

"Hell, I'd gladly make *twenty* kids with that man! And God knows he will be right there helping you with all of them."

They both laughed again, just as Ben, Tommy, Sasha, and Sid all walked into the room together. Ben headed straight for Carmen.

"Hey, look at you, awake and all bright-eyed!"

Carmen reached for him.

"Hold on," Sid told Ben. "Let me take a look at her eyes."

Bedlam ensued. Ben stood beside the bed and held Carmen's hand while Sid leaned down and kissed her cheek. "You're looking good, kid, and the MRI looks good, too." He shined a bright little flashlight into each eye. Another doctor told her that an ultrasound of her kidneys looked very good.

"My favorite former patient here drove me nuts with questions about your kidney function," he told Carmen. "I'm Dr. Yates, the doctor who took care of Ben after he was shot."

"I am glad to ... finally meet you," Carmen told the doctor. "You must be a miracle worker."

More soft laughter, hugs and smiles ensued as Sasha walked up and touched Carmen's cheek with her own. "Maybe now Ben will calm down and stop driving everyone in this hospital to drink," she joked..

Carmen started crying when she saw Tommy with his

arm in a sling. "Why did you and Ben ... jump down that cliff?" she sobbed, the words difficult to understand because they were half whispered.

"Hey, Caesar went down first," Tommy answered. "And there was no stopping Ben. He was not about to wait for the helicopter to lower him down. And once he went over, I was not going to be outdone by my little brother, so I went over, too."

Carmen cried even harder. "You could both ... have been killed."

"Do you really think we were thinking about that?" Tommy joked. "Ben has been gorging on Tylenol ever since."

"Oh, Ben!" Carmen looked up at him. "I want to talk to you alone."

More bedlam. Everyone understood. A barrage of "Get better" and "We'll be back" and "You're looking so much better" filled the room. The whole bunch of them walked out, and Ben pulled a big leather guest chair close to the bed, then carefully picked Carmen up, blanket and all, and sat down in the chair with her on his lap.

Carmen relished the feel of his strong arms around her. "Ben, you must be in so much pain." She curled against him, and he pulled the blanket around her.

"*Me?*" He kissed her hair. "Carmen, you are in a hospital bed with cuts and bruises on your entire body, a foot that looks like flayed meat, a bruised jaw, and a throat that will take several more days to get back to normal, let alone the mental trauma you have been through. And you are worried about *me?*" He reached down and pushed the leaver at the side of the chair that moved it into a partially reclining position. "Am I hurting you?"

"No. I mean, everything hurts, but it's like a full-body

ache. I don't care as long as you hold me." Carmen rested her head on his shoulder and kissed his neck, breathing in his familiar scent.

"You are okay now," he told her. "I made you a promise no one would ever lay a hand on you again. You have no idea how sick I am that someone I thought was my best friend ended up hurting you. I do not ever want you out of my sight after this. I am so damn sorry, baby."

"You didn't know. And it happened so quick." She broke into tears again.

Ben put a hand to the side of her head and kissed her battered face gently.

"Ben, I remember how you must have found me, but he didn't rape me. He ttried, but I hit him with a rock. I ... hit him hard ... right in the face a bunch of times."

"I know. I saw his face, and I knew you were the only one who could have done that to him. I felt pride at your strength and courage, but I did fear the worst. The doctors verified that he did not abuse you that way, but my God, Carmen, what he *did* do was bad enough. If we had not found you when we did, you would not be here in my arms right now. I was crazy with worry. I could not go through losing another woman I love. Just holding you here, alive in my arms, seems like such a miracle. We might not have found you at all if not for Caesar."

"Val told me about Caesar." She kissed his neck again, "Ben I am so sorry about Billy. He was your ... friend. It must ... break your heart to know the truth, that Billy k illed Talia. He's the one who shot both of you."

Ben gently rubbed her back. "I know all that. We suspected so when we realized it was Billy who had stolen you away. And we found out about Pat Daisy. Did Billy admit that, too?"

"Yes. They were going to ... take your money and run away."

"Pat has been fired. She did not know about all the other things Billy did, but she was helping him embezzle. I am just so sorry you got wrapped up in the whole mess."

"You ... didn't know. No one would ever have suspected Billy."

Ben kissed her hair again. "You have brought me closure, Carmen, the kind I needed. That is why the Great Spirit brought us together, for answers and so that I could love again. You brought me all of that. I will be glad to get you home. It is too lonely there without you. I cannot wait until you are well enough to make love. I feel a need to reclaim you, to show you gentleness and show you how sorry I am that I was not there to protect you. I would never have let Billy get his hands on you."

"I know that. I love you, Ben. I prayed you would find me." Carmen met his dark eyes and saw the adoration in them. "Thank you for letting Val stay with me for a while. I am so happy to have her here."

"She is your best friend. Of course she can stay. Sasha will be busy with rehearsals and helping get ready for the show before the Pow-Wow."

Carmen noticed he wore a blue collared shirt. His hair was drawn back at the sides, and he wore his usual silver earrings and a wide silver cuff bracelet. No paint. No feathers. Just that clean, handsome face, those broad, powerful shoulders.

"You look so nice," she told him. "I love how you look in a regular shirt ... but I have messed up the one you are wearing. I'm sorry I can't ... stop crying."

Ben smiled. "You are strong, but you cry so easily. Remember that first night at my house?"

"Oh, I keep ruining all our first times."

Ben smoothed back a piece of her hair. "You did not ruin the first time we made love. That makes up for everything else. And I look forward to when you are well enough to make love again. I was getting used to those almost nightly moments of exotic pleasure." He leaned down and kissed her eyes.

"I must be ... a bruised, swollen mess."

"You are the most beautiful thing I have ever seen. You are *alive*. That is all that matters." He kissed her lips gently again. "Tell me what you need, Carmen."

"You. Just you."

Ben stroked her cheek with the back of his fingers. "*Eenulah*. You are safe now."

He shifted a little, and Carmen heard those tiny bells.

I'm here. No one can harm you.

"When you come home, I will sleep beside you, so you never wake up alone or afraid," Ben said. "If you have bad dreams from this, I will be there to take them away. You have been through so much, Carmen. It is time you received all the love and attention and appreciation you deserve, for your beautiful spirit and beautiful heart. You have courage. That is one of the things I love about you. You can boss me around, and that is okay. I *need* bossing. I need you to help keep me out of the past to see the joy that lies in the future, in *our* future."

He kissed her again, and his eyes seemed to look right through her, into her very thoughts, just like they did that first night they met. Even then, he knew she would be his woman. She realized she'd not had one whit of control over her life from that moment on. And she knew he loved only her now. Just Carmen.

The ghosts from the past were gone.

CHAPTER THIRTY-FOUR

Sid and Val helped Carmen into an aisle seat in the front row of Talia's Theater of Dreams, leaving her wheelchair beside her. "Sid, I really don't need that," Carmen complained, frowning at the chair.

"Yes, you do," Sid answered. "Ben wants you off that foot so you will be able to stand on it later in the show." Sid and Val carefully moved in front of Carmen to sit in the next two seats beside her.

Carmen turned to Val. "Why will I be standing?"

Val shrugged. "I'm as curious as you are."

Carmen nodded to Dr. Yates and a couple of Ben's nurses, who sat in the front row. Why on earth were they here? She breathed deeply against nervousness. "You don't know Ben as well as I do," she told Val. "If he thinks he is going to get *me* up on that stage in front of a packed theater, he'll find out different. He's got me a nervous wreck. Every time I asked him about tonight, he just grinned. He said he wants me to be here for the kids, but I suspect it's more than that."

"Then I guess we will find out, won't we?" Val patted

her arm. "Either way, you look gorgeous. That dress alone makes you look like a high-class model."

"I do like it." In spite of her worry over what Ben's plans were tonight, Carmen was anxious for him to see the form-fitting, black chiffon sleeveless dress Sasha and Val had bought for her. The plunging V-neck showed just enough tempting cleavage, and the belt at the waist glittered with Swarovski crystals. A ruffled flounce at the knees gave it a sexy feel, but she hated the fact that she had to wear tennis shoes instead of spike heels. Sasha had at least found her a pair of black tennis shoes that glittered with rhinestones. She wore a simple solitaire diamond necklace, tiny diamond drop earrings, and a diamond tennis bracelet. Her arms were still peeling from the bad sunburn she'd suffered in the Badlands, but she wore a healing lotion that softened most of the flaky edges.

"I'm proud of the job I did with your hair and makeup," Val told her, "although someone as beautiful as you makes it easy. You don't even *need* makeup, but Ben wanted you to have some extra color tonight."

"There! See? You only need lipstick and extra eye makeup and cheek color when you are going to be on that stage. I've learned that much from Sasha and rehearsals."

"Stop worrying. That dress will knock Ben out. Sasha and I never showed it to him. The cleavage alone will make him want to dive into it."

"You are such a brat, Val Ruben! Ben can be, too. I am surrounded by audacious brats."

"Meantime, I, for one, look forward to watching the warrior perform again," Val said with a grin. "From what I saw last time, those talent scouts you told me about were right on. That man could easily zoom right to the top with the right exposure. I'm glad Sid is here to watch this time."

"Just remember never to talk about that offer in front of the kids. Only Tommy and Sasha know about it, and they are so proud of Ben's decision. I only told you about it so you would understand him even better."

By seven o'clock, the theater was full, with a few extra people standing in the center aisle and at the sides. Capacity was five hundred, and it was obvious more than that had packed themselves in to see Ben Coulter and the Y.E.S.S. Native youth group, probably because what happened with Billy had been in the news.

The lights dimmed, and Sasha stepped out in a strapless, sequined hot pink dress with a wide, glittering rhinestone belt and a full chiffon skirt. She looked as beautiful as ever. Tommy stood at one corner of the stage, wearing blue jeans and a simple black T-shirt, ever the plain and unassuming man. He held an electric guitar. Carmen knew he was forcing himself to play tonight, in spite of a still very sore shoulder.

Native drummers sat around the huge drum used for Pow-Wows, and the usual small orchestra was ready for tonight's performance.

Sasha introduced herself, then announced that this was a very special night. A recent tragedy involving Sunrise Reservation and Ben and his family had brought them and the youth group all together in love, and tonight was a celebration of life and answered prayers. Carmen could already see that this performance was going to be different from what she and Val had seen in Grand Rapids. Earlier rehearsals had not included Sasha's announcement, and Carmen hadn't seen Ben all day. He had purposely stayed at the theater to get ready there, which was another reason Carmen expected the *un*expected.

"I'm getting more and more nervous," she told Val.

"Our first set tonight will be Lakota song and dance," Sasha announced, "performed for all of you here who are Natives of many Nations from all over the country and from Canada. Each Nation is unique, yet we are one, and tomorrow we celebrate our Grand Entry!" Sasha held up her fist, and the audience erupted in war cries and women trilling while the drummers around the Pow-Wow drum pounded it with a thunderous, rhythmic beat for a full minute, chanting in the Lakota tongue.

"I feel like we are being attacked," Val joked.

"You are ... by Ben," Carmen answered with a grin.

Once the audience quieted, Sasha went on with the introduction. "You should know that our second set will show all of you how well our youth group can perform modern music and dance. For any of you who ever watched the television program *Glee* or movies like *Pitch Perfect,* you will get the feel of that same young talent tonight. These kids have worked very hard, so be sure to show them how much you enjoy their show, all choreographed by my brother-in-law, Ben Red Wolf Colter. Prepare to be amazed by what Ben has done for these young people." She put up her fist again. "*Weeusekee!*"

Everyone clapped and cheered as the lights went down and the program began. The first segment was very much the same as what Carmen and Val saw at the casino in Grand Rapids, except that this time there were no wolves involved. Ben feared the theater was too small and would be too packed. Again, the truly frightening look Ben could get in his dark eyes when portraying the proud warrior was a stark contrast to how gentle he was when alone with her. Last night they had made love for the first time since her ordeal. His every touch and taste and kiss and the feel of him pleasing her to her very depths had totally obliterated any remaining pain she had. Their lovemaking had been purely erotic, and watching him now made her warm with a desire to make love all over again tonight.

When Ben belted out the very Native-themed song called "Shouting Grounds," Native drumming shook the entire room. Most of the audience ended up standing and swaying and clapping to the wild Native rhythm. The song ended with chanting while Ben and the youth group whirled and stomped to the song, which was about defeating death and had the feeling of victory over the enemy to it. The audience whistled and cheered for a good two or three minutes after the rousing performance ended, and Ben stepped up to the microphone and announced their last song would be "When We Were Beautiful," a Bon Jovi song.

"All of you will recognize what the words mean to Native Americans," he added. Tommy and Sasha and all their sons held hands with Ben as the song began, with little Ben in front, dressed like a tiny warrior. Soon, tears and near silence enveloped the audience. The song was about a time when the Lakota were free and living wild and healthy on the high plains, hunting buffalo, spiritually alive and strong.

The audience watched a video of open plains, Native men dressed as warriors and riding bareback across grand landscapes, and happy families in tepees, all contrasted with today's poverty, cement-block houses, junkyards, and broken-down pickup trucks. At the end of the video the words We Will Rise Again lit up the screen. Ben held his little nephew high in the air, and the audience broke into cheers and thunderous applause.

After a short break, the youth group performed their second set, and Amy came through her song perfectly, looking lovely and confident, her voice strong as she sang the lead for "When Love Takes Over." The upbeat song had people bouncing in their seats. More songs of hope and fun followed, including "Love Can Move Mountains" and a rousing rendition of Daughtry's "Long Live Rock and Roll." Ben and Tommy played electric guitar together on that one, after which Ben turned around and talked about bringing love and support and attention to neglected and abandoned indigenous children. He sang Josh Groban's "You Are Loved" to the youth group.

"My God, Ben can sing *anything*," Val commented.

"The guy is a natural," Sid commented.

By the time the song ended, Ben had won every person in the audience, who all stood and clapped and cheered. When things calmed, Ben stepped up to the microphone and made an announcement Carmen did not expect.

"I have one more song before our third set," he told the audience. "It is dedicated to my first wife, who was killed tragically a little over three years ago. Most of you know the story. The wounds were reopened recently by the incident through which we learned who killed her and left me for dead." He cleared his throat. "Most of you read or heard about what happened in the local and national news."

He took a deep breath, obviously finding this moment difficult. "Several pictures of Talia hang in this theater because it was built in her memory. She is responsible for the success of the great and talented kids behind me, some of whom come from broken homes and poverty. This entire Sunrise Reservation and the School for the Arts are the product of one woman's dream to help indigenous youth. It has taken me a long time to live with what happened to Talia, but another woman came along who brought me back to life, and our next segment will be dedicated to her."

"Oh my God," Carmen whispered. "I knew it!"

"But right now, I feel I need to sing something in Talia's honor, a goodbye song, if you will," Ben continued. "The new woman in my life understands that I will always love Talia, and that she will always hold a special place in my heart. Talia was talented, caring, and dedicated to many indigenous causes.." He cleared his throat again and took another deep breath. "This song is sung best by Celine Dion, who sang the theme song from *Titanic,* 'My Heart Will Go On.'"

"Oh dear Lord," Carmen said softly. "This is just too sad."

Val grabbed her hand. "I'm not sure I can take this either."

Tommy played the opening to the song, using his own handmade Native American wooden flute, playing the opening just like the real one to "My Heart Will Go On." Carmen could tell Ben truly struggled to get through the song without breaking down. The curtains closed, and the audience was movingly quiet, not sure what to expect next. Sniffles could be heard throughout the crowd, mostly Native American, some dressed in various regalia of their tribe and many, Carmen was sure, who had known Talia.

Finally, the curtains opened, and the young men on stage were dressed in suits and ties, the girls wearing various fancy dresses as though they were going to a prom. Sasha wore a glittery white, ruffle-skirted dress and spike heels, and even Tommy, who hated to dress up, wore a slick black suit with a bow tie.

"Val, I think I am in for it," Carmen said.

Sid chuckled. "This should be good."

Out walked Ben, wearing an all-white tux. Everyone,

the kids on stage and the audience combined, broke into a roar of whistles and hoots and applause.

"Be still my heart!" Val exclaimed.

Carmen just shook her head. "What on earth?"

"Is he just gorgeous, or is he *drop-dead* gorgeous?" Val commented. "I thought he was heart-stopping that day he came to the lake house, but this beats all."

Ben's hair was slicked all the way back into clips at the back of his head and hung long down his back to his waist. He wore no paint and just one long, feather-shaped earring in each ear.

"Those scouts were right about Ben," Sid commented. "With those looks and the way he belts out songs he would go to the top so fast he'd leave dust behind him. It took a lot of courage for him to turn down that offer."

"That's part of what I love about him," Carmen answered.

Ben glanced at Carmen and smiled, then stepped up to a microphone, removing it from its stand. He walked back and forth as he spoke. "I know this is Pow-Wow time, and believe me, my heart and spirit are all Lakota. I will be announcing the Grand Entrance tomorrow, and I honor each and every one of you in the audience tonight who came here from many different tribal families. For the next three days we will be who we truly are : a People whose spirit and beliefs could not be removed from our hearts and blood by those who tried so hard to do just that."

More cheers and a few war cries and trills filled the theater.

"My god is Wakan-Tanka," Ben continued. "Yours might be Usen or Maheo, or the many other Native names for what we all call the Great Spirit. The fact remains we *believe* in that great power beyond, as does the woman I love, who is sitting down in front tonight. Her god is called Jehovah. That is fine with me. She is what some of us call an outsider, but I can tell all of you that she is Lakota at heart. She is kind, forgiving, understanding, tolerant of my religion and my customs, beautiful both in looks and in spirit, and she recently suffered trauma because of someone who was after *me,* not her. Again, I refer to the recent news stories."

Ben paused, taking a deep breath, obviously feeling deeply emotional. "This woman loves without rules, other than she laid down some rules for me not long ago that brought me out of a darkness I was not sure I could keep fighting. My head was barely above water before I met her, and now I am completely out of the water and walking on the beach of joy and emotional health. So, this part of our program is just for Carmen Wolfe. She is from Grand Rapids, Michigan, and she knew next to nothing about life out here before she came to visit," He grinned slyly. "And she never went back."

Hoots and whistles and laughter filled the theater. Carmen reddened and slunk down in her seat a little farther.

"The way we met in Michigan is a bit of a miracle in itself," Ben continued, "and since Carmen came here, she has been through things that would send any weaker woman running back home. But she stayed, and I am better off for it."

Young Amy walked up to Ben with a towel in her hand.

"Amy here is ready with a towel for my shoulder, because by the time I am done with this segment, I will likely have lipstick and mascara all over this white tux, and it is rented."

The remark brought more laughter.

"I will need this towel for Carmen to cry on because she

cries so easily, not from fear and weakness, but because she has a big, big heart."

Carmen covered her face. "Oh my God. Oh my God." she muttered.

"Carmen, this entire segment and the songs we will sing are for you," Ben announced.

Tommy struck an opening tune on his guitar, accompanied by a pianist, and Ben began singing "You Raise Me Up."

"Oh, Lord help me," Val exclaimed. "It's a good thing doctors are here, because I am going to have a heart attack."

While Ben sang, Amy walked down the stage steps with the towel and handed it to Carmen, who cried into it as Ben finished the song. On the last phrase he came down the steps and walked up to her, handing his microphone to Amy and leaning down to pick Carmen up in his arms. She wrapped her arms around his neck and put the towel on his shoulder to cry into as he carried her onto the stage while the audience cheered and clapped.

Carmen spoke close to Ben's ear. "I have already wiped off most of my makeup," she told him. "You knew what that song would do to me, Ben. I must look terrible."

Ben just grinned and kissed her, bringing more applause and whistles. "It is impossible for you to look anything but beautiful." He set her on her feet and stepped away, bowing to Carmen, then saying into the microphone Amy handed him, "Did I not tell you she is beautiful?"

Carmen could hardly see the faces in the audience because of the bright lights, but she could hear their appreciation. She looked at Ben. "You had better hold on to me before I pass out."

Ben smiled and moved an arm around her. He leaned

close to her ear and lowered the microphone. "Love the dress."

Carmen gave him a quick kiss. "Thank you." She wiped at tears with the towel.

Ben straightened and continued talking to the audience. "Carmen is the strongest, bravest woman I have ever met, but she cries over everything," he joked. "I swear, if I got a paper cut on my hand, she would cry about it and want to put a Band-Aid on it."

More laughter.

Ben told his nephew Matthew to bring out "the chair." Matthew left the stage and returned with a rolling desk chair. Ben told Carmen to sit in it.

"There is more to come," he told her. "Wipe off the rest of that makeup that you do not even need and try to stop crying for a few minutes." He turned to the audience as Carmen used the towel to wipe her nose and eyes. Ben began walking around her. "By Lakota custom," he told the audience, "this woman is already my wife. I think you know what I mean."

"You go, girl!" Val shouted, creating more laughter, whistles and applause.

"Carmen is an outsider," Ben continued, "but she is truly thirsty to learn more and be accepted as Lakota herself. She is very smart, and I recognize that she, too, has a culture and a background that deserves my respect, the same as she respects mine. So I have decided that when it comes to marriage, I will honor and respect her beliefs and desires."

Murmurs moved through the audience. Carmen sat in silence, not sure what to expect.

"This country's laws demand that we do this the legal way, and since I am a lawyer, I do not have much choice but to abide by those laws." The pianist began playing a tune Carmen could not quite place until Ben told the audience, "According to Carmen's best friend from Michigan, this song by Kane Brown is one of her favorites." He began singing "What's Mine Is Yours" as he kept walking around her chair. When he reached the chorus, he let the youth group sing as he knelt to one knee in front of Carmen, then handed out a black velvet ring box.

The musicians kept playing, but only a few of the kids on stage kept singing. Along with the audience, they burst into cheers and tears and applause, many in the audience jumping out of their chairs.

"Carmen, will you marry me?" Ben asked, into the microphone. He handed the microphone then to a smiling Sasha while Carmen opened the box, then sat there, dumbstruck. She knew jewelry, and this one was no ordinary ring from the average department store or even the common chain jewelry store. It was a round solitaire, a beautiful cut, and huge.

"Ben! Oh my God! When did you get this?"

He leaned closer. "I've been hanging on to that thing since we went to Denver," he told her. "It is from Darvier, and the design is by Moissanite. I just needed closure before I could go through with this, Carmen, and you brought me that. I sized it by trying that ruby ring you wear on my own little finger, so it should fit. Unless you are saying no?"

"Are you kidding?" She pulled the ring from the box, then hesitated, studying the joy in Ben's eyes. "My God, Ben, can you afford this?"

He broke into laughter. "Hell, I don't know. You're the bookkeeper, remember?"

"Well, affordable or not, I'm not giving this thing back!" Carmen slipped the ring onto her left ring finger, then held it up for all the kids and others around them to see. The Skycam moved in on it so the audience could see it on the monitor.

"She said yes," Sasha told the audience through a microphone.

The room came alive with cheers and war cries and trills, literal screams of joy from the youth group, and not a few tears. Carmen put the towel on Ben's shoulder, throwing her arms around his neck as he pulled her out of the chair and into his arms, keeping her feet off the floor as he turned her to Celine Dion's *I Love You,* which Tommy played over loudspeakers.

"Come on up here, Sid and Val," Sasha said over the microphone. "I know you want to see the rock on Carmen's hand."

"Ben, I love you so," Carmen wept.

"I love you more."

Carmen found his lips, and everyone cheered as they shared a long, deep kiss. When the kiss ended, Ben had tears in his eyes. "Thank you for putting up with a ghost this whole time," he told her.

They talked amid excited teenagers and Sasha and Val blabbing excitedly and commotion in the audience, and with *I Love You* continuing to play over the loudspeakers.

"Stop for a minute!" Val said as she stood behind them and grabbed Carmen's hand to look at the ring. "Holy moly, you could buy a Mercedes with this thing!"

Carmen looked at the towel on his shoulder. "This towel was a good idea," she told him with a smile. "It's a mess, and I am probably a mess."

"You will be more of a mess later tonight, woman. Val and Sid are staying at Tommy's house. Tonight, *I* am taking care of you ... in more ways than one."

"I will need lots of attention," Carmen teased.

"You will get it."

"And I'll need a shower."

"Definitely not a problem."

"What about your back? Don't tell me you are not in pain, because I know when you are."

"I will manage. Some things are more important, and you are better for pain than any damn opioid I've ever taken. If you thought last night was good, tonight will curl your toes."

"Just be careful of my left foot."

They laughed together, and Carmen felt lost in his eyes. "Thank you for the ring and the beautiful way you gave it to me," she told Ben. "I love you so much. I don't even have the right words."

"You do not need words. I see it in your eyes."

They kissed again. The concert was over, but a new life together, for better or worse, for richer or poorer, in sickness and in health, was just beginning.

CHAPTER THIRTY-FIVE

THE WIND BLEW Carmen's hair over her face. She pulled it behind her ears and readjusted her sunglasses against the bright day—a perfect day for sending Singing Boy to his mother.

This place in the Black Hills was a plateau on one of the higher peaks in the granite mountains. Forests of thick pine created the dark appearance of this region, an obvious reason this country was called the Black Hills. Shadows that changed constantly with the sun moved throughout the canyons, crevasses, and dazzling rock formations of the more than one million acres of fantastic lakes and scenery Carmen noticed on the way here. Buffalo grazed everywhere. Campgrounds and tourist attractions abounded, but up here, in this special burial ground set aside for burying the most holy chiefs and traditional healers and special Lakota women, was a place of simple, quiet beauty.

She doubted there was a dry eye here among the several who had come to help Ben send his son to a place far better than the chaos and hatred and divisiveness and hardships going on in the world below. Carmen still felt the devastation in Ben's heart that showed on his face when he finally had gone into the nursery this morning and removed Singing Boy's medicine bag from under the little pillow in the crib. He'd put the medicine bag around his neck, using its long leather tie cord so that it hung next to his heart. He'd been too distracted and heartbroken for the three-hour drive here, so Carmen drove, following Tommy up the winding mountain road. Ben did not speak most of the way here.

Carmen ached over the fact that Tommy had insisted Ben let him search him to be sure Ben did not have a knife hidden on him. In spite of how far Ben had come since the shooting, this tender and difficult moment for him would bring out his Lakota spirit, which Tommy feared might mean a sudden sorrowful slash to his arm. That was the deeper Lakota side to Ben that Carmen knew would take time for her to get used to and accept.

Val and Sid had gone home, but several teachers, Ben's legal assistants, Alice, and many of the youth who had known Talia were here, as well as Ben and Tommy's grandmother. Talia's parents were deceased, but several of her relatives were here. Lieutenant Bannon and Captain Hyer were also here. They stood back from the very holy ceremony, and from Caesar, who'd ridden in the back of the truck and now lay obediently beside Talia's grave. Ben had insisted the wolf be present for the ceremony and was helping train Caesar to be a personal guard dog for Carmen.

Out of respect for the very holy ceremony reserved for the Lakota, Carmen stood back and watched. She felt privileged to even be here, and she felt her heart moving deeper and deeper into Ben's world. Four Native drummers sat nearby around the big drum used at the Pow-Wow that had ended more than a week ago. She still could not get over the magnificent colors displayed in the hundreds of different dance regalia at the Pow-Wow. Sasha had painted Carmen's face with white stripes for the occasion, and Carmen had worn a beaded, fringed tunic Ben's grandmother made for her.

The dress was a surprise. Grandma Wanda had started the dress when Ben first took Carmen to see her several weeks ago, and receiving it as a gift from a full-blood Lakota woman was an honor, although because of her sore foot, she could not dance in the grand circle the morning of the Pow-Wow entrance parade. Sasha had pushed her in a wheelchair.

Now came a more somber occasion. Carmen's heart swelled with love and sorrow for Ben as Tommy played a rather mournful song on his Native-made flute, followed by soft drumbeats and a song offered by the drummers. Ben had explained the ceremony to Carmen several days ago, so she knew that the song was a prayer to Wakan-Tanka to take Singing Boy swiftly and safely to his mother. Through the singing, Ben remained kneeling as he held Singing Boy's little medicine bag in his hands. He was shirtless, and Sasha had painted his chest and face with white stripes. Tommy, also shirtless and painted, stood beside Ben, and Sasha stood behind Tommy.

The drummers' song ended, and Tommy raised his arms and sang a prayer song in the Lakota tongue. Finally, he looked down at Ben. "It is time, Little Brother."

Ben turned to look at Talia's gravestone, then up at the sky. He stood and said something to Tommy, who turned and waved Carmen over. She hesitated. Tommy nodded and motioned again for her to come. Wearing only a white blouse, a straight, denim skirt, and white tennis shoes, Carmen did as Tommy asked, limping a little on a still-sore left foot.

"Are you sure?" she asked Tommy.

"He wants you here. The one who mourns can have anyone he wants beside him."

"But this is too sacred."

"Not for you. You are Ben's wife." Tommy put a hand to his chest. "In here."

Carmen glanced at Sasha, who also nodded. She wore a buckskin dress today, with little tin bells tied into the ends of the fringes. It was her jingle dress, worn to celebrate life and joy ... joy over Singing Boy finally going to be in his mother's arms.

"What should I do?" Carmen whispered to Sasha.

"Nothing. Just stand beside him. The parting is only for Ben."

One of the drummers blew on a whistle, and the drumming and chanting began as Carmen moved beside Ben. Caesar sprang to his feet and moved beside her. *Does even Caesar understand what is going on?* Ben held the medicine bag in his right hand and took hold of hers with his left, speaking to her for the first time since about an hour before they arrived.

"I can't do it," he told her.

Carmen was surprised and touched. She thought he was ready. Here was this very strong, smart, educated, brave man who had survived horrible wounds and addiction, yet he could not open a little medicine bag and throw its contents to the wind. She prayed for the right words as she held his hand tightly and laid her other hand on his upper arm.

"Ben, you said that before you found me, you promised Yellow Robe you would do this. If a shaman said it was necessary, then it's right." She rubbed at his arm, fighting her own tears when she saw his own tears trickle down his cheek over the white paint. "What if Singing Boy were alive right now and crying for his mother? Would you hang on to him and refuse to let him go to her? That is what is happening now. You have kept him from Talia long enough. She needs her son."

She swallowed against a lump in her throat. "You told me once that if you let go of Singing Boy, you will be alone, but right now Talia is alone and you have *me*."

The wind stiffened, as though some Being above knew it would help blow the baby's hairs high and far. The drummers pounded rhythmically and continued singing. A few Native women in the background gave out intermittent trills, ululating in the way they had of expressing either joy or grief.

Ben finally let go and gently opened the little medicine bag. He reached in with his fingers and took hold of the hairs, kept them between his fingers, studying them. "They are so fine and soft," he muttered, more tears streaming down his face.

Carmen swallowed again and sniffed back the urge to break down completely. The hairs were so black and delicate. "The better to make sure they drift far in the wind," she said. "It's time to let go, Ben."

Finally, he threw the hairs as high as he could into the strong wind. They quickly disappeared. Ben went to his knees, weeping. Carmen knelt beside him, realizing that this was not just a matter of letting go of his son. The whole ceremony and being here beside Talia's grave, had brought back all the horror of the shooting, the memory of holding a dead Talia in his arms, and worst of all, the memory of Singing Boy's tiny leg moving just before he died.

Ben handed her the medicine bag. Carmen took it hesitantly.

"There are ... a few more hairs in there," he told her amid tears. "Take them and toss them for me. Then have Tommy turn the medicine bag inside out to be sure they all are gone."

"Ben, I don't have the right."

"You do if I say so." He wiped at his tears with his arm and sniffed. "You should be a part of this. Talia would want that."

Carmen felt a strange warmth as she took a few remaining hairs from the bag. Just touching them made her feel closer to Talia. These hairs belonged to a sweet child who had lived inside her. It was a moving, out-of-body experience to be a part of this. She stood and threw them into the wind, her own hair blowing forward over both sides of her face. She turned then, hardly able to speak, and handed the medicine bag to Tommy.

Tommy also had tears in his eyes as he took the bag. Carmen knelt beside Ben again as Tommy sent the hairs on their way, giving out a cry of mourning. Carmen could hear Sasha sobbing behind her. Tommy leaned down then and touched Ben's shoulder as he handed him the empty medicine bag.

"It is done," he said, "and Singing Boy and Talia are together and happy."

Ben closed a fist around the medicine bag and bent over, shedding more tears. Carmen reached out hesitantly and stroked his hair, and Caesar whined. The wolf was theirs now ... the wolf that had so terrified Carmen that night in

Grand Rapids. He licked at her face, and she hugged him with her other arm.

The drumming and chanting continued, Native spirits all around them. The grass and surrounding rocks and trees seemed to come alive, announcing that this place, Paha-Sapa, would always belong to the Great Sioux Nation.

Grandmother Wanda walked up behind Ben then. She asked Tommy to help her kneel, and Carmen moved aside slightly so the old woman could put an arm around Ben's shoulders and lean close to speak to him in Lakota. Carmen did not understand, but the old woman cried as she pulled Ben's hair away from the side of his face and leaned in to kiss his cheek. She said something more, and Ben nodded. Grandmother handed him a handkerchief that had Native designs around the edges. Ben used it to wipe at his nose and eyes while Wanda turned to Carmen and patted her shoulder.

"You will be number one wife now," she told Carmen. "Good woman. You will make my grandson happy." She handed Carmen another handkerchief before Tommy helped the old woman rise and walk back to a lawn chair she'd been sitting in during the ceremony.

Carmen felt deeply touched by Grandmother's words of acceptance, but she had to smile even through her tears at the comment. *Number one wife* harked back to the days when Native men could have more than one wife.

Not a chance.

The drumming stopped, and the drummers and others began packing up and walking to their vehicles. Tommy knelt behind Ben and Carmen. He touched Ben's shoulder. "Tell me you will be all right, Little Brother. I am leaving you and Carmen alone here for as long as you need to stay."

Ben drew a deep breath and threw his head back, tossing his hair behind his shoulders. The wind had stopped. Whatever great Being had sent it knew it was no longer needed. Streaks from tears had cut through the paint on Ben's face. He said something in Lakota, and Tommy replied as he rubbed Ben's shoulders. He turned to Carmen then.

"Stay with him until he is ready to leave.," Tommy told her. "We have dug a small hole over Talia's grave. He must bury the medicine bag there before you go." He patted her shoulder and rose. "You did well, *meeton.*"

Tommy left with a still-crying Sasha, and Carmen felt deeply moved by the fact that Tommy had referred to her as a sister.

Carmen remained quietly knelt beside Ben, feeling Talia's presence ... a woman so full of life and vitality, beauty and generosity, so devoted to helping others. It made no sense that she'd died so needlessly while Billy had lived long enough to do so much harm to others.

After several minutes, Ben moved an arm around her and pulled her close. "Thank you for what you did."

"I felt honored that you even asked."

"Give me the medicine bag and I will bury it," Ben told her.

She handed him the small leather pouch. "Are you all right? You won't do something I can't handle, will you?"

Ben took the pouch with a sad smile. "No." He turned and placed the pouch in the hole over Talia's grave beside him. He very softly sang something in Lakota as he covered the pouch and pressed the ground over it. A rush of warm air suddenly swept over both of them, followed by complete calm.

Ben closed his eyes. "That was Talia," he said confidently. "Singing Boy is with her now." He sat there for a few minutes, staring at Talia's gravestone.

"Talia Robin Daisy-Colter. Beloved daughter, wife, and mother, who gave heart and soul to those she loved, and to Lakota youth." The birth and death dates showed her as only twenty-eight when she died, the same age as Carmen was now.

Beneath those words was Singing Boy's English and Lakota names, Thomas Singing Boy Daisy-Red Leaf, showing both Talia's clan and Ben's mother's clan. Sadly, Ben had no idea what clan his father came from, so he had no bloodline to show. Carmen knew that cut deeply into his heart. At the bottom of the stone was Singing Boy's Lakota name, E-maha-Nemeneo-O. They Are All Singing.

Ben finally rose and helped Carmen to her feet. "I am sorry. I did not think about how hard kneeling must have been on your knees."

"It's okay. They are healed enough."

Ben took his grandmother's handkerchief from where he'd tucked it into the waist of his buckskin pants and again wiped his nose and eyes. Carmen used the other handkerchief to do the same, thinking how thin and old the handkerchief was, a piece of the past. Few people other than old ladies used handkerchiefs anymore. She would wash these gently and fold them as keepsakes.

She looked up at Ben, so deeply Native right now. In times like this, at Pow-Wows, or when he performed the war dance, it was as though he were another person, someone who'd walked out of the past to consume him.

Who lives in your soul, Ben?

"Are you really okay?" she asked.

Ben pushed some of her hair behind her ear, then leaned down and kissed her gently. "I need to leave here, but we need to come and visit every few weeks and bring flowers."

"Of course," Carmen agreed. She moved an arm around his back and urged him to start walking. "Come and put on the shirt we brought. Did you know that Detective Bannon and Captain Hyer were here?"

"I knew, and I was surprised. The FBI usually does not show much concern for these things."

"I think they were truly interested, Ben, probably because they were a part of my rescue. They had seen how hard all of this was for you. "

"Perhaps, but you still have much to learn about the FBI and the BIA and the damage they have done over the years. I appreciate certain things, Carmen, but do not think that most of those men and women have your good heart and understanding, because they do not. But I am not ignorant of the fact that some of them truly care. I have to work with them, so I have to remain tolerant."

They reached the truck, and he opened the back gate and urged Caesar to jump in. He closed the gate and turned to Carmen. He folded his arms, and a determined look moved into his dark eyes.

"I should tell you that I am going to join the Oglala Sioux Tribe as one of their lawyers in the lawsuit against the federal government, for failing to supply the reservations with adequate law enforcement. Something needs to be done about the disappearance of our women and sometimes our children. This situation with Linda Two Fists, and with you, might have turned out differently if we had more help. The council has asked for my help in representing them, and I told them yes."

Carmen knew there would be no stopping him. This latest event had taken him to a new level as a defender of the People. "If you think you need to do so, Ben, then do it. But please tell me before you commit to these things. I have been after you to do less, not more."

He put a hand to the side of her face. "I am sorry if this upsets you, but I assure you, something like this takes many months. Knowing the federal government, it could even take two or three years, with big gaps of waiting between filing briefs and arguments and appearing before Congress or in court. It will not interfere that much with my time at home with you and our children. I turned down that offer from the talent scouts because, as you heard me promise, I will not be an absentee father. This I promise."

"But you will make more enemies."

Ben pulled her close. "A man who speaks for the People will always have enemies. You wear a ring that says you understand this. There will be many times when I will abide by what you wish, Carmen, but in certain matters, I cannot go against what is in my heart and soul. There is much I can do to help legally, and I cannot let fear of making enemies stop me."

Sid's words from the day Ben took off to go after Jerry suddenly penetrated Carmen's thoughts. *Ben Colter is deep into his culture and the Lakota religion. If you two build a relationship, it's likely you are the one who will have to adjust to his way of life rather than the other way around. You need to be ready for that.*

How could anything Ben Colter did make her leave him or even *consider* leaving him? She could test his own resolve to make this work, but why would she do that to him? If his motives were not so sincere and heartfelt, it might be different, but he'd lost too much and sacrificed too much to ask him to do any less.

I am ready.

Carmen kissed his chest and looked up at him. "How about you give me some consideration for my opinion when it comes to having those ten kids you want?"

Ben leaned down and kissed her, then led her around to her side of the truck and reached into the front seat for a YESS shirt he'd brought with him. "I will think about it. I am willing to reduce that to eight."

"I was thinking more like two," Carmen said.

Ben pulled on the white shirt, which fit snugly over his broad chest. "How about seven?"

"I'll consider three."

Ben grinned. "Six?"

Carmen stood back and put her hands on her hips. "How about four, max? Let's stick to that and see how things are going by then. And since we agreed I should go off the pill, which I already have, we had better set a wedding date for sooner than later. I have no idea how easily I might get pregnant, and considering your very healthy appetite for sex, I could *already* be pregnant."

Ben pulled her close. "I sure do not mind all the hard work of trying."

Carmen laughed lightly. "Oh, you're a hard worker, all right. But for now, we need to set dates for two weddings. A Lakota wedding here and a traditional one in Michigan so my father can walk me down the aisle and I can show off my devastatingly handsome husband to all my friends and relatives back home."

"Now you embarrass me." Ben turned and helped her into the truck. "And I suppose you will choose the most expensive gown you can find, with a train that hangs halfway out the church door while you are already at the altar," he joked.

Carmen laughed. "Something like that. Val is going to fly out and go to Denver with me to shop for one. And I was thinking, how about a honeymoon that involves going to the lake house? There is no need to spend a lot of money on one, and we will already be in Michigan, so it will still be a getaway for you."

"I should have known an accountant would also be so frugal," Ben answered with a chuckle. "That sounds good to me, but I think we should also take a trip back here to the Black Hills when we have more time, maybe next summer, after we are truly settled in as husband and wife. There is so much here to show you, Carmen, so much power and spirit here, and incredible beauty. Sylvan Lake for one. I still have not taken you there. I will show you the reasons the Lakota People will never give up the Black Hills. They are magic, sacred, and full of spirits from the past."

"I can already tell how beautiful this place is. I would love to spend some quiet time here with you. I know how much the Black Hills mean to you."

"*You* mean much to me, and your beauty fits this land." Ben sobered. "You are a precious gift I never expected, Carmen. You have brought me to life." He ran a hand along her thigh under her denim skirt. "Do you know how much I love you?"

"I hope it's as much as I love you," Carmen answered. "You brought me to life, too. I didn't think I could ever be this happy or feel so gently loved by a man."

"You are easy to love. And out of all my travels, do you know where my favorite place is to be?"

"Where?"

Another kiss, longer and deeper. "Inside of you."

Another kiss.

"Mine is in bed … underneath a warrior," Carmen answered.

"Then we should get home so that you can visit your favorite place." He laughed as he shut the door and walked around to his side of the truck. The bells on the silver belt he wore tinkled softly as he climbed into the driver's side.

Caesar stuck his head through the back window they'd left open and whined. Carmen turned and leaned through the middle of the front bucket seats to open a picnic basket. She took out two pieces of baloney and fed them to the wolf. Caesar did not even bother to chew. The meat went down like a tiny bug, and the wolf looked at her as if to say, "Is that it?"

"Ben, are you sure this animal won't eat our baby when we have one?" she asked.

He chuckled. "Yes. In fact, it is more likely he will protect that baby so closely that we will have to ask his permission to pick up our own child."

Carmen pulled a banana out of the basket. "Want anything?" she asked Ben.

"No. All I want is to get you home and get started on making you pregnant."

Carmen chuckled and sat down. "Just that remark is turning me on. I had better stay healthy, so right now I am going to eat a Michigan banana. There are banana farms all around Grand Rapids, you know. We should go visit one sometime. We could look for a U-Pick and pick our own bananas."

They both laughed as Ben steered his way down the dirt road that led down the mountain to a paved road below. Carmen put a reassuring hand on his shoulder. Married to a man like Ben, what on earth lay in her future?

"I'm headed for a lot of trouble, aren't I?"

"Baby, you don't know the half. And by the way, I have chosen a Lakota name for you."

"Oh? I didn't know I needed one."

"Of course you do. You are my wife. I will call you Skeu-yay Wahnzheelah."

"And I am supposed to remember that? I wouldn't even know how to spell it."

"It means Sweet One. I will teach you how to spell it."

Carmen leaned back in her seat. "I think I need to sign up at the School for the Arts."

"Yes, you do, because I intend to teach you the language and teach you to sing."

"Oh, no! No, no, no, no, no. You can get that idea right out of your head. That will be one requirement for getting married. I will make you sign a contract to promise you will never, ever get me up on that stage to sing, not with you and not with those talented kids. If you heard me sing, you would laugh your head off."

"I *have* heard you sing, in the shower or when you are cleaning and you do not know I am listening. I came home early one day, and you were dancing around and singing to country music. I left and came back because I knew you would be embarrassed."

"God help me. Embarrassed because I can't carry a tune?"

"No. Just embarrassed that I caught you. You can carry a tune, and as long as you can do that, you can sing anywhere. Your only problem is, you need to learn to belt it out and not be shy."

"Ben, I repeat, I will never sing in front of you or those kids or on a stage."

He just grinned. "We will see, Skeu-yay

Wahnzheelah." He took off down the paved road toward home. A few tourists who were gathered near a table full of Native American souvenirs for sale stared at the truck as it went by. Carmen figured they were talking about the words painted on the side of the bed.

THE BLACK HILLS ARE NOT FOR SALE.

FROM THE AUTHOR ...

I hope you have enjoyed this, my seventy-fifth published book and my first contemporary story. My specialty is historical romance based on America's real history, real locations and events, but I do plan to write more contemporary stories as well. A full list of the books I have written over the past forty years can be found on my website at www.rosannebittner.com, where you can also join Rosanne Bittner's Heart of the West Street Team and talk to my friends and fans, as well as stay up to date on new stories to come.

Most of my older books, including my best-selling Savage Destiny series, are still selling and have been reissued with new covers. They are available at Amazon.com in print or for Kindle and other e-readers. Many can also be ordered through Barnes & Noble, Sourcebooks, and Diversion Books.

My husband and I have traveled the American West extensively, including the areas written about in this book. You can find me on Facebook, Instagram, Twitter, BookBub, Goodreads, and Google.

MUSIC SOURCES

I mention many songs in this story and am providing a full list here for you. Because legally I cannot include actual lyrics from these songs, which would lend to the emotion of *Dancing Beneath You*, I have listed the song titles and the versions I have. I recommend listening to these songs so you can get the feel of the kind of music the hero and his youth group perform in my story.

"Anthem," from the stage play *Chess*, sung by Josh Groban

"The Reason," from the 2016 TV Easter special, *The Passion: New Orleans*, sung by Prince Royce

"Let Freedom Ring," from the Gaither Gospel Homecoming Series Album *The Best of David Phelps*, sung by David Phelps

"Love Can Move Mountains," from the 2016 TV Easter special, *The Passion: New Orleans*, sung by The Passion Cast made up of several professional singers

"Shouting Grounds," from the album *Crowder * American Prodigal*, sung by Crowder

"When Love Takes Over," from the 2016 TV Easter special, *The Passion: New Orleans*, sung by Yolanda Adams

"You Raise Me Up," from the album simply titled *Josh Groban*, sung by Josh Groban

"Let's Make Love," from the album *Breathe*, sung by Faith Hill and Tim McGraw

"When We Were Beautiful," from the album *The Circle*, sung by Bon Jovi

"What Doesn't Kill You Makes You Stronger," from the album *Glee – The Complete Season Three*, sung by the Glee cast.

"Long Live Rock & Roll," from the album *Daughtry Baptized,* sung by Chris Daughtry

"I Love You," from the album *Falling Into You,* sung by Celine Dion

"You Are Loved," from the album simply called *Josh Groban,* sung by Josh Groban

"What's Mine Is Yours," from the album *Kane Brown Deluxe Edition,* sung by Kane Brown

"My Heart Will Go On," from the soundtrack for the movie *Titanic,* sung by Celine Dion

My "mood music" for envisioning Ben Colter and the youth group's Native American song and fancy dancing comes from the album *Ancient Visions,* by Ah*Nee*Mah (New Age 2005).

I also mention Bon Jovi's "In These Arms," from the album *Bon Jovi Greatest Hits (Deluxe Edition) Disc 2,* sung by Bon Jovi and "Drunk on You," from the album *Tailgates and Tanlines,* sung by Luke Bryan. I also listen to NATIVE VOICES/SACRED SPIRIT: TRADITIONAL NATIVE SONGS.

Most of my Lakota words/names came from the book "Lahcotah: Dictionary of the Sioux Language ," by J. K. Hyer and W. S. Starring, with the aid of Charles Geurreu, Indian interpreter, Fort Laramie, Dakota, December 1866. My version was ordered through Amazon and compiled by Historic Publishing, printed in Monee, Illinois in May 2022. I interpreted the Lakota words and names as best I could, and with a deep respect for Lakota culture and language.

Made in United States
North Haven, CT
14 October 2022

25458563R00261